BEAMING UP MR. *STAR TREK*

He was a struggling Canadian-born actor just starting to make a name for himself on Broadway when Hollywood called. Hugely ambitious, he decided to put off his goal of becoming the next Olivier to make a fortune in television . . . and became Captain James T. Kirk of the Starship *Enterprise*, the role that has haunted him ever since.

William Shatner. His name is synonymous with the most popular television show in history and the beloved hero he portrayed. But behind the scenes, Shatner was a man beset by demons—by an ego so huge he was disliked by just about everyone he ever worked with, by insecurities that had him screaming at extras and competing with co-stars as married as he was for the attentions of beautiful women, by a long-held belief that alien intelligence would soon be coming to earth . . . for him.

From his early days, when he defied his father to pursue an acting career, to the high of *Star Trek* stardom and the low of the disastrous decade after the series was canceled, to his resurrection as star of *Rescue 911* and *TekWar*, here is the inside story of the man who earned the name

Captain Quirk

CAPTAIN QUIRK

DENNIS WILLIAM HAUCK

PINNACLE BOOKS
KENSINGTON PUBLISHING CORP.

"Mr. Tambourine Man" reprinted by permission of Special Rider Music, New York, New York.

PINNACLE BOOKS are published by

Kensington Publishing Corp.
850 Third Avenue
New York, NY 10022

Pinnacle and the P logo Reg. U.S. Pat. & TM Off.

First Printing: October, 1995

Printed in the United States of America

My greatest fear is that my fans will find me out.
—William Shatner, 1991

Contents

Introduction   9

1. UFOs and Hollywood Stars   11

2. The Cosmic Connection   28

3. Toughy Takes 'Em On   46

4. A Tale Signifying Nothing   61

5. Horatio Hornblower, Meet Captain Quirk   82

6. Motorcycle Machismo   118

7. The Lost Years   134

8. The Captain's Return   158

9. Mutiny on the *Enterprise*   190

10. Sex, Aliens, and Palimony   228

11. The Mystique of *Star Trek*   250

12. What Does God Need with a Spaceship?   265

Notes and Sources   285

Acknowledgments   299

Introduction

William Shatner's role as Captain Kirk on *Star Trek* helped transform a struggling 1960s television series into an international entertainment phenomenon. The seventy-nine episodes of the original series have given birth to seven major motion pictures and three syndicated spin-off series and have generated over $2 billion in box-office receipts, rights sales, and merchandising. A recent poll indicates that throughout the world, William Shatner is more readily recognized than any other English-speaking actor. One out of every four people on the face of the planet knows who he is.

I first met William Shatner in 1976, during the filming of a documentary about UFOs. At the time, I was the editor of several newsstand magazines that dealt with the paranormal, and the producers asked me to work as a consultant. As the film's host, Shatner interviewed me on camera, and we traveled through New York and Virginia, tracking down UFO witnesses and talking with scientists involved in the search for extraterrestrial intelligence.

Surprisingly, I found the host of the documentary as fascinating as its subject matter. I had always thought of William Shatner as a John Wayne type—a macho hero who lived by an unbending moral code. Instead, he had a mercurial personality and could change in an instant from a deeply sensitive person into an egotistical child.

Shatner often exhibited the same self-centered preening behavior that had been Capote's trademark. Moreover, both men seemed consumed by deep-seated passions and shared the neurotic temperament one expects of artists.

Later, I discovered that others had formed the same first impressions of William Shatner that I had. Many of his co-workers described him as being pompous, difficult to work with, and totally self-consumed.

Paramount production crews and even some of his fellow actors started calling him "Captain Quirk" behind his back. (Here's an odd bit of *Trek* trivia. A 1967 issue of *TV Guide* in which Shatner predicts his fame as James T. Kirk will be "ephemeral" lists its publisher as "James T. Quirk.")

When I decided to write a popular biography of Shatner, I undertook a nationwide survey of hundreds of *Star Trek* fans to see what they thought of the man. I discovered that even his most devoted fans sensed something "different" about the real Captain Kirk. Only 8 percent thought he was a good actor apart from his work on *Star Trek;* nearly 25 percent described him as a *terrible* actor off the *Enterprise.* On the other hand, almost 65 percent called his portrayal of Kirk excellent. However, when asked to judge Shatner's personality, almost 40 percent described him as "arrogant/aloof," and another 35 percent went so far as to label him "quirky/odd."

Shatner has done little to dispel these impressions. He often ignores personal questions from the media or feigns loss of memory. He derides fans and sometimes makes light of questions by telling outrageous lies. His so-called memoirs contain stories about everyone's personal life except his own.

I decided to find out everything I could about this charming, arrogant, sensitive, macho paradox of a man. What I found out surprised even me.

Chapter 1

UFOs and Hollywood Stars

Well, if I were a little green man in a flying saucer and wanted to get publicity—who would I contact faster than Captain Kirk of the Starship Enterprise?
—William Shatner on his UFO encounter

"Goddamn airlines!" William Shatner cursed through clenched teeth. "How the hell am I supposed to go on without makeup or clothes? Goddamn airlines." Shatner's suitcase, containing his makeup and wardrobe, had not arrived with our flight. "Why me?" he mumbled. "Why does this have to happen to me?"

The enraged star paced back and forth, his brisk footsteps echoing through the marble lobby of Dulles Airport. He interrupted his frantic pacing just long enough to look up at the vaulted ceiling and shake his head in a gesture of total exasperation.

Only William Shatner's luggage had disappeared. Cameraman Eddie Marritz carried his equipment with him on the short flight to Washington. My suitcase and two bags belonging to director Chuck Romine arrived safely with the other checked baggage. The four of us had flown down from New York to continue filming a docu-

mentary about ancient astronauts and UFOs entitled
Mysteries of the Gods.

At the moment, however, we were caught up in a
spontaneous production that might more appropriately
have been called *Conspiracies of the Airlines.* The volatile
Shatner was convinced his missing bag was part of a plot
by some faceless airline employee to sabotage his career.
The source of his paranoia, I learned later, was a series of
delayed flights and lost luggage that had plagued him for
many years.

Chuck tried to fall into step at his side, but Shatner kept
darting to and fro like an angry dog trapped behind a
fence. Finally, the director positioned himself in the middle of the actor's path and was able to get his attention.

"Look," Chuck said calmly, "we can get some cosmet-
ics and clothes at a department store first thing in the
morning."

When he heard the suggestion, Shatner grimaced and
looked like he was going to burst into tears. His shoulders
sank, and he twisted his head down to one side. From that
odd angle, he looked me straight in the eye.

"Designer clothes?" It was all I could think of saying.

"Yeaahzzz!" he intoned, as if I were the only one in the
world who understood the seriousness of the situation.

"Maybe we should get checked into the hotel," Chuck
quickly suggested. Before Shatner could resume his com-
pulsive pacing, the director stretched out his arms and
herded all of us toward the nearest exit.

Chuck Romine was a tall man with long gray hair and
puffy, world-weary blue eyes. A respected investigative
reporter, Romine had written and produced for Edward
R. Murrow. Now, in September 1976, he was directing a
documentary about space aliens.

Luckily, the director had taken charge, however, because the host and narrator of the film was not talking to
anyone. Shatner just stood empty-handed and watched
silently as the rest of us slid our luggage into the trunk of

the limousine. I could not help feeling a twinge of guilt. When we reached the Hotel Wellington, I made sure the porter carried my bag.

After registering at the front desk, we agreed to meet later for dinner and headed for our individual rooms. I followed an elderly porter down a narrow first-floor corridor whose walls were decorated with flowered red-felt wallpaper. My room was small and overfurnished, with an unnerving maroon-and-white color scheme. The porter tossed my suitcase on the bed and lingered patiently while I fumbled through my wallet for a tip. On his way out, he pulled the door shut, exposing a tiny closet.

I unzipped my suitcase and took out a stack of folded shirts and trousers. As I draped my clothes neatly over the hangers, I imagined Shatner in similarly garish quarters, sitting on the edge of his bed with nothing to unpack. Captain Kirk might have had a handsome new wardrobe beamed down immediately, but William Shatner was sitting alone, pissed off and frustrated, in an antebellum room in the middle of the nation's capital.

I had gotten involved in this project almost by accident. At the time, I was working in New York City as the editor of *Official UFO, Ancient Astronauts,* and three other monthly magazines dealing with paranormal topics. Pamela Childs, an executive for Hemisphere Pictures, had seen me on a local cable television show and suggested that I make an audition tape for the film.

When the producers asked me to appear in the movie and serve as a consultant, the first advice I gave them was to get a bigger name. I suggested they contact space scientist Carl Sagan or Dr. J. Allen Hynek, the government astronomer–turned–UFO investigator. They told me they had already talked with them and decided that I had a "fresh approach that deserved a larger audience." What they did not tell me was that both men had already declined to be in the movie.

I accepted primarily for the opportunity to work with

William Shatner, whose characterization of Captain Kirk had fired my imagination while I was still a student in college. Like many *Star Trek* fans, I had found the show's optimistic message, the idea that our species would one day conquer its earthbound problems and travel to the farthest reaches of the universe, welcome relief from the everyday world of petty wars, prejudice, and corruption. I wanted to believe that some cosmic intelligence was ready to communicate the Big Idea, to let us in on nature's secrets, or at least help us get beyond ourselves. *Star Trek* had made that seem possible.

But I did not find Captain Kirk in William Shatner. In the few days I had worked with him, I found the man to be driven and self-centered. He ran off gut energies that sometimes surfaced out of control, distorting his whole personality. At such times, his voice became pinched and high, and he spoke in short, rapid bursts. Then he became petulant or pompous, swinging between nitpicking perfectionism and condescending boredom. Yet at other times, he could be absolutely charming and extremely sensitive to other people's feelings.

It was as if Shatner were made up of two distinct personalities. One was the gallant and beguiling Captain Kirk. The other was the insensitive and twisted person whom others have dubbed "Captain Quirk." Unfortunately, I had never mastered the Vulcan grip that Spock had used to subdue the malicious Kirk when faced with a similar problem in "The Enemy Within," an episode of *Star Trek*. Instead, Shatner was free to vacillate between his two opposing personas in a split second and for no discernible reason. But one thing was certain: whoever the man really was, he was much more complicated and fascinating than the two-dimensional character I had admired on the tube. I looked forward to talking with him more that evening.

At the Captain's Table

At the dinner table in the restaurant of the Hotel Wellington, Captain Quirk sat with his legs tightly crossed on a chair at least four feet from the edge of the table. He was obviously still upset about his luggage. Except for cursory greetings, we all sat in silence for several minutes. The first words Shatner spoke were detailed instructions he gave the waiter about the preparation of his red snapper. Slowly, as the wine was poured and the dinner progressed, Shatner loosened up, and we all started to relax a little.

"I suppose we should go over what we're going to shoot tomorrow," he said. It was the first indication that the host of the film was willing to continue, and Chuck jumped at the opportunity.

The director said he planned to drive to COMSAT, the Communications Satellite Corporation, a few hours outside Washington. Dr. John Billingham, who worked nearby at NASA's Ames Research Center, would meet us there. Billingham headed the Extraterrestrial Intelligence Division, and the plan was to interview him on the roof of the COMSAT building, against the backdrop of an impressive array of gigantic satellite dishes. Chuck hoped we would have enough time in the afternoon to drive to a radio telescope site, tucked away deep in the Virginia hills, to interview me.

There was no mention of a script or even a list of what topics we might cover. Shatner was a firm believer in spontaneity and did not want to discuss the specifics of the interviews any further. He felt it best to let things unfold on screen. Instead, he changed the topic of conversation to something that really interested him.

"What do you think of the Crystal Skull?" Shatner asked, turning to face me. He was referring to a life-sized quartz skull and jawbone found in 1927 during the excavation of an ancient Mayan city in Honduras.

"I know it's quite a work of art," I answered. "There are no tooling marks, so it must have been made by hand rubbing over hundreds of years. Some people have suggested it was fashioned by ancient astronauts using some kind of laser. I read somewhere that if you shine a light up through the base, the light is projected out through the eyes. But I've never seen it up close."

"We went up to Kitchner, Ontario," Chuck commented, "where we interviewed Anna Mitchell-Hedges, the daughter of the archaeologist who found it."

"I got the chance to actually hold it!" interjected Shatner. The memory rekindled his enthusiasm and he huddled closer to the table. Then he really opened up: "She has it sitting in her apartment. I held it in my lap and tried to psychically tune myself into it. I tried to go back in time to when they used it in their ceremonies. I tell you, I really felt something. It was eerie!"

"Didn't the priests use it in some kind of death ritual?" I queried.

"She said the high priest used it to will the death of certain people," Shatner replied, "and they used it in a ceremony to transfer knowledge from a dying priest to a young boy."

"That's fascinating," I said. "Can you imagine what something like that is worth? And she has it in her apartment!"

"She's not worried," said Shatner. "She thinks it's cursed! She told us about a group of students from Australia who visited her father to see it. One girl picked up the skull and made fun of it. Anna's father felt insulted and put it back in the case. The girl died mysteriously a few months later, and just before her death, she told her friends she believed the Crystal Skull was the cause of her ill health!"

Eddie rolled his eyes. At least he kept his mouth shut.

This was the most enthusiasm Shatner had shown in the last three days. But Chuck was ready to change the subject.

"While we're here in Washington," the director said, "we're going to interview Jeane Dixon. She's predicted UFOs are going to land and make contact with earthlings."

I felt uncomfortable about Jeane Dixon being in the film. I wanted to concentrate on more "scientific" speculation, but the film was loosely based on Erich von Daniken's *Miracles of the Gods,* a book that stated that the impulse to produce visions and psychic phenomena is of extraterrestrial origin. One of the chapters even contained an interview with Jeane Dixon. Though I said nothing, Shatner sensed my unease.

"Don't you believe in psychics?" he asked.

"Well, Jeane Dixon? I don't know," I hedged. "She was right about the death of Marilyn Monroe and the assassinations of the Kennedys, but she was way off on other things. I was hoping we could interview some heads of UFO organizations."

"Jeane believes UFOs are going to land on earth in August of 1977," Chuck countered. "That's one hell of a prediction." He glanced over at Shatner and continued: "Besides, I'm sick of trying to work with ufologist groups."

Chuck, a hard-nosed reporter who had survived military actions and Mafia exposés, told me that he had never encountered such obstinate and backbiting types as he'd come across in UFO organizations. After the Air Force had officially stopped investigating such phenomena in 1956, an alphabet soup of nonprofit organizations took over the responsibility. The oldest group, APRO (Aerial Phenomena Research Organization), would not work with anyone from MUFON (Mutual UFO Network), whose founder had left APRO to form his own splinter group. NICAP (National Investigations Committee on Aerial Phenomenon) was thought to be infiltrated by the

CIA in a plot to discredit UFO research. CRUFON (Citizen's Radio UFO Network) was run by the IUFOR (International UFO Registry). No one trusted them because they had set up a national toll-free UFO hotline, in what looked like an attempt to hog all the sighting reports. CUFOS (Center for UFO Studies) would not work with anyone from the Ancient Astronaut Society. It was ludicrous. UFO organizations were wasting their energies arguing about who should best handle a problem that most people denied even existed.

"Everyone has their own wagon to push," Shatner said, smiling. "The funny thing is that there's most likely intelligent life in outer space, but I'm not sure about here on earth!" After that bit of levity, Shatner suddenly turned serious.

"What do you know," he asked me, "about these people who are going around saying they're in contact with aliens from space?"

"I guess you mean the HIM couple," I replied, assuming he was referring to a pair of UFO cultists currently making the rounds. "They're called Bo and Peep, or simply 'the Two,' by their followers."

"What's HIM?" Shatner queried.

"Human Individual Metamorphosis. That's what they call their blueprint for saving souls on our planet. This couple, a man and woman in their mid-forties, claim they are really ageless UFO beings come to earth to help humans evolve to the next level. I heard them speak in Waldport, Oregon."

"What did you think?" Shatner said eagerly.

"Well, they're quite impressive. They dress in identical outfits and speak in slow, measured tones. Mostly, they talk about the need for a leap in human evolution, which is something that's hard to argue with. But then they ask everyone to give up all their possessions and meet them at a remote camp in Colorado, where everyone will be picked up by a UFO and taken to another planet. Once there, people will undergo psychic training and be returned to earth as seeds of a new consciousness. Supposedly, Christ, Elijah, Ezekiel, and all the saints left earth the same way. In fact, the Two say they are the 'two witnesses' described in Revelations. It's an enticing message. Out of 200 people at the meeting, 20 joined up."

"They gave up everything to join them?" Shatner asked.

"Oh, yes. There was a millionaire in Durango who gave up his real estate company to join them, and lots of people who sold their homes and donated the money to the movement. There must be over 150 members by now. Both Jackie Gleason and musician Steve Halpern came close to joining the group."

"And why didn't you go with them?" Shatner remarked.

"Well, the Two travel around in a 1964 Pontiac and communicate with members by a network of secret post office boxes. It just doesn't seem all that advanced. Plus, the Oregon police say they have identified them as a couple from Texas. He is allegedly the son of a Presbyterian minister, and she worked as a nurse. Both have had some minor run-ins with the law."

"I see," said Shatner. "Are they the only ones you know of?"

Shatner seemed to have something specific in mind, but I really could not understand what he was driving at. True, there were a few fringe elements who said they were in contact with space aliens, but they were not the subject of study by reputable scientists. It would take another fifteen years before reports of contactees and abductions would become so commonplace that they would be discussed openly among reputable researchers.

"I've heard of another group called the Nine," I offered, "but they only communicate telepathically to certain people. They're supposed to be sort of a consortium of extraterrestrial intelligences."

I paused to sip some wine, expecting he'd drop the subject, but Shatner pressed me to go on.

"Well, Uri Geller, the Israeli psychic, says he has been in contact with the Nine. I've talked with him, and he believes they are the driving force behind his psychokinetic powers. But for me, this all gets to be a little bit too much. I'm trying to be scientific about the UFO problem so people will realize it's something real."

That high-minded statement was obviously the wrong stance to take. Shatner leaned back in his chair and abruptly changed the subject. The contactee controversy was a touchy issue and one reason why Hynek and Sagan had refused to be in the film. However, less than three months later, I discovered that Shatner had probably learned about the Nine from Gene Roddenberry and was trying to find out what I thought about them. After a little more digging, I was surprised to discover that Shatner thought himself to be an alien contactee.

William Shatner's Close Encounter

In the summer of 1967, Shatner observed a UFO in the Mojave Desert northeast of Palmdale, California. During the encounter, he seemed to have engaged in psychic contact with extraterrestrials, and some evidence suggests that he may even have been abducted.

At the time, a flap of UFO sightings was occurring near Palmdale, in the area between the San Gabriel Mountains and Edwards Air Force Base. Sightings included both unidentified nocturnal lights and odd, disk-shaped objects seen during the day. There were also reports of close encounters. At least one witness claimed to have communicated with the aliens prior to Shatner's experience.

Every so often, Shatner would ride his Suzuki Titan 500 motorcycle in the same area to get away from the hassles of Los Angeles and relax in the sun. He had heard of the UFO reports and sometimes looked skyward, wondering if the alleged space visitors could tune into his thoughts.

One day, he was riding through the desert with four friends when his motorcycle hit a hole and he was thrown off. The heavy bike fell on top of him, striking his head, and he lost consciousness for a short time. Oddly, the other riders saw none of this. They later said the fourth figure on the bike behind them, which they assumed was Shatner, was never out of their sight. The identity of the mysterious rider has never been determined.

Just as he was coming to, Shatner felt and heard something strange. He later described it as "like when you have a nightmare and you feel something crawling over your body or wrestling with you." Whatever the "shadowy phantom" was, Shatner immediately felt better, as if he were infused with fresh energy. He got up, righted his motorcycle, and tried to get it to start. But the machine stubbornly refused to engage.

Shatner suddenly realized he was stranded in the middle of the desert at the hottest part of the day. Still, he did not want to leave his expensive motorcycle lying in the sand, so he picked it up and started to push it along the desert trail.

It was 110 degrees, and Shatner was wearing a leather jacket and heavy clothes. He kept removing the hot, padded helmet from his head, only to put it back on to protect himself from the blazing sun.

Suddenly, his motorcycle seemed to acquire a mind of its own. He could push it in only one direction—it was as if an unseen force was directing it.

On the horizon, directly in front of him, he kept seeing a mysterious dark figure waving him on. Seeing the figure caused Shatner to push forward with renewed vigor. Finally, he arrived at an old gas station just off a paved road. Nearly six hours had passed, but he had reached safety.

At that moment, far off in the distance, he observed a pie-pan–shaped object glistening in the sky.

His buddies eventually realized Shatner was missing and began a frantic search. They found him relaxing with a cool drink at the gas station. He almost certainly would have died had he not been guided to safety by the unknown presence.

A Transformed Man

Shatner's close encounter in the Mojave Desert was so real to him that he planned to produce a half-hour film to document his experience. Unfortunately, the film project never got off the ground, although Shatner did begin to question openly the general lack of progress in identifying the real nature of "flying saucers." Though not a religious man, he became convinced there were superior intelligences in the universe capable of interacting with our species.

"I can't prove UFOs exist," he told the press at the time, "but anyone who denies they exist is as foolish as the person who denies that God exists. The mystery is definitely there . . . We humans aren't as yet all-knowing creatures, and therefore I would not say that unidentified flying objects aren't what some believers say they are. There are still some mysteries that none of us can solve."

A few months after his UFO experience, Shatner worked out a deal with Decca Records to record his first album. Charles Bud Dant served as producer, and Don Ralke arranged and conducted the music.

Titled *The Transformed Man,* the recording was Shatner's attempt to express his feelings about his strange experience in the desert. He begins by reading King Henry's charge to his troops from Shakespeare's *Henry V,* in which the king beseeches his reluctant men not to lose their courage even though they are overwhelmed by in-

CAPTAIN QUIRK

credible odds. Next, Shatner renders "Elegy to the Brave," which describes a pale young man lying unconscious on the ground in a valley as shining diamonds fall from the sky. The scene is reminiscent of Shatner's loss of consciousness after being thrown from his motorcycle in the Mojave Desert.

Then, after reading Cyrano de Bergerac's pledge never to be false to himself, Shatner goes into a rendition of "Mr. Tambourine Man" that has left listeners dumbfounded ever since the album was released. Because of it, Shatner's fledgling singing career took a crash dive and he became the butt of scores of jokes that continue to this day. In 1991, a group of New York publishers offered him $10,000 to sing it at their convention (Shatner refused).

In fact, the song is very personal. It is about William Shatner's close encounter with a tambourine-shaped craft in the desert. Haltingly, with tremendous feeling, he sings to the alien presence:

In the *jingle-jangle* morning,
I'll come *following* you.
Take me on a *trip* in your magic, SWIRLING
   ship.
My senses have been stripped.
My *hands* can't feel to grip.
My *toes,* too numb to step, wait *only* for my boot
   heels to be wandering.
I'm *ready* to go ANYWHERE.
I'm ready to fade—into my *own* parade.
Cast your *dancing* spell my way.
I *promise*—to go under it.
I'm not sleepy and there is no—place I'm going
   to.
Mr. TAMBOURINE MAN. Mr. Tambourine
   Man. *Hey, Mr. Tambourine Man!* MR.
   TAMBOURINE MAN!!!

After that, Shatner centers himself with a quote from Hamlet's "to be or not to be" speech and then intones a down-to-earth version of "It Was a Very Good Year." But his composure does not last. Before long, he is carried away by Romeo's description of Juliet's sparkling eyes and how they "speak without words." With breathtaking emotion, Shatner describes how Juliet came to Romeo like a "winged messenger of heaven that sails upon the bosom of the air."

Could Shatner's Juliet have been a telepathic alien? Whether the star's UFO encounter was real or sprung from some unconscious archetypal energy, Shatner's alien is very similar to entities described by other witnesses. In fact, instead of diminishing, the contactee phenomena has mushroomed over the last quarter century. Some recent studies suggest that as many as 3.7 million Americans have had an alien abduction experience.

In the album track entitled "How Insensitive," Shatner goes on to describe his feelings of inadequacy in dealing with the telepathic entity he encountered. To the Latin beat of "Insensatez," he laments how insensitive and cold he must have seemed when "she spoke to me," and admits that the memory of her parting look will stay with him forever.

Shatner's last song, "Lucy in the Sky with Diamonds," sounds like a modern abductee's description of almond-eyed beings on a mother ship. His emotional tribute to "the girl with ka*leid*oscope EYES" makes it sound like he really misses the alien.

Not surprisingly, people had a hard time figuring out exactly what Shatner was trying to convey in *The Transformed Man*. Reviewers dubbed his interpretations "bizarre," "psychedelic," and even "drug-crazed."

In 1990, the recording was featured in a book entitled *The Worst Rock 'n' Roll Albums of All Time*. That same year, two selections from the album ("Mr. Tambourine Man" and "Lucy in the Sky with Diamonds") were released by

Rhino Records in their tongue-in-cheek collection of celebrity singers called *Golden Throats*.

But of *Transformed Man*, Shatner has said: "The thrill I got from making this album was deeper and more satisfying than anything I have ever experienced. I was really in orbit." So Shatner's first album was a serious effort, and critics had totally misunderstood his deeply personal interpretations of Shakespearean narratives and modern lyrics.

In the title track for *The Transformed Man*, Shatner concludes: "Then, one day, in the split of a moment, the shutter within flashed open and a rush of light flooded my being. I became as a pure crystal submerged in a translucent sea, and I knew that I had been awakened. I had touched the face of *God*."

Spokesman for Extraterrestrials

"I believe in UFOs," Shatner declared in 1968. "The time is long past when the Air Force or the scientists or the government can say that what people are seeing in the sky are nothing but hot-air balloons or the planet Venus. That kind of doubletalk won't wash any longer. There has been too much evidence over the years that UFOs exist.

"Although I believe in UFOs, I must admit that I fail completely to understand what their purpose is. I just can't find the answers to the intriguing questions that they raise. For example, if these vehicles are piloted by intelligent beings from outer space, then why have they made no effort to contact heads of government or other responsible agencies?

"They have kidnapped farmers in a Georgia swamp and a couple driving a car, but have made no effort to contact the people of earth on a large scale. Perhaps soon, they'll make their purpose known."

Shatner's own UFO experience was part of his motivation for making *Mysteries of the Gods.* In fact, he worked on several projects aimed at expanding the public's awareness of extraterrestrial life after the *Star Trek* series was canceled.

In a 1975 television special called *The Star Trek Dream,* he described humankind's yearning to return to the stars. In 1976, he recorded part one of Isaac Asimov's classic trilogy, *Foundation,* which told the adventures of a small colony of humans created by a dying galactic empire. The course of the colony's growth was plotted according to the science of psychohistory, in which prearranged crises force the people to evolve rapidly. It was an elegant exposition of the ancient astronaut theory, and Shatner's popular recording was nominated for a Grammy Award.

That same year, he recorded Henry Kutner's science fiction short story "Mimsy Were the Borogroves." The premise was that alien beings would have thought processes so different that no adult human would be capable of understanding their behavior. For instance, what seem like random events to us would be entirely predictable by their logic. Only very young children would be capable of learning an extraterrestrial's viewpoint of reality. The album jacket shows a photo of Shatner with a young child in pajamas gazing up at the stars. Both of Shatner's sci-fi albums were re-released in the *Science Fiction Soundbook* collection by Caedmon Records the following year.

After the release of *Mysteries of the Gods,* he began his *Evening with William Shatner* tour to 45 college campuses with audiences ranging in size from 3,000 to 10,000 people. The content of the one-man show centered on man's dream of freedom from earth and his own species' limitations. After asking the audience to relax and listen to the "stars talking to you," he contrasted Aristotle's and Galileo's views of cosmology. Then he presented a variety of concepts about space travel by portraying characters from Cyrano de Bergerac, Shakespeare, Rostand, and Brecht. He read "Earthbound" by poet Irene Jackson,

"Galileo" by Bertoldt Brecht, and selections from H. G. Wells's *War of the Worlds*. Other titles included "Go With Me," "High Flight," "Summer Spaceship," and "Three-Way Alchemy: The Brain."

Although critics asked such questions as "Has Captain Kirk Become a Poetry-Reading Punk Rocker?" the college tour proved very popular. Audience members came away with the impression that Shatner was trying to expand their mental horizons by demonstrating how our historical concept of space travel is linked with the cultural and scientific norm popular at the time. A recording of his performance at Hofstra University was released by Lemli Productions, Shatner's own company.

Within a few months of completing *Mysteries*, Shatner started work on another documentary that explored our place in the cosmos. The NASA-sponsored film, *Universe*, was nominated for an Oscar and won many prestigious awards.

In August 1976, during a speech at a *Star Trek* convention in Oakland, California, two scientists rushed into the auditorium and interrupted Shatner to announce that NASA had discovered life on Mars. It turned out to be a false report, but everyone started screaming and applauding in a frenzy of amazement.

"You have just been told that alien life has been found on Mars," he told the quieted assembly, "but you and I knew it all the time!"

Chapter 2

The Cosmic Connection

Man conceives of God in his own image, but those
images change from generation to generation,
therefore he appears in all these different guises.
—William Shatner on God

William Shatner's belief in extraterrestrial life was based
on his own intuitive feelings about a godlike cosmic intelligence and his telepathic experience with a UFO in the
Mojave Desert. But *Star Trek*'s cosmic connection did not
begin until May 1974, just after Gene Roddenberry got
the nod from Paramount Studios to work on a proposal
for a *Star Trek* motion picture.

Roddenberry was approached by the representative of
a psychic research organization known simply as Lab 9.
They wanted him to write a movie about the Nine, a
group of telepathic extraterrestrials whom the researchers
believed actually existed. They hoped the movie would
make the world aware of the Nine and of their plans to
visit our planet in the near future. Whatever they represented, the mysterious Nine were quite popular among
alien contactee groups during the period I was working
with Shatner.

To prove their claims, Lab 9 asked Roddenberry to

undergo preparation for "the right frame of mind." Their representative, Sir John Whitmore, would introduce Gene to the Nine through psychic channeler Phyllis Schlemmer. But first, Gene would have to travel to universities and research centers around the country witnessing paranormal experiments to open his mind to "higher possibilities." The organization would pay his travel expenses (which ended up being around $25,000), plus $50,000 for the completed script.

"Gene was told to do considerable research into psychic phenomena," recalled screenwriter Jon Povill. "I was around for that, and there was no doubt it was very credible. He couldn't dispute research he had done and witnessed. We even did some ESP experiments around the office and found duplicatable evidence."

Many of the experiments Roddenberry witnessed took place at the fifteen-acre estate of Dr. Andrija Puharich in Ossining, New York. Puharich was a noted neurologist who became interested in parapsychology in the 1950s. He founded the prestigious journal *Parapsychology Review* and wrote *Beyond Telepathy*, about his experiments with the famous psychic Eileen Garrett. In 1960, he led an expedition into Oaxaca, Mexico, to collect hallucinogenic mushrooms that reportedly enhance psychic abilities. He recounted those experiences in his second book, *The Sacred Mushroom*. He also traveled to Hawaii to study Kahuna shamans and to Brazil to investigate the famed healer Arigo. However, little in his background prepared him for meeting Uri Geller, the Israeli psychic and metal-bender.

Geller supposedly developed his powers after being enveloped in the bright light from a UFO at the age of three. Puharich documented Geller's psychokinetic powers and arranged to have the young psychic tested at eighteen university research centers worldwide. Nearly all the tests confirmed Geller's unusual ability to bend metal and sometimes even dematerialize it.

Geller's manic, almost hysterical, personality caused

people to share his passionate belief that something strange was about to happen. His brand of magic seemed to work through the suspension of adult belief systems, much as described in Shatner's recording of "Mimsy Were the Borograves." Too bad the two men never got to meet. Geller is an avid fan of *Star Trek*. Shatner has had a lifelong interest in psychics and consults them even today.

Within a few months of discovering Geller, Puharich would become convinced that the same extraterrestrial intelligences that seemed to play such a mysterious role in Geller's life were also communicating to him.

They identified themselves as the Nine, a community of telepathic aliens headed by an entity known as "Ja Hoovah." They were supposedly communicating from a spaceship called *Spectra* located deep in space—53,069 light years from earth, to be exact. The Nine communicated only with children and selected adults who opened their thoughts to them.

Gene Roddenberry did not know what to make of the alleged extraterrestrials and the people from Lab 9. Some of the things he witnessed were just mind-boggling. During one session at Puharich's estate, Roddenberry was interviewing a group of young psychics. During a break for ice cream, spoons and other utensils started bending. Some spoons bent just as they got near a person's open mouth, and ice cream toppled to the floor. Afterward, Roddenberry examined all the crooked cutlery, mystified by the spontaneous psychokinetic event.

Another time, Puharich started receiving coded messages on his wristwatch. The watch would regularly stop and start again for no apparent reason. Each time, the hands formed a letter of the Hebrew alphabet. Taken together, the letters formed a secret message. As each message neared completion, Puharich would be able to predict exactly when the watch would stop and what configuration the hands would take. Roddenberry witnessed the phenomenon and was much amazed by what looked like direct communication from the Nine.

Other communications with the Nine were channeled through Geller or trance medium Phyllis Schlemmer. In one session, as reported by Joel Engel in his biography of Roddenberry, Gene asked the Nine, speaking through Schlemmer, how he could be certain that they were not using him to implement some evil plan.

"By that of their knowledge, by that of their benefit to planet Earth, you will have understanding," came the channeled reply, in the typically convoluted Nine way of speaking. "We had explained that there would be of those that could create of difficulty, that of the power cannot sustain. Within that of your ear, within that of your heart, within that of your mind—if it feels not right, then that of the essence of which they convey to you, then we give to you our assurance, it is not right."

All the Schlemmer communications were recorded on audiotape. In later sessions, the Nine informed Roddenberry of his past lives as the grandson of Moses and the father of Peter the Apostle. They also spoke of his Jovian characteristics and related his soul to that of the Roman god Jupiter. This was long before fans started calling Roddenberry "the Great Bird of the Galaxy."

But the Great Bird was having great difficulty accepting what he was witnessing. While most of the psychic research seemed credible, Roddenberry never could accept that he might be in actual contact with extraterrestrials. His close friends and fellow writers Ray Bradbury and Isaac Asimov were very much opposed to the idea that UFO intelligences were visiting our planet and would have thought him crazy had he told them about the Nine.

On the other hand, William Shatner was very interested in the search for extraterrestrial life and had voiced concern about government secrecy and UFOs. He was one of the few people with whom Roddenberry could speak freely about the Nine.

In the first draft of the movie script that Roddenberry wrote for Lab 9, a character called Jim MacNorth, the cynical creator of a canceled science-fiction television series, is approached by a group called Second Genesis, who want him to write a screenplay about other life forms trying to contact earthlings about the future of the human race.

Despite convincing demonstrations of paranormal phenomena, MacNorth cannot accept the evidence. His experiences, however, do change his character to the point that he is able to appreciate the profound mystery of life.

But Roddenberry realized he was too closely involved in the story to write a good script. Shatner had already espoused his belief in UFOs and extraterrestrial intelligence. He had often talked with Roddenberry about new script ideas, and during this period the two were in close contact because of the evolving Paramount movie deal. It seems likely that Roddenberry at least mentioned the Nine to Shatner and might even have discussed writing the script with him.

In any case, Roddenberry eventually commissioned writer Jon Povill to produce the final draft. In the rewrite, MacNorth faces the central dilemma of what he would do if he really came in contact with extraterrestrials who had been attempting to guide his life, and moreover, the evolution of the entire human race. MacNorth cannot deal with the idea; he has a nervous breakdown in which he hallucinates that he is confronting ugly-looking aliens on the spaceship from his television series.

In February 1977, I visited Andrija Puharich at the Ossining compound, where he told me about his relationship with Roddenberry. Puharich had been studying a group of thirty-four psychokinetic "space children," whom he referred to simply as "the kids." He believed these children were part of a new race being introduced onto the planet by the Nine because man had proved to the cosmos that he is inherently dangerous.

"We wanted to do a movie about these kinds of kids," Puharich told me, "so we sent Roddenberry around the world for six months meeting kids, and we got them all together with Geller. We watched Gene seeing metal bending and listening to the testimony about teletransportation. But he couldn't handle it. He freaked out. The reality of it simply could not be handled, and I said: 'Gene, why, in the *Star Trek* series, did you have a transporter if you didn't believe in the concept of dematerialization? Do you believe in that?' He said: 'Hell, no! That was the cheapest way I could think of to get the actors from one set to another.' Gene Roddenberry has a very limited point of view."

Despite Puharich's disappointment, Roddenberry was affected by the many weeks he spent on the project. For one thing, he was forced to consider the possibility that alien civilizations might be interfering with our own species, and the Nine became a hidden theme in much of his later work.

In 1975, the first *Star Trek* movie script Roddenberry proposed was called *The God Thing*. It was about the *Enterprise* finding an alien God at the ends of the universe. Not surprisingly, that would be the same idea that Shatner chose when it came time for him to direct his own movie, *Star Trek V: The Final Frontier*.

"That script was very daring," said director Richard Colla, to whom Roddenberry had shown it. "They went off in search of that thing from outer space that was affecting everything. By the time they got to the spaceship and into its presence, it manifested itself and said, 'Do you know me?' Kirk said, 'No, I don't know who you are.' It said, 'Strange, how could you not know who I am? The time has passed and you should know me by now.' It shifts shape and comes up as Christ the Carpenter and says, 'Do you know me?' And Kirk says, 'Oh, now I know who you are.' And the presence says, 'How strange, that you didn't know these other forms of me.' Really, what Gene had written was that this 'thing' was sent forth to lay down the law, to communicate the law of the universe."

Just before Roddenberry's death, when it came time to script another *Star Trek* series about the most remote outpost in the galaxy, the title *Deep Space Nine* just happened to pop into the head of Rick Berman, the man who'd inherited Roddenberry's position as caretaker of the series.

Filming *Mysteries of the Gods*

Shatner's belief in the Nine or in other alien beings trying to guide the human race was also a hidden theme in *Mysteries of the Gods*. However, though he harbored a deep personal belief in the reality of extraterrestrial intelligence, it was the shortcomings of intelligent life on earth that gave him the most problems.

His luggage joined an ever-growing list of his personal items and clothing that would never be seen again. The trend began with his first appearance as Captain Kirk on television and would continue through *Star Trek VI*. Nearly $200,000 worth of *Star Trek* wardrobe items and Shatner's own personal belongings have disappeared from the face of the earth. Whether it represents a conspiracy by his enemies or his fans, or the efforts of some interstellar museum to set up an alien *Star Trek* exhibit, will probably never be known for sure.

The morning after we arrived in Washington to continue filming *Mysteries,* Shatner went shopping for makeup and new clothes to replace what he'd lost. The change in his wardrobe became obvious in the finished film. In earlier segments, he wears dark sportcoats and light-colored dress shirts, while later he appears in a black turtleneck or in a long-collared suede shirt and polyester bellbottoms. The host had undergone a significant change in his fashion sense while traveling cross-country.

When we finally began our long limo-trek through the rolling hills of Virginia, Shatner quickly became bored. He started questioning me about my education and hobbies, obviously searching for some entertaining conversation. My diverse background included several years in graduate school at the University of Vienna, studying mathematics. When I mentioned this to him, I assumed he might like to talk about his own travels through Europe. Instead, he asked me to teach him calculus.

That was a tall order, considering we were sitting in the back of a limousine and Shatner's only knowledge of math consisted of a few accounting courses he had taken at McGill University. But the captain insisted.

Thus, with neither blackboard nor textbook, I began my impromptu class with an introduction to infinite progressions. I used the back of the front seat as a graphic example. The leather stitching divided the seat back into a pattern of long rectangles whose tops met in a gently rising curve. While there is no simple way to find the total area under such a curve, it can be approximated by adding up the areas of the individual rectangles. If we could make the rectangles so thin that the curved tops became negligible, then we would have an even better estimate of the total area.

Shatner easily caught on to the basic principle involved. He saw that if we could stuff the area under the curve with an infinite number of rectangles, the curved area they did not fill would approach zero. The sum of all these ever-smaller rectangles tends toward a finite number, which is the precise area. The method, known as "integration," solves many types of equations that can be graphed as the area under a curve.

I used the same pattern of stitching on the back of the seat to demonstrate another method of calculus, called "differentiation." The curved top stitching could also represent a change over time, such as the growth of a child as he gets older. In that case, the vertical stitching would represent different measurements of the child's height, taken as he matured. The more measurements we'd take, the smoother the curve would become. A mathematician might say that a child's height is a function of his age, and the curve tends toward a limiting value, which is his adult height.

Shatner understood that the child's rate of growth could be represented by drawing a line from one measurement to another. He noted that the slope of the line would be steeper for a younger child than for an older one, because younger children grow at a faster rate. The slope of a line touching just one point on the curve gives a precise rate of growth at that instant. That line would probably be very steep at age three, but almost horizontal by age twenty-one, when we reach our adult height.

Shatner grasped such concepts intuitively. He took a tenacious hold of each new idea, trying to absorb the material on a gut level instead of understanding it intellectually. Whenever I attempted to prove a statement by appealing to some respected theorem, he cut me off and insisted I explain in a more immediate fashion.

The lively math of calculus is the foundation of modern physics and astronomy. That fact proved to be the reason for Shatner's interest. He knew calculus was a powerful tool for understanding acceleration and gravity, and he wanted to understand how it was used to navigate to the moon and guide space probes to Mars. For someone reluctant to reminisce about *Star Trek*, he was taking the perspective of a starship commander.

Shatner's enthusiasm for space science was nowhere more obvious than in his relationship with Jesco Von Puttkamer, a NASA scientist he interviewed for *Mysteries of the Gods*. Von Puttkamer came to the United States with rocket scientist Wernher von Braun and worked on the Apollo moon landing. His official title was Senior Staff Scientist for Advanced Programs of Space Flight, and in the film, he talked about the certainty of encountering intelligent life when mankind travels into deep space. Shatner became so enamored of the scientist that he later found a place for him as science adviser to *Star Trek: The Motion Picture.*

Jesco Von Puttkamer reminded me of Spock. He was very logical and precise, and these traits were underscored by a heavy German accent. He was in his early fifties and had thick white hair that contrasted sharply with his solid black eyebrows and mustache. He wore dark-lensed glasses that imparted a Dr. Strangelove look, although he was a straightforward and kind person.

Nothing in the highly disciplined scientist's years of training could have prepared him for the day when William Shatner kissed him while filming his interview.

"You have to be very tight," the German scientist recalled, "you know, for the interview, for the closeups—very close together—nose to nose. We had been working on it and I was not used to it. I was a little stiff or something. He wanted to loosen me up. All of a sudden Bill leaned forward and *he kissed me!* Well, you know, from *him* I take it. Nobody else."

Such spontaneous displays of emotion were not uncommon for Shatner. Once, at a party in Ottawa for the repertory theater where he was working, Shatner felt compelled to walk up to the Indian ambassador and pinch him on the cheek! He later explained that the ambassador had such perfect, round brown cheeks that he just had to squeeze them. Shatner's feelings—whether good, bad, affectionate, or loathsome—have always been close to the surface.

Part of the appeal of Captain Kirk came from Shatner's imbuing his character with an openness and range of emotions not previously associated with heroic figures. The popular male leads of the day, such as James Arness, Gary Cooper, Gregory Peck, or John Wayne, all portrayed strong, silent, stoic men. But Shatner's character revealed his deepest emotions and lived by his feelings. By contrasting Captain Kirk's emotional candor with his reserved, logical first officer, Spock, *Star Trek* became a weekly essay on the place of emotions in the ideal man.

However, it was our scientific discussion in the back of the limousine that set the mood for our visit to the COMSAT Technical Center. It was housed in a four-story yellow-brick structure that looked like many of the other buildings in the area, except that it had several odd-shaped antennae and satellite dishes on the roof. Inside, dozens of small offices were jammed with computer terminals and electronic gear.

Dr. Billingham was waiting for us in the office of a friend. Billingham was a thin, distinguished-looking man with neatly cut graying hair. His slight British accent complemented a natural politeness and cheerful demeanor. As chief of the NASA's Extraterrestrial Intelligence Division, he was responsible for directing the government's SETI project (Search for Extraterrestrial Intelligence). At the time, NASA's efforts were in the planning stages, and Dr. Billingham intended to outline some of the space agency's ideas for communicating with alien species.

We ascended a wide stairway to the roof, where Eddie set up his camera near the largest satellite dish and unfolded a white reflector to try to diffuse the harsh light from the midday sun. Shatner and Billingham took their positions near the satellite dish and walked approximately fifty feet in a practice run.

When filming started, Dr. Billingham began explaining the SETI program, and the two men strolled casually toward the camera. They stopped about halfway and Billingham opened a large, flat box containing artist's renderings of proposed SETI projects. At that point, Eddie zoomed into the paintings from over their shoulders while they talked about the futuristic designs.

Unfortunately, the bright sunlight made Shatner's long-haired toupee all the more obvious. The black hairpiece clashed against his blond eyebrows and yellow jacket, giving him the appearance of a Beatle doll. His natural light-brown hair had steadily receded over the last decade, leaving a bald spot at the crown of his head. His efforts to cover it were betrayed by his inability to decide on one style or color. This was the longest hairpiece he had ever worn, and the unkempt look and dark color were dead giveaways.

Despite the unflattering sunlight, Shatner seemed more comfortable on the high, flat roof of the building than at any other place we'd filmed. While he talked with Dr. Billingham, I thought back to a very different interview we had had a few days earlier.

We had driven north along the Hudson River to the small town of Stony Point, New York, where we'd set up in front of Town Hall to interview two policemen. The area had been the source of many UFO reports just a month earlier, and I arranged for Shatner to interview some of the witnesses. The two officers had observed several UFOs hovering over a nearby nuclear power plant.

When we arrived, shortly after lunch, the streets of the town were almost deserted. Still, Shatner seemed nervous. He huddled close to the officers in front of a parked patrol car and spoke in short, choppy sentences. He kept peering out of the corner of his eye, as if he were searching for someone.

Two blocks down the street, three teenaged girls walked out of an ice cream parlor and paused on the sidewalk. They looked innocent enough, standing on the sidewalk in their colorful flower-print dresses, slowly licking ice cream cones. One of them glanced down the street to see what was going on. That was all it took for Shatner.

"Thank you," he said abruptly to the surprised officers. Then, turning to me, he yelled: "Run for it!"

Shatner took off, running for the limo, which was parked in the shade a few blocks away. Without exactly knowing why, I started running after him. He kept glancing back over his shoulder, but I had no idea what he expected to see. When we reached the car, he motioned for me to get inside, then turned and waved for Chuck and Eddie to follow us. Neither of them could figure out what was happening, but they dismantled the camera equipment and started walking toward us.

Shatner got in the backseat and turned around to look out the rear window. The girls were still standing on the sidewalk, licking their melting ice cream cones and trying to figure out what all the commotion was about.

"What's wrong?" I asked.

"Didn't you see those girls? In another few minutes, they'd have gotten to us!"

My incredulous expression spoke for itself.

"I'm not kidding!" he said emphatically. "Before long, the word would get out, and we'd be besieged by hundreds of screaming teenagers."

I doubted if there were a hundred teenagers in the whole town, although I understood why Shatner was concerned. He had had some very scary experiences with his fans. He told me about being scratched by the fingernails of clutching teenagers and having pieces of his clothing ripped off by hordes of screaming admirers. Once, while he sat dining with friends in a fancy restaurant, a totally unknown woman jumped into his lap and started hugging him. Such behavior really frightened Shatner.

In addition to his overzealous fans, he was convinced that a small percentage of "Trekkies" actually believed he was Captain Kirk of the *Enterprise*. He said there was no telling what those people were capable of doing.

Back in the safe isolation of the COMSAT rooftop, Dr. Billingham had finished showing Shatner the last of his drawings. Most of NASA's plans required building orbiting radio telescopes ranging in diameter from 300 to 10,000 feet. The sensitive electromagnetic ears could eavesdrop on civilizations thousands of light-years away.

"What is your speculation that intelligent life from outer space has been here already?" Shatner asked the scientist.

"Probes from other civilizations," Billingham replied, "could have come here in the past. Life has been present on the earth for four billion years, and even if a probe came once every billion years, we would have been visited four times. However, all traces of the evidence of such visits, unless we were very lucky, would have long since disappeared."

Not according to Erich von Daniken, I thought. The bestselling author would insist that all around us there are signs left by ancient astronauts. In the film, Shatner narrated considerable footage presenting such evidence. Huge humanoid footprints were found fossilized next to dinosaur prints in Texas, Java, and China. Brazilian Indians and Arizona Hopis chant legends about the arrival of space-suited visitors. Cave paintings in Australia, New Guinea, France, and Italy seem to depict space-helmeted aliens. A stone relief found in the ruins of the Mayan city of Palenque is said to show an extraterrestrial piloting a spacecraft. Some unknown power arranged massive stones in strange patterns in Great Britain, Peru, and Costa Rica, and on several islands in the South Pacific.

Von Daniken's new interpretations of archaeological discoveries created a storm of controversy. It would have been much easier on everyone if the ancient astronauts had only left behind a phaser or a tri-corder.

After we wrapped up the Billingham interview, Shatner went into an unused office to change his clothes, while the rest of us prepared to head off for the next location.

When Shatner showed up at the limousine, he had traded his sportcoat and turtleneck for a reddish-brown suede shirt with high, pointed collars. He sported a gold chain around his neck, and his shirt was unbuttoned, exposing his chest hair. He must have expected a few comments about the new mod look, but no one dared say a word. We all got back in the car and drove to the radio telescope site to start my interview.

The huge dish-shaped antenna was concealed behind a clump of trees in a deserted meadow. We had to travel down a long dirt road to reach it, though there were no identifying signs or other indications of what was hidden there. It seemed to be an odd place to find a 100-foot-tall radio telescope. The only evidence that anyone worked there was a padlocked cinderblock hut underneath the dish support. Once again, we set up to do some filming.

The late afternoon lighting was more flattering, and Shatner looked handsome in his casual attire. At forty-five years old, he seemed in good physical shape. There was no evidence of the bone corset he was rumored to wear, but his massive chest seemed barely supported by his short legs and tiny feet. His shoes must have been only a size five or six. Close up, Shatner's long eyelashes and gentle hazel eyes gave his face a surprisingly feminine look.

As we strolled toward the camera, I told Shatner about my first UFO sighting. In December 1969, two companions and I went on a skiing holiday to Innsbruck, Austria. As we glided over a narrow ridge on the Nordketten Range, we came upon what looked like a metallic object hovering in front of a large boulder in a ravine about 250 feet ahead of us. The unsteady gray disk appeared to be spinning in mid-air. We threw off our skis and started walking toward it, but as we approached, it began to disappear right before our eyes. It was as if it pulsated in and out of existence.

The object could have been an optical illusion of some type, possibly caused by a reflection of light from the bright snow into the shadowy ravine. In any case, the sighting got me interested, and I began devoting a lot of time to the study of UFO reports.

After I told Shatner the story of my first encounter with a UFO, we paused for a moment and compared photographs of glowing or odd-shaped clouds, lens aberrations, and other explainable UFOs with photographs of truly unidentifiable flying objects. I was convinced that a small percentage of UFO reports represented an unknown phenomenon of some kind, although there was no evidence to suggest that the apparent intelligences behind them were here to save the world, or even destroy it.

If anything, the reported behavior of UFOs suggested that they had their own motives independent of human needs and goals. My opinion was not what Shatner had expected. He was looking for a more anthropomorphic viewpoint, something that suggested mankind was the subject of a grand experiment by extraterrestrial intelligence. I did not believe that UFO evidence suggested that, although the idea was certainly part of the ancient astronaut hypothesis.

Shatner got what he was looking for when we visited Tompkins Cove, a small settlement in upstate New York. I had arranged for him to interview Dan Cetrone, the director of the Parapsychological Research Institute.

An intense man with a round face and tight, curly hair, Cetrone headed a UFO research team that investigated nearly twenty-five sightings a week in New York and Connecticut. More important, he believed mankind was being prepared for a meeting with the same alien intelligences responsible for the ancient astronaut evidence.

"What will happen," Shatner asked him, "when the ancient astronauts return to contact us?"

"I think there will be an Eighth Day of Creation," Cetrone replied, "meaning our next stage. We have gone as far as we can on this particular planet by ourselves, and now we need help to get us beyond it."

"Do you have any thoughts about the possibility of our contacting them mentally, through telepathy?" Shatner might have been referring to his own UFO experience.

"I am totally convinced UFOs are going to land somewhere," Cetrone answered, "where they're going to be greeted by people who are in the right frame of mind and with the right interests."

(There was that phrase again: "the right frame of mind." Was it some kind of password with these people?)

"Do you mean there are people being prepared," Shatner queried, "to receive an extraterrestrial visitor?" I detected a slight quickening in the host's voice.

"To be specific," Cetrone replied, "*I* am being prepared for the frame of mind that is necessary to greet an extraterrestrial visitor. It is as specific as I can be."

That was what Shatner wanted to hear. He wanted to find out if there were people being prepared for contact with alien beings.

Later, he pursued the same theme in an interview with Dr. Richard Yinger, the director of the Exosociology Institute in Lake Worth, Florida. Yinger's head was totally bald, and his bushy black beard seemed to be attached to the horn-rimmed glasses he was wearing. He looked like a genuine egghead.

Yinger told Shatner: "I think there are some of us who have come to the point in our lives where our own consciousness has been literally raised to the level where the difference between us and the extraterrestrials is very, very narrow. I think these people feel the kind of sympathy that a person could project, and that sensitivity could actually be giving them messages. I have felt this very intensely myself."

Shatner ended the film with the unsettling question: "Are we somehow, in some inexplicable way, being prepared by an intelligence beyond our own for our first encounter with extraterrestrial beings? Think of it! Am *I* being prepared for this encounter? Are *you?*"

There is no doubt in my mind that Shatner thought he was one of a select group of earthlings who were being prepared for alien contact.

The mid-1970s saw the proliferation of dozens of groups promising to put people in the right frame of mind for extraterrestrial contact. Shatner's preparation for that "right frame of mind" came from going where no man has gone before in his portrayal of Captain Kirk. The role stretched his mind and imagination, imbuing him with a cosmic viewpoint. Throughout his life, he believed he was someone special. The thought of becoming one of the planet's "chosen ones" would be a natural progression for this gifted though egocentric man.

Of course, the source of Shatner's belief in a cosmic intelligence and the roots of his own complex personality can only be traced by traveling back to his childhood.

Chapter 3

Toughy Takes 'Em On

I never went through that off-putness, that adolescent, awkward puberty. I never had pimples on my face.
—William Shatner on his teenage years

The burly French-Canadian farmer heard the gang of boys rifling through his field, and by the time he reached them, he was pissed. When he came upon them yanking up his carrots and went after them like a mad bull, the kids dived over the fence rails like streaks of greased lightning. But one little boy could not make it in time. The farmer grabbed at the lad's tousled brown hair, missed, then kicked him in the rear with all his might. The man's hobnailed boot landed squarely on the tail of the boy's spine and sent searing pain throughout his body.

William Shatner's face still cringes when he thinks back to the incident. He remembers the pain like it was yesterday, describing the feeling as worse than getting hit in the balls because it lasts longer. The young Shatner would never forget what it was like to get kicked in the ass, and he would never let anyone do it to him again. He would grow into a real scrapper, a strong, athletic type who took no crap from anyone. Eventually, that would include even fierce Klingons.

William Shatner grew up in a large house at 4419 Girouard Street in Montreal, Canada. Born into an upper-middle-class Jewish family on March 22, 1931, he shared the attention of his parents with two older sisters, Joy and Farla. His father, Joseph, was preoccupied with the family's clothing business, the Admiration Clothing Company. His mother, Anne, stayed busy with neighborhood and household commitments.

The children's relationship with their parents was one of distance and respect. The Shatner children were well provided for, but as was the case in many families of the era, they were meant to be seen and not heard. Shatner recalls that even his mother's cooking was a way to keep them quiet.

"My mother made these matzoh balls. They were tightly packed, indestructible, and delicious. To prevent you from rising above your station, she put one in your stomach. It made it very difficult to rise at all."

Nonetheless, the high-spirited Shatner son would take a little longer to learn his station than did his sisters. Little Billy always seemed to be getting into trouble. Even the games he played had a way of running afoul of adults, because the boy's fantasies clashed head-on with the mundane world of his conservative Quebec town. Local farmers were always on the lookout for "that Shatner kid" who found their expansive fields irresistible. Sometimes he could be seen trampling their crops, running with other boys, or chasing invisible playmates by himself.

Besides getting kicked around by farmers, Billy got to know the sting of his father's belt. Once, the boy used a woodworking set he received as a gift to saw into the legs of an expensive dining room table his father had just purchased. While the family was eating dinner, the table suddenly collapsed, sending food and china crashing to the floor. What made the incident even more memorable was the beating his father gave him. Slowly removing his wide leather belt, he told his son: "This is going to hurt

me more than you." Billy learned never to take that
statement at face value again.

Lucky for his reddened rear end, the boy was very
young when he discovered an outlet for his imaginative
energy. William Shatner discovered the power of acting
when he was only six years old. It happened at summer
camp in 1937. Camp in depression-era Quebec was not
some privileged kids' retreat to Camp Coddle-Me. Summer camp meant fifty or so kids spending several weeks on
a real farm, working hard at chores and playing hard in
the outdoors. This particular farm was owned by Shatner's aunt and was located in the Laurentian Mountains,
ninety miles north of Montreal.

Every Sunday, the campers would put on a play for
visiting parents. In one of the amateur productions, Billy
was chosen to play a little Jewish boy in Nazi Germany.
To escape persecution, the child's family was abandoning
their home, and the little boy had to leave behind his pet
dog, who was played by another young camper. During
the scene where Billy was saying goodbye to his dog, tears
welled up in his eyes, and he started to cry. The audience
was profoundly moved by the portrayal of the sacrifices
being made by their friends and families in Germany at
the time. Many joined the boy and started sobbing
openly.

What the audience did not know was that little Billy
was crying because he really wanted a dog of his own, not
because he had any comprehension of the events in far-
away Europe. He just wanted a puppy, but his parents
would never allow it.

"All I remember was people were trying to take me
away from my dog," Shatner said many years later. "I
always wanted one, and my parents' argument was, in the
muddy streets of Montreal, the dog would run around
outside, come in, and dirty up the carpets and furniture.
They'd say, 'You can have a hobby horse, but you can't
have a dog!' So now that I'm an adult, I really got dogs,

I breed them—Dobermans—and so I remember my crying on stage as a kid, 'Don't take my dog away from me!!!'

"I didn't realize how meaningful the play was. At the end, I looked up and saw everyone crying. At that moment, I had a firm feeling of being able to get hold of people's emotions. So from that moment on, I wasn't interested in anything else but acting."

A Six-Year-Old Thespian

William Shatner's discovery of the technique of method acting at the tender age of six gave him quite an advantage over other child actors. Two years later, he made his professional acting debut, as Tom Sawyer, at the Montreal Children's Theater. Every weekend for the next five years, he appeared in a children's play at the popular theater. He also acted in more extravagant annual productions, which attracted families from throughout the province.

When he was ten, he started performing on the airwaves for the Canadian Broadcasting Corporation. The Montreal Radio Fairytale Theater was a live weekly show that featured Shatner reading the parts of fairy-tale heroes such as Prince Charming. He stayed with the radio program until he was thirteen.

During his childhood, Shatner continued to act at summer camp, which was usually located on one of the French-Canadian farms north of Montreal. Although there were between forty and a hundred other kids, and his older sister usually went with him, he was frequently homesick. His only consolation was the sheer physical exhilaration he got from farm life, like milking cows twice a day or gathering around to watch the pigs get slaughtered. The animals' blood was slowly drained out and collected, because blood soup was a favorite among the French-Canadian farmers.

There was plenty of time for more traditional camp activities, which centered in fallow fields and nearby rivers. Shatner excelled at swimming and became a champion boxer in contests with other boys. Young Bill eventually served as a camp counselor, and his impromptu campfire performances became legend.

One of Shatner's most popular campfire characters was a mad scientist. In November 1989, when he was the guest of honor on the *This Is Your Life* television show, host Michael Aspel coaxed him into reprising the role, complete with costume and props. Thousands of viewers witnessed the rebirth of a character Shatner had created as a teenager at camp.

In fact, summer camp had more of an influence on Shatner's life than any school he ever attended. It was at camp that he learned that both his acting talents and his athletic prowess could earn him the attention and admiration of those around him. Looking back, it is almost as if he based his whole life on developing those two talents. By the time he was a teenager, he was pursuing acting and sports simultaneously and relentlessly, as if nothing else mattered.

Tough and Tender

The young Shatner struggled to find a way to balance his passions for acting and sports with the normal activities and problems of adolescence. Like many teenagers, he wanted to be popular but was very shy around girls. He never attended any proms or had a steady girlfriend. There was no childhood sweetheart for William Shatner. At West Hill High School, his classmates thought of him as a very focused and dynamic kid who could also have a very short fuse.

Feelings always came first with Shatner, and he was quick to defend himself against any disparaging comments. Most of the students at West Hill High were Roman Catholic, and there was a hard core of antisemitism at the school. As a result, Shatner got in a lot of fights, sometimes with two or three kids at once. After a couple of semesters of taunting their swaggering classmate, his fellow students eventually nicknamed him "Toughy"— and they learned to watch what they said around him.

While Toughy relished the attention he received from his radio and stage work, he also loved the physical challenge of sports. He competed on the wrestling team and was active in the Skiing Club. He joined the football team and became a varsity letterman, despite the fact that he could not attend team functions on Jewish holidays. Once, he lost his position on the team because he could not attend a cutting session, where first- and second-team members were chosen.

"I was a bit small for a pro football career," player number 45 later admitted, "but I was mean."

Unfortunately, his passionate interests in acting and sports did not complement one another. His theater friends classified him as a "jock," while his athletic friends teased him about his "pansy" behavior on stage. The conflict became the central problem of his youth and undoubtedly contributed to the egotistical facade that would become a prominent feature of his adult personality.

Shatner's favorite play in high school was Clifford Odets's *Golden Boy*. He strongly identified with the main character, a boy torn between his two passions, boxing and playing the violin. Shatner felt the same tension between sports and acting, and he would often describe himself as feeling like he was caught "carrying a violin case past the gym" in high school.

"I had aspirations of being a football player and at the same time I wanted to act," he told one interviewer. "As a result, I was torn in two directions. The actors don't play football and the football players think the actors are sissies."

Even as an adult, he would have difficulty finding time for both the stage and his love of sports, although he would never give up either one. He strenuously worked out in order to be in top shape for new roles, and on movie sets he could usually be found hanging out with the stuntmen rather than with other actors.

Toughy stuck it out in high school and graduated in 1948. In his senior yearbook, he stated that his life's ambition was to become an actor. But his parents had always assumed their son's acting was only a youthful diversion, like his interest in sports. They fully expected him to go to business college, settle down, and enter the family clothing business in a few years.

Acting Like a Businessman

Heeding his parents' wishes, Shatner enrolled in the College of Commerce at McGill University in Montreal. However, his interests were not in the business and accounting courses on his schedule. He copied other peoples' notes and rarely showed up in class except to take exams. He devoted only enough time to his studies to keep from flunking out.

Most of his energies went into acting in off-campus plays and producing musicals for the student theater. He later estimated he devoted eighteen hours a day producing, directing, and writing musicals at McGill. In what little spare time he had, he worked as a radio announcer for the Canadian Broadcasting Corporation. With the extra money, he was able to pay for his books and fees.

Shatner held a deep distrust of things academic, believing one could learn only through direct experience, almost on a visceral level. He never undertook formal training in acting; he thought that acting could never be taught because it was not a discipline like other theatrical arts, such as lighting or set building. For Shatner, acting was the art of eliciting emotional responses from an audience. There was no way to put that in a book. If anything, acting classes destroyed one's natural spark by focusing on artificial techniques. Experience and adventure were the keys to developing character and true stage presence.

True to his beliefs, Shatner sought new experiences and adventures whenever he got the opportunity. When he was nineteen, Shatner and eight friends took a harrowing two-week canoe trip over the treacherous waters of Lake Champlain and down the Hudson River from Montreal to New York. Their feat landed them in a segment on American television. A year later, he took three months off from college and hitchhiked across the United States. He talked a friend into accompanying him, and with the princely sum of $200 in their pockets and a sign reading "Two McGill Students Seeing America," they hitchhiked from Toronto to Washington, D.C., then west all the way to Los Angeles. From there, the two went north to Vancouver, then over to Chicago, and ended up in Montreal.

In his junior year of college, Shatner became infatuated with a beautiful coed. Yet as their romantic relationship blossomed, it became clear that the two wanted different things from life. Shortly after Shatner told her of his dream to become a professional actor, the practical young lady dropped out of college to marry a businessman and move to New York. Realizing how foolish it had been to keep his real plans a secret from his parents, Shatner decided it was time to confess to them that he intended to make a career on the stage.

His father was absolutely furious. His son was going against all their plans and all hope of a solid, successful life. He insisted that William join the family business after graduating and put away such childish dreams. The theater was no place to make a living, and actors were held in low esteem. Economics dealt with the facts of life, his father said, and the stage was just for playacting. The bitter argument went on for weeks, but Toughy would not budge an inch.

One afternoon, the elder Shatner sat on his son's bed listening, while his son paced frantically back and forth, trying to explain his reasons for wanting to be an actor. Suddenly, deeply disappointed, he realized his son was adamant about his plans. They struck a deal: if in five years William could not find success in acting, he would come home to work with his father.

In his senior year, Shatner dropped all but one of his business classes and concentrated on improving his English and communication skills. He wrote and directed a college musical, *The Red, White, and Blue Revue,* which got good campus notices and national attention. He came to realize that the writers and directors are the ones who really make things happen in the theater. Actors only deal with the compelling rationale of their own characters, whereas writers and directors must deal with all aspects of all the characters.

"It's what we call the spine—or the core—of the character," he said later. "It's for the character what the theme of the play is to the play. A director must know the spines—or cores—of all the characters and see how they mesh or entwine or go against each other. And, of course, neither the actors nor the director can find them unless the playwright has put them there in the first place. As a writer, I've found from acting what I have to put in my plays to make them come alive for the persons who direct and act them so they'll come alive for the audience."

For the rest of his life, Shatner would want to write and direct as much as act. Unfortunately, his ambitions to do *everything* would often conflict with the actual writers and directors with whom he worked. The reason he ended up acting more than writing or directing was simply that he was a better actor than he was either a writer or director. But of course, that did not stop him from trying.

Shatner was graduated from McGill in 1952 with a Bachelor of Arts degree in commerce. He immediately looked around for a job in the theater, but the only thing he could find was a position as business manager for the Mountain Playhouse, a summer stock theater in Montreal. Shatner had never really learned anything about accounting or management in college, and he turned out to be a terrible manager. He misplaced money, lost track of tickets, and was very disorganized. He kept pleading for a chance to act, and out of sheer desperation, the owners let him audition.

It was clear that Shatner was a better actor than a manager, and the Mountain Playhouse was finally getting something for its money, even if it was not what they had expected. Shatner's acting talents saved his job. By the end of the first summer, the producer was so impressed that he recommended Shatner to the national theater in Ottawa.

The Canadian National Repertory Theater in Ottawa offered Shatner $31 a week to work as an assistant manager. Before long, they, too, realized that their new employee would end up spending far more time on stage than in his office. Although he played mostly the roles of children and adolescents, he appeared on stage in well-received productions such as *Skylark, Castle in the Air, Nightmare Abbey,* and *Mr. Bolfry.*

In Ottawa, Shatner lived alone for the first time in his life. During the frigid winter months, he could often be seen ice-skating on the fifty-mile-long Rideau Canal that runs through the city. At other times, he took long walks late at night.

On one of those walks, he was especially troubled and about to give up acting and return to his father's business. He stopped for a minute to listen to Christmas carols at the Peace Tower, near the capitol. Standing alone in the cold snow, he decided once and for all that being a great actor was more important to him than money, more important than anything.

"Those five years in Canada," he later told interviewer Robin Leach, "were starvation years. I'm talking about rope mattresses in attics and saving two dollars if I wanted to eat, or not doing my laundry if I wanted to eat—that kind of thing. Being hungry and in need is still always in the back of my mind. I paid my dues as an actor as I came up through the ranks."

Nearly all of his meager salary went to rent, and he learned what it means to be a starving young actor. His most frequent meal, sometimes twice a day, was the twenty-seven-cent fruit salad at Woolworth's lunch counter. To this day, he cannot stand the thought of eating fruit salad. But amid the noise and commotion of Woolworth's, Shatner studied his lines.

His fellow actors were not much better off. "They even had to make their own booze and I was the official taster," Shatner later admitted, "—which is pretty funny, as I'm a nondrinker. When I keeled over from the mixture, they knew it was ready for imbibing."

Shatner toured with the Canadian Repertory Theater and spent the summer months with the Mountain Playhouse. It was a hard life, but he was getting good reviews and that was all it took to keep him going. When his father asked him to come home and stay there until he got on his feet, Shatner turned him down. Reluctantly, his father realized his son was never coming home again and found another young man, someone outside the family, to help him with the clothing business. When his father died fifteen years later, the stranger took over the family business.

"Those days were hell," Shatner said later. "I got through them because in front of me was a dream. I hoped to become as fine an actor as Laurence Olivier." That was a challenging goal for any actor, but the young and inexperienced Canadian was determined to succeed.

From Businessman to Shakespearean

In 1953, Shatner got an offer to play juvenile parts at the newly formed Stratford Shakespearean Festival in Ontario. The festival's unique outdoor stage was a bowl-shaped pit in the ground covered by a huge tent that could accommodate 2,000 theatergoers. The company was under the guidance of Sir Tyrone Guthrie, one of the most respected directors in the world. Although Shatner's salary would be only $80 a week, it was his golden opportunity. The very first time Guthrie saw the young actor perform in rehearsal, he leapt from his seat clapping, then walked down to the stage and shook his hand. He became Shatner's mentor and promised the young actor that he could become "another Laurence Olivier" if he tried hard enough. That was all the aspiring lad had to hear.

Trying harder was exactly what he did. Shatner mastered nearly a hundred roles in sixty plays and rose from minor parts to important characters. His first major role came in June 1954, in the festival's production of *Measure for Measure*. He played a young lord in the bitter comedy about social mores and justice in old Vienna. James Mason played the lead. In July, Shatner played Lucentio, opposite Robert Goodier, in Shakespeare's comedy about the war of the sexes *The Taming of the Shrew*. In August, he was in the on-stage chorus for the festival's production of *Oedipus Rex*, the immortal tragedy by Sophocles.

Of Shatner's role in *The Merchant of Venice*, produced in July 1955 at the prestigious festival, the *New York Times* wrote: "As Gratiano, William Shatner has a boyish swagger that refreshes another commonplace part." Notices like that confirmed Shatner's belief that even in small roles, he could get the attention of critics and the audience if he had a commanding presence on stage. He developed an almost maniacal predilection for center stage, a trait that would perplex producers and directors who worked with him—both on stage and in movies—for years to come.

That same summer, Shatner played Lucius in *Julius Caesar* and appeared again in the chorus of *King Oedipus*, but his most significant part was Usumcasane in Christopher Marlowe's *Tamburlaine*, for it was that role that took Shatner to Broadway six months later.

The Stratford Shakespearean Festival's production of *Tamburlaine the Great* opened at the Winter Garden Theater in New York on January 19, 1956. The play was about the King of Persia's bloody conquests and his fragile truces with Turkey and Egypt. There was plenty of action—most of the scenes depicted violent battles, murders, and torture—along with primitive chanting and a stirring musical score. Anthony Quayle played King Tamburlaine and Shatner played the second male lead. The play ran for twenty-one weeks to good reviews.

Tamburlaine was Shatner's introduction to Broadway's theatrical life, and he loved every moment of it. He attended formal receptions by other theater groups, went to private parties, and made a number of important contacts. Although Shatner's main function in the play was to carry a sedan chair for Anthony Quayle, the young actor knew how to make the most of any role.

A talent scout from Twentieth Century–Fox went backstage and offered Shatner a seven-year exclusive movie contract at $500 a week to start. Just at that moment, a complete stranger, a man Shatner had never seen before or since, approached him and said simply: "Trust me—don't sign that contract." Then the man turned away and walked out of sight. Shatner did not know what to make of the strange occurrence.

He made an appointment with the talent scout and arranged for his cousin, a recent law school graduate, to represent him. But when Shatner showed up at the Twentieth Century–Fox office to sign the contract, he could not bring himself to do it, nor could he explain to anyone involved why. He stated simply that he had to follow his instincts. The only contract Shatner would sign that year would be to do a live television play for NBC's *Goodyear Playhouse.*

"I still had the idealistic dream of being an Olivier-type star," he said, searching for some explanation years later. "I didn't want to be a Hollywood actor."

Perhaps an even more significant incident in the young actor's career took place the following summer, during a performance of *Henry V* at the Shakespeare Festival in Stratford, Ontario. Shatner had landed the part of the Duke of Gloucester, but he was also the understudy to Christopher Plummer, who had the lead role. One day Plummer fell ill from an attack of kidney stones and was unable to continue. Shatner, who had never rehearsed the part, was asked to go on in the seasoned actor's place.

"I understudied Plummer in *Henry V,*" Shatner recalled, "and went on for him one evening very early on in the play's run with no rehearsal. I played in front of 2,300 people, and a coterie of critics happened to be there that evening. It was a play that I had not rehearsed with anyone, including myself. I had just learned the lines."

Shatner did not know the stage positions for the role and had to move about the stage without direction, although he instinctively gravitated toward center stage. What was worse, he could not remember all the lines. Surprisingly, the audience interpreted Shatner's halting, searching delivery of his lines and his intuitive movements on stage as a performance of tremendous depth. He received a standing ovation. Even the cast and stage crew applauded him, and the critics echoed the praise.

So what should have been a disaster was the birth of a dramatic style that would become Shatner's trademark. He developed a staccato way of delivering lines, and his movements on stage became even more dramatic than they'd been before. Some critics would condemn his unique style as blatant overacting, but Shatner believed he was really on to something. Eventually he would belittle the need for detailed rehearsals and emphasize the power of spontaneity in all his work.

Nearly forty years later, in trying to capture the essence of Shatner's style, comedian Kevin Pollak hit on the following key elements. First, command a presence much larger than called for. Adapt an attitude of supreme overconfidence, point a finger in righteous indignation, or just get in someone else's light. Second, start running around—then suddenly freeze at center stage. Thrust your elbows and hands straight out for added dramatic effect. Third, never forget those Shatnerian pauses at the most inappropriate moments. Stretch out every pronoun, pause for two beats, and finish at a rapid-fire clip. Open your mouth for at least four seconds before saying anything important.

Shatner's unique acting style was pretty much in place by the time he was twenty-five. He continued to expand his technique in *The Merry Wives of Windsor, Cymbeline,* and other plays with the Stratford company. In the summer of 1956, he received the Tyrone Guthrie Award for most promising actor and accompanied the famous director to the Edinburgh Shakespearean Festival in Scotland, where Shatner appeared in a production of *Henry V.*

But the accolades only heightened Shatner's ambitions. He was determined to move to New York City, where the Golden Age of live television drama was just getting started.

Chapter 4

A Tale Signifying Nothing

I hang on to the thought that there's
always Toronto. It's my security blanket.
—William Shatner on his "escape hatches"

Shatner realized how important working with the Stratford Shakespearean Festival was for his career. He had
moved to Toronto to be near the company. The city was
also the center of Canada's fledgling television industry,
and Shatner used the opportunity to approach executives
at the Canadian Broadcasting Corporation with several
teleplays he had written to showcase his growing talents.
The reviews for his television work were good, and Shatner was becoming something of a celebrity in Canada.
But at the same time, he felt very lonely.

"I learned about how terrible, debilitating, and mind-
numbing loneliness can be," he reflected on his days in
Toronto. "Fear of that has always been with me."

Then one day, while driving from Montreal to
Toronto, Shatner nearly lost his life in a car accident. His
small car was sideswiped by a semi truck and careened off
the road into a deep boat canal. As the automobile filled
with water, Shatner was certain he was going to drown.

His entire life flashed before him, and he suddenly realized that he had not really accomplished much at all. A
line from *Macbeth* kept ringing in his head: "A tale told by
an idiot—signifying nothing."

As the water level reached Shatner's chest, he felt
someone tugging at his arm. The truck driver had jumped
into the canal and sprung open the door to the vehicle. In
another minute, the two men were sitting on the bank of
the canal, watching the car slowly sink into the dark
water.

The experience changed Shatner on two levels. On one
hand, he decided it was time to find someone with whom
he could share his life. On the other, it caused him to
become even more determined to make a name for himself.

During the Broadway tour of *Tamburlaine,* Shatner had
met Gloria Rosenberg, a pretty, young Jewish girl who
seemed almost as lonely as he was. She had been living in
women's studio club apartments and was having a hard
time finding work as an actress. Her stage name was
Gloria Rand, and at the time, she was dancing in the
chorus line at the Copacabana. In April 1956, Shatner
arranged for them to star together in *Dreams,* one of the
plays he had written for Canadian television. While re-
hearsing a scene requiring the two to engage in an ex-
tended kiss, Shatner realized how deeply in love he was.

The two were married on August 12, 1956, and she
accompanied her new husband to the Edinburgh Shakespearean Festival in Scotland, where Shatner performed
a featured role in *Henry V.* Afterward, the newlyweds
honeymooned in London and Paris.

When Shatner and his wife returned to Canada, the
young actor put his career into high gear. Gloria had just
landed the role of the player queen in the Stratford Festival's *Hamlet,* but she resigned the part to move to New
York with her new husband. Shatner was convinced that

the only way he would become a commercially successful actor was to move to America.

Instead of using the $750 stipend from the Guthrie scholarship to study in England, as intended, he used it to set up housekeeping in the Jackson Heights section of New York City. Immediately, he started pounding the pavement looking for job opportunities.

He soon realized that his accent put him at a disadvantage in the American market, and he worked hard to rid himself of any trace of the Canadian sound. However, Shatner never became an American citizen. In fact, he attributed at least some of his eventual success in the United States to the fact that he was from Canada.

"I think we Canadians do well in acting," he told a reporter, "because we have the technique of the English and the virility of the Americans. We're in an advantageous position by being in the middle of the two."

Another reason Shatner's efforts paid off was simply that his timing could not have been better. He entered the American entertainment industry at the start of the Golden Age of Television, when the majority of TV fare was live drama. There was work enough for everyone, and over the next decade, Shatner would appear on television in nearly a hundred different dramatic roles.

Shatner's first major television appearance in the United States was on NBC's *Kaiser Aluminum Hour*, in "Mr. Finchley Faces the Bomb," broadcast live on September 25, 1956. He appeared with Roddy McDowell in another *Kaiser Aluminum Hour* production, "Gwyneth," in December. In October, he appeared with fellow Canadian Raymond Massey in the *Goodyear Theater* production of "All Summer Long." That same season, he played opposite Bert Lahr in "School for Wives," which was broadcast on ABC's prestigious commercial-free *Omnibus* series.

In January 1957, he was in another *Omnibus* production, "Oedipus the King," with Christopher Plummer, and in four installments of *Studio One*, CBS's equally respected dramatic anthology series. Later that year, he played the brother of a recently deceased spinster in an award-winning episode of *Alfred Hitchcock Presents* entitled "The Glass Eye."

The critics thought Shatner's performances were magnificent and were bestowing on him such flattering titles as "TV's Golden Boy" or "the Canadian Wunderkind."

In April of that year, Shatner decided to make a trip to Hollywood and test his luck there. His meeting with producer Pandro Berman at MGM was short and sweet. The movie mogul looked at the young actor, then glanced over to his assistant and commented: "Yes, he's the one."

Someone in casting had seen Shatner in a live television drama and suggested that he might do for a part opposite Claire Bloom in a new movie the studio was planning. Somewhere in the hidden recesses of the minds of Hollywood producers, Shatner's Canadian Shakespearean background seemed to mesh with that of the British actress. So the Canadian actor was cast with Claire Bloom, Yul Brynner, Lee J. Cobb, and Richard Basehart in the film adaptation of Dostoyevsky's monumental book *The Brothers Karamazov,* the classic story of a nineteenth-century Russian family ruined by greed and lust.

Shatner and MGM agreed to a nonexclusive two-movie deal valued at $100,000. He bought an Austin-Healey sports car, and in May 1957, drove from New York City to Hollywood with his bride of nine months. He almost splurged on a huge house with two fireplaces, a pool, a brick barbecue pit, and a glass-enclosed living room. However, his agent dissuaded him.

"Don't mortgage yourself to Hollywood," he warned the rising star. "Don't have to take roles you don't want just to meet the next house payment."

Instead, the Shatners set up housekeeping in a $125-a-month one-bedroom apartment in Westwood Village, a small community snuggled between Beverly Hills and Los Angeles. The couple's living room opened onto a sundeck and communal swimming pool. It was their first taste of the southern California lifestyle.

Shatner's official publicity bio, issued by MGM in September of that year, described him as "five foot eleven inches tall, 150 pounds, with brown hair and blue eyes." Even his closest friends would not have recognized him, given that description. Actually, Shatner was of medium height and build, with thinning dark hair and hazel eyes. MGM's description was actually closer to the fictional character Berman had had in mind when he'd first met the actor.

Shatner was chosen to play the spiritual Karamazov brother, Alexi, and it turned out Berman was right to follow his first impressions. Shatner's saintly performance was extremely well received. Said *Variety:* "William Shatner has the difficult task of portraying youthful male goodness, and he does it with such candor it is effective." Critics considered Shatner the leading choice to play opposite Elizabeth Taylor in Tennessee Williams' *Cat on a Hot Tin Roof,* although the role eventually went to Paul Newman.

The Crazy World of Suzie Wong

Shatner was restless. He wanted to star in something that would showcase his special talents, something that would make people view him as more than just a good supporting actor. He found what he was looking for in a script adapted from a popular novel by Richard Mason. *The World of Suzie Wong* centers on the life of Robert Lomax, a Canadian architect who takes a year off to see if he can make a living as an artist. He packs up his paints and easel and travels to Hong Kong, where he meets an eighteen-year-old Chinese prostitute with a heart of gold.

Though sold into prostitution at the age of thirteen, Suzie Wong has maintained a pure essence, isolating her love and innocence from the debauchery of her body. "Inside—still good," was the way she described it. Lomax resists his physical desire for the perplexing girl, and instead tries to reform her in a platonic relationship. Before long, however, Lomax falls in love with the prostitute, despite the efforts of a rich banker's daughter to lure him into a more respectable relationship.

Shatner considered the play poetic and wanted to act the male lead at any cost. He ordered his agent to get him out of his movie contract, a pay-or-play deal that awarded Shatner a huge lump sum even if he did not work. When his agent refused to cut him loose from the sweet deal, Shatner fired him and signed on with a more inexperienced agent, who agreed to see what he could do. Surprisingly, the agent had no trouble getting MGM to release the young star. The studio was in a slump at the time and had no new projects for the term of Shatner's contract.

So at the age of twenty-seven, Shatner returned to New York to begin what he thought would be a high point of his career. He auditioned for the role of Robert Lomax and was given the part within fifteen minutes.

But the perfectionistic actor soon locked horns with his leading lady, France Nuyen. The twenty-year-old actress had developed a style all her own, and she stubbornly resisted Shatner's attempts to turn her into a more seasoned, more graceful performer. He often accused her of being inexperienced and unreceptive to his suggestions, and their bitter arguments delayed rehearsals for hours.

Shatner had definite ideas on how scenes should be played and clashed with other actors, too. One time, a fistfight broke out between Toughy and fellow actor Ron Randell. Apparently, the misunderstanding stemmed from Shatner's suggestions as to how Randell should portray his character of Ben Jeffcoat. Shatner also reportedly treated his understudy, William Windom, like dirt. (Windom went on to become a familiar face in dozens of TV movies, but he would never forgive Shatner, even after the two worked together in a second-season episode of *Star Trek*.)

The backstage bickering became too much for *Suzie Wong* director Joshua Logan, who simply gave up and stopped going to rehearsals. By the time the play opened at the Broadhurst Theater on October 14, 1958, the actors were not speaking to each other off stage and were so emotionally drained that they lacked any spark on stage. To make matters worse, Paul Osborn's script had been changed so many times that it bore little resemblance to the original novel. Whole rows of theatergoers walked out in the middle of the performance, and highbrowed critics had a field day condemning it.

Said the *Herald Tribune:* "Its manly hero is played with an oddly melodramatic gloss and many a deepseated sigh by the normally interesting Canadian actor." Six other reviewers agreed, calling his performance "modest" and "wooden."

"Every night was a nightmare," Shatner later recalled. "I almost had a nervous breakdown."

Fortunately, the theater had banked nearly $1.5 million in presold theater parties, and the show had enough money to survive on its own for another three months. Shatner took advantage of the grace period to completely change the pace of the action on stage. Despite nearly losing his voice and being hurt by falling scenery, he never missed a performance and never gave an understudy a chance to take his place. By delivering his lines in varying tempos, with subtle changes in accentuation and facial expressions, Shatner stubbornly and single-handedly turned the play from a turgid drama into a lighthearted romance.

One reviewer described the invigorated stageplay as "a blend of sex and slush, a special treat for matinee ladies munching their tear-splashed caramels." Indeed, it was those maudlin matinee ladies who eventually made the play a huge success. Tickets started selling by word of mouth, and *The World of Suzie Wong* ran eighteen months for 624 performances. Shatner ended up getting best actor honors from Theater World and Theater Guild judges and also chalked up a Drama Circle Award.

Immediately after the Broadway run concluded, Paramount Studios started planning for the movie. They asked Joshua Logan to direct and France Nuyen to reprise her role as Suzie Wong. However, they passed over Shatner in favor of William Holden, an actor they believed had more name recognition. Shatner was absolutely incredulous that he could be passed over for a role he had worked so hard to develop. Unfortunately, it would not be the first time he would lose coveted roles to bigger names.

The movie *Suzie Wong* was a spectacular production, shot on location in Hong Kong. However, in just two weeks, France Nuyen quit the film and returned to the United States. She had heard rumors that her lover, film star Marlon Brando, was having an affair while she was out of the country, and she immediately flew back to tighten up the reins. Joshua Logan quit a few days later, and the new director, Richard Quine, hired Chinese actress Nancy Kwan for the title role.

Shatner was not free of his nemesis so easily. Nuyen was the arrogant princess to whom Captain Kirk attempted to teach social graces in the "Elaan of Troyius" episode of *Star Trek*. The teleplay re-created many of the backstage emotions felt by the two during rehearsals for *Suzie Wong* and turned out to be a cathartic experience for both of them. Shatner would later agree to work with Nuyen in a 1973 TV movie, *Horror at 37,000 Feet*, and a 1974 episode of *Kung Fu*.

A Coast-to-Coast Tightwire Act

Just before the birth of their daughter, Leslie Carol, in August 1958, the Shatners moved into a small house in Hastings-on-Hudson, a picturesque rural community just north of New York City, and Shatner began to see himself as something of a country gentleman. He bought an English sports car, and his typical attire was a Scotch tweed jacket and worsted slacks. He also started raising Doberman pinschers, a breed he admired for its fierce reputation. Sometimes his favorite dog, Dunhill, accompanied him and his wife to fancy restaurants, where Shatner insisted the animal be allowed to join them at their table.

At the time, Shatner was attempting to balance three separate careers: stage, screen, and television. On the East Coast, he pursued his stage and live television appearances. On the West Coast, he built a name in the movies and in filmed television series. He flew back and forth between them trying to further his career on all fronts.

In May 1958, Shatner appeared on television in his first role in a western, opposite Lee Marvin in *The Time of Hanging*. Then, co-starring with Rod Steiger, he played the ringleader of a lynch mob in the *Playhouse 90* presentation of "A Town Has Turned to Dust." Said the *New York Times* of his role: "Mr. Shatner gave one of the best performances of his career. He was the embodiment of hate and blind physical passion. His attention to detail in putting together the picture of an ignorant and evil social force was remarkable."

That same year, he appeared in three installments of the CBS dramatic anthology series *The U.S. Steel Hour*. One, "Old Marshals Never Die," was especially well received. He played a marshal torn between his duties to the town and his obligations to his family.

"This time I'm a good guy," Shatner said of the part.

"As a matter of fact, it's a western in which we're all good guys. The only type of role I've *never* had on TV is a young, romantic one, and this I'm getting on Broadway in *Suzie Wong*. What I do on TV is character work, and this is what a competent actor should be able to do."

In 1958, he appeared in four *Kraft Theater* presentations, including "Medic," in which he portrayed an intense, young doctor at a large medical center. The *New York Mirror* commented: "Shatner's been on most of the big TV shows, has written some himself, and if you haven't seen his recent brilliant effort on 'Medic,' you can get a good notion of his talents on other *Kraft Theater* presentations. He's good."

The young actor landed his first continuing role in a television series on CBS in 1959. Much to his chagrin, the role continued for only a few weeks. He played Archie Goodwin, the faithful right-hand man to a fey and fat detective, in the extremely short-lived *Nero Wolfe* series on CBS. But the demise of the series did not really worry Shatner. He was appearing regularly on television in a number of shows, including such family fare as *The Hallmark Hall of Fame, The Ed Sullivan Show, Family Classics,* and a variety of Sunday morning religious dramas.

He could also be seen in suspense and horror shows like *Alfred Hitchcock Presents, Twilight Zone, Thriller,* and *One Step Beyond.* In fact, Shatner was turning down prestigious roles at the Stratford Shakespearean Theater to pursue more lucrative commercial opportunities. Unlike other actors of his time, Shatner did not condemn TV work as being unworthy of his talent.

"Live television is exciting, a true art form," he told a reporter who asked him if he missed the stage. "You are performing for an audience, an audience of one, the director."

"They don't teach this in school," he continued, explaining his approach to television acting, "—the whole technique of sustaining the emotional impact while coolly keeping track of the technical state of affairs. You see cameras moving in on you, creeping up like animals. Then you hear their cooling mechanism humming and the director growling softly as you work yourself to a pitch of emotion for the closeup." Even on camera, Shatner's whole point in acting was to get a hold on other people's emotions, exactly as he had done as a boy at summer camp.

Shatner's passionate ambitions drove him at a frenzied pace. He had insatiable desires and seemed always eager to experience everything the world had to offer. He was naturally "wired,"—performing a tightwire act that stretched from coast to coast and would have exhausted most men.

"You've got to keep moving and seeing what's going on in the world," he told a newspaper columnist. "Otherwise, whatever you write or act or direct won't have the genuineness and truth it must have to communicate to your audience."

As if balancing all facets of his acting career was not enough, Shatner still wrote and directed for television. He was hoping to create parts suited for his particular style of acting, but his efforts rarely bore fruit. When he sold a script to the CBS *Checkmate* series, he wrote the guest star's part with himself in mind. However, the show's sponsor wanted a bigger name and even tried to get Bob Newhart, a popular comedian who had never done any acting. Only Shatner's persistent pleading caused the producers to give in and let him play the part.

That was not the only time Shatner locked horns with sponsors. In an episode of *Arrest and Trial*, Shatner played a young executive who rises up the corporate ladder by copying the habits of his boss. Shatner wanted one trait he copied to be the use of a cigarette holder, but a sponsor of the show quickly snuffed the idea. The guest star later found out that cigarette holders were generally taboo on TV because they implied there was something in cigarettes that was not good to put directly into your mouth. Before they were outlawed, commercials from cigarette manufacturers made up a large portion of television revenues. The incident did not really bother Shatner, who chided snobbish New York critics who believed television was the only commercialized entertainment medium.

"One would think," he said, "that the stage is a vessel of culture, but is it? The producers of *The World of Suzie Wong* saw the sex angle and pressured the playwright into cutting and rewriting it so the emphasis was almost totally shifted to the prostitutes, and theater party agencies in New York even demand and get a say in casting many of the plays."

Shatner knew from firsthand experience that Hollywood movie producers cast leading roles based on box-office draw, which is kind of a built-in collateral for financing major films. And the situation was not much better in regular television work.

"If you do a TV series," he told one entertainment editor, "it's got to be for the money, because it is impossible to get quality from it. There never is enough time for rehearsal, or for the writer to work on the script. If you don't do a series, then there is the waiting between jobs. It doesn't leave much choice for the actor today."

However, in 1961, Shatner made three controversial movies that would stretch his talents even further. The twenty-nine-year-old actor had turned down several television series in order to appear, in his own words, "in exciting feature films that had something to say." The most widely known of these was *Judgment at Nuremberg*, Stanley Kramer's probing docudrama about Nazi war criminals. The black-and-white movie blended horrible scenes from concentration camps with intense courtroom drama and raised sensitive questions about the responsibilities of government servants to humanity as a whole. The film received two Academy Awards and was nominated for five others.

In it, Shatner plays an American liaison officer whose most difficult job is to help the tribunal's chief justice understand the German people. On trial are several judges who bent Germany's legal system to support Hitler's mandates. One of them, played by Burt Lancaster, refuses to defend himself against any of the charges. His proud stance forces the American judge to take a closer look at the evidence and consider weighty issues about the duties of the judiciary in any political system.

Spencer Tracy played the American judge. Shatner truly respected the seasoned star and, as a stage actor, was impressed with Tracy's ability to remember long monologues and deliver them with tremendous impact. After delivering his dialogue in the film, Tracy could remember his lines long afterward for retakes. Even Laurence Olivier admitted to having difficulty recalling lines.

One day, in an attempt to ingratiate himself with Tracy, Shatner confessed how amazed he was at the actor's ability to remember lengthy and complicated lines. Unfortunately, Tracy mistook the statement as a sarcastic comment about his age. He walked away in a huff, and the two men hardly spoke to one another after that.

The rambunctious Shatner tackled another sensitive subject in *The Explosive Generation*. Director Buzz Kulik's film was based on a real-life incident that occurred in a Van Nuys, California, high school. Shatner portrays a teacher who attempts to teach sex education to a class of inquisitive teenagers. He instructs them to write unsigned essays on their sexual experiences and plans to use the papers as a focal point for class discussion. But the PTA finds out about the project and the teacher is told to destroy the essays and not talk about sex in the classroom. He refuses and is fired, but the students rally on his behalf. The parents finally realize that the project was the students' idea in the first place and conclude that nothing unsavory has taken place. The teacher is reinstated and ends the film reading the essays aloud to his class. The film became a rallying point for frank discussions about adolescent sexuality, although some parents believed Shatner was trying to incite youthful discontent.

Riots would become an actual part of Shatner's next "say something" film. Roger Corman's *The Intruder* was based on an incident in the life of ultraconservative racist John Kasper. Shatner played the provocative orator, who incites the population of a small southern town to protest the integration of their high school by ten black children. A black leader is killed when a bomb is thrown through the window of his church, and a boy is almost murdered by a mob after Shatner's character convinces a white girl to falsely accuse the boy of raping her.

But much of the action during the filming took place off camera. The movie was shot on location in the town of Charleston in the bootheel of Missouri, and the residents were none too happy to be depicted as bigots. When they found out what the movie was about, they revoked permission to shoot in certain locations and did everything they could to thwart the filming of the controversial script.

"We were in fear for our safety," Shatner told one reporter. "We were chased out of five locations. We shot scenes with Ku Klux Klan uniforms, burning crosses and . . . blowing up . . . a Negro church. Roger had to sneak back with a hand camera in his own car to take an establishing shot of one school. But we needed the southern smalltown atmosphere."

"Discrimination was worse than in the Deep South because there the white southerners have taken a position—the lines of war are clearly marked," he said to another reporter. "But here it was a fringe area and therefore more explosive. Literally, this movie was made at the risk of our lives. We even had escape plans. The state militia had to be called in when we shot scenes depicting the Ku Klux Klan bombing a Negro church."

Shatner said he modeled his character after one of America's most famous demagogues. "Joe McCarthy was the idol of people like Kasper," Shatner told an interviewer, "and I tried to get something of McCarthy's quality in my oration in front of the courthouse. I must say I felt sorry for Kasper. He was so obviously wrong, so obviously trying to compensate for his own inadequacies by showing the supposed inadequacies of others. Why, it's the whole history of racism in a microcosm."

Reviews of Shatner's portrayal of the bigot were full of praise. Said the *New York Times:* "William Shatner is unctuous and deceitful in a provokingly superficial way as the determined rabble-rouser." Famed critic Arthur Knight called the movie one of the best American films ever made. Shatner won the Best Actor Award at the International Peace Festival and considered the role the best acting he had ever done.

The Intruder premiered at two New York art houses to glowing reviews. The *Herald Tribune* said of the movie: "People with something to say put it into a film without being fey or pretentious about it." The *Los Angeles Times* went even further, calling it "the boldest, most realistic depiction of racial injustice ever shown in American films."

Sadly, for 1962, the film was just too hot to handle. Because of the subject matter, few distributors wanted to touch it, and the producers kept changing the film's name, hoping people would forget about its controversial subject matter. It was later released under the title *I Hate Your Guts!,* and in 1966, it appeared as *Shame.* In Great Britain, it was shown in theaters as *The Stranger.*

Roger Corman, whose previous credits included such cult classics as *Swamp Women* (1955), *Attack of the Crab Monsters* (1957), and *Teenage Caveman* (1958), produced *The Intruder* for around $160,000. It took under four weeks to complete, and Shatner was paid only about $200 above his expenses. Still, it remained one of the actor's proudest accomplishments.

Years later, when a friend informed him that the film

was playing in Los Angeles under the name *I Hate Your Guts!*, Shatner took his wife to see it. The luridly advertised film was shown after another gem that went by the name of *Rat Fink*. In the dark anonymity of the theater, both sat with tears running down their faces, as they watched the once significant film being treated like some racial war flick, exploiting people's fears.

Back to Broadway

Shatner's second daughter, Lisabeth Mary, was born in June 1961, and the vagabond father decided to stay close to home and help raise a family. His third daughter, Melanie Ann, would be born at New York's Lebanon Jewish Hospital in August 1964.

Shatner's return to Broadway was in Leland Hayward's production of *A Shot in the Dark*. The lighthearted mystery also starred Julie Harris and Walter Matthau. In the stage play, Shatner is an examining magistrate in a Paris courtroom, and Julie Harris is a saucy parlor maid under indictment for the murder of a chauffeur. She is found naked and unconscious next to the body with the murder weapon clenched in her hand. Shatner's character senses a refreshing candor in the simple woman's testimony and undertakes an exhaustive investigation of the case. He uncovers a shocking history of sexual indiscretions in the respected and privileged household but cannot believe the girl is capable of murder. He eventually exposes the real murderer, and the maid is so grateful that she offers herself to the magistrate as a reward.

A Shot in the Dark opened at the Booth Theater on October 18, 1961, and ran for 389 performances, until February 1963. "The eager, earnest magistrate," said the *New York Times*, "is played attractively by William Shatner," but other critics described the play itself as a "boulevard comedy" revolving around "the staple theme of infidelity" and "spiced with a little harmless sex." Most of the accolades went to Walter Matthau, who received a Tony Award for his portrayal of the lecherous patriarch of the family in which the maid was employed.

Shatner was devastated when Matthau stole the limelight in "his" play and garnered most of the critic's attention. Once again, his Broadway experience left him "with all the symptoms that appear in a person just before a nervous breakdown."

Still, Shatner reprised his role in another Broadway production of the same story, *L'Idiote*. That was the title of Marcel Archard's original play, upon which Harry Kurnitz had based *A Shot in the Dark*. The popular second effort ran on Broadway for over a year. However, when it came time to make a movie of the play, Shatner was passed over for another Hollywood star, Peter Sellers. The 1964 movie *A Shot In the Dark* was directed by Blake Edwards and also starred Elke Sommer and Herbert Lom. It would be the first in the highly successful *Pink Panther* series.

At that point, a frustrated Shatner made the decision to seek financial success first and then, after he was secure, return to the stage to hone his artistic talents. Even Laurence Olivier's illustrious stage career did not peak until he was 45. So Shatner turned down starring roles in such classics as *Romeo and Juliet* and *King John* at the Stratford Festival to do television in New York and movies in Hollywood. He was still picky about what roles he appeared in and turned down about three out of every four scripts offered him. He tried to remain free to choose parts that really interested him. At the time, one reporter described the high-strung actor as "a husky, compact young man with passionate beliefs and emphatic opinions." But Shatner was also approaching the point in his life when he realized he had to compromise.

"When I say I decided it was time to grow up," he reflected on the period years later, "I mean I recognized the fact that great parts come rarely to an actor. Most of the time it's slugging away in run-of-the-mill endeavors. You do the best you can with all your resources. You work to make a living and to support your family."

Nonetheless, Shatner tried to keep from becoming stereotyped by playing a single character type. For that reason, he turned down several series roles, including the lead in the *Dr. Kildare* series. Shatner would spend the next five years watching Richard Chamberlain soar to stardom on the popular show.

However, Shatner did accept a wide variety of guest star roles on television. He played a cowboy on the run for a murder he did not commit in an episode of *The Outlaws*, a temperamental artist and crude Burmese sailor on two different installments of *Naked City*, a prodigal son confronting his father in *Route 66*, a playboy spy in a *Man from U.N.C.L.E.* episode, and a businessman involved with the Mafia in a five-part episode of *77 Sunset Strip*. He portrayed a variety of doctors in episodes of *Ben Casey*, *The Doctors*, *The Nurses*, and *Dr. Kildare*.

Shatner also played a number of different characters in five episodes of *The Defenders*, a Herbert Brodkin production about father and son lawyers. Shatner had played the son (opposite Ralph Bellamy) in the two-hour pilot movie broadcast on CBS in 1957, but Robert Reed and E. G. Marshall were chosen when the series finally made it to the air in 1961. Four years later, Brodkin offered Shatner the lead in another dramatic series about the law called *For the People*.

In many ways, *For the People* was a successor to *The Defenders*. Shatner played assistant district attorney David Koster, whose passion for justice always landed him in trouble with his boss, played by Howard DaSilva. Koster's cultured, socially sophisticated wife was portrayed by Jessica Walter. Naturally, Shatner's strong-willed character clashed with everyone, and like *The Defenders*, the show depicted both the professional and personal lives of the characters realistically. Unfortunately, the critically acclaimed series was lined up against the smash hit *Bonanza* and lasted only thirteen weeks.

In 1963, Shatner decided to try his luck with another television series. Although he was still concerned about being stereotyped, he accepted the title role for a possible ABC series called *Alexander the Great*. The epic production would depict the life of the Macedonian military genius. Shatner thought the unique character would be a perfect showcase for both his acting and his athletic abilities. He prepared diligently for the pilot and spent months learning fencing, riding, and how to leap around in short togas without exposing too much derrière.

The $750,000 film also starred Adam West, John Cassavetes, John Doucette, and Joseph Cotton. It was a spectacular success when it was released in European theaters four years later, but no sponsor could be found to pick up the proposed television series in the United States. Even Shatner admitted that the show was one of the silliest concepts in television history and compared it to *Combat* in drag.

However, Shatner's work in Hollywood opened the door for other opportunities. In 1964, he signed another contract with MGM. He agreed to portray a disillusioned preacher in *The Outrage*, which was a western remake of the classic Japanese film *Rashomon*.

Shatner was a rising young star, still turning down more offers than he accepted. He was so desperate for good parts that he even formed his own production company to purchase promising scripts and try to turn them into movies. His goal was to act and direct in his own productions. Shatner called the company Lemli Productions, a composite title made up of the names of his three daughters, Leslie, Melanie, and Lisabeth. Although he purchased the rights for screenplays from such notable writers as Jerry Sohl, Jay Simon, and Richard Matheson, he found it hard to find the financing necessary to bring their works to the screen.

"I feel half the job of producing a picture is getting the property and its ingredients," he commented. "From then on, it's a matter of coagulating the elements."

He tried "coagulating the elements" with Warner Brothers and several other studios but had a hard time getting their attention. He asked only to make low-budget films in the $250,000 to $500,000 range and planned a three-way payback for their investment. First, there would be revenues from the theatrical release, then came the eventual sale to television, and finally, a movie would be turned into a regular TV series. But none of the major studios was interested in partnership productions with smaller companies. All Shatner got for his efforts was the cold shoulder.

"Major studios which have again and again evinced their interest in young blood because the old blood is dying of old age," he lamented, "have made it almost impossible for young blood to get into that activity." Before long, the disappointed producer had put up over $100,000 of his own money without seeing any return on his investment.

In April 1965, Shatner escaped his business worries with another unique acting role, this time in a surrealistic art film about the eternal battle between good and evil. He played a decent man seduced by evil in the form of a succubus, a female demon. But Shatner's character is so pure that the demon falls in love with him—a situation that infuriates the dark powers. In an act of revenge, they send forth a male satyric demon, known as an incubus, to seduce the man's angelic sister.

The Incubus takes place in the mythical land of Nomen Tuum and was filmed along the Big Sur coastline. It had English subtitles, and all dialogue was in Esperanto, an artificial language invented in the nineteenth century and promoted as a new, world tongue.

Critics compared the film to the works of Ingmar Bergman. Famed critic Henri Chapier was so taken by the film that he made it his pet project and arranged for the world premiere to take place in Paris. It was first shown in the United States at the 1966 San Francisco Film Festival, where Shatner made the enigmatic promise that theatergoers would think the film incredible regardless of whether they liked it or not.

"I can afford to take chances," he said at the time, "because I haven't got a name to live up to. Most actors feel they can't afford to gamble once they've reached the top. That's why many of the big stars look back on their early days as the best time of their lives. The more successful you are, the more in danger you are of becoming stultified."

But as he approached his thirty-fifth birthday, Shatner realized he was running out of options. He started losing parts and went into a career slump. He saw his dream of becoming a great actor dissolve before his eyes.

"My dream of success was hollow," he admitted. "All the things I thought went along with it—good parts, money, and acclaim—weren't happening. As a star, I was one step down from Paul Newman—a good actor, but not popular enough to bring in big audiences. I started losing parts—something that had never happened to me before. I had lost movie after movie to kids who had been on TV and had virtually no experience or talent."

Shatner realized that he would either have to give up acting or accept the danger of becoming "stultified" in some limited but commercially successful role. For the first time in his career, he was prepared to give up acting and take a normal job like "selling ties in Macy's."

But his next decision would take him beyond any fear he could ever have imagined of becoming stereotyped. William Shatner was about to become an icon of popular culture.

Chapter 5

Horatio Hornblower, Meet Captain Quirk

My favorite roles in *Star Trek* were any ones
in which I played two different characters.
It gave the viewers twice as much of me!
—William Shatner's reply to an oft-asked question

By early 1965, William Shatner had reached a crossroads
in his career. His series *For the People* had just been canceled, his pilot for *Alexander the Great* had failed to attract
any interest, and his private production company had
gotten off to a bad start. He was living in New York and
looking ahead to the stagnant prospect of an endless succession of guest appearances and character parts. Then,
just two days after *For the People* was canceled, he got a
phone call from a man named Gene Roddenberry.

The producer asked if Shatner would fly out to Los
Angeles to view a failed pilot for a new sci-fi television
series. The network had given the show another chance,
and Roddenberry wanted to know if Shatner would be
interested in playing the lead in the second pilot.

Gene Roddenberry was a very tall, large-framed man
with piercing blue eyes. He had a reputation as a man not
easy to ignore, both physically and for his persistence in

getting what he wanted. For nearly two years, Rodden-berry had been pitching his idea of a futuristic *Wagon Train*-to-the-Stars to MGM and a half dozen other Hollywood studios, and it looked like the series would never find a home. Not only did the television studios believe science fiction was too expensive, but they also thought the genre could not succeed using continuing characters. A series called *UFO* had run only a few weeks before it was canceled, and producers were even more skittish about anything that had to do with outer space.

But Roddenberry kept making the rounds, hoping to interest someone in his proposal for the daring new television program. Then, seemingly out of the blue, Desilu Studios agreed to take on Gene's "baby" and nurse it into a TV series. In reality, the desperate production company hoped to use *Star Trek* to bring an infusion of badly needed cash from the networks.

CBS was the first to express an interest in the new series, but after picking Roddenberry's brain for new ideas, decided to produce their own series, *Lost in Space*. In their show, the *Jupiter II* had a five-year mission to explore a distant star system, until the ship's navigational controls were sabotaged by a hapless stowaway by the name of Dr. Zachary Smith.

Actor Jonathan Harris's characterization of the childishly self-centered Dr. Smith quickly became a favorite of viewers. Shatner had worked with Harris a decade earlier in an installment of *Kraft Mystery Theater* called "The Man Who Didn't Fly," but now the two would be vying for the attention of television audiences in two very different series. The comical and often puerile *Lost in Space* was on the air for about the same length of time as *Star Trek*, but it was never able to attract as fanatically dedicated fans.

Just a few weeks after CBS started production of its lighthearted space odyssey, NBC agreed to invest $630,-000 in the first *Star Trek* pilot. It would be the most

expensive TV pilot ever done up to that time, although it
took only nine days to complete.

That effort, titled "The Cage," is about the crew of a
spaceship answering a distress call on planet Talos IV.
The ship's leader, Captain Christopher Pike, is taken
prisoner by telepathic aliens who create all sorts of stun-
ning illusions to get him to mate with a human female.
But the beautiful woman is really a horribly deformed
survivor of a scientific expedition that had crashed on the
planet twenty years earlier.

The Talosians are weak, sterile creatures—survivors of
nuclear war who have gone underground. There, they
developed their mental capabilities to the maximum.
They now use their powers to blur the captain's sense of
reality, hoping to breed the humans and repopulate their
wasted planet. Luckily, two members of the captain's
competent bridge crew beam down to free him from the
clutches of the deceitful aliens.

Lloyd Bridges was the first actor considered for the part
of Captain Christopher Pike, but he feared the role would
ruin his credibility and refused flat out to act in anything
that had to do with outer space. Roddenberry eventually
signed Jeffrey Hunter, best known for his role as Jesus
Christ in *King of Kings* (1961). For the role of the green-
blooded alien crewman Mr. Spock, Roddenberry approached both Martin Landau and dwarf actor Michael
Dunn. Dunn was too busy with his role in the series *Wild,
Wild West* to take on more work, and Landau had just
committed himself to do *Mission Impossible*.

However, Landau did recommend a good friend with
whom Roddenberry had already worked. Leonard
Nimoy had had a small role in *The Lieutenant*, Rodden-
berry's one-season-long dramatic series about life in the
U.S. Marine Corps. Nimoy, intrigued by the possibilities
of playing a half-human alien, accepted the part. Majel
Barrett, who also had worked on *The Lieutenant*, played
Number One, the cool, logical first officer of the *Enterprise*.

John Hoyt was the ship's cynical but paternal doctor, Dr. Bones Boyce.

While NBC lauded the quality of the "The Cage," they rejected it as being "too cerebral" for television audiences. To everyone's surprise, the network was willing to invest another $300,000 in a second pilot, provided it was spiced with more action and adventure. They also insisted that Roddenberry dump the "uninteresting characters" of Mr. Spock and Number One. The network executives felt that audiences would not identify with an extraterrestrial character nor be comfortable with the hard-minded female role of Number One.

Much to his credit, Gene Roddenberry refused to drop the alien crewman. He did agree to trade off Number One, although he would later imbue Mr. Spock with many of the attributes originally carried by that character. For Roddenberry, Spock was the most interesting personality in the series. In the early scripts, the alien officer evolved from a red-tailed creature who never ate (absorbing energy from a red plate in his belly) into a pointy-eared, human-alien hybrid in whom the opposing forces of logic and emotion were constantly at war. Instinctively, Gene realized that Spock could be the vehicle for great insight into the human condition, as well as adding an interesting alien presence on the monotonous bridge set that for economic reasons would come to dominate the show.

Her character of Number One sacrificed, Majel Barrett would go on to become Nurse Christine Chapel in the ensuing series, although she had to dye her hair blond so the network would not catch on. Luckily, she had used her maiden name (M. Leigh Hudec) to play the first character. George Takei, who had just moved from New York to appear in an episode of *Perry Mason,* was originally cast as physicist Hikaru Sulu and would later become chief navigator. James Doohan joined the crew as the chief engineer, Montgomery Scott, after being recommended by his friend James Goldstone, director of the second pilot.

John Hoyt's character, Dr. Bones Boyce, was replaced by the cantankerous Dr. Mark Piper, played by Paul Fix. It would not be until the second production episode that DeForest Kelley would replace him as the equally cantankerous Dr. Leonard "Bones" McCoy. Kelley had worked with Roddenberry on another unsold pilot and played a doctor in *Police Story*. Grace Lee Whitney, who had also worked in *Police Story*, would play Yeoman Janice Rand. Nichelle Nichols, who had had a small role in *The Lieutenant*, signed on as Lieutenant Nyota Uhura.

The real problem was with Jeffrey Hunter, whose wife had convinced him that the role of captain of a spaceship was beneath his dignity. By mutual agreement with the producers, he left the show. Roddenberry tried to sign on Jack Lord (of *Hawaii Five-0*) as the new captain of the *Enterprise*, but he wanted fifty-percent ownership of the show.

Roddenberry then decided to give William Shatner a call in New York. Shatner was known to be picky about his roles and was seen as an accomplished actor in the entertainment industry. After viewing the first pilot episode, Shatner agreed to play the captain in the second pilot. He signed on for $5,000 per episode (Nimoy signed on for $1,250 per show). Although Shatner probably would have done as well financially by continuing in television guest roles and movies, he was thrilled with the prospect of steady work and truly believed the new show had potential to prove that science fiction could be an accepted dramatic form.

"Gene was very happy that he was able to get Bill Shatner," said Bob Justman, associate producer of the second pilot. "I had worked with Bill on *Outer Limits* and he had a good reputation well before the second pilot of *Star Trek*. He was someone to be reckoned with, and we certainly understood that he was a more accomplished actor than Jeff Hunter was, and he gave us more dimension. The network seemed to feel that Jeff Hunter was rather wooden. He was a nice person, everyone liked him; but he didn't run the gamut of emotions that Bill Shatner could do. Shatner was classically trained. He had enormous technical abilities to do different things and he gave the captain a terrific personality. He embodied what Gene had in mind, which was the flawed hero. Or the hero who considers himself to be flawed. Captain Horatio Hornblower—that was who he was modeled on."

Where No Star Has Gone Before

The series' second pilot was called "Where No Man Has Gone Before," and Shatner portrayed the bold and adventuresome Captain Kirk for the first time. It was an entirely new direction for William Shatner. In fact, no star of his caliber had ever played a continuing character in a science fiction series. Yet his acting career was in the doldrums; he felt he was not going fast enough nor far enough. Shatner knew he had to make this new series work. From the beginning, he showed an indefatigable interest in the day-by-day production of the show.

"I'll never forget Bill Shatner coming into my office," Roddenberry told a reporter, "holding a copy of our first script, saying he had some suggestions. I was understandably apprehensive—I had never worked with Bill before and I wondered if this would be an ego-centered list of selfish demands. I was delighted, pleased, then admiring, when his observations turned out to be shrewd dramatic points which improved the whole story immeasurably."

During production, all the attentions of the director and crew were focused on the star. Everything revolved around Shatner, who sat imperially in the large Naugahyde captain's chair at the center of the set. From that position, he shouted out suggestions to director Jim Goldstone while cracking jokes with the camera crew. According to George Takei, Shatner laughed the loudest at his own jokes, responding with "a bright, lilting, surprisingly high-pitched giggle."

"Bill, who had a weird sense of humor," agreed Nichelle Nichols, "would regale us with some stupid story. We'd all laugh because the stories were so stupid, but Bill, who thought they were hilarious, laughed the whole way through, sometimes so hard he couldn't finish telling us anyway."

In Shatner's pilot, two members of the Starship *Enterprise* crew acquire superhuman abilities after the spaceship drifts through a mysterious radiation belt. The crew members are played by Gary Lockwood, another veteran of Roddenberry's *The Lieutenant* series, and Sally Kellerman, who had appeared on television in several dramatic supporting roles. The radiation exposure causes the two humans to evolve at an accelerated rate and acquire astonishing psychic abilities, which Lockwood's character uses to take over control of the ship. Spock urges Kirk to kill him before he grows any stronger, but Kirk hesitates, not wanting to hurt an old friend. It all boils down to an old-fashioned fist fight between Kirk and his empowered subordinate. After a protracted and fierce battle, the crewman dies a painful death.

In an interview on the set a few months before the series premiered, Shatner described the basic concept of the show: "The *Enterprise* is a spaceship patrolling somewhere out there, in much the same way that naval vessels of the eighteenth century patrolled the outer reaches of the British Empire. And we perform the same tasks: the dispensing of justice, supply, medicine, war."

In many ways, life on the Starship *Enterprise* was similar to life on ships manned by the crew of the humane yet courageous Captain Horatio Hornblower, only four centuries later. That theme became central to the development of the *Star Trek* concept. Director Nicholas Meyer made everyone on the set of *Star Trek II* watch *Captain Horatio Hornblower* (1951), starring Gregory Peck, and producers presented a copy of C. S. Forester's *Commodore Hornblower* to Patrick Stewart when he continued the voyages of the *Enterprise* in *Star Trek: The Next Generation*. Still, Captain Kirk was very much William Shatner's creation.

"Captain Kirk behaved as William Shatner would," the star of the show recalled, "or rather, how the ideal William Shatner would behave in the face of danger, love, passion, or a social situation. So all of me was invested in him, because I had no other choice. I couldn't plan ahead because I didn't know what was coming next."

Shatner's *Star Trek* pilot was shot in only eight days during the summer of 1965, but postproduction editing dragged on until December. Nonetheless, within weeks of seeing it, NBC executives slated the new series for their fall 1966 lineup. Production began in May 1966 with an episode called "The Corbomite Maneuver." The uncomplicated script gave the actors a chance to concentrate on their new characters. It featured Captain Kirk bluffing his way out of impending disaster when the *Enterprise* wanders into an area of space controlled by an evil alien warlord.

Associate producer Bob Justman had set up a six-day production schedule for each episode. That called for filming an unheard-of twelve-to-fourteen pages of script every day. He set aside the seventh day for rewrites and corrections. The directors had only one week of preproduction for each episode, and that included guest-star casting, props and scenery, and script refinement.

Because of the grueling schedule, *Star Trek* evolved some of the most creative and efficient production techniques in the history of television. Everyone worked hundred-hour weeks, and Gene Roddenberry worked until the wee morning hours each night, keeping very tight control over the first thirteen episodes to ensure that his personal vision of *Star Trek* was coming through.

Some of the best episodes were made during the first

season. "Mudd's Women" introduced Roger C. Carmel's fast-talking con man character. The show was such a hit that two more Mudd episodes were planned and NBC asked for a spinoff series. Unfortunately, Carmel got involved in other projects and only one other episode was made with his unique character.

Robert Walker, Jr., portrayed a disturbed psychokinetic teenager in a powerful episode called "Charlie X." According to people on the set, Shatner had a number of run-ins with the director and the associate producer about this episode, in which he felt Walker was given too many good scenes.

Shatner was happier with "What Are Little Girls Made Of?" because he got the opportunity to play dual roles. In the show, he is duplicated in android form by a mad doctor who wants to take over the *Enterprise*. Fans also liked the episode for its arcane references to the mythos of science fiction writer H. P. Lovecraft.

Another dual role for Shatner came in "The Enemy Within." A transporter malfunction splits Kirk into two persons, one with his positive aspects and the other with his negative aspects. Shatner's performance in a fight scene between the two halves of his personality was so stirring that the whole crew broke into spontaneous applause.

Footage from the series' first pilot, "The Cage," was used to compile the two-parter "Menagerie." In the hybrid episode, Kirk is forced to court-martial Spock, who has commandeered the *Enterprise* to take the now paralyzed Captain Christopher Pike to a forbidden planet where the inhabitants use their psychic powers to help Pike lead a fulfilling life.

Susan Oliver's seductive performance in it as a green-skinned Orion animal woman who appeared to Captain Pike while he was under the control of the aliens was deemed overtly sexual by several critics and even banned by a station manager for KXTX in Dallas. That only served to increase the episode's notoriety.

Shatner volunteered to wrestle a truly ferocious creature during the filming of "Shore Leave." The episode has the *Enterprise* crew stopping off at an extraterrestrial amusement park that entertains visitors with images from their own minds. NBC thought the Theodore Sturgeon script too abstract, so Shatner looked for some way to add a little excitement. Since most of the filming took place at a wild animal park, he volunteered to wrestle a full-grown tiger that had been used in one of the earlier scenes.

But Roddenberry did not think it was such a good idea, and the producer made his point when he took Shatner to watch the animal tear apart fresh meat during feeding time. The intrepid star quickly changed his mind, making it one of the few times that Shatner compromised his "anything-for-the-show" philosophy.

Shatner's daughters appeared in "Miri," an early installment about a planet inhabited by centuries-old children. He embraces his youngest daughter, Melanie, in the final scene. Shatner was able to showcase his Shakespearean talents in an episode entitled "The Conscience of a King," which is about a traveling troupe of actors who are concealing an escaped war criminal.

In what is widely considered to be the series' best episode, "City on the Edge of Forever," Kirk goes back in time to undo an act that has tragically altered the future. In 1930s New York, he meets a beautiful woman, played by Joan Collins, with whom he falls in love. In some of his best acting, Shatner realizes it is her surviving an accident that has changed the future; he must let her die. It is the only episode in which censors allowed his character to curse. (Kirk utters an innocuous "Go to hell.") The script won the Writer's Guild Award for outstanding teleplay and the International Hugo Science Fiction Award.

For the season opener, however, the network chose a mediocre episode called "The Man Trap," about a shape-shifting creature that gets aboard the *Enterprise* and starts sucking the salt out of crew members' bodies. The network thought viewers would go for the straightforward plot and creepy Salt Vampire monster.

They were wrong. The initial reviews were terrible. *Variety* predicted flatly, "this series won't work," and *TV Guide* commented, "the sky's not the limit on this Trek." Sagging ratings seemed to confirm the critics' judgments. In fact, in its entire run, *Star Trek* would never rise above fortieth place in the Nielsens.

Nonetheless, those who thought it was good thought it was *really* good. Even before it went on the air, the show was awarded a special citation at the 1966 World Science Fiction Convention, where Roddenberry had arranged a special preview of both pilots. By the end of its first season, *Star Trek* had been nominated for five Emmy Awards and received nearly 30,000 pieces of fan mail. It was not really such a bad start for a totally new offering.

Everyone at Desilu, from the head of the studio to members of the stage crew, were contributing to making the show a success, but Shatner still had his misgivings. Story editor John D. F. Black remembers encountering a morose Shatner leaning against Black's car one night in the parking lot. Black remembers the look of enormous innocence on Shatner's face as the star looked at him and said simply, "It's so damn important to us." Trying to cheer him up, Black said, "Yeah, we've got a hit!" "I hope so," Shatner replied, as he walked away.

But NBC brass did not appreciate the Herculean efforts being made on the set of the new series. They were fixated on the bottom-line Nielsen numbers, which were tied to advertising revenues. The bean-counting executives detected no improvement in the show's ratings and even considered canceling the show in the middle of its first season.

Then, the first in an amazing chain of fan-inspired actions took place. Noted science-fiction author Harlan

Ellison, who had written the well-received "City on the Edge of Forever," initiated a campaign to keep *Star Trek* on the air. He sent out 5,000 letters to his fellow writers and *Trek* fans.

The unique challenges the series was facing at the time are best summarized in Ellison's original letter, dated December 6, 1966:

It's finally happened. You've been in the know for a long time, you've known the worth of mature science fiction, and you've squirmed at the adolescent manner with which it has generally been presented on television. Now, finally, we've lucked out, we've gotten a show on prime time that is attempting to do the missionary job for the field of speculative fiction. The show is *Star Trek*, of course, and its aims have been lofty. *Star Trek* has been carrying the good word out to the boondocks. Those who have seen the show know it is frequently written by authentic science fiction writers, it is made with enormous difficulty and with considerable pride. If you were at the World Science Fiction Convention in Cleveland, you know it received standing ovations and was awarded a special citation by the convention. *Star Trek* has finally showed the mass audience that science fiction need not be situation comedy in space suits. The reason for this letter—and frankly, its appeal for help—is that we've learned this show, despite its healthy growth, could face trouble soon. The Nielsen Roulette game is being played. They say, "If mature science fiction is so hot, howzacome that kiddie space show on the other network *(Lost in Space)* is doing so much better?" There is no sense explaining it's the second year for the competition and the first year for *Star Trek;* all they understand are the decimal places. And the sound of voices raised. Which is where you come in.

Star Trek cancellation or a change to a less adult format would be tragic, seeming to demonstrate that real science fiction cannot attract a mass audience.

We need letters! Yours and ours, plus every science fiction fan and TV viewer we can reach through our publications and personal contacts. Important: not form letters, not using our phrases here; they should be the fan's own words and honest attitudes. They should go to (a) local television stations which carry *Star Trek;* (b) to sponsors who advertise on *Star Trek;* (c) to local and syndicated television columnists; and (d) to *TV Guide* and other television magazines.

The situation is critical; it has to happen now or it will be too late. We're giving it all our efforts; we hope we can count on yours.

The letter-writing campaign worked, at least temporarily. Over 116,000 letters were received by NBC, and *Star Trek* was renewed for a second season.

Romance in the Captain's Quarters

Although he was extremely busy, Shatner was living exactly the kind of life he'd always hoped for. He was able to pursue his sporting interests, family life, acting career, and affairs of the heart simultaneously.

Rumors were rampant about Shatner's romantic escapades. It was said that Andrea Dromm, the curvaceous, pug-nosed blonde who played the captain's yeoman, had quit the show rather than put up with Shatner's amorous advances. In any case, she was quickly replaced by Grace Lee Whitney, who had a reputation for being on the wild side. Whitney had gotten her start in Hollywood as the original Chicken of the Sea mermaid, then she appeared in *Top Banana* (1954) and *Some Like It Hot* (1959).

"Janice Rand's duties on the *Enterprise*," Whitney recalled, "were that of a right-hand woman, a girl Friday. In other words, she took care of Kirk's personal needs, like a valet would do. I had a pet name I used to call myself: a space geisha."

Whitney had been abused as a child and she grew up a nymphomaniac. When she drank, her defenses crumbled. Although she never admitted to being Shatner's lover, he was the only member of the cast to stand by her when the studio decided to get rid of her at the end of the first season. David L. Ross, who played a security officer in the series, recalled what it was like then.

"I remember Grace Lee Whitney going through some bad things," Ross told me. "She was loud and would tell dirty jokes. She liked to laugh and be one of the guys, too. And there was sex on the set. But she did the best she could. She always showed up, but she was going through some personal changes and got drunk. Bill tried to help her. He kept warning her to get her act together. He told her to get it together because it was coming down to the line. But she was canned in the middle of the first season. In the last weeks, when everyone knew Grace was going to be cut, she was taboo. No one would talk to or even look at her."

(After she was fired, Whitney hit rock bottom as a prostitute on Hollywood's skid row. Gradually, she pulled her life together and today lectures at substance-abuse seminars. In a triumphal return, she reprised her role as Janice Rand in all the *Star Trek* movies except *The Wrath of Khan*.)

Several former members of the cast and crew of *Star Trek* have insinuated that Shatner made a habit of bedding female guest stars on the series. One cast member, who asked to remain anonymous, stated that only four or five female guest stars resisted his amorous intentions.

Of course, it is hard to believe how any red-blooded man could resist going after such beauties as Angelique

Pettyjohn (who played the sensuous Shahna in "The Gamesters of Triskelion"), or Antoinette Bower (the seductive alien witch in "Catspaw"), or Tania Lemani (the alien nightclub dancer in "Wolf in the Fold"), or the flame-haired Leslie Parish (who played Lieutenant Carolyn Palamas and ended up wearing an alluring pink chiffon gown in "Who Mourns for Adonais?"). And what about the ultimate virgin, the android Rayna, portrayed by Louise Sorel in "Requiem for Methuselah"?

How can one forget the cache of luscious female flesh that were "Mudd's Women" (Karen Steele, Susan Denberg, and Maggie Thrett), or the curvaceous series of android twins (Rhae and Alyce Andrece and Maureen and Coleen Thorton) in "I, Mudd"?

Like his alter ego Kirk, Shatner became enamored of Joan Collins after working with her in "The City on the Edge of Forever." The alluring actress played Edith Keeler, the 1930's social worker with whom Kirk falls deeply in love. Shatner's attraction to the actress may have been one reason he was able to give one of his most emotionally charged performances in the entire series.

As for Joan Collins, she says their relationship soured the day she walked into his dressing room and caught him without his wig on.

"Bill Shatner was a great flirt," recalled Tasha Martel, another guest star on *Star Trek*. The exotic actress, who appeared in many TV shows, including *The Outer Limits* and *Have Gun Will Travel*, played Spock's wife T'Pring in the "Amok Time" episode. She recalls giggling and flirting with Shatner like two kids in school, until director Joe Pevney had to step in to put a halt to their bubbly antics.

But Shatner had to compete for her attentions with the episode's writer, Theodore Sturgeon. Martel said Sturgeon started "gazing amorously" at her from off the set, and before long, the two were an item.

Obviously, Shatner was not the only person messing around behind the scenes of *Star Trek*. Even Leonard

Nimoy had his moments of passion. It is said that he and Shatner battled over the attentions of Jill Ireland, who played Spock's love interest, Leila, in "This Side of Paradise." Gene Roddenberry had a long affair with Majel Barrett, who played Number One in the first pilot and Nurse Chapel in the series (which didn't stop him from having a short romance with Nichelle Nichols during the same period). In 1968, he left his wife and moved in with Majel. The following year they were married.

Nobody Upsets the Star

Although Shatner seemed to have everything he could ask for, he wanted even more, and the scheduling of a second season for *Star Trek* represented yet another opportunity for him to achieve it. Shatner knew the second season was a reprieve, one more chance to achieve his greatest dream: to become the preeminent stage actor of his generation.

"Although I've compromised my dreams," Shatner admitted at the time, "I haven't given up on them entirely. If *Star Trek* is a long-running series, it will mean that in five or six years I can go back to the stage and do what I choose. If the series isn't successful, I'll just begin slugging it out again."

Of course, the Toughy in him was always ready for a fight, and he would certainly fight to make *Star Trek* a success. In his pilot for the series, Shatner's character had been called James R. Kirk, but the name was changed to James T. Kirk by the second episode, when it became obvious that "Tiberius" was better suited to the imperial character Shatner was creating. Nerves started to fray as the lead actor's royal bearing showed up behind the camera.

In "The Deadly Years," for example, Kirk, Spock, McCoy, and Scotty are infected with a disease that causes accelerated aging. Shatner realized he was not very good at portraying an old man, but DeForest Kelley was excellent at it. When Shatner copied many of the things Kelley did to appear older and then demanded more time on screen to show off his newfound talents, Kelley exploded. Director Joe Pevney said the episode was "strife with behind-the-scenes conflict" because of it.

For William Windom, who played Commodore Decker in the "Doomsday Machine" episode, William Shatner's royal bearing was familiar. Windom had understudied Shatner in the Broadway play *The World of Suzie Wong* and experienced firsthand the power of his ego. During the *Star Trek* filming, Windom harbored deep resentment against Shatner and the two hardly spoke off camera.

In the original script, Windom's character was considerably stronger. Instead of being discovered weak and confused, slumped over the console of his destroyed ship, he was to show up glaring out of the *Enterprise*'s viewscreen full of anger. Shatner felt that Decker overshadowed Kirk, and he had his lines reduced and toned down.

"I've gotten great insight into the omnipotence of the series lead," Shatner commented at the time. "Everybody does his best not to upset the *star*. It's an almost unique position few in the entertainment industry achieve. It's like absolute power.

"In television, the star of the series has much more power, to use a bad term, than is ordinarily given an actor. It's equivalent, I would think, to the power that a big star in a film has, and it takes a very strong, powerful director to curb that star. That power can corrupt, I am sure, but at this point I don't feel it has. If it does happen, I hope someone stops me fast."

It would have been very hard to stop him. The energetic Shatner came in to the studio between four and five in the morning and stayed until nearly everyone else had left. He took an active interest in every aspect of the show's production and always spoke out when something seemed wrong, whether it was the lighting or someone else's lines. Although he never hesitated to criticize, he also was quick to praise good efforts.

"Shatner was never late," actor Dave Ross remembers, "never made you wait like some stars. He didn't do those things because he was a professional. Even with guest actors, Bill worked with them. He showed up, had his lines pat, was always there. Sometimes on the set, when you're shooting, with all the lighting set up and timing, you often make a mistake. At such times, there was always a joke from Bill. We had these stupid plastic phasers that broke to pieces right on camera, and he always had something to say about that, always trying to keep the mood up. Leonard would never instigate it but would jump in. Bill was always the one who had something funny to say about whatever was going on. That's carrying the show, keeping up the morale. Bill was for the show, it was his ticket. He always wanted what was right for the show and got along with anybody who was 'pro' the show—that's the bottom line. If you were against the show or were in some way jeopardizing the show, then you were Bill's enemy.

"And he was always around if you had a problem. He was always there if you were facing down a director when something was not right, and you didn't feel it. Bill wouldn't necessarily take your side, but at least he'd be there to see that things didn't get out of hand. My first show was 'Miri,' and I had a problem with the way I was doing something. I was arguing with the director, Vincent McEveety, and Bill came over and took his side. Then, he showed me how to work the scene to make it right. I don't know if his contract gave him a say in directing, but he was always interested in everything that was going on."

But Shatner's aggressive interest in the show was not appreciated by everyone. For some, Captain Quirk was a neurotic mother hen on the set of *Star Trek*. Instead of relying on the producers and directors to do their jobs, Shatner set up a table next to his dressing room where he gathered the actors, associate producer, and director to discuss script alterations. He insisted that everyone meet at the table outside his dressing room before moving onto the set. The so-called rehearsal table, while giving the actors a chance to go over their lines, proved to be a kink in the show's tight production schedule.

Director Joe Pevney recalled: "Like a producer himself, Bill would arrange the table and seats and would talk the property man into moving the thing over to the side. Well, when you're doing television in five or six days, there's no time for this constant rehearsal—with pencils in hand and making changes. Because once you start making changes on the set, they have to be approved by the producer. It also destroys the disciplinary control of the director. I'm an angry guy when it comes to this kind of shit. I come from a disciplined school where everything is in the script. The director's responsibility is to tell the story as the writer intended it. Once that's interfered with, he loses all control. So, anyway, every time you would hear 'Cut. Print,' you'd have these guys rushing over under Bill's command to the table to work on the next scene."

Shatner also felt responsible for the general mood on the set. As Dave Ross said, he was the first to crack a joke or try to lighten the heavy burden of producing a show a week. One prank Shatner is very fond of telling concerns lunch breaks.

Unlike the cafeteria at Desilu, which was usually empty, the commissary at Paramount was always crowded. Since everyone from *Star Trek* broke at the same time, they would all rush over and get in line for lunch. It became a real challenge to get a bite to eat and find a few moments to relax. Shatner usually headed for the commissary at a fast trot, often arriving at the head of the line. That is, until the day Leonard Nimoy brought a bicycle to work. By outpacing everyone at lunchtime,

Nimoy was able to enjoy a leisurely meal and rest in his dressing room afterward.

Shatner decided to sabotage Nimoy's neat scheme by chaining the bike with a padlock. Nimoy had no idea who was locking up his bike, but he found a pair of boltcutters and kept them handy to cut the chain should it ever become necessary. Once, Shatner hid the bike in George Takei's dressing room, and the confused Mr. Sulu was at a loss to explain to Nimoy how it had got there. Another time, Shatner put the bike in his own dressing room with his dog, a Doberman pinscher named Morgan. When Nimoy asked what had happened to his bike, Shatner volunteered that he saw someone put a bicycle in his dressing room. Nimoy strolled over to Shatner's quarters and opened the door, only to find the ferocious dog guarding the bike. Spock prudently decided to walk to lunch that day.

Not long after that, Shatner asked the electricians to suspend the bike in the rafters with a spotlight shining on it. When Nimoy inquired about his bike, Shatner said simply: "Lift your eyes to the stars, Leonard!" Nimoy finally figured out who was behind the continuing prank and began keeping his bicycle safely locked away in the trunk of his car. Of course, that only encouraged Shatner, who then arranged to have the car towed away.

Nimoy got even when it came time for Shatner to play a scene that required full body makeup. The flesh-toned powder is mixed with water in a bucket and applied with a sponge all over an actor's skin. A few hours before Shatner's turn, Nimoy placed the bucket of water in a refrigerator to chill. The screeching Shatner could hardly stand still as the icy concoction was sponged everywhere on his body. Only afterward did he realize who was responsible for his tortured makeup session.

In an attempt to put an end to the practical jokes, Shatner brought in a Safari grill and started preparing lunches for Nimoy and Kelley in a storage lot just behind the soundstage. That way, their lunch periods were much more relaxing and a lot less competitive. The portable cooker used rolled-up newspapers for fuel, and Shatner became proficient at cooking quick meals. Their favorites were "Vulcan veal sandwiches" and cheese-filled "space-burgers."

Who's the Star, Anyway?

However, the two stars were not always on such amicable terms. The friction started in the middle of the first season, as the popularity of Nimoy's character grew rapidly. He started receiving noticeably more fan mail than Shatner. Even NBC, who had previously asked Roddenberry to get rid of the Vulcan, was now telling him to feature the alien crewman more. One tobacco company sponsor asked the network to have the increasingly popular character start smoking "space cigarettes."

The breaking point came when the *Saturday Review* published an article that suggested since Spock was so much more interesting than Kirk, the alien character ought to be made the captain of the *Enterprise*. Shatner was absolutely livid.

"Well, nobody was near Shatner for days," recalled writer David Gerrold. "He was furious. He had been hired to be the star of the show. All of a sudden, all the writers are writing all this great stuff for Spock, and Spock, who's supposed to be a subordinate character, suddenly starts becoming the equal of Kirk. Bill definitely feels he was lessened by that. On the other hand, Leonard is a very shrewd businessman, a very smart actor, and recognized that this Spock business was a way to be more important than an 'also ran,' and he pushed."

Not long afterward, a photographer from *Life* showed up on the set to document the arduous makeup routine that Leonard Nimoy had to sit through each day. George

Takei remembers Shatner walking into the makeup room, doing a double take, and promptly turning around and leaving. It had been rumored that Shatner's contract gave him preapproval of any photographers on the set. Sure enough, in a few minutes, someone from the front office came in and asked the photographer to leave immediately. The man packed up his camera gear and left.

It was obvious what had transpired. Nimoy, with his makeup half applied, retreated to his dressing room and refused to go on unless the photographer was brought back to finish his work. Studio executives were seen dashing back and forth between the two stars' dressing rooms, and the feud delayed production for over four hours. Finally, another appointment was made for the photographer and filming of the show got under way.

"Bill Shatner's problem," mused scriptwriter Norman Spinrad, "was that he wasn't given as interesting a character to play as Nimoy was. He was the lead character, but he couldn't be the most interesting. That led to all the line stealing and all the crazy, lunatic stuff in any number of scripts where the captain went crazy because somebody was trying to take away his ship. This gave the character of Kirk more depth. It gave Kirk a little edge somewhere that was really Shatner, which is a good way to use it."

Before long, both Shatner and Nimoy were counting lines and each had become very protective of his character. Writers and directors were terrified of submitting new scripts, because the two stars would make such a fuss about their parts. Nimoy felt he was not getting the recognition he deserved, probably because the studio was trying to downplay his popularity, fearing he would demand more money and perks.

Neither star wanted to play the straight man to the other, and both wanted more lines. Nimoy's character suffered, because Spock working alongside Kirk has a magic that plays very well, driving off Kirk's energy and Spock's alternative points of view. Spock alone comes off aloof and ponderous, as in the "Galileo Seven" episode, where he takes charge of a shuttlecraft mission. Nimoy admitted the episode was a failure, but he still demanded more opportunities to command, while Shatner fought tooth and nail to keep from sharing his character's responsibilities.

The situation got so bad that Roddenberry asked Isaac Asimov for assistance in making Kirk more appealing to viewers. Asimov suggested having Spock and Kirk do more things together, so people would come to associate Kirk with Spock. He also thought it would be a good idea to expand on Shatner's character.

"Mr. Shatner is a versatile and talented actor," Asimov wrote Roddenberry, "and perhaps this should be made plain by giving him a chance at a variety of roles. In other words, an effort should be made to work up story plots in which Mr. Shatner has an opportunity to put on disguises or take over roles of unusual nature. A bravura display of his versatility would be impressive indeed and would probably make the whole deal a great deal more fun for Mr. Shatner."

The shift in emphasis raised Shatner's dampened spirits, and he started to show new enthusiasm for the show. However, the backstage tensions would eventually send Leonard Nimoy into therapy. A sensitive man, Nimoy became possessed by the character of Spock, although he was ultimately able to come to terms with his obsession.

"I didn't get close to Leonard until after the third or fourth show," David Ross revealed, "after he heard that I had turned down being a regular character. I remember from Leonard's scripts that he had been circling words and there would be a count of dialogue. But on a personal level, Leonard had a line, and he would never cross that. If anyone was the snob of the show, it was him. He was into health food, organics, and off-the-wall stuff. If you didn't have a lot of things in common with him, you didn't have much to talk about with Leonard. He was certainly not the kind of guy Shatner could go to if he was really down and out and needed a shoulder to cry on. The difference between Bill and Leonard was simple enough. Leonard was calculating. He thought before he said a word. Shatner, being real, said what he was feeling, and it sometimes got him in trouble."

Most people who worked on *Star Trek* would agree with Ross's unflattering assessment of the man who played Mr. Spock. Nimoy himself later admitted that he behaved in a cold and superior way on the set, but he said it was part of his getting into character. Unlike Shatner, who was very spontaneous, Nimoy spent hours trying to become Spock and maintain his persona as the technicians prepared for the day's shooting. The last thing he wanted to do was joke around or fraternize.

Nimoy spent so much effort trying to stay in character that he found himself having difficulty shaking Spock even when he was away from the studio. Finally, his Vulcan moods began affecting his wife and children, and the actor sought professional help. It was the beginning of a decade-long struggle to shake the power of Spock. In a statement of triumph, he titled his autobiography *I Am Not Spock*.

DeForest Kelley never got involved in the off-camera power struggle. According to Ross: "Kelley was very savvy in the ways of Hollywood. He went way back. He was a close friend of Audie Murphy and had co-starred in many of his westerns. Kelley had experienced the ups and downs of the business and banked his money. He was very careful and always gracious. He never took sides with either Shatner or Nimoy."

The Plot Unravels

The personality conflicts and grueling schedule took their toll, and *Star Trek* was beginning to look like another *Suzie*

Wong-type fiasco. Director Joe Pevney eventually left the show rather than continue to try to work with Shatner and Nimoy, and even Gene Roddenberry felt he was losing control of *Star Trek* to its two leading actors. Early on, producer and writer John D. F. Black had quit and was replaced by Stephen Carabatsos, who lasted only another few weeks. Associate producer Bob Justman had a nervous collapse and had to take time off to recuperate.

That was followed by a similar breakdown by Gene Roddenberry, who also had to leave the show to recuperate. When Roddenberry returned, he made himself executive producer in an attempt to lighten his load and distance himself from the bickering on the set. Shatner was upset that Roddenberry had "jumped ship" in the middle of the second season, and the relationship between the two grew even more strained.

"Roddenberry didn't abandon *Star Trek*," Nichelle Nichols told me. "He went away to take care of his health, so he wouldn't die in 1968 instead of 1992. There was never a sense of abandonment on the part of the supporting cast. They felt that was a *good* thing for him. I'm telling you that you couldn't get to the studio earlier than Gene Roddenberry and you couldn't leave later. It was a constant battle to get him off that lot for his own good. Many nights, he ended up sleeping on the couch in his office."

According to Nichols, Shatner tried to take over Roddenberry's position. "Without anyone's consent," she said, "Bill stepped into the role, bossing around and intimidating the directors and guest stars, cutting other actors' lines and scenes, and generally taking enough control to disrupt the sense of family we had shared during the first season."

In the meantime, Roddenberry elevated writer Gene Coon to the position of producer. Coon's contribution to the show was enormous. He was responsible for humanizing the characters and injecting humor into the scripts. Coon worked hard to make *Star Trek* happen on a daily basis, but he sometimes was forced to make last-minute changes without Roddenberry's input. Sometimes their animated discussions spilled over onto the set. Another problem was that Coon tended to feature the Big Three (Shatner, Nimoy, and Kelley) at the expense of the rest of the cast. He usually consulted only with Shatner, Nimoy, and the director, rarely talking with the other actors. In his memoirs, Shatner emphasized the hard feelings between Roddenberry and Coon, although several cast members have since taken exception to his view.

Nichelle Nichols said, "I was *shocked,* as were my colleagues from *Star Trek,* when we read Shatner's portrayal of the tension between the two Genes. We kept asking ourselves, what is he talking about? They were not at each other's throats. There was not a negative relationship between them. They were absolutely devoted to each other, and the devotion had to do with their mutual respect, talentwise, since they were coming from the same place, both creatively and politically.

"I was in and out of that office and had the greatest relationship with Gene Coon. My friendship with Gene Roddenberry—which by the time *Star Trek* began was totally platonic—was deeply warm. I used to marvel at these two men, at their creativity, how they laughed and thought together. I used to joke: 'If you guys' names were both Pete instead of Gene, I could call you "Pete" and "RePete."' Roddenberry welcomed and celebrated Coon's input. At the same time, one must understand that *Star Trek* was Gene Roddenberry's baby, his life's blood. Nothing happened that he did not condone and have his hands on. But the entire relationship between those two men was collaborative, easygoing, laughing, and fun.

"Their offices . . . were across the hall from one another, with their secretaries seated in between. Their doors were always open, and they used to yell at each other. We're talking a half-block apart and yelling across at one another rather than picking up the phone. They were saying things like: 'Did you figure out such and such?' or 'I'm tied up with this!' or 'Have you figured out where the Klingon's attitude is coming from?' One would be yelling at the other with great glee and joy in the creative process. Sometimes one would walk over to the other's office, and they would work together for hours. That's the kind of relationship they had.

"Where that business Shatner talks about came from, I have no idea. In fact, Gene Coon's second wife, Jackie, was equally shocked by it. These men were the closest of friends. It was an easy friendship—they could have been brothers."

Before the end of the second season, however, even Gene Coon, "the Fastest Typewriter in the West," said that he could not keep up the frantic pace of the show, and quit. The real reason for his leaving, however, might have been that he was tired of dealing with William Shatner and Leonard Nimoy. His managers, Doris and Reece Halsey, certainly thought so. Jackie Coon also commented that her husband thought the two stars of the show, like many leading actors, were "just too needful and egocentric." John Meredyth Lucas, the man Roddenberry picked to take Coon's place, attested to the tensions on the set.

"When I joined the show," Lucas said, "there was a great deal of tension with the actors. Not civil war, but a great deal of tension among the cast and company. As a matter of fact, Gene Coon took me out on location to introduce me as producer. . . . When they'd gotten a particular shot, we walked over and Shatner walked away from us. He would not speak to Gene or to me. They were feuding over something, though I've no idea what the problem was. There was tension among Shatner and Nimoy and Gene. Just a great deal that had built up."

Coon would die of cancer four years later, but a number of people connected with the show would continue to praise "*Star Trek*'s unsung hero" for years to come.

"There was great sadness when Gene Coon left," Nichols told me, "but it was because of his health. Just as it was because of Gene Roddenberry's health that he originally asked Coon to come aboard."

John Meredyth Lucas tried to ignore the hard feelings on the set and concentrate on revitalizing the show. He returned to the original Horatio Hornblower idea of action and warfare on a ship at the boundaries of the empire. At the same time, he tried to work more closely with Roddenberry, incorporating his higher concepts without letting the storyline stagnate.

The Seven Dwarves

If the producers and directors of *Star Trek* felt it was difficult dealing with Shatner and Nimoy, they sometimes experienced equally trying times with the remainder of the cast. While the Big Three were guaranteed a role in every episode, the others were promised only seven out of every thirteen shows. They were actually hired on a weekly or even daily basis. This created another division among the actors. In fact, Shatner would come to call his supporting troupe the "Seven Dwarves."

The situation was especially challenging for Nichelle Nichols, who had given up a promising singing career to act on *Star Trek*. She had to put up with backstage prejudice as well as the frequent bickering between the actors. Desilu executives initially opposed having a black woman in the cast, so Gene Roddenberry had to hire her on a daily basis to make it seem like she was not a regular. The studio even went so far as to hide bags of fan mail from Nichols so she would not get the idea that she was one of the cast. One executive, who started out working with Roddenberry but ended up as an assistant to one of the top brass at Desilu, regularly taunted her with racial slurs. It got to the point where she finally decided to quit.

"My pain came in petty ways," she confided to me. "It's fascinating now but was very painful then. I was leaving because I had a singing career that was really moving and I didn't need all this. It was extremely frustrating, but at the same time, it was very rewarding. I know that might sound contradictory, but it really was like that. Besides, very shortly I realized that I was involved in something very important. That Gene's dream was a step forward and had social impact. I'm talking about the original series, which still speaks to the same socioeconomic situations, prejudices, and advancements that affect the people of today."

It took a chance meeting with Martin Luther King, Jr., to convince Nichols of the importance of her role in *Star Trek*. After all, despite her circuitous bookings on the show, she was the first black woman to hold a regular role in a major television series.

Nichelle decided to stay with *Star Trek* and try to strengthen her character's position. That was a formidable task, considering the powerful egos already staking claim to the bridge.

"Bill Shatner began to make it plain to anyone on the set that he was the Big Picture and the rest of us were no more important than the props," Nichelle Nichols related in her memoirs, *Beyond Uhura*. "Anything that didn't focus exclusively on him threatened his turf, and he never failed to make his displeasure known."

Most of the former cast members agree that Shatner forbade even the most minor ad-libs or any additional lines in their parts. His most frequent excuse was that they were detracting from the "rhythm of the scene." Shatner's personal relationship with them was condescending at best, and he rarely mingled with the other actors on the set, choosing instead to spend his spare time with the camera or lighting crews, or hanging out with the stuntmen. When cornered by one of the other actors, he would suddenly become overly affectionate and extremely charming, as if they were long-lost friends. Then, within a minute or so, he always found a way to excuse himself, often dismissing the person with an insincere squeeze on the arm.

George Takei summed it up: "Shatner was the one who made life trying for all of us." While the polite Takei never confronted the star during the *Star Trek* years, he made his true feelings known in his autobiography, *To the Stars*. Takei was especially galled by Shatner's habit of flashing a big smile after he had cut someone's lines or succeeded in an underhanded power play.

"He always managed to keep that smiling, charming facade up, as if nothing out of the ordinary had happened, joking, giggling, and bantering," Takei recalled. "And always, that sunny, oblivious, rankling smile. That smile as bright, as hard, and as relentless as the headlights of an oncoming car. You just had to get out of its way."

To help relieve the tension on the set, Takei often imitated Shatner, imagining what the star would be like after he had achieved his ultimate goal of delivering all the lines of the entire bridge crew. Nichelle Nichols remembers laughing until tears ran down her cheeks as she witnessed Takei's impersonation of Shatner's halting, staccato style: "Hail! Ing! Fre! Quencies! O! Pen! Cap! Tain! / Fas! Cin! A! Ting! / He's! Dead! Jim!"

A native of Vancouver, British Columbia, James Doohan had never had much use for his fellow Canadian actor. They were never good friends during the *Star Trek* years and eventually became outright enemies. Once, Jimmy decided to give Shatner a call. On answering the phone, an incredulous Captain Quirk demanded: "How did you get my phone number? Don't you ever call me at home again!" And Doohan made sure he never did.

The addition of a new actor to the bridge crew at the beginning of the second season only served to exacerbate the situation. NBC had pressured Roddenberry into finding a cute actor to attract eight- to fourteen-year-old viewers to the show. The network was courting the teenybopper market, and the ideal candidate would look like bubblegum idol Davy Jones of the hit show *The Monkees*. At about that same time, *Pravda* had published an editorial asking why there was no Russian on the bridge of the *Enterprise*. After all, the Russians were the first in space. In a brilliant move, killing two birds with one stone, Roddenberry created a youthful Russian character, Ensign Pavel Chekov.

Walter Koenig had worked with Roddenberry in *The Lieutenant* and had played a Russian exchange student in an episode of *Mr. Novak*. He also looked a lot like Davy Jones. That was all the qualification he needed. To cover up his short haircut until he could grow longer hair, the studio gave him a ridiculous-looking wig to wear. So, armed only with his Beatlesque toupee, Walter Koenig was tossed onto the bridge of the *Enterprise* to sink or swim.

His reception was anything but warm. The scripts now routinely featured the relationships among Kirk, Spock, and McCoy at the expense of the other characters, and everyone was extremely covetous of his own screen time. Adding another character to the bridge only made matters worse.

"Walter Koenig was a kid they brought in," David Ross remembered, "and a lot of people didn't like that. If the cast felt threatened in any way by a new cast member, they didn't like you, no matter what. Walter was like a lost puppy. He did well with his Russian accent for the few words they gave him in tryouts, but we experienced delays because he couldn't get it right during shooting. He spent lots of time in voiceover trying to do it a second time. Three times, casting head Bill Costilla said he wanted Koenig replaced. He was not even the first choice for the role of Chekov. Two ahead of him turned the role down because they knew they would never star."

One example of the tense undercurrents on the set of *Star Trek* was the "high chair confrontation," in which the folding canvas chairs used by the actors took on added significance. Each chair was like a mobile office, with a pouch for scripts and personal items. The chairs also gave actors a place to relax while waiting for the next scene. The director always had a chair that sat higher than those used by the rest of the production crew, and Shatner, Nimoy, and Kelley all had chairs that were higher than those of the other cast members. Most often, a production gofer would carry the chairs from set to set for the stars and director, while those with regular chairs carried them themselves.

Walter Koenig did not even have a chair when he first arrived on the set, and the lack of a place to sit made him feel like an outcast from the beginning. But after only a few episodes, the young actor was receiving over 600 letters a week from fans, and it became obvious his new character was becoming very popular. At that point, Koenig insisted on having a chair as high as the ones used by the Big Three. When he finally got his towering seat, Koenig kept watch and would not let anyone else sit in it. Of course, the other cast members became jealous, and before long, everyone was sitting in "high chairs."

Koenig's first impression of Shatner was one of deep respect. "He's a gentleman and a gentle man," Koenig described his captain, "and a leader. If any member of the cast is unhappy about the show, Bill will speak to the producer for him. He's also a very loose guy. He tells very cool jokes and keeps everyone relaxed during the tensions of the day. It was Bill who helped me to develop the character of Chekov."

Shatner's public stance was that if the Chekov character added to the show, and could pick up the young audience, why not? Privately, he lamented Koenig's unpolished performances and his inability to get his accent down. Shatner never admitted to feeling threatened by Koenig's growing popularity, but as an experienced actor, he understood the attention young players command on stage. Moreover, Shatner's own character had embodied many youthful characteristics. It must have seemed that the captain's preeminence was once again threatened.

On at least one occasion, however, Shatner got to bask in his own importance. During the second season, rumors circulated that the captain had an offer to do another show and was thinking of leaving *Star Trek*. Several of the cast members panicked. Everyone realized that a new lead character would hurt the series. Shatner played it cool, though. He told a friend: "I don't know where these rumors are coming from, but no one asked me, so I'm not saying anything."

Another time, during filming of the episode "Return of the Archons," director Joe Pevney playfully called for the *Big Four* to come to the set. Everyone knew who the Big Three were, but no one could imagine who had been elevated to the new status. Was it Doohan? Koenig? A few minutes after Shatner, Nimoy, and Kelley showed up, Pevney announced over his loudspeaker: "Hey, Dave Ross, come out here!" The director and stars enjoyed the moment of levity, but the rest of the cast hated it.

All the cast members were lobbying Gene Roddenberry for more time for their individual characters. At one point during the second season, the executive producer issued a memo about everyone's counting lines that ended with the exasperated admonishment that they were all acting like a bunch of spoiled brats. I asked Shatner's friend David Ross what he recalled about the supporting actors.

"I never got along with Jimmy Doohan," Ross said. "He was not the kind of guy to open up. He was always worried about his career, and it was something he really wanted. He wanted his parts to grow, and there was confusion and arguments because of it. Jimmy would go so far as to figure out how much more screen time he could add by using his accent on the words and stretching it out. But I guess that's part of the business. All George

Takei wanted was something more to grow in his position. But he was what he was in the show, and there was no getting around that. If you had a minor part, just how many ways could you deliver it?"

"There was a lot of stress at the end about who's the greater star," Ross summarized. "Even makeup was terrible. Every one of them thought they were stars. They were all doing that number. They were figuring out how many lines they had compared to the other characters. They had good jobs but never learned that they just weren't that important. Other than Leonard, Bill could have had any of them fired. I learned from Bill that a lot of times, some of these guys would try to step in front of your key light and shadow you. He had to say things to protect guests or some of the more innocent actors."

Obviously, most of the other cast members had a different view. They were warning guest stars and extras to watch out for Shatner.

Star Trek Synchronicity

Despite all the battered egos and growing pains, *Star Trek* got through its second season. Perhaps viewers sensed the backstage tensions, which seemed to surface in a few of the scripts. Kirk faces being replaced by a talking computer—though not Spock—in "The Ultimate Computer" episode. "The Changeling" is a man-sized computer programmed to destroy all inferior life forms. It thinks Kirk is its creator. In "Who Mourns for Adonais?" a Spock-like Apollo wants the crew to worship it, but Kirk must destroy the false god. In "Journey to Babel," Kirk gets sick but must fake his recovery so Spock will relinquish control of the *Enterprise*.

"Mirror, Mirror" posited the existence of a parallel dimension where their evil personalities replaced the bridge crew. "The Trouble with Tribbles" was the show's badly needed comedy relief episode.

Could "By Any Other Name" be Paramount Studios, where Kirk plots to regain control when a bunch of aliens hijack the ship? Are the "Gamesters of Triskelion" really network executives and not the distant disembodied brains for whose amusement Kirk must fight deadly games?

Whether or not backstage tensions were creeping into the storyline during Shatner's rehearsal table meetings, the second season's twenty-six episodes were overall the series' best. The higher-quality scripts, however, did not improve the show's Nielsen ratings.

Star Trek had to rely on luck and a prayer to survive. The prayer came during the first episode of the second season ("Amok Time"), in which the famous split-fingered Vulcan salute "Live long and prosper" came into existence. No more fitting prayer could have been conceived for the struggling show. Leonard Nimoy delved into his Jewish background to come up with the hand sign, which is used by rabbis to bless their congregations during certain prayers. The rabbinical blessing proved quite appropriate for the cast and crew of _Star Trek_, because by the middle of the season, NBC had decided to cancel the show.

Luckily for the series, there was more synchronicity at work on the set of _Star Trek_. Two dedicated fans, Bjo and John Trimble, happened to be visiting the set on the day the cast found out about the network's plans. Shatner and the other actors were very depressed but carried on as best they could.

"It was very disheartening to watch," Bjo Trimble said later, "because people would go on and do their lines and be 'up' and cheerful members of the _Enterprise_. And then they'd come out and go 'Uggh! . . .' It was really a sad thing."

The actors were in the middle of filming the fortieth installment, "The Deadly Years." In the story, Kirk is relieved of his command after being exposed to a mysterious radiation that causes him to age rapidly. At the very last minute, an antidote is found that saves him, and ultimately, the *Enterprise*.

As it turned out, that is exactly what happened to *Star Trek* itself. On the way home from the studio, Bjo and John Trimble, the two fans who just happened to be on the set that day, decided to launch a campaign to save *Star Trek*. It snowballed into the biggest fan response in the history of television. Meanwhile, William Shatner was having the time of his life.

Chapter 6

Motorcycle Machismo

Hell—I'll do anything once.
—William Shatner on his lifestyle

"We would go down to San Diego and ride our dirt bikes over Turkey Rut," *Trek* actor David Ross told me, "and that's pretty rough going. I've seen Shatner fly off his motorcycle and really take a tumble, then get right back on. A lot of people don't know this: William Shatner was much more macho than Steve McQueen ever was, but it was never publicized. And I knew both of them."

David Ross played several small parts in *Star Trek*, including a security officer, the transporter chief, Lieutenant Galloway, and Lieutenant Johnson. The writers killed off his characters and brought them back a number of times in the three years he was with the show.

Ross had his own fan club and even today is asked to participate in *Star Trek* merchandising events, like those held on the QVC cable network. He always declines such invitations. For Dave Ross, *Star Trek* was just another job.

Gene Roddenberry asked Ross to become a regular in the series and, later, to appear in the first motion picture, but the highly trained Vietnam veteran was never really interested in acting as a career. He owned a Hollywood construction business, building houses for producers and celebrities such as Barbra Streisand, and he was close friends with Marlon Brando and Michael Caine. In his spare time, Ross worked as a contract actor with a number of Hollywood studios and appeared in episodes of *Combat* and *Wild, Wild West*. He and Shatner hit it off and became good friends during the *Star Trek* years.

"Bill and I would find our place," he continued, "normally with the stuntmen in Bill's dressing room, and everyone in that clique would hang out. We went motorcycling, scuba diving, and off on other trips. He was really a man's man, the kind of guy who does the macho thing for the pleasure of it—not to tell *Variety* all the time: 'Look what I did.' I worked with a lot of actors and most of them were real jerks, but not Shatner. He used to come over to my house a lot, and if I had a visitor or relatives, he was always willing to sit down and be nice. Bill was like part of the family. He'd go to the icebox and help himself. He didn't act like a god, like they say. More than anything else, he liked to be treated normally."

It was Dave who taught Shatner to scuba dive. They trained for weeks in a swimming pool, and Shatner gradually picked up the underwater techniques. Ruggedly handsome actor Christopher George, known at the time for his role as Sergeant Sam Troy in *The Rat Patrol*, was invited along for Shatner's oceanic baptism. Unfortunately, on the day that Ross, Shatner, George, and another diver arranged their underwater excursion, the ocean was exceptionally choppy.

Their first problem, however, was getting air for Shatner's tank. The group stopped in Santa Monica to fill tanks, but Shatner was not a certified diver, so the store refused to put air in his scuba tank. Finally, an employee recognized Shatner and agreed to give him air if he promised to be careful. "The owners would not want to be blamed for killing Captain Kirk," he cautioned.

By the time the four men reached the seashore, an

offshore storm was churning up to twenty-foot waves.
Once underwater, the divers were beat against rocks by
the strong currents, and they were all a little unnerved by
the rough conditions. Shatner kept reminding everyone
that he was counting on the buddy plan in case he got in
trouble, but the other divers were too busy steering clear
of the jagged rocks to worry about anyone else. Fortunately, Shatner handled himself well and came away with
only a few bruises.

Shatner and Ross planned fly-in fishing trips to Alaska
and once went so far as to get a sponsor and vehicle to
compete in the grueling Baja Motor Race. However,
something in Shatner's busy schedule always interfered
with their plans. The two men dreamed of sailing around
the world and settling down on a tropical island, yet most
of their excursions were on the spur of the moment.

On one occasion, Shatner went on a desert motorcycle
trip with Dave Ross and Gary Lockwood, who played the
deranged but superhuman officer in the second pilot for
Star Trek. Shatner hit a rut, was thrown off his bike, and
landed on top of a big barrel cactus. The star's rear end
was peppered with painful thorns. He dropped his trousers and straddled his bike while his two companions
yanked out the sharp thorns.

About that time, two young female hikers happened by
and stood back relishing the "em-bare-assing" scene.
Shatner kept shouting, "Get them out of here," but the
giggling girls would not leave. One nail-like thorn was so
deeply embedded in Shatner's posterior that Lockwood
had to use pliers to pull it out, while his companion yelped
in pain. Shatner was bleeding and too sore to ride. He had
to walk his bike all the way back to town.

The next morning, the adventuresome trio was having
breakfast when the same two girls walked into the restaurant. Dave Ross thought it would be funny to let them in
on the secret. But when the girls realized just whose naked
butt they had seen, they ran screaming over to the star,

who happened to be in the middle of downing his scrambled eggs. Shatner immediately dropped his fork and rushed out of the restaurant, giving Ross a hard shove out the door in front of him.

Cameraman Al Francis also became a close friend of Shatner's. He joined the show in the second season and was being groomed to replace first cameraman Jerry Finnerman. Al Francis was a professional motorcycle racer and would go out on weekends with Shatner to instruct him in the tricks of the trade.

Sometimes Ross, Francis, Shatner, and a few other cameramen or stuntmen went bar-hopping together in Los Angeles. They usually just had a few quiet drinks together, but sometimes they were bothered by tough guys who wanted to pick a fight with Captain Kirk. In such confrontations, Shatner never backed down, although ex-marine Ross sometimes stepped in to try to head off a fight. One time, Ross defused a dangerous situation by asking the combatants to step out back into a dark area, where no one would witness his lethal Special Services skills. Another time, a brawl broke out and Shatner's cronies formed a ring around him to keep him from getting hit.

In fact, Shatner had a penchant for getting into trouble with guys bigger than he. Sometimes, he felt his Corvette Stingray gave him unwritten priority on the highways, and he almost came to fisticuffs with other drivers on several occasions. Even in a golf cart, he believed he always had the right of way. Once, when he bumped into another moving golf cart, he yelled at the three burly men inside that they should have yielded to him. When they got out, Shatner ran up to one of them and gave him a flying drop-kick to the chest. But the man did not budge, and Shatner ended up lying on his back on the ground. From that position, he proceeded to apologize for his hasty action.

Shatner met his match again, when he took his three

daughters to a Hollywood amusement park. They were riding in miniature cars when three young punks in different cars suddenly started slamming into Shatner's car from all angles.

"One of them hit me and almost hit my girls," Shatner recalled. "When the ride was over, I picked up this man and bounced him on the floor. I thought I could take on all three guys, like Captain Kirk had done in many fights. All three came at me and began to pound on me. Blood was spurting all over. One of them kept yelling: 'Don't get your blood all over me!' Captain Kirk was all over the floor." The embarrassed father ended up begging for mercy in front of his three daughters.

Bill Theiss to the Rescue

Most of Shatner's bruises came not from brawls but from his favorite sport, motorcycling. Off-road biking was a dangerous sport, and it was not uncommon for guys to come back with broken arms, legs, and shoulders. Shatner took a lot of nasty falls from his bike and could have been seriously injured.

That could have jeopardized the filming of *Star Trek*, and the studio would have been furious had they known what he was doing. But Shatner was able to keep it a secret until the final year of *Star Trek*, when his contract was rewritten to preclude the star from participating in any risky sporting activities.

In the meantime, it was up to *Star Trek*'s costume designer, Bill Theiss, to wrap Shatner's pulled muscles and attempt to hide his swollen joints and bruises. Theiss also kept tab on everyone's weight and gently prodded the actors to keep trim. It was a constant battle, because the uniforms shrank when washed, and several actors, including Shatner, had started putting on weight.

When Theiss suggested to Grace Lee Whitney that she

lose twenty pounds, the actress lost the weight but ended up hooked on amphetamines. The situation got so bad for James Doohan that the front office told him to maintain a decent weight or leave the show. Theiss just kept altering Doohan's uniform, hoping to hide the excess pounds. He performed the same magic for Shatner, though the star's weight did not fluctuate as dramatically as Doohan's.

The real problem was Theiss's tight-fitting and scanty costumes. How he got them past network censors probably had something to do with the fact that the show took place in the distant future, and who could guess what trends fashion would take? In Theiss's view, women would start showing skin in unexpected places on their bodies and a girl's sexiness would be judged by how close her garment was to slipping off. For men, he designed tight-fitting stretch trousers and ultrashort tunics.

Ten years later, when it came time to make the first *Star Trek* movie, Theiss designed a new line of uniforms that gave the aging actors a little assistance with their protruding bellies. The designer added a wide elastic band to the trousers that fit tightly over the abdomen and helped pull it in.

"Bill Theiss was a funny guy," Dave Ross recalled. "He always had some quip about someone, usually something like, 'What a bitch.' He stepped on some toes and was supposed to be fired several times for one reason or another, but Gene Roddenberry said no way. Theiss was a great designer and could repair or replace any garment in a few seconds. Thanks to Theiss, very few people on the set were aware of Shatner's injuries or the real reason Captain Kirk was so slow moving about on certain days."

Theiss collaborated on other Roddenberry projects and won an Emmy for his costume designs on *Star Trek: The Next Generation*. He also was nominated for three Oscars for his work in the motion picture industry.

A Human Dynamo

During Shatner's *Star Trek* years, his friends were amazed at his boundless enthusiasm for activities outside the show. Despite long hours on the set and doing publicity, Shatner always found time for a number of other projects. The phone in his dressing room was always busy with calls from people who wanted him to buy scripts, invest in spaceships or other weird projects, do interviews, or just perform.

One part Shatner could never resist was a dual role. In March 1967, during a hiatus from *Star Trek*, he traveled to Spain with Joseph Cotton to film *White Comanche*. The movie is a classic evil-twin story retold as a spaghetti western. The twins' mother is Indian and their father is white, and the babies are separated at birth. One boy is raised by Indians; the other is brought up by white settlers. The cowboy twin grows up and is accused of a murder committed by his Indian brother. He tracks down his lookalike, and the two end up fighting a duel to the death. Unfortunately, Shatner's short haircut is the same for both the cowboy and the Indian characters, so he comes off looking pretty silly.

After he returned from Spain, Shatner purchased the rights to Hank Greenspun's autobiography, *Where I Stand: The Record of a Reckless Man!* The flamboyant New York attorney became a powerful figure in the publishing world when he founded several newspapers, including the *Las Vegas Sun*. Shatner talked *Trek* director Joe Pevney into becoming his partner in the film project. He also tried to produce a film he had previously purchased, a Jerry Sohl script titled *The Twisted Night*. Shatner hoped to star in both films, but financing fell through at the last minute, and his scripts never made it to the screen.

About the same time, Shatner came across a script

about a true incident during the war in Vietnam that he desperately wanted to produce. In the lead role, he planned to cast his friend Christopher George, who was starring in ABC's *The Rat Patrol* at the time. Shatner even scouted a tropical location in Mexico in which to film the story. He took the script to Alan Ladd, Jr., at 20th Century-Fox, then over to Universal and a few other large studios, but they all turned it down. The studio executives were convinced that nobody wanted to see a movie about the Vietnam War. Of course, the string of smash box-office Vietnam movies that soon followed proved them wrong and frustrated Shatner no end.

The actor-producer-writer spent the rest of his spare time pursuing his varied athletic interests. Shatner was a veteran boxer and spent many hours sparring in gyms when he first arrived in Hollywood. But from 1966 to 1969, he actively pursued karate training with screenwriter and black belt expert Terry Bleecker.

"His memory is incredible," Bleecker said of his pupil. "His discipline as an actor and his gift for total recall make him a prime student of karate. He is strong, coordinated, and fast. If we miss a week of work, when he returns, he finds it easy to remember exactly what he has learned and where we left off. He's right on all the time."

Archery, wild boar hunting, canoeing, skiing, golf, tennis, and flying (he soloed in a Cessna 150 after only eight hours) were just a few of the other activities Shatner enjoyed. It was a physical routine that would have exhausted anyone else.

"Looking back on the things I've done," he said at the time, "I must be a little crazy. But I'm constantly testing myself, both in athletics and acting. I've always believed that if you don't define your limits by trying everything, you'll never know your capabilities."

The Trouble with Trimbles

William Shatner was against Bjo and John Trimble's letter-writing campaign to save *Star Trek*. He felt their efforts to force network executives to change their minds diminished the cast as actors. It would be many years before Shatner could graciously accept the role fans played in keeping *Star Trek* alive.

The Trimbles launched their campaign to save the show with only 800 addresses from a science fiction convention. Within a month, they had added more names from Roddenberry's files and fan clubs and ended up with a mailing list of about 6,000 addresses. However, the key to the Trimbles' success was that they asked the recipients to copy each letter and send it out to as many of their friends as possible.

By the time the chain-mail avalanche ended, NBC had received nearly a million protest letters. At first, the network tried to downplay the response and officially admitted to receiving only 60,000 letters, but before long, the spectacular effort was making news all around the country. Over 500 Cal Tech students held a torchlight vigil at NBC's Burbank studios, and students from MIT picketed the network's headquarters at Rockefeller Center.

Most of their placards read "We Want Spock," and 90 percent of the letters specifically asked that *Leonard Nimoy* not be taken off the air. That fact irritated Shatner and was probably part of the reason he described the actions of the fans as "demeaning."

One fanatical Trekker infiltrated the New York headquarters of NBC and pasted *"Star Trek* Lives" signs in the lobby and elevators. Then she sneaked into the parking area and stuck scores of *Trek* bumperstickers on automobiles belonging to network executives and stars. Johnny Carson could not figure out the meaning of the "Grok

Spock" sticker on his limo until one of his writers explained it to him. (The word "grok" means to understand someone thoroughly because you have empathy with him or her. It is from Robert A. Heinlein's science-fiction classic *Stranger in a Strange Land*.)

Before long, NBC's corporate offices started receiving hundreds of letters from angry stockholders demanding the series continue. It was an unprecedented response that has never been duplicated.

The network was forced to announce on the air, in the middle of the second season, that *Star Trek* would be renewed for a third season. NBC received another 100,-000 letters thanking them. The network's top brass even promised Roddenberry that the show would be moved to the coveted 7:30 PM slot on Mondays, which would virtually assure better ratings and the continuation of the series.

But Shatner was tiring of his *Star Trek* battles and secretly hoped the series would not be renewed. For ten years he had been turning down supporting roles in television. His whole point in accepting the role of Captain Kirk had been to star, not to end up usurped in popularity by a green-blooded alien with pointed ears or some teeny-bopper idol.

Shatner's wife, Gloria, also hoped the series would end. The pressures of the show had taken a toll on their marriage, and she wondered if her husband's bruised ego could survive another year on the show. Her daughters would also have loved to see the series end. They were taking a lot of teasing at school and felt their father had abandoned them when *Star Trek* began.

"I stood on the front porch, begging him not to go," said Lisabeth, looking back on that day in 1966 when Shatner began the series. "He appeared only once or twice a week after that to see me and my sisters."

The Shatners' secret hopes were answered when the network suddenly went back on its promise to move the show to Monday nights. The producers of *Rowan & Martin's Laugh-In* had vigorously protested being pushed ahead a half hour, from 8 to 8:30 Monday evenings, to accommodate *Star Trek*. Since the comedy show was the number-one-rated program on television at the time, NBC executives quickly acquiesced to their request.

Within two weeks of renewing *Star Trek* for a third season, the network rescheduled it for 10 PM Fridays, commonly referred to as the "death slot." It was widely believed that the only people watching television at that hour were elderly people on fixed incomes. College students, young marrieds, and affluent homeowners were not watching television during that period and sponsors knew it.

Furthermore, marketing executives were leery of science-fiction audiences in general. The viewer group was thought to be composed of free-thinking counterculture types not likely to rush out and buy a new brand of deodorant just because they saw it on TV. It was clear NBC had taken another look at the bottom line and decided there was no money to be made by going along with the wishes of a small core of fans, no matter how vociferous they were.

Roddenberry saw the writing on the wall and told NBC he would not actively participate in producing third-season shows unless a better time slot was found. When the network failed to respond, he carried out his threat. Although Roddenberry kept the title executive producer, he moved his office from Paramount to MGM, where he began work on a movie project and pulled himself out of the daily production of *Star Trek*. Almost immediately, the network cut the budget for the show. Shatner would never forgive Roddenberry for "deserting his sinking starship" a second time.

Shortly after Roddenberry's departure, producer John Meredyth Lucas decided to quit the show and was replaced by Fred Freiberger. Oddly enough, Shatner suddenly found an ally in Freiberger, and the two were in close agreement on how to run the show. Freiberger, who had worked on *Wild, Wild West* and was known for his ability to bring shows in under budget, was looking for action scripts with simple sets. Both Shatner and Freiberger believed that heart-pounding and violent action, with the characters running around all the time, should become the basis of *Star Trek*.

More important, Freiberger considered Shatner the sole star of the show and ignored much of Nimoy's concern for his character. In the course of the third season, Spock was forced to lighten up considerably. A variety of unlikely plot twists had the normally stoical Vulcan cracking smiles, bragging about his sexual prowess, eating meat, abandoning his nonviolent behavior, and even singing. Nimoy was humiliated. He appealed to Roddenberry and studio head Doug Cramer, but in the end, the actor was told to go through channels and take all his complaints directly to Freiberger.

But just as Shatner was regaining his starring position, the creative talent behind *Star Trek* began to vaporize before his eyes. He was already devastated by Roddenberry's perceived abandonment at the beginning of the season. Then, director Marc Daniels and cinematographer Jerry Finnerman, both with the show since the beginning, quit. Associate producer Bob Justman gave up in the middle of the season. Some of the series' best writers stopped submitting material, and the quality of the scripts suffered. To make matters worse, the budget had been drastically reduced and location shooting became a luxury. Several of the shows were filmed entirely on the *Enterprise* set. *Variety* commented that the show's characters were turning into empty caricatures of themselves. Even diehard fans realized the show was going downhill.

Whom Gods Destroy: The Third Season

The series' third season opener was a sample of things to come. In the story, Spock's brain is taken out of his head by curvaceous female aliens and wired up to run their underground civilization. Kirk steals it back, and as McCoy attempts to surgically reimplant the slimy organ, Spock awakens to guide him. While Spock got back his brain, the prestige of *Star Trek* took a nosedive.

In all fairness, the last season did offer a few good shows. In "All Our Yesterdays," Nimoy and Kelley were able to deepen their characters' relationship while traveling back into the past of a dying planet, and most fans enjoyed the surrealistic western tale, "Spectre of the Gun," which pitted the Big Three against Wyatt Earp at the OK Corral. In another entertaining episode, "The Tholian Web," Kirk disappeared into a parallel dimension, and Spock sailed the *Enterprise* through a rift in space-time to save him.

In a psychologically powerful installment, "And the Children Shall Lead," Kirk fights a malevolent force that feeds on the energies of innocent children. (That episode was so disturbing to one Dallas station that they refused to air it, saying it encouraged children to believe they could conjure up spirits.)

In another episode with supernatural undertones, "The Lights of Zetar," a cosmic spirit takes over the body of a woman passenger, Lieutenant Miri Romaine (played by Jan Shutan). The entity is attacking Memory Alpha, a library containing all the knowledge of the galaxy, when Lieutenant Romaine makes psychic contact with it and is able to predict its moves. She is then possessed by the evil force and has to be confined to a hyperbaric chamber, where she undergoes a space-age exorcism.

"The *Star Trek* set was like being in another world,"

Shutan recalled. "It was so filled with fantasy, I was able to *not* be 'me.' But I do remember being embarrassed about wearing that short costume because I had chubby thighs. That's why my family and I get hysterical at what I look like in that stupid costume. Everyone on that show had long, gorgeous legs and I only had cute little thighs. I didn't think they belonged on television.

"Someone brought my two children to the set and William Shatner was great—he was so wonderful to them; he threw them around, played with them, he was just terrific! They adored him. Shatner really knew how important the set visit was to my kids, so he paid special attention to them and teased me a lot, in order to make them feel I was important on the show! That was very nice."

Actress Lee Meriwether, best known for her role as the Catwoman in *Batman,* was also impressed with Shatner. She played Losira, the computer-generated temptress who prevents the *Enterprise* from exploring an unusual planet in the episode "That Which Survives." The former Miss America, who once admitted she went into show business so she could meet movie stars, spent most of her time on *Star Trek* in the company of Shatner.

"I got to know Bill Shatner," she recalled, "and it was great fun working with him. He had that same brand of devilish, boylike humor that Adam West [of *Batman*] had, always upbeat and full of jokes."

Three third season episodes ("The Empath," "Plato's Stepchildren," and "Whom Gods Destroy") were actually banned by the British government for too much violence, and several American television stations complained to the network about the series' sexual undertones. As for overall quality, most critics agreed that *Star Trek*'s third season was simply not up to par.

Except for Shatner, most of the cast blamed the dismal season on Fred Freiberger. Walter Koenig was infuriated that Freiberger would cast one of his close friends (lawyer

Melvin Belli in "And the Children Shall Lead") but not pay any attention to the supporting cast members, and James Doohan has described Freiberger as a no-talent businessman who lacked inventiveness.

"Fred came in and to him *Star Trek* was 'tits in space,' " said Margaret Armen, a writer whose work spanned seasons two and three. "I was in the projection room seeing an early episode when Fred came in and watched with me and said, 'Oh I get it. Tits in space.' Fred was looking for all action pieces, whereas Gene [Roddenberry] was looking for the subtlety that is *Star Trek.*"

While Roddenberry foresaw the demise of the series, he also realized the huge potential of merchandising *Star Trek* after it was canceled. His gut instincts told him that the fans were not going to let go that easily. In 1968, he formed Lincoln Enterprises to sell *Trek* memorabilia. He put ownership in the name of Majel Barrett and appointed Bjo and John Trimble to run the company. That way, he could protect his assets from his wife, whom he was divorcing. Nine months later, after he had married Majel, he summarily dismissed the Trimbles.

Roddenberry felt that the Vulcan creed of IDIC (Infinite Diversity in Infinite Combinations) fascinated many of the fans, so he had a medallion designed to symbolize the idea and wrote a scene in the episode "Is There in Truth No Beauty?" to promote it.

In the scene, Kirk would describe its significance and present the IDIC medal to one of the crew. Shatner vehemently protested the obvious commercialization of the show and refused to participate. Roddenberry simply rewrote the script and had Spock perform the ceremony. Nimoy also refused, but when the actor realized how important the marketing ploy was to Roddenberry, he agreed to wear the IDIC insignia and explain its meaning on the air.

The final episode of *Star Trek* was called "Turnabout Intruder." Filming was completed on January 9, 1969, and in fitting irony, NBC decided to broadcast it at 7:30 PM on a Tuesday. That last day of filming was a traumatic one for the entire cast.

Shatner was so emotionally upset that he suffered from dizziness and nausea all through the shooting. But at the farewell party that evening, he was the center of attention and cracking jokes as usual.

In his autobiography, George Takei thought back to that evening: "The last three years had given me a wonderful gift of shared experiences and rich relationships. Colleagues had become synonymous with friends. But Bill, in his single-minded drive for personal success, had made himself oblivious to the human riches surrounding him. With his shining armor of charm and wit, he had only taken and not experienced. In his unrelenting determination to protect what he had gotten, he had only isolated himself and made himself the poorer. An actor not without considerable talent, he probably would go on to the next series or the next film. He would probably continue to 'succeed.' And yet, I couldn't help hearing the faint sound of melancholy in his raucous merriment and loud hilarity."

Chapter 7

The Lost Years

I was insane, like the way an animal is insane,
because I had lost my family, I'd lost everything,
and I was scrambling, clawing to get everything back
and put it together.
—William Shatner on his life after the cancellation of
Star Trek

The year 1969 represented a major turning point in the career of William Shatner. After the demise of *Star Trek*, his professional and personal life took a nosedive. It was the beginning of what some researchers and collectors of Kirkiana have referred to as Shatner's "lost years."

The roots of his problems can be traced back to a few months after he moved from New York to California to work in the television industry. It seemed that the temptations of Tinseltown were just too much for the thirty-something star, who had spent so many years vociferously condemning the freewheeling Hollywood lifestyle.

Among the dozens of business calls Shatner received every day in his dressing room were many from admiring females, and witnesses recall being amazed at his unabashed flirting over the phone.

Before long, he was spending less and less time with his

family and his ten-year marriage started to unravel. Nearly every Sunday, he was off in the desert, cavorting with his motorcycle pals. The rest of his time off he spent scuba diving, kayaking, skiing, car racing, flying, skydiving, playing tennis, or engaged in other less sporting but equally physical endeavors. All his life, Shatner had used strenuous physical activities to release his pent-up energy and unwind.

When asked why he spent so little time at home, he freely admitted to being a selfish man who required a lot of time doing things that truly interested him. But when he went to Spain alone for three months in 1967 to make *The White Comanche*, his wife never forgave him for not taking her and his daughters with him.

Shortly after his return from Europe, he moved out of the family ranch house in Sherman Oaks. Within five weeks, he was back home, only to move out again by the end of the year. His press agent blamed the separations on the grueling schedule of the weekly TV series, but everyone connected with *Star Trek* knew the real reasons.

To make matters worse, Shatner's father had died unexpectedly in the autumn of 1967, just as the two men were becoming closer after years of feuding. Shatner had drifted apart from his cousins, aunts, uncles, and other family members, who had begun to treat him like a big Hollywood star. At family gatherings, they would crowd around him asking for his autograph, and nobody wanted to hug him. But he felt his father was finally realizing that his son could be successful as an actor, and the two men, who had always loved one another deeply, were finally growing closer.

Then, Joseph Shatner suffered a fatal heart attack while playing golf on vacation in Florida. Shatner got the bad news at Desilu Studios, where he was working on the episode "Devil in the Dark." Shatner was devastated but also surprised at the show of support he received from the cast and crew, especially Leonard Nimoy and cameraman

Jerry Finnerman. Their heartfelt concern was a great comfort, and he was able to finish the day's shooting. That evening he flew to Miami to pick up his father's body and accompany it to Montreal for the funeral. During the lonely flight to Montreal, Shatner got a frightening glimpse into his own personality.

"I remember banking over the city and looking out the window. But what I was really doing was looking into myself. What I saw was an empty pit—and it terrified me. I suddenly saw how the insane go insane. They see reality for one terrifying, fleeting moment. They take off the rose-colored glasses. Maybe we'd all go insane if we took off the rose-colored glasses."

Living on the Edge

Yet Shatner was quick to put back on the rose-colored glasses. He was back at Desilu, ready to work again, the following Monday morning, joking and clowning around as usual. The star was putting up a good front, but inside he was hurting. His father's death, combined with the problems at home, were becoming too much to handle. His close friend David Ross knew what it was really like in Shatner's dressing room during that period.

"Only a few times was he late, when he was going through some real hard times," Ross told me. "You have to accept that because of what he's going through. Sometimes, boy, you knew he was hurting inside. I mean, he was hurting, and he didn't even open himself up to Leonard.

"If he went into his dressing room and there was no wardrobe change, I knew something was wrong. I'd go in to see if there was something I could do. I walked in sometimes, and he would look me straight in the eye, and I knew, oh boy. I would see little tears in his eyes. When I asked if there was anything I could do, he always said no.

In private, he would get a grip on himself, take a hold of whatever it was, and the next thing, you'd see him composed and ready to work."

By January 1969, production on the *Star Trek* series had halted. Three months later, Shatner divorced his wife of thirteen years, leaving their three daughters in her care. The settlement with Gloria was based on his salary from *Star Trek,* and his alimony payments were enormous. All his shares in their community property (valued at under $250,000) were consumed in the divorce process.

All he had left of his family were weekend-visitation and child-support obligations. The simultaneous failure of his marriage and the loss of *Star Trek* nearly crushed Shatner. The divorce settlement left him penniless and alone, and the cancellation of his television series left him without a job.

"There's such a terrible void, such a loss," he told an interviewer for *TV Guide.* "I find myself clinging to times when life was a joy, a thing to cherish. Today, I'd characterize success as security and love."

Desperate to have a place where his daughters could spend weekends, he scraped together enough money to make a down payment on a two-bedroom house in Los Angeles. He furnished the house for only $300 by buying damaged and used furniture and converting crates into tables. He lived more like a hippie than a former star of a major television series.

By his fortieth birthday in 1971, the onetime TV star was a cynical and defeated man. Shatner was convinced he had sacrificed both his career and marriage for the temporary fame Hollywood had offered him. He felt betrayed, both emotionally and financially. Even the alien presence Shatner believed had visited him in the Mojave Desert had never returned to help him. Shatner, the eternal Golden Boy, finally realized he would never become the Chosen One. Instead, his feelings began to turn paranoid.

"Somehow, I can't help but feel like the victim of some grand cosmic plan whose sole purpose is to kick the shit out of me," he said of the lonely years after *Star Trek*.

He accepted any type of acting work he could find, sometimes driving half a day to earn a couple hundred dollars. While he worked in summer stock productions on the East Coast, the former spaceship captain lived in the back of an old Chevy truck to save money on airfare and motels. If the play was to last more than a few days, he removed the camper shell on the back of the pick-up truck and set it up on metal legs, usually in a campground. Then, he drove the truck back and forth to the theater. For nearly seven years in the 1970s, Shatner spent two-thirds of every year on the road looking for work.

In August 1969, he set up his freestanding camper shell in the driveway of a friend in Millburn, New Jersey. He was working at the Papermill Playhouse, playing the part of Charlie Reader in the *The Tender Trap*, a romantic comedy about married life.

Early one morning, a six-year-old boy knocked on the door to his camper. The lad had spotted the podlike contraption sitting on its spindly metallic legs and wanted to know if it was a spaceship. Of course, when Captain Kirk came to the door, the answer was obvious. Shatner offered to show the amazed boy through the Planetary Landing Module, pointing out the sophisticated Sony communications equipment and transporter-tube shower stall.

Shatner was just beginning to understand the extent to which *Star Trek* had touched people's lives. Occasionally, during his performances, someone in the audience would toss a Tribble doll or other *Trek* memorabilia on the stage. At other times, people just shouted out how much they still cared for Captain Kirk. Shatner did not know *Star Trek* was in reruns until a friend told him he had seen it on TV at a local bar.

That same winter, Shatner met a young lady and took

her on a weekend skiing getaway to Mammoth Mountain, California. One evening, while he was walking through the lobby, he heard the familiar music from *Star Trek* coming from the bar. Someone had gotten a hold of a fifteen-minute "blooper" reel that was being circulated at *Star Trek* conventions.

As he watched, Shatner saw himself making bizarre faces at the camera, breaking into uncontrollable laughter, and crashing into automatic doors that would not open. In a scene from "Squire of Gothos," actor William Campbell asks Shatner in a high, female voice, "Are you challenging me to a duel?" He replies in his best soprano falsetto, "Yes, if you have the courage." In another sequence, Shatner pretends he is hit in the groin with an arrow, and a native pulls out the imaginary arrow with a quick jerk. As the laughter subsided, they start the next scene. A wounded Shatner is carried off to a cave where Kelley runs over and starts examining him. "You shouldn't have to find out what's wrong with him," yells one of the stage crew, "He must know what's wrong with him." Everyone breaks up.

Caught up in the fond memories, Shatner suddenly realized the film was part of a forty-five-minute collection of outtakes made up by series editors and shown for the entertainment of the cast. He thought that the film had found its way into the trash, but Gene Roddenberry had saved it, and now the film was making the rounds among fans.

"This may strike you as unbelievable," Shatner told an interviewer, "but the whole *Star Trek* thing just sort of snuck up on me. I only became gradually aware of it when people started calling me 'Captain Kirk' on the streets."

The popularity of *Star Trek* continued to grow, even though no new episodes were being made. Thousands of people attended the first *Star Trek* convention held in New York's Statler-Hilton Hotel in February of 1972, and that proved to be just the tip of the iceberg.

But Shatner's contract with Paramount limited "residuals," or payments for reruns, to just five shows and provided no payments for the massive merchandising that followed the cancellation of *Star Trek*. The series was being rebroadcast on 150 independent stations in the United States and in over 100 foreign countries, but Captain Kirk was hardly receiving anything. His total annual residuals varied from none to $40.

Running Away from Kirk

In an effort to raise money and break away from his *Star Trek* stereotype, Shatner accepted any stage play, B-movie, or television appearance that came his way. He guest-starred in over fifty episodes of various television dramas in the five years after the cancellation of *Star Trek*.

He appeared in episodes of *Ironside*, *Mission Impossible*, *Medical Center*, *Hawaii Five-O*, *The FBI*, *Mannix*, *The Bold Ones*, *Barnaby Jones*, and other popular programs. Yet he was never offered a continuing role in any of them.

In 1971, Shatner took a chance on another television series. He co-starred with Arthur Hill in the pilot for *Owen Marshall, Counselor at Law*. Shatner played Dave Blankenship, a district attorney who faced talented defense attorney Owen Marshall in the courtroom. The film was first broadcast on ABC as a TV movie and later released on videotape under the title *A Pattern of Morality*. Once again, Shatner was not chosen for a regular part in the successful television series that was based on his pilot.

However, he continued to find work in a number of other TV movies, including *Vanished* (1971), *The People* (1972), *Hound of the Baskervilles* (1972), *The Guardian* (1972), *The Revolution of Antonio DeLeon* (1972), *Incident on a Dark Street* (1973), *Go Ask Alice* (1973), *Horror at 37,000 Feet* (1973), *Pioneer Woman* (1973), *Indict and Convict* (1974), and *Pray for the Wildcats* (1974). Most of these movies were considered run-of-the-mill television fare by viewers and critics.

His personal life at the time was a shambles. He took full advantage of the free and easy lifestyle of the 1970s and got involved in a number of tawdry love affairs. One of the few he remembers was with a beautiful, smart young lady with whom he spent several months. All he will say now is that she was a member of Mensa and ended up marrying a very famous person.

"I was in a terrible state all those years," he confessed. "I don't know *where* I was—I've heard things that have happened to me from 1968 to 1974. I have no recollection. People come up to me—I see people I met then and knew, in fact, I had a whole relationship with them—and *I don't remember them.* I don't remember what I did. I don't remember what I felt. Some people say, 'You were awful then.' "

During that same dark period, Shatner made a string of exploitation films that would also haunt him for the rest of his career. The most distasteful example was *Want a Ride, Little Girl?* (1972), in which he portrayed a sexually tormented psycho killer. The film opens with a primal sex scene involving his character as a boy. The perverted lover of the boy's mother tries to bring the child to their bed, and the boy ends up killing the man with a sword. The abused child grows up psychotic and stalks girls and young women who resemble his mother.

In one tawdry love scene, Shatner appears with his future wife, actress Marcy Lafferty, who plays an anonymous motel clerk. During the filming of another scene, Shatner broke his finger trying to rescue Harold Sakata, the 250-pound wrestler-actor famous for his role as Odd Job in *Goldfinger.*

In the fateful scene, Sakata was hung from a clothesline a few feet above the ground while Shatner used him as a punching bag. Suddenly, the rubber-coated line got twisted around Sakata's throat and cut off his air. The crew thought the actor's pleading movements were part of the script, but Shatner realized what was happening and quickly found a knife to free his strangling co-star. Unfortunately, when he cut the rope, Sakata dropped like a lead weight and broke Shatner's finger.

Reviewers unanimously condemned the film, accusing Shatner of shameless overacting and being allowed to "run amok on camera." Two years later, the film was rereleased under the title *Impulse*. "I've forgotten why I was in it," Shatner later said of the film. "I probably needed the money. It was a very bad time for me. I hope they burn it."

Equally embarrassing were Shatner's three nude love scenes with Angie Dickinson in *Big Bad Mama* (1974). The scenes were so prurient that photographs were published in men's magazines. Although made by well-known producer Roger Corman, the film was really just a sexy knockoff of *Bonnie and Clyde*. Fortunately, by the time efforts for *Big Bad Mama II* were under way in 1987, Shatner's career was back on track, and he declined to repeat his role.

"I'm not terribly proud of some of the features I've made," he explained to an interviewer years later, "but they were offered to me at various times when better movies weren't being offered. If I were in the position of Robert Redford and able to pick and choose from among a dozen scripts and then turn them all down because they weren't up to the quality I like, I would be one of a half-dozen people in the industry. I am not in that position."

Light at the End of the Tunnel

Luckily for Shatner, his friend and producer Lewis Freedman offered him the lead role in a prestigious public television production. In *The Andersonville Trial*, Shatner portrayed the prosecutor in America's equivalent of the Nuremberg trials.

Andersonville was a Confederate prison camp where Union soldiers were treated like animals. They were kept in an open compound, and many had to resort to cannibalism to survive. Captain Henry Wirz, who really had no control over the deplorable conditions, was the scapegoat tried as a war criminal. The ninety-minute special premiered on May 17, 1970. Shatner's explosive, sarcastic portrayal of the prosecutor was called "staggeringly brilliant," and the show received the coveted Peabody Award plus three Emmys.

During the taping of *The Andersonville Trial*, Shatner grew closer to an aspiring young actress by the name of Marcy Lafferty with whom he had acted in *Want A Ride, Little Girl?* The beautiful dark-eyed, long-haired brunette had also worked opposite Shatner in an episode of *Medical Center* a few months earlier.

Marcy was the daughter of producer Perry Lafferty, West Coast program chief for CBS-TV, and Mary Frances Carden, a nationally known radio personality. On the set of *The Andersonville Trial*, Marcy was an assistant to director George C. Scott and helped Shatner rehearse by reading lines with him. For her, it was love at first sight. The first time Shatner kissed her (during a lunch break at the studio), her knees actually buckled and she fell to the ground.

"I fell for him, hook, line, and sinker," she reminisced. "Bill had just been through a terrible divorce and a folded series. He didn't want to get involved. But I hung in there and wormed my way into his heart."

As for Shatner, he was looking for "a girl who's capable of giving love as well as receiving. One who can cook but also eat her own food with relish, one who plays tennis, has a sense of humor to counter my straitlaced manner, and one who likes to go horseback riding."

Marcy fulfilled all those conditions, but at first Shatner

felt he was not ready to get married again. While he enjoyed playing the field, he realized how good Marcy was for him. To everyone's surprise, especially Marcy's family, Shatner proposed to her in July 1973. They were married on October 20 at the lavish Brentwood home of her father. It was a traumatic day for Shatner, and he admits he cried at his own wedding—not out of happiness but out of sheer panic.

He was 42 years old, and she was 27. The newlyweds pooled their resources and bought a house south of Beverly Hills, in the Hillcrest area of Los Angeles. Their new home, at 2729 McConnell Drive, was a medium-sized ranch house with a long, curving driveway in front.

Their marriage was difficult at first. According to Marcy, Shatner had great difficulty sharing his life and opening up to her. Though fifteen years younger than her husband, Marcy provided the consolation and support so necessary for his psychological recovery. Gradually, he learned how to trust someone again.

Shatner had been living in such a daze that he had difficulty remembering the names of people with whom he had been associated for years. Not only had he lost his mental energy and drive, but his physical condition had seriously deteriorated. His face appeared puffy on camera and even his bone corset could not hide his bloated belly. Under the direction of Dr. Ernst Duynder of the American Health Institute, he undertook a health and diet regimen that he believes saved his life.

He also began an intense workout routine centered around his karate training with Terry Bleecker, a screenwriter and martial arts instructor. Shatner had always enjoyed boxing, wrestling, and fencing, but he saw in karate a combination of mental and physical discipline that really appealed to him. Moreover, he thought the training would make his fights on screen all the more believable. In fact, he drove his new wife crazy when he insisted on going to see cheap Japanese karate movies rather than more substantial film fare.

The Comeback Kid

A few months before he got married, Shatner had invested another $50,000 into his film production company. He was hoping to acquire scripts, novels, and true-life stories to make high-quality films in which he could star. He even hired a writer to produce a script titled "Time of the Tempest," a drama in which he hoped to play the lead. In the meantime, he attempted to make a respectable comeback on television.

"In show business today," he summarized, "most of the action is in television. And television, by its nature, has to appeal to as many people as possible. Which means the lowest common denominator. Occasionally—and those are the occasions *I* watch TV for—television will do something extraordinary. Quite a lot of competition exists for those occasional roles. In the past I've been successful in getting some of those parts, but in some instances I have not been successful."

In an effort to improve his image, Shatner started hosting public service television specials and documentaries. In *Secrets of the Deep*, he led viewers on a twelve-part odyssey investigating underwater life. He talked about the same subject in another syndicated documentary series called *Inner Space*. In *Space Age*, he narrated a one-hour special about the effects of new electronic items on the American lifestyle. Then he hosted ten segments of a Canadian talk show called *Flick Flack*, in which he interviewed celebrities from both Canada and the United States.

But his favorite job was hosting sports shows. He once said that of all his roles, it was in the real-life adventures he underwent for *American Sportsman* that he came closest to being the real William Shatner. He hunted down a Kodiak bear with just a bow and arrow on a ten-day excursion to Alaska in one of the early installments. Then, he kayaked down the Salmon River in Idaho. Much of the time he was upside down in his tiny kayak, bobbing down the roaring river, and he almost drowned twice. In another episode, he flew a Pitts Special airplane in dangerous stunts, including a couple of twirling, flat spins.

Then, there was the time he had a three-foot-tall Bald Eagle perched on his forearm in a show about endangered species. When his arm dropped slightly from the heavy weight, the powerful bird sank its sharp talons deep into his flesh. The bird's claws cut to the bone and severed a large vessel in Shatner's arm. He passed out and dropped to the floor, although he later depicted the incident as a glorious moment—one in which he was able to experience directly the savage power of nature.

After *American Sportsman,* he hosted another real-life adventure series called *Breakaway.* That show also featured a variety of daredevil sports—like skydiving, hot-air ballooning, and race car driving—that people use to escape the workaday world.

Cartoon Kirk

Less exciting, for Shatner, at least, was his entry into the fantasy world of Saturday morning cartoons. In the early 1970s, reading the part of Captain Kirk in an animated *Star Trek* series became Shatner's only regular job on television.

Two years after the cancellation of *Star Trek,* a demographics expert proved to startled NBC executives that Nielsen ratings for the show had been wrong. The truth was that *Star Trek* was one of television's most successful shows, and it was reaching exactly the same young-adult consumer market that the network had targeted. The embarrassed executives scurried to revamp the show but concluded that rebuilding sets and replacing props and costumes would be too expensive. Instead, they opted for an animated series to be produced by Filmation Enterprises.

In June 1973, Shatner joined the rest of the cast from the original *Star Trek* to record the first voice-overs for an animated series. Originally, only Shatner, Leonard Nimoy, DeForest Kelley, James Doohan, and Majel Barrett were invited back, but when Nimoy found out that Nichelle Nichols and George Takei had been left out, he insisted they be included.

Gene Roddenberry served as executive consultant, and writers' credits included several names from the original series, including D. C. Fontana, David Gerrold, and Walter Koenig. The first installment of the syndicated show was broadcast exactly seven years to the day after the premiere of the regular series.

Shatner was embarrassed to be connected with a cartoon series; it certainly seemed a long way from his goal of becoming another Laurence Olivier. He never took much interest in the new animated series and simply went along with most of the scripts. Shatner felt the show degraded his character and admitted to recording at least one episode while sitting on the toilet at a remote movie location.

But critics gave Shatner's cartoon captain a better reception than they did his character in the original series. "NBC's new animated *Star Trek*," said the *Los Angeles Times*, "is as out of place in the Saturday morning kiddie ghetto as a Mercedes in a soapbox derby. It is fascinating fare, written, produced, and executed with all the imaginative skill, the intellectual fare, and the literary level that made Gene Roddenberry's famous old science fiction epic the most avidly followed program in TV history, particularly in high-IQ circles."

The *Star Trek* animated series was on the air from

September 1973 until August 1975, for a total of twenty-two episodes. Many reviewers said that it should have been run during prime time instead of on Saturday mornings, and the show received an Emmy Award for its 1974–1975 season. The irony of the situation sent Captain Quirk to the verge of another breakdown.

A Master of Disguise

In the spring of 1975, Shatner was offered the lead in a pilot for another ill-fated television series. Inspired by *Wild, Wild West,* the new show was called *Cash and Cable.* Shatner played Jeff Cable, an undercover agent in gold-rush San Francisco, and Doug McClure played Cash Conover, a casino owner who helps Cable fight crime in the rough Barbary Coast section of the city. Paramount built an extravagant set depicting 1880s San Francisco, complete with waterfront, on seven acres of studio property.

Shatner's character was a master of disguise, and he thought the role was an actor's dream. The series was picked up by ABC, who changed the name to *Barbary Coast.* Shatner made thirteen episodes that summer, although production was delayed in the middle of July when a horse he was riding fell on him.

Shatner had insisted on personally doing a stunt involving falling off a stumbling horse. The horse was trained to fall with a jerk of the reins, but it slipped and fell on a freshly plastered surface on the set. The animal landed on Shatner's right leg, breaking the star's tibia and fibula, and putting him in a fiberglas cast for two weeks.

The pilot episode was shown as a two-hour TV movie in May 1975. The regular series began three months later but lasted only until January 6, 1976. In that short time, Shatner got the chance to play fifty different characters. It is hard to imagine a role better suited to the actor, who always loved makeup and portraying multiple characters.

Shatner was fighting hard for his comeback. He described a typical week's schedule to one reporter: "We worked on *Barbary Coast* until 11 PM on Friday; then, at 12:45 AM, I took a plane to Houston to do a public appearance. From Houston I went to New York to hold a press conference about a CBS-TV *Playhouse 90* called *The Tenth Level* to be shown on December 18. That same day, which was Monday, I flew to Miami to be there for the opening of the pro game to publicize *Barbary Coast*. Tuesday morning at 4 AM Los Angeles time, I got on a plane to return to Hollywood to be in front of cameras Tuesday afternoon. And it just keeps going—I will work late Friday night and then I fly out of here to Chicago."

Unfortunately, his new series was part of ABC's new "family hour" concept, which placed restrictions on the types of conflicts and action that writers could portray in their scripts. The producers were forced to concentrate on gaudy scenery and nonviolent crimes, a formula that attracted few viewers.

The response to *Barbary Coast* from the *Los Angeles Herald-Examiner* was typical: "A couple good actors and various gaudy ingredients should add up to a vibrant western swashbuckler in *Barbary Coast*—but it doesn't. The show fell into fragments. There was an absence of togetherness of people and atmosphere. The Shatner-McClure relationship was too vague. There were innumerable stories twisting across each other's path. You knew what the filmmakers were after and you also knew they were still fumbling around in their search for it."

"We can't have any man-to-man combat, even for the fun of it," Shatner explained at the time. "We're throwing mud pies at each other in an effort to get in some action. We're into nonviolent crimes committed in nonviolent ways. . . . we can do mud in the face a lot. However, mud in the face works only for a while. We need more tension in the stories and that comes from conflict between stalwart people."

The cancellation of yet another promising television series caused Shatner to reevaluate the direction of his career. He was convinced that episodic television had nothing left to offer him.

"Most of the people who are good in TV don't do a weekly show. I have taken myself out of that market long ago. I don't do weekly television anymore. But that leaves very, very few opportunities to exercise my craft. So I am trying to invent my own work—both by buying scripts and books to make into movies or television and by putting together touring shows in which I'm trying to invent an entertainment that people will enjoy watching."

Shatner's idea of entertainment that people would enjoy turned out to be him, sitting on a stool absolutely alone in the middle of the stage.

Shatner Live!

Shatner's one-man shows actually proved very popular, especially on college campuses. In 1976, he began a national road tour of *An Evening with William Shatner,* a presentation of readings about space travel with selections from Shakespeare, Rostand, Bertholdt Brecht, and H. G. Wells. His performances in forty-three cities included a laser light show.

Lasers were also part of the show two years later, when he toured with *Symphony of the Stars: Music from the Galaxies and Beyond.* He was accompanied by the philharmonic orchestras of several major cities, as he read selections from Arthur Clarke, D. H. Lawrence, and H. G. Wells. Using some of the same material, he then produced another series of one-man shows called *Star Traveler.*

"It was a totally new idea to me: a one-man show," Shatner said, shortly after beginning his first road tour. "I had no experience in it at all. I had to find out what made it work—and indeed if I could make it work. I did excerpts from authors like Rostand—the 'Moon' speech in *Cyrano de Bergerac*—and Shakespeare, and some original prose and poetry related to the way science fiction grew— how man's imagination was soaring even when his technical knowledge was limited or totally aberrated—when man thought earth was the center of the universe and later thought not and later thought so again; it's been a peculiar transformation of man's ego. We did a history of the imagination and how it's been limited by various forces like religion and science."

Working with live audiences again proved exhilarating for Shatner. By performing so many one-man shows, he also gained new insight into his acting technique.

"I used to learn lines and leave them half-unlearned so that I could react," he told a reporter in 1978, "developing the role as I came into the scene. But because I've had to learn in terms of monologues with no response, I've come to deal with concepts. In other words, I try to think of what the concept must be and how I can best effect it. So now I'm kind of amplifying my vision from what used to be learning a scene by words to kind of a larger picture."

Smashing Stereotypes

The theme of stretching people's imaginations and belief systems became a standard part of Shatner's repertoire. Just before the final telecast of *Barbary Coast*, Shatner appeared in a special *Playhouse 90* presentation called "The Tenth Level," in which he portrayed a psychiatrist who conducted experiments on the limits of human obedience with a group of unsuspecting volunteers. The teleplay was an original script based on the work of Dr. Stanley Milgram, a psychologist who, while pretending to test learning methods, induced volunteers to give electric shocks of increasing severity to one another. Shatner's dramatization generated a storm of controversy about medical ethics.

In 1976, Shatner hosted two documentary films investigating the idea of life in space. *Mysteries of the Gods* looked at ancient and modern UFO encounters. In NASA's *The Universe*, he traced the evolution of the cosmos from the primordial "big bang" and was nominated for an Oscar for his narration of the film.

The following year, he received more kudos for his rendition of excerpts from Edgar Lee Masters' *Spoon River Anthology* in a public television poetic gallery called "Anyone for Tennyson?" That same year, he was asked to present awards at such prestigious industry gatherings as the Photoplay Gold Medal Awards and the Science Fiction Film Awards.

Later in 1977, he appeared in a chiller about an Arizona veterinarian who discovered that tarantulas were killing people and livestock. The movie, *Kingdom of the Spiders*, drew good reviews for Shatner and his 10,000 tarantula co-stars. He later agreed to direct and star in a sequel, *Kingdom of the Spiders II*, but the project fell through before it reached the big screen.

Shatner guest-starred in three television miniseries in 1978. He was Paul Revere in *The Bastard*, a two-parter about an illegitimate Frenchman who meets Benjamin Franklin and joins the American revolution. In *Testimony of Two Men* he played the brother of a surgeon who recounts his life and passions in nineteenth-century Pennsylvania. That project was part of Operation Prime Time, an effort in which a group of independent stations pooled their resources to make quality dramatic programming.

A few weeks later, he played the husband of Jo March (played by Susan Dey) in the television adaptation of Louisa May Alcott's classic *Little Women*. While the roles

Shatner responds to a question from a member of the audience at a
Star Trek Convention in Charlotte, North Carolina, in 1994.
Although he still refuses to sign autographs, Shatner tends to treat his
fans with more respect in recent years.   (Credit: Steve Healey)

William Shatner's boyhood home was this large house at 4419 Girouard Street in the Notre Dame de Grace section of Montreal. The building has since been converted to condos. (*Credit: Chris Merciari, 1994*)

Shatner attended West Hill High School, now called Royal Vale School in Montreal. (*Credit: Chris Merciari, 1994*)

Shatner's McGill University yearbook picture. He served as president of the Radio Club and wrote, produced, and acted for the campus theatrical company. (*Credit: McGill University*)

Playbill for an evening of three one-act plays written and performed by students at McGill University in 1950. Shatner appeared in all three plays. Afterward, the Canadian Marconi Company broadcast a scene from the theater in a test of Canada's rudimentary television system. (*Credit: Margot Howard*)

SEASON OF 1949 - 1950
ENGLISH DEPARTMENT OF McGILL UNIVERSITY

The DRAMATEURS
ELMER HALL - DIRECTOR

present

Three Student Experiments Toward Playwriting

MOYSE HALL — ARTS BUILDING
Friday, March 31st at 8:30 p.m.

¶ These student efforts should not be considered as "plays", but rather as exercises. In no other field of art is a student obliged to display his first classroom exercise before an audience in order that his effort may be evaluated.

¶ If he fails completely to impress the audience, reports submitted are unanimously in condemnation. A sensitive student-writer may then never again to attempt writing in play form.

¶ The pieces presented tonight represent the first attempts of three students who all feel that you submit brief notes of constructive criticism.

¶ In an attempt to focus audience attention on the writing, neutral back-grounds are used throughout. It is suggested that you try to view this presentation as a "pre dress-rehearsal." The players are ready, dressed and made-up — but the lights can't be set until the scenery arrives!

¶ Although students have been encouraged to write of things they know personally, and fully understand, these scenes have been "dramatized". Any similarity to persons living or dead is coincidental.

Publicity still used by
William Shatner when
he first arrived in
New York in 1957.

Shatner played a high school teacher trying to teach kids
sex education in *The Explosive Generation*.
(Credit: United Artists, 1961)

William Shatner, Angie Dickinson, Susan Sennett, Tom Skerritt, and Joan Prather are all members of an immoral gang of bank robbers in *Big Bad Mama* (1974). *(Credit: New World Cinema)*

Herbert Rowe, of NASA's Office of External Affairs, accepts a copy of *Mysteries of the Gods* from Shatner. Jesco von Puttkamer, Senior Staff Scientist for Advanced Programs of Space Flight, is on the right. *(Credit: Hemisphere Pictures, 1976)*

William Shatner takes a break to pose for photographers during a production of *The World of Suzie Wong* in New York. (*Credit: AP/ Wide World Photos, 1959*)

Shatner's hilltop home at 3674 Berry Drive in Studio City. The Hebrew prayer post calls for peace on earth. (*Credit: D.W. Hauck, 1994*)

Shatner steps from the backyard pool at his first home in California. (*Credit: Archive Photos/Shere*)

Daddy strums a tune for his three daughters. From left to right: Lisabeth, Melanie, and Leslie. His first wife, Gloria, sits behind the girls. (*Credit: Archive Photos/Shere*)

A sweaty Shatner finishes a 10-mile workout along the ocean near Malibu. *(Credit: Wayne Williams/Shooting Star)*

Dean Martin? No—it's Captain Kirk in a seductive 1970s pose. *(Credit: Zimm/Shooting Sta*

A topless Shatner looks ready for anything. At 64 years old, he is still a ladies' man.   (Credit: Sato Ri/Shooting Star)

The cast looks like one big, happy family at the opening of the Star Trek Exhibit at the Smithsonian's Air and Space Museum in Washington, D.C. From left to right: George Takei, Walter Koenig, Leonard Nimoy, Nichelle Nichols, William Shatner, DeForest Kelly, and James Doohan. *(Credit: AP/Wide World Photos, 1992)*

The original Star Trek control console does not look like much closeup. The bridge set toured the country in 1994.
(Credit: D.W. Hauck, 1994)

At unveiling ceremonies on May 19, 1983, Shatner posed next to his star. Fans raised $5,000 to have the bronze memorial inlaid on the Hollywood Walk of Fame. Shatner's star (the 1,762nd) is located just east of Mann's Chinese Theater. (*Credit: AP/Wide World Photos*)

WILLIAM SHATNER

Leonard Nimoy and Shatner at a party in honor of the 20th anniversary of Star Trek. (*Credit: AP/Wide World Photos, 1986*)

Shatner rehearses his infamous 1986 "Saturday Night Live"
skit with Kevin Nealon and Dana Carvey.
(Credit: AP/Wide World Photos, 1986)

Grand Marshal Shatner
rides one of his favorite
horses to lead the 105th
Tournament of Roses
Parade on January 1,
1994. (Credit: AP/Wide
World Photos, 1994)

Marcie and Bill arrive at London's Heathrow Airport for the British premiere of *Star Trek: The Motion Picture* in December 1979. (Credit: AP/Wide World Photos, 1979)

Signing autographs in the concrete at Mann's Chinese Theater became a test of egos. Shatner was upset after DeForest Kelly took up so much room with his signature, and when Walter Koenig added his handprints, the captain was livid. He quickly added his own handprints to his signature. (Credit: D.W. Hauck, 1994)

The "T.J. Hooker" cast: Adrian Zmed, William Shatner, Richard Herd, and of course, Heather Locklear. *(Credit: ABC Television, 1984)*

Belle Reve, Shatner's farm near Versailles, Kentucky. *(Credit: James E. Rainbolt, 1994)*

William Shatner reluctantly poses with Patrick Stewart at Paramount's
25th Anniversary of Star Trek celebration.
(Credit: AP/Wide World Photos, 1991)

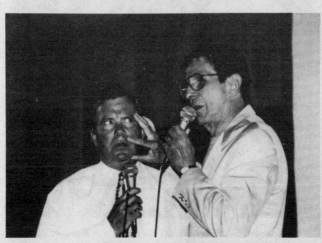

Leonard Nimoy performs a mind-meld on a suspicious-looking
William Shatner during their Star Trek farewell tour
appearance in Chicago.

An animated Shatner addresses the crowd at Paramount's Great America in Santa Clara. The audience would have never guessed how upset he was at missing a dog show to attend the event.
(*Credit: AP/Wide World Photos, 1991*)

gained him further prestige, they were a little slow paced for the adventuresome Shatner.

However, he found plenty of action in a series of four adventure films. In *Land of No Return* (1978), he fought exotic circus animals to rescue an animal trainer whose airplane had crashed in the mountains of Utah. He was an FAA investigator in *The Crash of Flight 401* (1978), which dramatized the events surrounding an actual airliner crash in the Florida Everglades. He portrayed another dedicated expert, this time a Secret Service chief trying to rescue the President of the United States in *The Kidnapping of the President* (1979).

But the intrepid actor could have been killed doing his own stunts in *Disaster on the Coastliner* (1978). He played a con man who proves his worth when he finds himself in a passenger train that is running out of control on a collision course with another train. One dangerous stunt involved him climbing onto the top of the lead car of a moving train. He did not realize how dangerous it was until he tried it and nearly lost his balance. By the time the film crew got it right, he had had to climb onto the roof of the car fifteen times.

Also in 1978, he acted in a well-received psychological drama filmed in Canada. *The Third Walker* followed the lives of family members dominated by an obsessed mother who believed one of her sons had been accidentally switched at birth. In another psychological study, *The Babysitter* (1980), he played a husband whose weaknesses are used by an amoral young housekeeper to get her way. Patty Duke Astin played his wife, who slowly realizes what is happening. When the psychotic babysitter's plans are thwarted, she tries to murder the entire family.

According to critics, most of these films were "mediocre" or even "disappointing," yet at the same time, Shatner was becoming a ubiquitous film and television personality. Even during station breaks, he could be seen in commercials for Wish Bone Salad Dressing, KeroSun, and Commodore Computers. He and his new wife, Marcy, appeared in a number of commercials for Promise Margarine.

He became a popular guest on talk shows and game shows. He appeared several times on *Hollywood Squares.* In one installment, titled "Storybook Squares," he showed up dressed as Captain Kirk. A few of the other game shows on which Shatner spent his afternoons were *Liar's Club, To Tell the Truth, Tattletales, The $10,000 Pyramid, Don Adams' Screen Test, Celebrity Bowling,* and *The Match Game.*

It was on one of those game shows that the extreme tensions of Shatner's UFO experience would surface once again—this time in front of millions of viewers. He was working on *Mysteries of the Gods,* spending a lot of time thinking back on his own close encounter. He was still trying to produce a short film about his UFO experience but could not come to terms with what it all had meant. Was he being chosen? Could he raise the consciousness of an entire nation? Would he become the perfect vessel of the Nine, or whatever cosmic force seemed to be directing his life?

Shatner was taping five segments of Dick Clark's *$10, 000 Pyramid* show at the Ed Sullivan Theater in New York. He had just concluded a long interview in his dressing room with Timothy Green Beckley, editor of a science-fiction newspaper called *Tomorrow,* regarding that encounter with a UFO in the Mojave Desert eight years earlier.

Shatner at this point is still thinking about the interview when he walks on stage. He seems a little tired, a little preoccupied, but finally he and his contestant partner win a chance at the $10,000 pyramid.

Shatner is able to come up with the correct answers right up to the very last question.

He looks over at the emcee's podium with its golden pyramid—that powerful symbol of cosmic knowledge— and becomes distracted for a moment, perhaps considering larger questions. Suddenly, he snaps back, but he fumbles the answer, saying only part of the right word. Appalled that he has lost, that he knew the answer but could not get it out, he jumps to his feet and looks as if he is about to explode. He has failed at his only chance at the pyramid!

Shatner picks up his chair and heaves it over the railing to the studio floor, where it smashes to pieces. As they quickly cut to commercial, Shatner keeps shaking his head in disbelief, trying to find words to apologize to his amazed partner. Leonard Nimoy, also a contestant, breaks into raucous laughter. When they return, Shatner and Nimoy are holding up pieces of the chair, trying to make light of the incident.

Kirk's Painful Resurrection

"It's been tumultuous," Shatner summed up the decade since *Star Trek* had been canceled. "It's gone from the mediocre to the marvelous. Gradually I became a member of the haves rather than the have-nots and of that small group known as the happily married. I became more conscious of the art that's necessary in what I do, more conscious of my health. I've not made a lot of films because I was offered the wrong things. Most of my work has been in television and on stage. I've been very busy."

In 1975, while Shatner was at Paramount Studios filming an episode of *Barbary Coast*, he decided to take a stroll through the deserted sound stages where *Star Trek* had been made. To his surprise, he came across Gene Roddenberry, sitting in his former office, pounding away at the keys on an old typewriter. "Hey, Gene!" he joked, "Didn't anybody tell you? We got canceled!"

What Shatner did not know was that Roddenberry had signed a contract with Paramount to write a script for a feature-length *Star Trek* movie budgeted at a modest $3 million. Originally, the film was to be a low-budget theatrical release or pilot for a new television series.

However, by mid-September 1976, when the first space shuttle was christened the *Enterprise* by NASA and the *Star Trek* resurgence was in full bloom, the studio had not yet decided on a script. A year earlier, George Lucas had approached Paramount about purchasing the film rights to *Star Trek*, and they'd decided not to sell. In the meantime, Lucas had proceeded with his own version of a space movie.

The studio's delay cost them dearly. In the summer of 1977, Twentieth Century–Fox released *Star Wars* to unprecedented box-office receipts. That same summer, Los Angeles and Oakland *Star Trek* conventions drew 16,000 fans apiece—a feat that garnered the attention of studio executives. That would be followed by the instant success of Columbia's *Close Encounters of the Third Kind*, directed by Steven Spielberg. At a time when the public was clamoring for outer space adventure stories, Paramount had obviously missed the boat.

After the shock of the phenomenal success of *Star Wars* had worn off, jealous executives at Paramount started toying with the idea of bringing back *Star Trek* on a larger scale. The studio decided to go ahead with a spectacular *Star Trek* movie that would rival the special effects seen in *Star Wars*. They went so far as to pay Shatner an advance for being the first to sign for the project, in order to encourage other cast members to sign on, too. But by the end of August 1977, after reviewing the cost of special effects for such a movie, the studio got cold feet and abruptly canceled the project.

Just three weeks after canceling the film, the fickle studio proudly announced that William Shatner had agreed to reprise his role as the captain of the USS *Enterprise* in *Star Trek: Phase II*, a new version of the classic television series. Gene Roddenberry was lined up as executive producer, and work was begun on a remodeled

Enterprise set. The series would have been the flagship of the new Paramount Television Network.

Unfortunately, the television project was canceled in November, when Paramount's parent company, Gulf + Western, scrapped plans for the new network. Shatner was absolutely livid. He was especially upset about the cancellation of the motion picture, which he believed would have been a tremendous success.

"I feel that it was an idiotic decision by the people at Paramount," he said at the time. "A *Star Trek* feature would be an entertainment and financial success, and its blockage stands as one of the greatest monuments to stupidity. As far as I know, the movie has been canceled, and in the light of the success of *Star Wars,* I just can't understand it."

But Captain Quirk would be vindicated. *Star Trek* was about to become the most profitable motion picture franchise in the history of filmmaking.

Chapter 8

The Captain's Return

In the beginning, Kirk is not very nice.
He is more driven. Ten years have gone by,
and he is different just as I am different.
—William Shatner on *Star Trek: The Motion Picture*

In 1978, Shatner received another propitious phone call from Gene Roddenberry. Gene asked him if he would be interested in joining the original *Enterprise* cast to make a motion picture. After canceling their plans several times, Paramount regained their confidence and felt that a *Star Trek* film would do well.

What Shatner did not know was that the producers had planned to kill off Captain Kirk in the first few scenes and introduce a new crew of big-name stars. Roddenberry stubbornly refused to go along with the idea, saying he felt Shatner was an "extraordinarily fine actor."

It took time, but *Star Trek*'s creator finally convinced the studio to bring back Shatner and the original cast. With the exception of Leonard Nimoy, all the former cast signed up within a few weeks. DeForest Kelley, James Doohan, Nichelle Nichols, George Takei, Walter Koenig, and Majel Barrett all agreed to reprise their roles. Even Grace Lee Whitney returned as Janice Rand.

Nimoy's reluctance to be in the motion picture soon became a sore point. He demanded more money than Shatner had signed for, as well as a higher percentage of any profits from merchandising the movie. Surprisingly, Shatner supported his fellow actor.

"Leonard Nimoy has a beef," Shatner said at the time, "and it is a legitimate one. It's about merchandising, and it's something that irks me as well. Our faces appear on products all over the country, all over the world, and we've not really been compensated fairly for it. Right now Paramount wants Leonard, and Leonard wants fair recompense. Someone has made a lot of money from the show, and the people who *were* the show have seen very little of it."

By signing first, Shatner had locked himself into his terms, although that legal fact did not stop Captain Quirk from threatening to quit the film. The reason he gave was Paramount's dropping of the original script in favor of one with more special effects. The first script had the *Enterprise* coming face-to-face with God at the ends of the universe in *The God Thing*, with a theme very similar to that of *The Final Frontier*, which Shatner would direct.

"It was a mind-boggling script," Shatner lamented, "something along the lines of *2001*. The dialogue was incredible. Spock was questioning the logic of a supreme being whose actions appeared questionable and inconsistent. It would have made a classic science-fiction film."

Shatner quickly lost his enthusiasm for the alternate script. He was just finishing *Kingdom of the Spiders*, and the bullheaded star had overloaded his schedule with several plays and film projects. He made it abundantly clear that as far as he was concerned, the *Star Trek* movie could happen without him.

"Having followed this film for so long," he angrily commented, "I have now really gotten tired of wondering what's happening. I would like to see a *Star Trek* film and another series happen again, but I'm no longer interested in being Captain Kirk."

But Leonard Nimoy suddenly agreed to make the movie. Although his acquiescence might have had more to do with the fact that the studio had signed on a replacement to play the ship's Vulcan science officer, Nimoy told reporters that his decision was based on artistic considerations.

The major factor, according to Nimoy, was that Robert Wise, who had directed *The Day the Earth Stood Still* (1951) and *The Sound of Music* (1965), had signed on as director. Nimoy believed having a director of Wise's stature would guarantee the film's quality. David Gautreaux, the actor who would have played Xon, Spock's replacement, was recast as Commander Branch of the *Epsilon 9* space station.

Not long after Nimoy had signed on, Shatner also changed his mind. While his enthusiasm was sorely dampened, he was still excited about the prospect of a *Star Trek* feature film.

Unfortunately, the decade since he'd last played Captain Kirk had taken its toll. He had gained twenty-five pounds, most of it in a spare tire that hugged his waist. The crown of his head was completely bald, and other assets that had made him the heartthrob of millions were now noticeably sagging.

Shatner decided to tone up and hide as many of the signs of aging as he could. The old Toughy in him returned in his best fighting spirit. Shatner's strenuous training regimen included jogging six miles a day, frequent weight-lifting sessions, and long visits to saunas and steam rooms. His meager diet consisted mainly of sprouts and plain yogurt. Giving up sugar and coffee, he put himself under the care of famed nutritionist Dr. Ernst Duynder of the American Health Institute.

Some suggested that Shatner resorted to some less natural means of regaining his youth, such as liposuction, a facelift, and a new hair weave. Looking back over the first few *Trek* films, *Newsweek* commented that while the rest of the actors were getting "jowly and gray," Shatner appeared to be growing "curiously smooth-skinned and hairy."

"I worked hard to get into shape for the picture," Shatner commented. "It was no accident I looked the way I did. I knew I would be compared to a decade ago. That's a difficult position to put anyone in, especially an actor who, like every actor, has vanity."

The hard work seemed to pay off. When Nichelle Nichols saw Shatner on the set for the first time, she commented on how young and skinny he looked. He could not contain his glee. The captain grabbed his surprised communications officer and kissed her right on the mouth.

So, with the help of aerobics workouts, Vaseline facials, flattering camera angles, gauzy lens filters, and possibly a little plastic surgery, Shatner and the rest of the aging crew returned to the bridge of the *Enterprise* hoping to appear about ten years younger. It was all part of one of the biggest glossovers ever perpetrated on moviegoers.

Star Trek: The Extravaganza

It took Gene Roddenberry five years—ironically, the same length of time he'd set for the *Enterprise*'s original mission—to bring *Star Trek* to the big screen. *Star Trek: The Motion Picture* would be the biggest movie project ever undertaken at Paramount Studios. It took the efforts of nearly a quarter of Paramount's work force and required eleven of the studio's thirty-two soundstages. Four of those studios were devoted exclusively to sets of the *Enterprise,* which included views of the bridge, the sick bay, a transporter room, engineering, a hanger deck, and a recreation hall never before envisioned by fans.

Special effects and sets dominated the movie, and the state-of-the-art screen magic ate up two-thirds of the film's budget. Comprehensive blueprints for every level of the enormous spaceship were prepared with the help of NASA scientists, including Shatner's buddy from *Mysteries of the Gods,* Jesco Von Puttkamer. Von Puttkamer was NASA's program manager for space industrialization and advance long-range planning. At the time he said, "I take *Star Trek* to be NASA's longest-range plan."

With meticulous detail, interiors of the ship were created three-football-fields-long. The operation of all nine stations on the ship were computerized, and all controls were standardized. Actors were issued technical manuals on the correct operation of pushbuttons, lights, screens, instruments, and other control circuitry.

The film's players were outfitted in over 500 totally redesigned costumes and uniforms. Costume designer Robert Fletcher's new form-fitting jumpsuits did away with the possibility of the infamous pair-of-socks prop used surreptitiously by some male members of the cast to augment their "equipment" in the original series. In *Star Trek: The Motion Picture,* all the male actors appeared quite equal when it came to their physical endowments.

In deference to the shifting contours of the older actors, Bill Theiss, costume designer from the original series, added a wide elastic band in the trousers that fit snugly around the upper abdomen. Instead of ending at the waist, the new trousers went all the way to the diaphragm, and in order to keep them from sagging, the actors had to keep their pants pulled up tight over their bellies. That tightened the crotch so severely that male cast members were often heard yelping in pain for no obvious reason. During breaks, actors rarely dared to sit down for fear of endangering the "family jewels."

Robert Abel & Associates, originally hired to do the special effects, was fired when costs rose from the estimated $4 million to over $16 million. A number of companies were called in to complete the work, but they all had to work seven days a week to make deadlines.

Security at Paramount was doubled during production, with security patrols working around the clock. Even the FBI was called in to investigate possible industrial espionage involving the scripts, special effects, and sophisticated electronic equipment borrowed by the studio from NASA, Boeing, and Lockheed. All the actors had to sign oaths not to reveal the scripts, and visits by relatives and fans to the sets were no longer allowed. After filming was complete, all scripts were destroyed and master films were locked away in a vault.

The complicated special effects were almost too much to handle. Two weeks before the film premiered, Shatner was still recording seemingly nonsensical voiceovers in an attempt to provide some continuity between the script and the special effects. Originally budgeted at $10 million, the film ended up costing a staggering $45 million.

The movie opens with the old *Enterprise* sitting in drydock, undergoing a two-year modernization. However, before reconditioning is complete, Kirk is asked to take the ship out to investigate a massive energy cloud that has been detected drifting toward earth. The captain, recently promoted to the rank of admiral, recruits most of his original bridge crew and launches the *Enterprise* to rendezvous with the mysterious cloud. Even Grace Lee Whitney, banned from *Star Trek* a decade earlier, returns as the captain's yeoman. Shatner's real-life wife, Marcy Lafferty, has joined the crew as an assistant to the ship's bald-headed Deltan navigator, played by Persis Khambatta.

Shatner later described Khambatta as "a stunningly beautiful model, a stunningly bad actress" and tells of once standing by for nineteen takes while she tried to master the single line "No." In his book *Star Trek Movie Memories*, Shatner implies she was hired off the casting couch for her looks alone.

There is no doubt that the beautiful young woman was the source of much sexual tension on the bridge of the *Enterprise*. George Takei recalled how "up—and aroused" all the actors on the set were when she took her place on the bridge. Takei had an especially hard time because Khambatta sat at the navigation console right next to him. His character's physical arousal became part of Roddenberry's novelization of the film, although the scene never made it to the big screen.

"Persis had a very refreshing narcissism," recalled Walter Koenig. "She was very candid about it. She thought she looked beautiful and she was the first to mention it. That was okay. She did look great."

Much of Shatner's ill will toward Khambatta can be traced to the fact that she vigorously declined his sexual advances on the set of the movie. Her character, Ilia, hailed from the planet Delta, where constant sexual activity was normal; the character had to sign a vow of chastity just to be allowed on the *Enterprise*. No doubt actress Khambatta was convinced that similar vows should have been required of the ship's captain, too.

Back on screen, the *Enterprise* is nearing its destination when Khambatta's character suddenly dematerializes from the bridge. She returns a few minutes later as a zombielike mechanized probe under the control of a superintelligent force at the center of the cloud. (In the original script, Khambatta rematerialized nude in Kirk's shower—much to the captain's surprise.)

The Ilia probe communicates that the alien being is returning to earth to find its creator. Spock, in the middle of a long Vulcan ceremony to strip him of his human emotions, senses the approaching danger and joins the *Enterprise* en route. In an effort to clarify matters, he performs a mindmeld with the space entity, which he discovers is actually a living machine from far away in the galaxy. Kirk decides to bluff and tells the alien that he knows the identity of its creator. The alien then allows

Kirk, Spock, McCoy, and Decker (Stephen Collins as the latest commander of the *Enterprise*) to travel to the heart of the cloud and meet with it face to face. The four men are amazed to discover an old earth satellite called *Voyager*. The primitive device has been transformed by an advanced civilization into a self-aware machine.

The checkerboard set for the embellished *Voyager* was designed in a sixty-foot octagon-shaped bowl to resemble the inside workings of a computer. The whole thing was suspended five feet off the floor to access lighting and electrical fixtures. During his scene, Shatner fell through one of the flimsy panels and could have been fatally injured. He dropped through all the way to his armpits and had to be hoisted back up by Nimoy and McCoy. Only a few days earlier, two lighting technicians had fallen through the set and one of them had received a life-threatening jolt of electricity.

In the film, just as the superintelligent machine is about to rid earth of its "carbon-based human parasites," Decker volunteers to join the female navigator and be assimilated by *Voyager*. In that way, the errant satellite completes its mission by uniting with its human creators. The hybrid life form—one that Spock calls the next step in the evolution of mankind—then continues its solitary exploration of the universe.

Shatner played Kirk with a distinctly sour disposition that was never seen in the television series. It appeared that Admiral Kirk had taken on some of the characteristics of a neurotic Julius Caesar. He had fiery confrontations with everyone including his old friend Leonard Nimoy. To his fellow actors, it seemed that the forty-eight-year-old actor had further distanced himself from them both on screen and off.

Five weeks into production, a clause in Shatner's contract that gave him story and dialogue approval kicked in. A similar clause was included in Nimoy's contract. Every morning, Shatner met with Roddenberry, Nimoy, screenwriter Harold Livingston, associate producer Jon Povill, director Robert Wise, and Paramount representative Jeffrey Katzenberg to go over the script. Some of those meetings became quite heated as Shatner fought for changes that put his character on more solid footing.

The biggest changes involved Stephen Collins's character, Captain Decker. According to the storyline, he was the grandson of Commodore Decker (portrayed by Shatner nemesis William Windom in the "Doomsday Machine" episode of the original series). From the start, Shatner felt crowded by newcomer Collins, and the two men had several arguments right on the set. Shatner suspected Collins's character was being groomed to replace Kirk. Only after Captain Decker was sent off into oblivion in the final version of the script did Shatner feel placated.

"I enjoyed working with Collins," Walter Koenig noted. "We had some interesting soul-searching conversations about working opposite Mr. Shatner." In fact, it soon became obvious to everyone that Shatner had turned very testy over the years and was more defensive than ever.

"I like Kirk. Really I do," he replied, when asked if he was getting bored with the character. "I modeled him on Horatio Hornblower. They were similar in many respects. Kirk's [and Shatner's?] problems of command were just as real as Hornblower's. And those problems *were* real. I've even had some Navy submarine commanders tell me that—how they could get close to their men, but only to a point, and how they had to be at arm's length after that."

Star Trek: The Motion Picture premiered on December 6, 1979, at the MacArthur Theater in the Kennedy Center as a benefit for the National Space Club. The next day, it opened at 900 theaters nationwide and achieved the second-biggest weekend draw ($20 million) up to that time. But the fact that Shatner and Doohan both fell asleep at the film's preview in Washington should have served as a warning. The critics would not be kind.

"In this post–*Star Wars* era, stories are created merely to provide a feeble excuse for the special effects," Richard Schickel pointedly noted in *Time*. "*Star Trek* consists almost entirely of this kind of material: shot after shot of vehicles sailing through the firmament to the tune of music intended to awe. But the spaceships take an unconscionable amount of time to get anywhere, and nothing of dramatic or human interest happens along the way."

"The producers want to keep the rhythm and intimacy of the TV format while latching on to the epic advantages of the movie format," chimed in *Newsweek*. "But in making this maneuver, they fall on their asteroids. The deliberate pace that can be perversely hypnotic on TV expands to a large soporific cloud on the giant screen."

"Shatner dominates, as usual," observed former *Trek* writer Harlan Ellison in *Starlog* magazine. "Stuffy when he isn't being arch and coy; hamming and mugging when he isn't being lachrymose; playing Kirk as if he actually thinks *he* is Kirk, overbearing and pompous. The saddening reality is that it is a dull film, a stultifyingly predictable film, a tragically *average* film."

"*I am Captain Kirk!*" Shatner responded. "Whatever I do is what Captain Kirk does. And his [Ellison's] percentage rating sounds like 50 or 60 against my 75. We don't seem that far apart. I don't agree with his adjectives, though. They're a little strong, but then, so is Harlan Ellison—he's *little* and he's *strong*."

The Wrath of Quirk

Despite catcalls from critics, the worldwide gross receipts of the first *Star Trek* movie ended up a respectable $178 million, about $50 million of which went back to Paramount. But that was not enough for the studio's executives, who were disappointed with bottom-line profits from the costly project. At the same time, they realized that there was a large audience of *Trek* fans and science-fiction buffs who wanted to see more of the *Enterprise* crew.

They decided that the next *Star Trek* film must be done for a lot less money, even if it ended up as a made-for-TV movie. They called in television producer Harve Bennett, who promised them he would bring the second *Star Trek* movie in under budget. Based on his assurances, Paramount agreed to release the sequel in movie houses rather than on television. As it turned out, the methodical producer would make *Star Treks II, III, and IV* for what it had cost to make the first motion picture.

After the first *Trek* movie, it became obvious that the visions of Gene Roddenberry and the down-to-earth studio executives were in direct opposition. Oddly enough, the Great Bird of the Galaxy was now preaching the gospel of the Nine, the group of alleged extraterrestrials he had been put in contact with in the 1970s.

Roddenberry adhered to the idea of the perfectibility of man. He believed that mankind could, with effort, fundamentally change in the near future and overcome its warrior ways. His vision of the twenty-third century was one of evolution, bliss, and peace. That was in direct conflict with the Horatio Hornblower concept held by the studio. They wanted human nature to remain the same throughout history, with plenty of action, human frailties, and conflict to bring audiences to the edges of their seats.

Moreover, Roddenberry wanted to saddle future generations with a certain amount of karma for the sins of our species' past. For each of the next five films, he pushed for scripts based on the idea of the *Enterprise* crew going back in time to the year 1963 and finding a way to foil the assassination of President John F. Kennedy. (According to communications from the Nine channeled to psychics at the estate of Andrija Puharich, Kennedy's assassination was a profoundly negative turning point in the history of our planet.)

To ensure such outlandish ideas never made it to the screen and to give Harve Bennett complete authority on the set, Gene Roddenberry was removed from the front lines. Banished to his office with the title of "executive consultant," Roddenberry communicated with writers and producers via an endless series of memos in which he expressed his views on characterization and plot. His viewpoints, however, were now treated as suggestions, not orders.

Shatner was very pleased with the new chain of command and later credited Bennett for being "the man who got *Star Trek* back on track." Although Shatner never said whether or not he was aware of Roddenberry's communications with the Nine, the actor certainly never shared his executive producer's elevated vision for the future of humanity. Shatner's vision, as played out in *Star Trek V*, was to locate the alien God responsible for the human condition and confront him with his misdeeds.

Still, Shatner fretted over the script for the second *Trek* adventure almost as much as he had for the first: "I was nervous about it, especially after the first film. The success of your performance rests in the words. As this script developed, I swung wildly from awful lows to exalted highs, (yet) by the time we were ready to shoot, I knew *The Wrath of Khan* would be great."

The preliminary subtitle for *Star Trek II* was *The Undiscovered Country*. The phrase is a quote from Hamlet's famous soliloquy and referred to death—in this case, Spock's. It was changed to *The Wrath of Khan* by a nervous studio executive, who was looking for something more exciting. (The original subtitle would be used later for *Star Trek VI*, this time referring to the promise of a new future formed by the death of old political alliances.) Production of *Star Trek II: The Wrath of Khan* began on November 9,

1981, and continued until January 2, 1982. The film opened in 1,600 movie theaters on June 4, 1982.

In *Star Trek II,* the producers decided it was time to stop fighting the aging process and allow the cast to start showing their years. It required some effort on the part of Harve Bennett to convince Captain Quirk to give up his fear of aging. After much cajoling and many carefully reasoned discussions, Shatner finally agreed to show his wrinkles. It would be a mid-life crisis shared by both the actor and his character.

"At a certain point in everybody's life," he commented, "presumably in Kirk's and certainly in mine, you begin to see the end. Life's no longer immortal. It's like going to a high school reunion where everybody's gotten so old you can't believe it. But of course, it doesn't apply to you. I think it's a very good dramatic element to play to in *Star Trek.* You have to play up those elements that are universal to human beings."

The movie opens on Kirk's birthday, with the graying admiral trying to get used to his granny-style reading glasses. Dr. McCoy presents him with a vintage bottle of blue wine, and Spock gives him a tattered copy of *Tale of Two Cities,* noting the admiral's "fondness for antiques." The deskbound Kirk is going through a mid-life crisis, and his friends persuade him to take the *Enterprise* out on training maneuvers for one more spin through outer space. The dominant subtheme of the film is Kirk's coming to terms with old age and finally taking responsibility for the "wild oats" of his misspent youth. One reviewer went so far as to dub the movie *On Golden Galaxy.*

Leonard Nimoy preferred that his character, Spock, not only age, but be killed off for good. Playing the character had always been a psychological drain, and Nimoy was now fearful that *Star Trek* would become a long series of sequels. The producers went along with Nimoy's wishes and rewrote the script eight times, eventually adding a replacement half-Vulcan, half-Romulan character by the name of Lieutenant Saavik (played by Kirstie Alley).

Although Gene Roddenberry was cut off from the production of the film, he found ways to make his input felt. When he leaked the news that Spock would die in the film, Trekkers went wild. Fan clubs threatened a nationwide boycott. The once-beloved Nimoy started receiving hate mail, and there was even a death threat against his daughter. One group, called the Concerned Supporters of *Star Trek*, placed full-page ads in Hollywood newspapers warning that the studio would lose at least $28 million in profits from ticket sales if they carried out the planned "murder." The emotional protest caused producers to rewrite the script in such a way that Spock could be brought back to life in a sequel.

Surprisingly, *Wrath of Khan* proved extremely popular with Trekkers and received glowing reviews. It broke all previous records for opening weekend box-office receipts. In our survey, the movie was voted the second-best of all six *Trek* films. It ran just a few percentage points behind *Star Trek IV*, which was considered the best of the series.

What saved the movie for devoted fans was that Spock died in such a way that he could be resurrected in the next installment. The movie cost a mere $13 million to make. It made that back in the first three days, and after a few weeks, it had grossed over $80 million. It proved much more of a moneymaker than the first *Trek* movie. Of all the *Trek* films, *Wrath of Khan* came closest to the tradition of a Horatio Hornblower adventure story.

Commented reviewer Michael Sragow: "*Star Trek II* happily accents the qualities that made the TV series addictive to adolescents of every age: garish parables of good and evil, improbable adventures in tacky but colorful surroundings, and posturing actors in their hambone glory. Best of all, this movie retains the series' benign aura. It makes you feel that common sense, intuition, and the great books of the Western world can overcome every cataclysm in the universe."

The movie was based on the "Space Seed" episode of the television series. In that installment, Ricardo Montalban introduced viewers to Khan Noonian Singh, a genetically altered superman exiled from earth for trying to take over the planet. Khan and his followers are accidentally released from their suspended-animation prison when their vessel crosses paths with the *Enterprise*. Kirk welcomes the group onto his ship, but in the end is forced to maroon the treacherous Khan and his crew on a desolate planet.

Fifteen years later, while the *Enterprise* is on training maneuvers, Kirk meets up with his archenemy once again. He receives a distress call from a former lover, Dr. Carol Marcus (played by Bibi Besch). Dr. Marcus now heads the Genesis Project, a device that generates life from inanimate matter through a top-secret process of molecular reorganization. Carol was one of Kirk's many romantic liaisons, although this one resulted in the birth of a child about whom the captain was never informed.

When he arrives at the Genesis site, Kirk meets up with Khan, who has seized a Federation starship that mistakenly landed on his prison planet. Aboard the starship is Commander Pavlov Chekov, former navigator of the *Enterprise*.

Using a terrifying "truth bug," a voracious parasite known as the Ceti Eel that burrows into Chekov's brain, Khan discovers the potential power of the Genesis device. The crazed Khan takes the commandeered spaceship directly to the *Regulus* space station, where the device is being tested. Luckily, the scientists have hidden the equipment deep within a nearby asteroid.

That is where Kirk eventually finds Carol. The aging captain is also introduced to his illegitimate son, David (Merritt Butrick). But before long, Khan locates the sequestered group and beams Genesis aboard his vessel, leaving Kirk and the others stranded in the underground cavern in the heart of the asteroid.

Fortunately, Spock is able to lock the ship's transporter on the entire group and beam them back up to the *Enterprise*. In the ensuing battle, both ships are disabled and drift helplessly in space. Knowing more Federation vessels will arrive soon, a desperate Khan sets off the Genesis device, which can easily destroy both of the helpless ships.

Just four minutes before the device is set to go off, Spock enters the reactor chamber and repairs his ship's damaged warp drive. The heroic science officer dies from exposure to radiation, although the *Enterprise* manages to escape from the Genesis energy wave. At the end of the film, Spock's body is placed in a spacecoffin and interred on the newly formed Genesis planet.

Even though Shatner was very nervous about the film, he was quick to claim credit when it proved critically successful. He felt vindicated about all those times he'd been passed over for leads in major films for actors who were considered bigger draws at the box office.

In an interview with *People* magazine, he crowed: "I am the fulcrum, and I really wanted this popular validation. I always knew there was a large audience that wanted to see me."

If Shatner was the fulcrum, then Ricardo Montalban was the lever that made the film work. His portrayal of the ruthless Khan caught the attention of many critics and moviegoers. He played the part in the style of the classiest comic book villain, with great relish and flamboyance.

Moreover, the cast really enjoyed working with the considerate actor, who stood out in stark contrast to their own Captain Quirk. Walter Koenig felt very lucky to be spending his time working with Montalban instead of Shatner. *Starlog* magazine commented that for Koenig, facing the Ceti Eel was easy compared to working with Shatner.

"It was great, not having scenes reblocked by our leading man," said Koenig, "which I found very oppressive. Montalban was always there for your closeup and always very giving. The two weeks I worked with Bill as the leading man weren't as much fun."

Only one person on the set had any problems with Montalban. Afraid he was being upstaged, Shatner treated the kind-hearted actor with contempt. He lobbied hard to insert a scene where Kirk would defeat Khan in violent hand-to-hand combat, but the studio nixed the idea.

Captain Quirk also felt threatened by Merritt Butrick, the handsome actor who played his long-lost son in the movie. Shatner felt the young actor, whose claim to fame was the role of Johnny Slash in the short-lived television sitcom *Square Pegs*, was much too "uppity." Despite their bickering, when Butrick died from AIDS the following year, Shatner was one of the first to eulogize the "lovely, gentle young man."

For different reasons, Shatner had unpleasant dealings with Kirstie Alley, who played Lieutenant Saavik. Rumors were that Shatner was trying to hit on the temperamental actress, who certainly possessed all the features Shatner found attractive in women. But Alley did not respond to Shatner's advances.

While filming a scene on the Eden Cave set, Shatner accidentally stepped on one of the round styrofoam balls that were painted to look like space warts. "I've crushed a ball," he yelled out. "Yours or theirs?" Nicholas Meyer shouted back facetiously. "Certainly not mine," Shatner replied in a mockingly deep voice. "Too bad!" Kirstie Alley is said to have murmured from off the set. The backstage pressures got so great that Alley refused to reprise her role in *Star Trek III*, saying she would not return unless her salary matched Shatner's.

Shatner's relationship with the other cast members was not much better. Several believed Shatner was responsible for deleting whole scenes in *Star Trek II*. Shatner himself admitted that he refused to film anything unless he was a hundred percent satisfied with the script. George Takei nearly quit over his reduced role in the film, and even DeForest Kelley came close to leaving when his character was neglected.

"When you have one actor so dominating the proceedings in terms of participation," observed Walter Koenig, "regardless of how good he is, I don't think it's possible for the other actors to feel totally comfortable about the situation. The sense of ensemble playing wasn't there. In most cases, Bill dominated *every* scene he was in, and that's the way it was photographed.

"Bill has a very strong sense of his value to *Star Trek*, and he explores and exploits it to its zenith. He will do whatever he can to make the picture better in terms of his performance. On the one hand, that's meritorious, but on the other hand, it may be at the sacrifice of the other performers."

One scene where a dead ensign (played by Ike Eisenmann) is identified as Scotty's nephew was completely severed from the theater version of the film. To this day, James Doohan believes Captain Quirk removed the scene because it gave Doohan a chance to add some dramatic depth to his character. Director Nicholas Meyer restored the scene when the film was first shown on ABC television.

"It is ironic," commented Meyer, "that as a director of a feature I may not have final cut, but as a director of the television version, no one gives a fuck. Places where I was overruled, rightly or wrongly, I get to have the last word. I am not persuaded that artists are the best judges of their own work."

From J. T. to T. J.

In 1981, Shatner tried to shed his James T. Kirk stereotype with a new character named T. J. Hooker. In the *T. J. Hooker* television series, he portrayed a tough detective who surrendered his desk job at the precinct to walk the beat of a street patrolman. In addition to keeping peace in the neighborhood, Hooker was assigned the added responsibility of working with rookies and training them in proper techniques.

Overall, Hooker was a very human character. He lost his partner in the line of duty, had difficulty forming relationships with people, and was divorced from his wife. Yet Hooker always stayed close to his daughters and always stood for traditional values. He was also athletic, known for pursuing automobiles on foot or grabbing onto car hoods and not letting go. In many ways, the character was a carbon copy of the real William Shatner.

In typical fashion, Shatner poured himself into the new role and used it as an excuse to lose weight and get back in shape. Following a strict diet and exercise program, he reduced his spare-tire abdomen, losing seventeen pounds. He even warned the wardrobe department that his uniforms would have to be taken in at the beginning of each season. (He did not mention that the uniforms would have to be let out by the end of each season.)

"I spent five years in *T. J. Hooker,*" he reflected, "in which most of it was shot at night and most of the time I was running, so everything else seems vacation-like by comparison. I mean, we would go to work at sundown and leave at sunrise. We did a lot of fights and stuff like that, but I didn't find that exhausting."

Of course, with Heather Locklear on the set, no man would want to look bad. The perky blonde got her start in show business doing commercials while she was still a freshman at UCLA. After college, she landed the role of Officer Stacy Sheridan on *T. J. Hooker*.

Shatner was immediately attracted to Locklear, even though she was thirty years younger. He paid her a lot of attention and developed the habit of rubbing seductively against her during rehearsals. Then he tried becoming a father figure to the aspiring actress. Although his tactics were rumored to be successful at first, Locklear eventually made it clear to Shatner that she was interested in starting a family, not messing around. The two had a strained but polite relationship after that.

There was also gossip about Shatner's relationship with another Heather—Heather Thomas, from the television series *The Fall Guy*. Shatner and Adrian Zmed, the swarthy young actor who portrayed Officer Vince Romano, were said to have fallen over each other in an attempt to get the attention of the gorgeous twenty-seven-year-old blonde when she guest-starred in an episode about a murdered cop on the take.

Actress Molly Cheek, who was a regular on *It's Gary Shandling's Show*, stirred up the set in a different way when she guest starred in a *T. J. Hooker* episode. She and Shatner never hit it off.

"When I did *T. J. Hooker*," Cheek recalled, "Shatner said, 'Now, let me tell you about your motivation in this scene.' And I thought: 'God, next to Charlton Heston, this is the last person I want to get acting notes from.' Shatner is the luckiest man in show business. Who *couldn't* play Captain Kirk? He just happened to be there, got the part, and he's never stopped working since. And he wears a girdle and a terrible hairpiece and is the male counterpart to a *grande dame*."

More respectful was actress Teresa Saldana, who appeared in a 1982 episode of the show. A year earlier, the beautiful, long-haired Saldana had nearly been killed in a knife attack, and *T. J. Hooker* was her first acting job after her recovery. Shatner spent a lot of time with her, and she credited him with helping her get over the tragedy.

But in 1984, Shatner met a guest star on the set of *T. J. Hooker* who would change his own life forever. Actress Vera Montez played a bank clerk who was raped, and it was up to Hooker to track down her assailant. The twenty-five-year-old had long dark hair and a fantastic body. Shatner could not keep his eyes off her.

"It was clear almost from the very beginning," Montez recalled, "that he was quite taken by my body. We were at close quarters a lot, and strangely, Bill just kept bumping into me. He especially kept making sure our chests kept rubbing together. I was very attracted to him, and who wouldn't be? He was very attentive and very complimentary. The romance just flared from there."

On her second day on the set, Shatner asked her to lunch in the studio cafeteria. After work on the episode was completed, he asked Montez out to dinner to a more fashionable restaurant. When he found out she loved horses, Shatner started asking her out almost every other day. Before long, they were sharing her bed together.

"I cannot believe what a fantastic lover he is," she confessed. "He makes me feel like no other man has made me feel. He is like no other man in my life, and nobody has ever had that effect on me. No one has ever handled me like Bill."

At first, Montez did not even know that Shatner was married. Later he told her his marriage was in name only and had been deteriorating for some time. In 1987, when news broke of their affair, Shatner's manager told reporters that there was no relationship of any kind between them. But Shatner's wife had walked out on him and had returned only when he'd promised to stop seeing Montez. Unbeknownst to his wife, Shatner had bought a house for Montez and would continue seeing her for the next three years.

In the meantime, *T. J. Hooker* proved to be Shatner's

most successful television series. It was one of the first cop shows to mix the personal lives of policemen with their public image and focus on the ethics of police work, as well as their family lives. *T. J. Hooker* was first broadcast on March 13, 1982, and stayed on the air until 1987. Initially broadcast on ABC at 8 PM, it moved to 11:30 PM, CBS's "late prime time," in 1985.

"Viewers think of Hooker as the archetypal conservative cop fighting for justice," Shatner said of the role, "which Kirk does, but on a higher plane. They are both universal characters doing what they can to preserve peace and justice. They share similar qualities, but there are differences, too. Kirk has a thoughtful, analytical approach to problems. Hooker is an angry man who reacts to stress with action. Actually, I'm centered on both of them. And the core of each of them, of course, is within myself."

The Gritz Affair

On the set of *T. J. Hooker*, in the fall of 1982, Shatner befriended a forty-four-year-old ex–Green Beret, Lieutenant Colonel James "Bo" Gritz. Enthralled with the man's adventuresome life history, Shatner paid him $10,000 for the rights to his story. Shatner himself hoped to play Gritz in a made-for-TV movie. The venture capital came from a partnership between Shatner's Lemli Productions and Paramount Studios.

The two men shared a concern about the well-being of American soldiers still missing in action when our country withdrew from Vietnam. In fact, Shatner had done a public service spot for the National League of Families of American Prisoners and Missing in Southeast Asia.

In November 1982, Gritz pooled Shatner's $10,000 with another $30,000 from actor Clint Eastwood and formed Operation Lazarus, an expeditionary mission into communist Laos to rescue American MIAs. He also said he had backing from the U.S. government.

"Some of the money," Gritz told reporters, "isn't private money. The FBI has helped me; the CIA has helped us; the U.S. Embassy in Bangkok has helped us; President Reagan stands ready to support us if and when we produce an American."

The group was outfitted with extremely sophisticated equipment. They had night-vision sights on all their weapons and carried "nuclear fire plan boxes" which allowed direct, coded communication with Gritz's backers in Washington. The $750,000 boxes were provided on loan by a major defense contractor, Litton Industries.

The strike force, consisting of four Americans and fifteen Laotian guerrillas, entered Laos from Thailand and planned to travel 185 miles to a small town near the Mekong River. Gritz had information that 120 U.S. servicemen were being sequestered in a large cave outside the village of Sepone. Another 30 MIAs were supposedly being held near the town of Namrath.

Tragically, 60 miles into Laos, the team was ambushed. Three of the group's Laotians died in the half-hour battle and one American was captured. He was released a month later, after a ransom of $17,500 had been paid.

The Thai government vigorously protested the action and charged Gritz with illegal entry and arms possession. The Justice Department undertook an investigation into the raid and questioned the legality of Gritz's actions. Shatner admitted to knowing of his efforts to rescue MIAs but denied knowing how the money was to be used. As a result of the controversy, "Bo" Gritz's life story was never filmed.

The Search for Sequels

After the success of *The Wrath of Khan*, Paramount executives finally realized they had a winner on their hands. The only problem was how to keep the actors happy and find interesting scripts for the movie series. They went so far as to offer Leonard Nimoy the chance to direct if he would return as a resurrected Spock. In private, Paramount President Michael Eisner admitted that having Nimoy direct was an immediate audience and publicity grabber.

Production of *Star Trek III: The Search for Spock* began on August 15, 1983, and lasted only forty-nine days. Fans were so eager to find out what happened to Spock that the scripts were chemically treated so they could be traced in case they ended up on sellers' tables at *Trek* conventions.

All of the actors agreed to return with the exception of Kirstie Alley, who demanded almost three times the money she'd received for *Star Trek II* to work with Shatner again. The studio refused to meet her demands, which would have been more than some of the series regulars were receiving. Alley was replaced by Robin Curtis, who would also play Lieutenant Saavik in *Star Trek IV*.

To complicate matters further, the remaining cast had serious reservations about Nimoy's ego getting in the way of his directing. Fortunately, their concerns turned out to be groundless.

"There were apprehensions at the beginning," said George Takei. "When you're working as an actor, you're always fighting for your place in the sun. Now he's the big boss, making the final decisions about who gets closeups and what gets cut. The one you used to be competing with is now in charge."

Despite the backstage tensions and short schedule, Nimoy elicited excellent performances from the entire

cast, including a somewhat reluctant William Shatner.
Shatner found it especially difficult to take orders from his
former co-star.

"We were brothers in flesh and spirit," Shatner admitted, "and now, suddenly, my brother was saying 'You
should do this,' and I would say 'I think I should do that.'
It was more awkward in the beginning than any of the
other films."

Shatner also feared the producers were killing off characters too soon, in effect surrendering future plot development for short-term dramatic appeal.

"I thought the loss of the *Enterprise* and David's death
were very clever devices used to create drama in a situation," he said at the time. "The problem is that, in a
continuing series of movies where the characters appear
through all the films, we have to raise some jeopardy. In
fact, the real problem is, what else can we kill? We're
looking around for people to die! It's like court-martials
where you come into a room, and if the knife is pointing
to you, you're dead."

Perhaps what he feared most was that the smoking gun
would point toward him next. Early in production, Shatner insisted that Harve Bennett and Leonard Nimoy attend a weekend meeting to be held at his house. When the
producer and director arrived, they found Shatner, his
agent, his lawyer, and a burly bodyguard, who stood by
silently with his arms folded across his chest. Both men
were somewhat intimidated by the show of force. Shatner
said bluntly he was unhappy with the script and would
quit unless specific changes were made. His major com-
plaint was that there was not enough of him in the material.

For the next six hours, the group went over the
changes, generally adding more time for Kirk on screen.
One change that Shatner wanted was for Kirk to get
between Spock and McCoy in the "remember" scene,
where Spock passes on his soul for safekeeping. But Ben-

nett and Nimoy refused to sacrifice Kelley's big moment. Finally, Shatner felt satisfied and agreed to continue in the film. Before leaving, Harve Bennett summed up the thoughts of everyone connected with *Star Trek*.

"Bill," he said, "you *know* you're the quarterback on this team, but the problem is you want to call the play, take the snap from center, block the defensive lineman, backpedal into the pocket, toss the perfect spiral, run downfield, catch the pass, fake out a safety or two, score the touchdown, do the victory dance, and captain the cheerleading squad all at the same time."

"You're absolutely right," replied Captain Quirk, visions of young cheerleaders dancing in his mind. "But I can't handle all those cheerleaders by myself."

Shatner was temporarily at ease with the *Star Trek III* script, and his paranoia subsided. But rumors that Kirk would be killed off at the beginning of the next movie caused Shatner to revamp his aging image. Once again, he started a strenuous exercise program, but by now costume designer Robert Fletcher knew the routine.

"We had twelve shirts made for Shatner," Fletcher said. "He diets before a movie and shows up looking terrific. But he would slip as it went along."

This time Shatner also opted for a much younger hairstyle. The thick locks he suddenly sprouted prompted many a snide remark. One reviewer suggested retitling the movie *Star Trek III: The Search for a Good Toupee*.

In reality, it was not the appearance but the humanity of the actors that became the film's best selling point. Fans looked on the *Enterprise* crew almost as family and relished the longstanding friendships they watched develop over the previous eighteen years. When Kirk uttered the incredibly hokey line "This time we've paid for the party with our dearest blood," he might as well have been talking about anyone's brother or closest kin in the audience. No one thought it overly sentimental at the time.

In fact, it is that unwilling payment that the crew of the

Enterprise seeks to take back in *Star Trek III*. After the *Enterprise* limps back to space port, Kirk is informed that the ship is to be scuttled and only the engineer, Scotty, will be reassigned to a new ship. It should be remembered that the *Enterprise* has always been a member of the cast with fans. The ship actually starred in *Star Trek: The Motion Picture*, and whenever it is threatened with destruction, fans react as if it were a member of the crew. Captain Kirk's consuming love affair with the inanimate vessel became a theme in several episodes of the original series.

The film's melancholy mood is broken when Spock's father visits Kirk and informs him that Spock's spirit may still be alive, if he was able to perform a mindmeld with one of the crew just before he perished in the ship's reactor room. Kirk is convinced the crew member host to Spock's spirit is none other than Dr. McCoy, who has been acting stranger than usual. The rambunctious Kirk steals the *Enterprise* out of drydock and heads for Vulcan with a minimal crew.

At the same time, Lieutenant Saavik (Robin Curtis) and Kirk's headstrong son, David (Merritt Butrick), discover a young Vulcan boy on the Genesis planet. Apparently, the youth has been regenerated from Spock's corpse. Before the landing party can leave, however, they are attacked by a Klingon force headed by the ruthless Commander Kruge (played by Christopher Lloyd). The Klingons have arrived to steal the secret of the Genesis effect, and David is killed in the process.

In what Shatner has called his finest acting as Kirk, the captain learns of his son's death and, in a moment of unaccustomed vulnerability, stumbles backward on the bridge of the *Enterprise*, devastated by the news. At first, Shatner insisted on playing the scene more stylistically, with less overpowering emotion, but in the middle of the scene, director Nimoy stopped the action and asked everyone but Shatner to leave.

"He and I kind of got ourselves off into a corner,"

Nimoy remembered, "and discussed it slowly in a relaxed atmosphere, and privately. I said, 'You have to decide how far you want to take this reaction. My opinion is that you can go pretty far and get away with it; maybe strip off some of the veneer of the admiral, the hero, always in charge, always on top of the situation, and show us a vulnerable person.' We did several takes and used the one where we really thought Bill lost control and fell. I'm very moved by it. He looks deeply hurt."

Of course, grief over David's death does not keep Captain Kirk from engaging in a violent confrontation with the Klingons. The damaged *Enterprise* is unable to put up much of a fight, and Kirk must surrender his beloved ship—though not before rigging it to self-destruct with the Klingon boarding party trapped on the bridge.

Before long, the former *Enterprise* crew members have taken over the Klingon vessel and are heading for Vulcan with the resurrected Spock on board. In a moving finale, Spock regains his spirit and memories during an elaborate ritual presided over by a Vulcan high priestess (none other than Dame Judith Anderson, in a rare screen appearance).

Two days before the wrap of *Star Trek III*, one of the oldest sets on the Paramount lot, the twenty-building Old New York set caught fire. The inferno quickly spread to Stage 15, which housed the Genesis planet set. Knowing he had to shoot his final scenes on the set the following day, Shatner rushed to a water hose and started dowsing the fire. By his own account, he had things pretty well in control by the time firefighters arrived. News reports told of how Captain Kirk single-handedly directed the fire-fighting effort.

That, at least, was the official story. According to witnesses, Shatner never really got involved in fighting the fire. He had been excused from filming a scene in *Star Trek III* when publicity people had fetched him to pose for photographs at the fire. They drove him to the fire, where he struck a variety of impressive poses from outside the fire safety zone. Then he got in the car and was driven back to the set.

Fortunately, the Genesis set was repaired and available for filming by the next morning. Amazingly, the third *Trek* movie was completed one week ahead of schedule.

"*Star Trek III*," wrote Kevin Thomas in the *Los Angeles Times*, "is so much a sequel that it might confuse some who haven't seen the earlier film. Yet it has genuine spirituality, and at its end, you may be surprised, especially if you're not really a Trekkie, to realize how moved you've been."

The *New York Times* agreed: "The humanity of the *Star Trek* series, unexpected as it is in a sci-fi setting, remains the series' best feature. The members of the *Enterprise* crew, a too-perfect interracial and sexual mix, share a longstanding friendship by now."

Shatner's acting, whether on the set or fighting fires, was some of his best. In reviewing the first six *Trek* films, *Cinefantastique* singled out *Star Trek III* as his shining moment: "The real surprise here is Shatner, who aside from a few scenery-chewing moments gives his finest performance as Kirk in all the feature films."

Time also noted Shatner's unexpected depth: "Above all, the emotions are as broad and as basic as anything this side of Rigoletto. Principally, these are the province of William Shatner's character. His attempts to answer the cries for help that Spock transmits by means of a Vulcan mindmeld forces him to the most anguishing command decisions. These involve the life and death of his son and the fate of his beloved starship *Enterprise*."

The budget for *Star Trek III* was $16 million. It was released in June 1984, and the initial box office return was $76 million. In spite of intense competition from *Ghostbusters* and *Indiana Jones and the Temple of Doom*, it was another highly profitable *Trek* film. In our fan survey, it placed fourth in popularity in the first six movies. Slightly over 10 percent of the respondents considered it the best in the series.

At the end of *The Search for Spock*, the former *Enterprise* crew members are renegades from the Federation in a stolen Klingon spaceship. There was no doubt in anyone's mind that another sequel was going to be made.

Voyage to the Box Office

It slowly dawned on Paramount executives that some of the best moments in the *Trek* films were the comedic exchanges of Kirk, Spock, and McCoy. Realizing that these warm-hearted interactions played a major role in the success of the films, they decided the fourth *Star Trek* film should reflect that new insight, and they demanded more lighthearted scenes.

At one time, comedian Eddie Murphy was slated to play the role of an eccentric college professor in the film. The plan was discouraged by Paramount executives, who saw no reason to mix their two biggest box-office draws in a single project. Murphy got busy with *The Golden Child* (1986), and his professor part evolved into that of a marine biologist played by Catherine Hicks. Hicks was hired after a long-drawn-out process that included a trip to a horse ranch to meet Shatner and his favorite horse.

Shatner did not sign on to do the picture until the very last minute. His bitter contract negotiations dragged on for months, and Harve Bennett started pushing for a prequel called *Starfleet Academy*, which could be done without the classic cast. The idea was dropped when Shatner finally agreed to a $2 million deal, though Nimoy received $3 million because he was once again asked to direct. The other regular cast members each received under $100,-000 this time around—actually a cut in salary. The studio realized that the crew was so severely typecast by now that they would have a hard time finding other work. They were all made to understand that they could be written out of the script at any time.

Once again, Roddenberry pushed his Kennedy assassination idea. While the final script would be based on time travel, it was not the idea that Roddenberry had had in mind. Leonard Nimoy proposed the storyline, which contained a strong message about respecting other species on the planet. The first script was completed in August 1985 and required several rewrites.

Shooting was supposed to begin in November but was delayed until February of the following year because of Shatner's previous commitments to *T. J. Hooker*. The TV series was canceled by ABC, then unexpectedly picked up by CBS in September 1985. As a result, *Star Trek IV: The Voyage Home* did not appear in theaters until December 1986.

In the film, a megalithic space probe disables the entire planet Earth in an attempt to communicate with humpback whales, a species that had become extinct in the early twenty-first century. In order to keep civilization from being destroyed, Kirk must take a starship back in time to 1986 to try to retrieve living whales to answer the alien's call.

The time travelers find "an extremely primitive and paranoid culture" but are able to pass themselves off as contemporaries despite a few blatant transgressions, most involving old-fashioned fish-out-of-water routines. Kirk's observation that "nobody pays any attention to you unless you swear every other word" elicits a series of hilarious gaffes by Spock. In another example, Kirk tries to explain Spock's behavior by saying his friend did a little too much "LDS" while a student at Berkeley in the 1960s.

At the end of the film, Admiral Kirk is demoted to the rank of captain again, ostensibly for sacrificing the *Enterprise* at the end of *Star Trek III*. However, everyone realizes that the rank of captain means Kirk will once again return to Starfleet to take command of another starship.

The fourth *Trek* flick cost $23 million to make, but total box-office receipts were $126 million, making it the most profitable film of the series at the time. In fact, it turned out to be the most critically acclaimed installment in the entire series. Our survey showed it to be the most popular *Trek* movie. Slightly over 38 percent of the respondents favored it. Apparently, Paramount was dead-on in its hunch to add more levity to the script.

"We discovered something in *Star Trek IV* that we hadn't pinpointed in any of the other movies," Shatner admitted. "It's as though the characters within the play have a great deal of joy about themselves, a joy of living. That energy, that *joie de vivre* about the characters seems to be tongue-in-cheek but isn't, because you play it with the reality that you would in a kitchen-sink drama written for today's life."

Walter Koenig thought it was the best film in the series for two reasons: "For the first time I felt the dialogue was indigenous to my character, that only Chekov could say these lines. And I had the opportunity to work away from Bill Shatner."

Critics agreed that the supporting cast contributed more to the movie, even as they downplayed Shatner's contribution. Wrote Mark Altman in *Cinefantastique:* "Shatner plays too broadly and the film camps up its time travel story a little too much, but the witty banter works for the most part and the supporting cast's star turns make this the best showcase for the ensemble."

But the ensemble cast would soon lose the progress they had made for their characters in *Star Trek IV*. The next film in the series would be directed by William Shatner, and at one point, he wanted to get rid of all of them.

Chapter 9

Mutiny on the
Enterprise

If I knew what a jerk he was gonna turn
into, I wouldna saved him so many times!
—James Doohan on William Shatner

During contract negotiations for *Star Trek III*, lawyers for
Shatner and Nimoy worked out a special contract with
the studio that gave both actors equal salaries and benefits. While Shatner had received more money for the first
two *Trek* films, the two stars were now guaranteed equal
salaries. That simple agreement made negotiations with
the studio considerably easier. However, the agreement
also provided equal benefits, and since Nimoy had directed both *Star Trek III* and *Star Trek IV*, Paramount had
no choice but to offer the director's position to William
Shatner in the fifth film.

Shatner immediately divulged to the press that he was
in the director's chair and would provide the storyline for
the next *Trek* film. He hinted that he would take the
Enterprise crew to the ends of the universe to meet God.
Unfortunately, no one had informed Gene Roddenberry,
who insisted he had final director and script approval.
Roddenberry was still pushing his Kennedy assassination

angle and was vehemently opposed to Shatner's *Enterprise*-meets-God idea, despite the fact that he had proposed a similar idea for the first *Trek* movie. Called *The God Thing*, it was about an alien presence that was projecting a Christlike consciousness into the universe. At the time, Roddenberry was told the script was too controversial.

Of course, the basic idea was that of the Nine, the telepathic alien committee guiding the galaxy, that both Roddenberry and Shatner had pursued in the 1970s. Some openly accused Shatner of stealing Roddenberry's ideas, and the behind-the-scenes battles led to bruised egos all around.

"Roddenberry did come down strongly against the story," Shatner admitted, "and set up circumstances that were negative and unfortunate. There's nothing wrong with a good story about the search for the meaning of life that's basic to any great storytelling no matter what form it takes."

Roddenberry was fed up. He told Harve Bennett: "Shatner is your problem now, not mine." Bennett told reporters that Shatner had jumped the gun with his claims for story credit. The producer said only that Shatner had a vision which "may or may not come true." Nonetheless, Shatner continued to push Roddenberry into the background and used the news media to spread the notion that he had full control over the next *Trek* movie.

Actors' contract negotiations and a writers' strike that lasted through most of 1988 delayed the start of production for *Star Trek V*, and Shatner used the additional time to develop two separate story ideas for his *Trek* movie. One of his ideas had the *Enterprise* crew finding God at the center of the universe. His other idea had them finding the fountain of youth, with everyone growing much younger on screen.

Both scenarios were very close to Shatner's heart. He was getting to the point in his life when he felt longing for the exuberance of his lost youth. And he was still looking for "Mr. Tambourine Man," the alien presence he had sensed in his close encounter in the Mojave Desert twenty years earlier. Shatner's idea of God was a superior extra-terrestrial intelligence.

"I hope the end result will reflect certain life experiences that I am going through," the fifty-eight-year-old Shatner admitted to one interviewer, "because as we take these characters through the aging process, there are certain inevitable questions one asks oneself through each passage, each decade that we pass through, roughly. We ask ourselves questions which are universal that don't occur when you're younger. So I hope that the end result will reflect some of these questions that I want the characters to ask."

"I've always been *fascinated* by people who believe that God talks to them and why God would choose that individual over someone else," Shatner told another reporter. "If I were an entity who crashed my UFO in a Florida swamp, I'd want to be talking to the White House, not to an ordinary individual. That's what provoked my idea of *Star Trek* looking for God."

He further teased reporters with promises of break-through special effects—he called them "philosophic effects"—that would have to be seen to be believed. Shatner predicted his movie would be more profound than any previous *Trek* film. That was a big promise, considering that the other films dealt with death, resurrection, eternal life, and the survival of earth and our species. It was true that only meeting God face-to-face could top all that.

"Just the fact that you're no longer twenty-five and that things are no longer in front of you," Shatner told reporters, "just the fact of that weighs on your thinking. Out of that stage of my development, I wanted to make a *Star Trek* movie. I think God is the final frontier, what is beyond death, what is beyond the great barrier."

Facing the Final Frontier

Shatner finally got permission to develop his *Enterprise*-meets-God idea. He immediately brought in novelist Eric Van Lustbader to write the script. Lustbader's bestselling books blend action-suspense and Eastern philosophy with ninja warriors, and Shatner was greatly impressed by his ability to write in a "wonderful, mysterious vein." But when the writer asked for $1 million plus publishing rights, the studio balked and told Shatner to find someone else.

Shatner was extremely upset and threatened to quit the film, but finally, he sat down himself and wrote a four-teen-page summary of the film. He chose two possible subtitles: *An Act of Love* and *The Final Frontier*. Shatner reviewed the script with his close friend Harve Bennett and agreed to use David Loughery as the writer. (Loughery had written the script for *Dreamscape*, a 1984 film about a telepathic dream researcher's efforts to sort out the president's nightmares about nuclear holocaust.)

Production was delayed another six months because Leonard Nimoy was busy directing another film called *The Good Mother* (1988). Shatner was very upset, but when Nimoy suggested that his co-star make the movie without him, Shatner exploded, "You know I can't do *Star Trek* without Spock!"

Another disappointment for Shatner concerned the casting of the role of Sybok in his film. He wanted Sean Connery to play the part of the mystical leader, but the actor had already agreed to do *Indiana Jones and the Last Crusade* (1989).

To complicate matters further, producer Harve Bennett decided he did not want to do any more *Trek* films, to a large degree because he felt that director Leonard Nimoy had bullied him during the filming of *Star Trek IV*.

Nimoy went so far as to ban Bennett from the set at one point. But Bennett also had reservations about the story-line for *Star Trek V*. He felt finding God would be an anticlimactic trick and the only suspense for the audience would be finding out the nature of the trick.

"The problem was to take a talented and wonderful man, Bill Shatner, and try to dissuade him from doing the story he wanted to do," Bennett explained. "I was told Bill was going to direct, and that he had story approval, which I said was a terrible situation, especially once I heard the story he wanted to do. No one is going to find God because that's like finding the fountain of youth—which was, incidentally, Shatner's backup story."

"I was devastated," Shatner recalled. "Harve had been vital to three of the *Star Trek* films, and I needed him as a producer and friend. I set out to talk him into doing it. I wanted this to be a joyous time, I told him. I felt I was too old to face the risk of having idiotic fights with a strange new producer. I knew that with Harve we wouldn't argue, we would *discourse passionately*, for the good of the film. I promised Harve he would enjoy this project more than any other. I wanted it to be the most enjoyable, rewarding moment in my career.

"At first, Harve was adamant about quitting, but I changed his mind. I started talking about how we felt about God and the afterlife, deep questions between friends. And we both concluded that God exists in the heart, and we struck a new rapport and sensitivity toward the idea."

Their rapport did not last very long. When Harve brought Shatner the first-draft script, the two argued for the next two days. Shatner was "devastated" once again but was able to finally "get it back on track." The biggest change came when they did away with Shatner's idea of featuring both God and Satan in the film and substituted an evil alien pretending to be God. It was a compromise that Shatner regrets to this day.

Another major change was made while Shatner was in Nepal filming a public broadcasting special called *Voice of the Planet*. Bennett and Loughery decided to alter the script to give the enraptured Vulcan, Sybok, a more important role. The entire *Enterprise* crew, including Captain Kirk, were now part of Sybok's cult, following the mystic to a land where no one grows old. The peaceful far-off country was called Sha Ka Ree, a play on "Sean Connery," whom they hoped would take the part of Sybok.

But there was no peace at Paramount on the day Shatner returned. Captain Quirk went through the roof. He argued with the two men for most of the day and finally convinced them to restore the original idea of an alien God, although he agreed to keep the concept of Sha Ka Ree as the place where Sybok would find his bliss.

Shatner prepared for his directorial debut in typical fashion: "I got myself into the best shape I've been in for years, with aerobics, strength exercising, and stretching. My body woke me up every day by four-thirty AM no matter what time I got to sleep, and I'd lie in bed for an hour before I got up—dreaming, running the film through my mind, trying to hone a moment so that when I came to the set I knew exactly what the camera should be doing, and what I should be doing, and what the actors should be doing."

On October 10, 1988, the night before location shooting was to begin, Shatner nearly had a collapse. "That night was *very* nervous for me," he confessed. "I've always had a great capacity for denial, and even though I had been preparing for the film for a year and a half, I had blocked out the pressures that directing it was going to entail. I suddenly realized that we're going on location the *next day* and there would be hundreds of people asking me hundreds of questions. The prospect of coming up with hundreds of answers made me awfully nervous."

"I told him to stop talking so fast," said Leonard Nimoy, thinking back on Shatner's first few days. "It's a sign of a first-time director. If you want to find a first-time director, you look for the guy with the sweaty palms and he's hyperventilating and he's talking too fast. Shatner thought that by talking fast it would speed up the schedule, but you couldn't understand a word he was saying."

Somehow, Shatner managed to slow down and start coming up with the right answers. Gradually, he won the respect of his cast mates. His main problems with the film turned out to be financial. The budget for *The Final Frontier* was set at $30 million, and nearly half of that went to the actors. Shatner and Nimoy each received $6 million, and DeForest Kelley got $500,000. The other crew members got $125,000 each, which represented a twenty-five-percent "goodwill" increase over the previous film's fees.

Special effects cost another $7 million. Unfortunately, Industrial Light & Magic, which had done such a great job on the previous *Trek* films, was approached too late to accept work on the fifth film. With only three months left to complete the special effects, the contract was finally awarded to Bran Ferren and Associates of New York, who had to put in overtime to meet the deadline.

Location shooting also proved much more expensive than anticipated. The Paradise City set was constructed from scratch on Owens Lake, a dry lakebed near Ridgecrest in the Mojave Desert. Construction took over a month and cost $500,000. A Teamsters' Union strike was called a few days before location shooting was to begin and nonunion drivers had to be hired. One of the camera trucks was blown up on the lot, and tensions were so high that a police escort was necessary to get the film crew out of the studio in the middle of the night.

Other unplanned expenses plagued the film, including the theft of over $60,000 worth of costumes from an unmarked trailer. *The Final Frontier* ended up going $3 million over budget. The project would have certainly been a complete disaster had it not been for Shatner's indomitable willpower.

"Energy is something I believe in," he said at the time, "and it exists at different levels. When I get up in the morning, I hit it running, and that's how I approached directing. I energized myself and dragged others along by force of will. I wanted to make the others run at the same pace. I wanted to make things happen quickly. The waste of time is a tragedy, because the older we become, the less time we have. Each moment becomes vitally important.

"Every scene in a film has what I call theatrical energy that is stronger and faster than real life's energy. The motion picture camera derives that energy from within a scene, and the scene thrusts and drives the movie, a certain theatrical energy that rivets you and keeps you watching."

"This is a Shatner film," Leonard Nimoy commented during filming, "which obviously means there has been more running and jumping than in all the previous *Star Trek* films put together. All the other films have been relatively contained, but in this, we're riding horses, climbing mountains, and stunt flying on wires and rigs."

However, Shatner's boundless energy and relentless drive were not always appreciated by his co-workers. To complicate matters further, ever since his close encounter with a UFO, something about working in the dry heat of the Mojave Desert really bothered Shatner.

Once, while directing a scene, he got so worked up, he stumbled over a large rock and fell to the ground. The force of the fall flung his hairpiece across the set, and as the mortified director got back to his feet, a group of extras in the scene started laughing out loud. Shatner fired them all on the spot, with no further discussion.

Not long afterward, the entire crew almost walked off the job during a day of desert shooting that recorded Sybok's triumphant march through the desert. In the 110-degree heat near Cuddeback, just northeast of where his UFO encounter had taken place, Shatner cracked again. Without provocation, the director started attacking and berating everyone around him. He screamed at the producer, insulted the head electrician in front of his crew, told the cinematographer that he did not know how to do his job, and nearly drove everyone else crazy. Just as things were about to explode, executive producer Ralph Winter and Leonard Nimoy took Shatner aside and managed to calm him down. By the next day, he seemed fine.

There were also some problems during the initial editing of the film. Shatner was very impatient with traditional cutting-room methods and wanted to experiment from scratch. Some of the editors felt insulted and wanted to quit, but a few brave ones simply told the pushy director that his ideas would just not work. The crew had been doing this for thirty years and knew what worked on the big screen.

"During the first few weeks of filming," said Harve Bennett, who witnessed some of the cutting-room debates, "Bill shot himself in the foot time after time. It's a different game being in front of the camera than behind it, and directing multiple episodes of *T. J. Hooker* just did not prepare Bill Shatner for the wide screen's demands. It took Bill time to graduate from an actor and television mentality to a director and motion picture mentality. A year of verbalizing things to him did not have the same impact of the first few days of working on the *Star Trek V* film cut together. It's funny how first-time directors try to be pioneers in the craft."

When asked what he thought of Bennett's criticisms, Shatner agreed, blaming the whole experience on his "youth" as a director. Shatner likened himself to a youthful person who knows no boundaries, trying to make the camera do things it was not supposed to do.

"There's lots of problems acting and directing," Shatner summarized. "There's lots of problems in just acting in a picture and lots of problems in just directing as well. Combined, there's lots and lots of problems. But none that I foresee as insurmountable in that I have a wonderful backup team and my main man, Harve Bennett, whom I rely on implicitly, is always there."

Shatner also admitted to upsetting a lot of people on the set and being aware that some "lesser" members of the cast did not enjoy making the film with him. But one potentially mutinous problem involving the Big Three arose with some early scenes in the script.

Both Leonard Nimoy and DeForest Kelley refused to allow their characters to betray Kirk and follow Sybok, as described in the original script. Shatner really wanted a falling-out to occur among the Big Three. It would have given his own character an independence he had always yearned for and added fresh dramatic depth to his film.

Yet despite days of begging, arguing and histrionics, Nimoy and Kelley refused to compromise their characters. Nimoy had already seen Spock's screen time cut in half and was not about to budge. Shatner was forced to rewrite the script and preserve the triumvirate of friendship that had become the basis of *Star Trek*'s humanity. In order to explain Spock's kindness to Sybok in earlier scenes, it was decided to make Sybok Spock's half-brother.

In the film, Sybok is played by Laurence Luckinbill, who was a regular in *The Blue and the Gray* and *The A Team*. In *Star Trek V*, his character wants to hijack the *Enterprise* to travel beyond the Great Barrier at the center of the universe and meet face to face with God. The charismatic leader launches an attack on the planet Nimbus III in order to lure the *Enterprise* into a trap. At the same time, the Klingons have also decided to take on the *Enterprise*.

Meanwhile, Kirk, Spock, and McCoy are enjoying some quality time together camping out in Yosemite Park. Their holiday is interrupted when they are ordered to take the *Enterprise* to Nimbus III to try to free the hostages taken by Sybok. But Sybok has the uncanny ability to free people's souls by looking into their eyes and saying: "Each of us has a secret pain. Share yours with me and gain strength from the sharing." He uses his hypnotic talent to subvert the *Enterprise* crew and take over the ship. Even Spock cannot fight against him, when Sybok reveals that they are actually half-brothers.

With the Klingons in hot pursuit, Sybok hijacks the *Enterprise* and takes it to the ends of the universe, to an immense cluster of stars known as the Great Barrier. Crossing the final barrier, they arrive at a magnificent planet which is home to a powerful force that takes on many godlike forms.

But it turns out God is really an alien life form that wants to spread its power throughout the universe by using the starship. Kirk's impudent question, "Excuse me, what does God need with a spaceship?" exposes the ruse and enrages the powerful creature, who hits the captain with a bolt of lightning. Sybok realizes God is not what it appears to be and sacrifices himself in a futile attack on the creature. Meanwhile, Kirk orders a photon torpedo hit, which has no effect.

Just as the landing party begins transporting off the planet, the Klingon battle cruiser attacks the *Enterprise,* leaving Kirk stranded on the surface. The ruthless alien creature finally corners Kirk on a jagged mountaintop and closes in for the kill. Just in the nick of time, Spock shows up in the commandeered Klingon vessel and saves his captain's life once again.

As it became obvious the film was running over budget, Paramount told Shatner he would have to speed up production and cut some scenes to save money. His initial reaction was anger at being put in such a position. Then he realized this was his only opportunity to make a big-budget movie and that he could fail at it.

"I started to sweat," he confessed. "When an actor was five minutes late getting to the set from the makeup trailer, my stomach would start turning. I resolved in my own mind that I would not get overwhelmed by the filmmaking process and just do the best possible job I could."

Nearly $350,000 was saved simply by eliminating one dramatic camera shot. It was planned to have the camera focus on Kirk rock climbing, then pull back until he became a mere speck on the sheer cliff. The camera work would have required another full day on location in Yosemite National Park. Shatner was also forced to cut a river of fire scene, eliminate a host of angels, and gargoyles, and slash the number of extras in the Paradise City scenes, making the shots much less impressive.

Another $300,000 was saved by cutting a final scene involving six rockmen monsters who were to emerge from the barren mountainside and chase the landing party. Most of the cost was in making the six rockmen costumes, so only one rockman ended up in the final cut.

In all fairness, those missing scenes would have added badly needed continuity and visual effects to the film. Shatner planned to have the landing party descend into the equivalent of hell, after the angels of God turn into terrifying gargoyles that chase them into a chasm of hellfire. Scotty leaves Kirk stranded on the surface when he mistakenly beams up one of the gargoyle monsters. To escape, Kirk climbs up the side of a mountain, but the monsters multiply until their numbers become legion. Those interesting scenes were all cut to save money, and the studio threatened to cut even more scenes, unless the director/writer/actor caught up on his production schedule.

"I felt this grand, epic movie I had envisioned had suddenly been reduced to an ordinary film," Shatner said. "It took me a while to realize that the movie in my head would not be the movie on the screen. It was my first big lesson as a director."

After the final scene was filmed, Shatner broke down and cried. He said that he cried out of relief that it was finished and sadness that such a wonderful experience was over.

"I thought the film was flawed," he confessed later, "and that I hadn't managed my resources as well as I could have. And I didn't get the help in managing my resources that I could have! We experimented and I had to learn a great deal, not only about film but about the politics of film on that picture."

Star Trek V: The Final Frontier became the highest-grossing film in history for one short weekend in June 1989. Then, *Batman* and *Indiana Jones and the Last Crusade* premiered. Both films ate into the profits of *The Final Frontier*. In fact, box-office receipts for *Batman* were five times those of Shatner's film. Among respondents to the survey for this book, the film tied with *Star Trek: The Motion Picture* as the least liked of all the *Trek* movies.

The total box office for *Star Trek V* was only $52 million, down about 18 percent compared to the first three movies and 50 percent compared to *Star Trek IV*. Shatner settled on a flat fee of $1 million for directing and another $1 million fee with percentages for acting, but his percentages never kicked in, since the movie did not earn sufficient box office receipts.

Reviewers did not forget Shatner's grandiose predictions for his film. *"Star Trek V* is absolutely baroque," wrote Caryn James in the *New York Times,* "borrowing snatches of *Mad Max, Star Wars, The Greatest Story Ever Told, 2001,* and *The Wizard of Oz* while diffusely chasing after a plot best described as 'Indiana Jones Finds a Field of Dreams in Space.' The film's references are not auteurist allusions to the cinema—*Star Trek* has not drifted that far from its pulpy origins—but part of an unwieldy, misguided attempt to make this the biggest, grandest *Star Trek* yet."

But that same reviewer gave the novice director some unexpected credit: "Shatner's direction is smooth and sharply focused. He has a sure feel for keeping *Star Trek* just this side of camp, and for the slightly tacky, artificial look that lets us know this is all a game."

Not all the critics agreed with that assessment. "With Shatner in command behind the camera as well as in front of it," wrote Brian Johnson in *Maclean's*, "*Star Trek* has finally run aground."

Other critics, sensing the director's mid-life crisis, were taken aback by the mood of the picture. "For all its intergalactic cliff-hanging," noted Kevin Thomas in the *Los Angeles Times*, "*Star Trek V* is a mellow experience, a contemplation of life's possibilities and rewards in maturity, tinged with an awareness of mortality." *Time* agreed: "The atmosphere on this voyage is a lot like late night at an Elks' smoker, all bleary sentimentality and nostalgia for the past. Maybe we will never find God, Kirk suggests at the end, but, by golly, male bonding is a swell substitute."

Shatner had no illusions about his film. He felt that it was full of the major joys and major sorrows of anything he had ever done.

"I see *Star Trek V* as a failed but glorious attempt to make a picture full of character growth and a deep philosophical base," he wrote in his memoirs, "delving into man's universal desire to believe. I really wanted to use *Star Trek* as a means to tell a story that would've taken these beloved characters into waters they'd never before tested, simultaneously making them question their own beliefs and ultimately their faith in one another. Obviously, it didn't come out as I'd hoped . . . I ultimately came away feeling like the big brass ring had somehow eluded my grasp."

However, poor box-office receipts and lukewarm reviews did not deter old Toughy. He still wanted to be a Hollywood director. He soon announced plans to direct a sequel to *The Kingdom of the Spiders*, the 1977 killer-tarantula movie in which he had starred. Financial backing could not be found, however, and the sequel never made it to the screen. But Shatner has never given up on his ambition to be a film director. After all, he had been trying to take on the responsibilities of both actor and director ever since he'd entered the entertainment industry.

"I love the idea of having a dream, bringing it to fruition, and putting it on the screen," he told Joan Rivers in 1991. "Now, if that means that I have to act in it, I will. I still think directing is the best job in entertainment."

Mutiny!

On December 28, 1988, near the end of filming for *Star Trek V*, Shatner arranged for the entire cast to pose for publicity photos on the $250,000 *Enterprise* bridge set. Amazingly, it was the first time they had ever gathered together on the bridge off screen. The purpose: to toast the success of his film and provide at least a facade of one big happy family for photographers.

In truth, behind the smiles were a lot of hurt feelings. The supporting cast, the ever-loyal bridge crew of the *Enterprise,* were getting fed up with Shatner's self-centered antics. They recalled that after Shatner had found out he was slated to direct the fifth movie, he was almost hoping that Nimoy's *Star Trek IV* would fail. If that happened, Shatner would appear to be the savior of the film series. He was even planning to slash costs by dumping all the characters but Kirk and Spock.

When *Star Trek IV* started breaking box-office records, Shatner was quick to announce that all the classic cast members would have "special moments" in his film. However, Shatner's grasp of their characters was flawed. Most of the supporting cast felt they were being mocked in *Star Trek V*. Scenes depicting Sulu and Chekov getting lost, Scotty's awkward professing he'd been attracted to Uhura after two decades of working together, Uhura dancing on a hilltop to provide a distraction, and cheap laughs (such as Scotty hitting his head after boasting how well he knew the ship), did not sit well with the actors.

"There is really only one person on the show that nobody can stand," was James Doohan's assessment. "He tried to do too much in *Star Trek V,* and look what happened—it wasn't a good story and it wasn't a good movie. He can't even act. He doesn't act: he makes faces. He'll wrinkle his nose like a rabbit and that's supposed to mean, 'Oh look, I'm about to cry.'

"*Star Trek V* doesn't have enough of all the characters. We all have what are called 'cheap shots.' The fans are starting to demand more of all the characters. They just absolutely adore all the banter that goes back and forth. Forget this ego stuff and let's get down to telling a story."

"Bill has a big, fat head," Doohan elaborated later. "To me, Bill is selling Paramount a bill of goods which is rotten. I don't know why. He's got power somewhere. He shouldn't have it. No one should have it if they don't have the goods. One of Bill's problems is that Bill thinks of Bill, whereas Leonard thinks of the show first and thinks of himself second.

"Bill doesn't like anyone to do good acting around him. I can remember DeForest Kelley complaining about that when we were doing the series. The scripts would come in with Kelley having major parts and somebody talked them out of it. And there were parts where I was favored during the second year that were all cut out. I'd end up with six lines. Kelley is very diplomatic and won't say anything bad about Bill, but he snickers behind his back."

"Shatner was a lot better to work with as a director than he was as an actor," admitted Nichelle Nichols, "but *Star Trek V* wasn't a good story. You go in search of God, and if you don't find yourself, what the hell are you going to find? What they came up with was a bit of a sham, a cop-out. If you won't make a statement on who or what God is, then why do it?"

"I think Shatner's difficult," Walter Koenig added. "He's the epitome of the star in many negative ways. He's totally preoccupied with himself and his career and his work on the show. I want it understood that I respond to the working relationship, not the man. He can be congenial and enormously seductive. It's very difficult to dislike him if he decides he wants you to. He has incredible charm. In fact, I have to keep slapping myself!"

"From the beginning," Koenig summarized, "Bill believed the credits—that there were three actors above the title and the rest of us below. The rest of us were not significant, not only as actors, but as people."

Other cast members and production crew, who wish not to be identified, have agreed with Doohan's and Koenig's assessment of Shatner. Most chalk it up to Shatner's "oppressive ego." Few believe that the superstar is out to hurt anyone deliberately. In fact, Shatner seems genuinely puzzled at the criticism.

"I don't understand that," he told a reporter in early 1992. "I'm not even aware of it, quite frankly. Occasionally I'll hear something and it bewilders me because I have no trouble with them—nothing certainly bad, nothing particularly good, either. We have done our job and gone on, and I have never had bad words with anyone. I don't know what vitriol is spilling out."

In the epilogue to *Star Trek Memories,* Shatner reports being genuinely surprised at the negative feelings he uncovered while interviewing the cast for his book. Nichelle Nichols and Walter Koenig both revealed their harsh feelings to him. A polite George Takei found it difficult to confront his former captain, while James Doohan refused even to meet with him, fearing things would get out of hand and Shatner would distort his comments. Shatner wrote an open invitation for Doohan to contact him and devoted an entire epilogue to dealing with personal criticism from the other cast members. An apparently mystified Shatner implied he always thought the cast was one big happy family.

"I was shocked that Bill thought we were a big happy family," Nichelle Nichols confessed to me. "I mean, we all knew we were one big happy family—but it didn't include Bill. He distanced himself from us, whether it was deliberate or just from a lack of concern. He just didn't know what he was doing. Maybe he didn't realize that he was hurting anybody.

"I always put on a great face to the public, and really, ninety-nine percent of the things that went on were wonderful. But like all families, we had our problems and showed a united front. I used to disagree and have battles royal with Jimmy Doohan about saying things against Shatner. And I think I might have been the cause of my friend Walter Koenig's holding back. I told him it just did no good. One day he said to me: 'You know, you're right, Nichelle.' Really, it serves you no good to harp about something. If it hurts you that bad, then sue the bastard. Do something about it. Otherwise, shut up."

Walter Koenig seems to have accepted Nichelle's advice. Now, when reporters ask him how it was to work with Shatner, he usually responds with something like: "I really don't have a lot to say about Bill."

Nichelle believes the problems between Shatner and the cast go back to the early days of the series: "Initially, *Star Trek* the series and *Star Trek* the films were designed for an *ensemble* of stars who would each be given equal time," she had said years earlier. "But at some point, the decision was made to separate Bill and Leonard from the rest of us. And I'm not happy with that situation. I don't mind Bill and Leonard being the stars. But in light of the fact that we were totally typecast through *Star Trek*, I felt the least they could have done was not totally defuse our characters."

"What Gene had said he wished to do was periodically highlight each person," Nichelle explained to me, "so that as the show went on, you got to know more and more about the person. There would be one episode that featured Uhura and Christine, or Uhura and Scotty. And then, as you go along, it would *truly* be an ensemble piece.

You would still have the *Star Trek* show with the triumvirate, but the other people would be strong, too. That is not what happened.

"Bill Shatner helped keep the bridge crew in their place, not letting the other actors realize their characters. He had a *lot* of control. I *do* know that nothing ever got done without his approval. I *do* know that during shooting, suddenly Bill would stop, and we couldn't get any further. Then, the producers would meet with him, and we would come back and they would go on to something else. When you came to do that scene again, you'd find your part was cut. It got so that we—the cast—knew what to expect the moment he stopped, so we would just go sit down somewhere. If the director wouldn't agree with him, then we simply could not get that scene done until Bill was satisfied. Finally, everyone just threw up their hands and said something like: 'Well, this is the star of the show. Just do it. We only got six days to get this!' That's essentially the way it went on."

But the final straw for Nichelle came just after the publication of Shatner's memoirs, when she received an invitation to a Thanksgiving get-together at Shatner's beach house in Malibu. She accepted the once-in-a-lifetime offer, thinking it was a cast party designed to smooth some ruffled feathers. Shatner's secretary called Nichelle four or five times to confirm she was still coming. In the meantime, Shatner was on TV talk shows denying there was any real tension between him and the cast and using Nichelle's dinner date as an example of how well they all got along.

When Nichelle arrived at the beach house on Thanksgiving Day, she was surprised to find no one else from *Star Trek*. Then, when she asked Shatner why the whole world knew she was coming to dinner, he replied it was "time to put this fucking thing to rest."

Nichelle was "stunned and then hurt" at being used to foster the appearance of friendship for the press. At the end of her own book, *Beyond Uhura,* she writes: "As for Bill personally, I say, with some regret and much hurt, 'This communication channel is now closed. Uhura out.' "

Majel Barrett Roddenberry, who played Nurse Chapel in the television series, has also closed her communication channel. Gene Roddenberry's widow is incensed at the way Shatner portrayed her husband in his memoirs. Like several other ex-colleagues of Shatner's, she believes he exaggerated his own creative input.

"The only thing that surprises me about Bill's book," Majel said, "is that he managed to get it in the nonfiction category!"

George Takei summed up the views of the cast when he told an interviewer for *USA Today:* "Shatner is victimized by his ego. What he essentially did was build this invisible wall—and that's sad, to see someone do that to themselves."

Shatner canceled some interviews rather than field questions about the mutiny on the *Enterprise.* Finally, he could ignore the reporters' queries no longer. During a November 1994 appearance on the *Tonight Show,* host Jay Leno asked Shatner what he thought about all the negative comments by former cast members.

"They love me," Shatner replied. "They just don't know any better. They love me. A couple of them, they're a little bit . . . , but they love me. It's just family squabbling."

"But you have a good relationship with them, then," asked Leno.

"Everybody *loves* me," Shatner repeated.

"So, any minute," said Leno, "one of them could walk out and kiss you."

"Well, I doubt that," said Shatner.

Then, from behind the curtain, Walter Koenig walked on stage, shook Shatner's hand, then kissed him firmly on the mouth.

"I love you, you son-of-a-bitch," shouted an obviously touched Shatner during their embrace.

But Koenig pulled away and turned toward the audience: "Don't you love him? Don't you *just love him?*"

Koenig had not returned Shatner's "I love you." Instead, he slapped Shatner three times in the face. The last blow was quite hard and surprised Shatner. Fortunately, Koenig was off the stage before Shatner could do anything but point a finger after him.

"I love Walter," countered an embarrassed Shatner. "He's a great guy, and he told me he loved me [he didn't] and then he hit me a smack on the face! That was incredible. And the movie which he was *in . . .*" Shatner seemed to be implying that the fact Koenig was in the latest *Star Trek* movie was further proof of their reconciliation.

That same month, when asked what he thought of books by former members of the *Trek* cast, Shatner said sarcastically: "Why, I'm having a big picnic and barbecue for all of them." Then, the angry captain declined to comment further, saying he did not want to talk about the artistic endeavors of others.

The Undiscovered Commodity

After the poor performance of *Star Trek V,* Shatner was convinced that his directorial debut represented the last of the *Star Trek* films. Paramount executives had always based their decision on whether to make another *Trek* film on the financial performance of the previous film in the series. Producer Ralph Winter and others had tried unsuccessfully to get the studio to shoot multiple films at once, as filmmakers did with the *Superman* films. The method would have been less costly and allowed more continuity between films.

Yet despite the lackluster performance of *The Final Frontier,* the silver (twenty-fifth) anniversary of the *Star Trek* television series gave Paramount marketing heads one last chance to cash in on the *Trek* phenomenon. They decided to make one more film dedicated to the original series.

Harve Bennett, who had produced *Star Trek III*, *Star Trek IV*, and *Star Trek V*, proposed making the next film a prequel, titled *Starfleet Academy*, which would introduce new characters and look at the early lives of the bridge crew. Kirk is back on his father's Iowa farm, spending his spare time rolling in the hay with young ladies, while McCoy is spending his youth tending to his terminally ill father. Spock has left Vulcan against the wishes of his father. They all meet up at Starfleet Academy.

Bennett's idea met stiff opposition from Shatner, Roddenberry, and *Star Trek* fans in general. Although Paramount executives were all for the prequel, Martin Davis, the CEO of the studio's parent company, Gulf + Western, squashed the idea. Although he was offered $1.5 million to do *Star Trek VI*, a disheartened Bennett withdrew from the project entirely. Ralph Winter and Steven Charles Jaffe took his place as co-producers.

"I certainly felt the sting of *Star Trek V* not doing very well," Winter acknowledged. "So the approach we took from the beginning was to distance ourselves from the last film's poor performance. After [*Star Trek*] *V*, many people felt that this picture shouldn't even be made. But people close to *Star Trek* felt it *had* to be. Some cast members were initially skeptical about another movie, but as we went along, everyone got on board."

Leonard Nimoy declined an offer to direct the film, although he served as executive producer and came up with the final story idea of "the Berlin Wall comes down in outer space." Nicholas Meyer, who had directed the popular *Star Trek II: The Wrath of Khan*, was chosen to direct the sixth picture. The script would be written by Meyer and his longtime associate Denny Martin Flinn.

However, a budgetary dispute between Meyer and the studio actually canceled the whole project in January

1991. Paramount had lost over $400 million on other projects since 1988 and wanted to reduce the *Star Trek VI* budget from $30 million to $25 million to save cash. Meyer refused to go along. Luckily, a change in studio management raised the budget to $28 million and *Star Trek VI* once again breathed life.

Jack Palance was offered the part of the Klingon chancellor, but he wanted too much money. The role went to David Warner, who had worked with Nicholas Meyer as Jack the Ripper in *Time after Time* (1979). Shatner's youngest daughter, Melanie, played the role of assistant navigator.

Christopher Plummer signed on as General Chang, the Klingon Chief of Staff. The actor was born in Montreal about the same time as Shatner, and the two are good friends. Both have Shakespearean backgrounds, and they appeared at the Stratford Festival together. In fact, it was Christopher Plummer whom Shatner had replaced in his own career-making breakthrough in *Henry V*.

Once again, the producers approached Kirstie Alley, now playing Rebecca in television's *Cheers,* about reprising her role as Lieutenant Saavik. Once again, she asked a million-dollar fee to work with Shatner. In response, Paramount dropped that character from the script, and Kim Cattrall signed on to play the role of the traitorous Vulcan, Valeris.

Cattrall, who played the libido-driven cheerleader coach in *Porky's* (1982), quickly became the center of attention between Shatner and Nimoy. But she had worked with Shatner in a 1978 miniseries (*The Bastard*) and knew what he was like, so she started developing a "real affinity" for Leonard. The two spent a good deal of time together trying to develop the very special relationship between their characters. The result was the groundbreaking scene in which Spock performs a mindmeld with Valeris. It is an extremely erotic scene and depicts a "mental rape" of the Vulcan woman. Cattrall admits that because of the chemistry between them, the scene took on a life of its own. But for some reason, Cattrall did not feel much chemistry with William Shatner.

"He was a gentleman with me, and it doesn't matter how I feel about him personally," she said. "I never had any problems with him or his outcries. I found him respectful. He runs his lines a lot, over and over and over again, which is kind of annoying. But everyone has their own way of working."

As filming neared completion, the adventuresome Cattrall posed nude (except for her pointed Vulcan ears) on the empty bridge set of the *Enterprise* while a photographer clicked away several rolls of sultry stills. She reclined *au naturel* over Captain Kirk's command chair and then assumed a variety of seductive positions at other locations on the helm. When she showed the pictures to Leonard Nimoy, the enraged executive producer ripped up the prints and destroyed the negatives, fearing the photos might somehow become public.

As if sexual tension on the set were not high enough, international supermodel Iman joined the cast as the shape-shifting alien, Martia. The beauty's film credits include *Out of Africa* (1985), *No Way Out* (1987), *House Party 2* (1991), and *L.A. Story* (1991). In one of the film's most dramatic effects, called "morfing" by ILM technicians, her chameleon character melts and becomes Captain Kirk in mid-sentence.

Shatner wasted no time staking his claim on the alluring woman. In response to rumors that the two had "morfed" together in real life, Iman would only comment that her leading man possessed an "uncontrollable" passion for women.

Star Trek VI: The Undiscovered Country began filming April 16, 1991, under extremely tight security. Shatner insisted it would be his last *Trek* film, and everyone assumed it would be the last of the series. Rumors were rampant that Kirk would be killed off in a final blaze of glory, or that

Spock would fall uncontrollably in love with a sexy alien.

Surprisingly, the film had a much more mundane plot than Kirk's death or a Spock love affair. The story mirrored political changes taking place in the contemporary world, specifically, the fall of Communism.

The Klingon Empire is doomed after the fiery destruction of one of its moons. Forced to focus on problems at home, the Klingon leaders seek a lasting peace with the Federation. At the request of the Klingon leader, Admiral Kirk is asked to lead the peace delegation. "We have an old Vulcan proverb," Spock quips. "Only Nixon could have gone to China."

Christopher Plummer's character has conspired with a Starfleet admiral to block the peace initiative by assassinating the Klingon High Chancellor. All the circumstantial evidence points to Kirk and McCoy, and a Klingon tribunal sentences them to life at hard labor on a frozen planet.

They finally escape with Spock's help and make it to the peace conference just in time to meet up with a Klingon Bird of Prey. In the nick of time, Captain Sulu arrives to assist in the destruction of the Klingon vessel. That allows the renegade band to beam down to the planet and foil another assassination attempt—this time on the Federation leader.

Sulu's integral part in *Star Trek VI* was a gratifying reward for actor George Takei. He looked forward to one scene in particular, in which Captain Kirk acknowledges Sulu's promotion to captain. However, Shatner read his lines with such perfunctory dismissal and lack of feeling that Takei was shocked. He approached Shatner and told him what an important moment it was to his character, pleading with Shatner to at least look him in the eye when he spoke the lines. "Of course, George," was Shatner's reply. But in the final take, Kirk never looked at Sulu and spoke with offhanded coldness. The scene had to be cut from the film.

Fortunately, most of Kirk's negative feelings were directed toward Klingons in *Star Trek VI*. In fact, the dichotomy between Kirk's personal hatred of the Klingons and the possibility for galactic peace became the dominant theme of the movie. Composer Cliff Eidelman tried to capture Kirk's dilemma in his score for the film.

But Kirk was not the only one to hate the Federation's archenemies. Gene Roddenberry was extremely upset over the Klingons' portrayal as civilized good guys in the film. He felt the Federation characters came off in a bad light.

Nichelle Nichols would simply not allow her character to be seen as less enlightened than a Klingon. In a scene where the bridge crew is searching for some good things to say about the Klingons, she refused to speak the line: "Yeah, but would you want your daughter to marry one?"

The supporting cast suffered enough when Paramount decided to save money by cutting the first fifteen pages in the original script. The opening scene was to show a retired Admiral Kirk making love to Carol Marcus, his paramour from *Star Trek II*, with whom he has now reconciled. Their lovemaking is interrupted by a mysterious messenger with a glowing hand. He informs Kirk he has been summoned back to duty.

The following scenes show Kirk and his alien envoy traveling through San Francisco, rounding up the classic crew for one last mission. He finds Chekov at a social club, playing a tedious game of chess with a Betazoid alien. Professor Montgomery Scott is found lecturing a group of college students about the inner workings of the Klingon Bird of Prey. Uhura is hosting a call-in radio show, fielding questions from a female colonist on Mars who is complaining about how much weight she has gained.

None of the former crew members has any problem being whisked away from his or her boring life back to the

Enterprise, and certainly none of the actors who portrayed them would have given up the chance to expand his or her character on screen. Writer Denny Martin Flinn, who originally planned separate entrances for the entire cast, fought hard to keep the scenes in place. But Paramount threatened to halt production unless $1 million was cut from the budget, and something had to be sacrificed.

While Shatner admitted to being relieved he was out of the director's chair in *Star Trek VI,* he found it very hard to give up control. On several occasions, Shatner stalked off the set, after he and director Nicholas Meyer locked horns over the direction of the film. After production was over, Shatner revealed his strategy for handling Meyer.

"Nick is a very funny, sardonic, ironic human being," Shatner said. "He's very loving and very nervous! He also has a very strong point of view. He's very frank about what he likes or doesn't like. But he's a pussycat to work with—you just have to pet him the *wrong* way!"

Of course, Meyer had his own way of manipulating the actors. During the banquet scene in *Star Trek VI,* everyone was asked to eat blue-painted squid, but nobody even wanted to touch it. He offered the actors twenty dollars for every mouthful. Shatner made a quick eighty dollars, though he got sick afterward and "had the blues for days."

Even after the film was completed, Shatner kept insisting on changes. In the closing scenes on the bridge, Shatner felt his derrière was a little too wide-beam to be sexy, so he insisted that it be air-brushed to suitable proportions. It is said that the frame-by-frame butt-tightening was done at great expense to the studio.

"I feel a sense of great relief in that I don't have any responsibilities other than knowing my lines and hitting my marks," he confessed to one reporter, "and a fear and trepidation that I'm not in control. Somebody *else* has got the controls. It's like being a driver in a car for so long and then you sit down in the passenger seat and somebody else is driving."

In one improbable twist of the script, Shatner managed to insert dual roles for himself. By this time, his propensity to play dual roles had become legend. In fact, cast members joked for years about his playing *all* the roles if he could. In this case, he wrestles a mirror-image of himself after the shape-shifter Martia takes on his form. His alter ego quips: "Bet you've always wanted to do this!"

Still, it is Shatner's indomitable presence that gives *Star Trek VI* its unique flavor. Film reviewer John Boonstra observed: "Shatner, looking a full decade younger than his sixty years, rips into this frolic with a smug twinkle that can't help looking like center-cut hambone, but what the hell—his overbearing, world-beating James Tiberius Kirk is surely what separates First Trek from cooler, cannier Next Trek."

By borrowing sets from the TV series *The Next Generation, Star Trek VI* kept within its $26 million budget and became one of the twenty-five top-grossing films of 1991. Box office receipts were nearly $150 million.

Gene Roddenberry suffered two strokes in 1991 and was confined to a wheelchair. Just two days before his death in October of that year, he previewed the movie and was very upset with some of the more political scenes. He felt that the militaristic thinking displayed by Federation characters was more in tune with our own century's problems than any developments that would take place four hundred years in the future. Although he indicated his approval of most of the footage, he immediately contacted his lawyer to request that at least fifteen minutes of the film be removed. Despite the fact that the film was dedicated to Gene Roddenberry's memory, his last wishes were ignored and it was released as screened.

Theatergoers and critics apparently agreed with the producers' decision to leave the film intact. One exit survey reported that nine out of ten people rated the film "outstanding" or "above average." Six out of ten said they would see it again. The film earned a respectable $60 million, about 20 percent above *The Final Frontier* but nearly 70 percent below the average earnings of *Star Trek II*, *Star Trek III*, and *Star Trek IV*. Our own survey of Trekkers showed that they considered *The Undiscovered Country* a distant third in the series, behind *The Wrath of Khan* and *The Voyage Home*.

"Hardcore Trekkies will get their rockets off with *Star Trek VI*" piqued *People* magazine, while Susan Rosini noted in *USA Today:* "You don't have to be a Trekkie to savor this timely plot. Even though Scotty looks like he's hiding a meteor under his shirt, Kirk looks like a squirrel is napping on his head, and Spock's ears aren't quite as perky, this is quite a suitable send-off."

Indeed, most critics agreed with the *Chicago Tribune*, which called the film "an unassuming and affectionate farewell." Everyone believed that the crew of the classic *Star Trek* series had finally retired. The last entry in the ship's log made it clear that Admiral Kirk had seen his last voyage and the "next generation" was waiting in the wings to take over:

> This ship and her history will shortly become the care of a new generation. To them and their posterity will we commit our future. They will continue the voyages we have begun and journey to all the undiscovered countries, boldly going where no man, where no *one*, has gone before.
>
> —James T. Kirk.

(Executive producer Leonard Nimoy had the reference to the "new generation" replaced with "new crew" in the final version of the film. He was upset with Michael Dorn, who had declared in an interview that *Star Trek VII* would definitely feature *Next Generation* cast.)

At the well-planned wrap party, Captain Quirk was

also a little perturbed. While everyone was gathering for a final photograph of the entire cast, Shatner realized George Takei was missing.

"We were all hanging around, waiting for the day to end," Shatner recalled, "but George Takei forgot and went home. So, instead of being loving and friendly, we were rather irked. Instead of being magical and sentimental, as the moment required, the ending was filled with, 'For goodness' sake, how long is it going to take him to get back?!' "

You're Dead, Jim!

But within just a few weeks of the release of *Star Trek VI*, Shatner began pitching his own idea for a possible *Star Trek VII* to Paramount chairman Brandon Tartikoff. Shatner's storyline centered on a passionate romance between an aging Kirk and an irresistible young woman. There would also be a falling out between Kirk and Spock in which they become mortal enemies. Shatner even invoked the equal-benefits clause in his contract to be allowed to direct the film. While the Kirk-centered script might have proved psychologically soothing for William Shatner, the studio chief did not think people would pay to see it, nor did the studio want Shatner to direct it.

Instead, Paramount decided to use the next film to introduce *The Next Generation* characters to the big screen. The whole idea of a new generation of *Trek* actors had never sat too well with any of the original cast members. In my private conversations with them, most agreed that the new series lacked the character development of the original series. Shatner, however, felt genuinely threatened by *The Next Generation*.

When a hapless Wil Wheaton, who played ensign Wesley Crusher in the new series, walked onto the *Star Trek V* movie set to pay his respects to the first captain of the

Enterprise, the lad encountered an icy Captain Quirk. When Wheaton mentioned that he had a position on the bridge of the new *Enterprise,* Shatner told him that he would never allow "a child" on *his* bridge. "If this were my bridge and my ship," he shouted at the embarrassed actor, "you wouldn't be allowed on." Wheaton did a prompt about-face and exited the sound stage without looking back. The upset lad informed Gene Roddenberry about the incident. He asked Harve Bennett to talk to Shatner, who eventually apologized to Wheaton.

"I've never liked the idea of the new television show," Shatner admitted. "I think it's a dangerous thing to call something *Star Trek* which, when asked, 'What is *Star Trek?'* and you enumerate the various things that are *Star Trek,* none of the things you enumerate apply to that particular series. What a shame it would be if they fail."

Of course, one of the things not enumerated in the new series was the name of William Shatner. He always felt that the name *Star Trek* should apply only to the original series and the original characters. Shatner vowed with other cast members to stay away from *The Next Generation* and was flabbergasted when he heard that Leonard Nimoy and James Doohan were contemplating appearing on the show.

Shatner was especially concerned over questions about who made the better *Enterprise* commander, Captain Kirk or Captain Picard, played by Patrick Stewart. (In the survey for this book, 55 percent preferred Kirk over Picard.) For many years, he refused to acknowledge Stewart, saying things like, "Stewart is not the captain, he's just a wonderful actor." One of the conditions of Shatner's appearing in *Star Trek VII* was that he receive top billing over Patrick Stewart. Shatner gave his reasons why Kirk was superior in a televised interview in December 1991.

"Kirk was the better captain," said Shatner, "because he was more three dimensional. He was a wonderful leader—not only an intelligent [man] but an emotional man. He was a passionate man, and he felt for his troops—and they knew it!"

In another interview, Shatner further contrasted the two captains: "Given a dire situation, Captain Kirk says 'Drop that gun. I'll count to three. One, two, three,' and he fires. But Captain Picard says, 'Drop that gun. I'll count to three. One, two, three. I'm not kidding.' "

Shatner got to know Patrick Stewart just a few weeks before filming of *Star Trek VII* began. The two captains shared a private Paramount jet for over an hour. They had just appeared at ShoWest, a theater owners' convention in Las Vegas, and flew back to Los Angeles together.

"It was a little awkward," Stewart revealed. "There had been certain reports that Bill had made negative remarks about our series and so forth. We had always felt a little bit uneasy about that. Fortunately, that awkwardness was all but gone when it came time for he and I to do the movie."

The two men talked about their very similar Shakespearean backgrounds but had different feelings when it came to *Star Trek*. Stewart was glad to be out of the television series, happy to be able to work on other projects as well as have a future in *Trek* films. Shatner felt like he was being put out to pasture. He related a story about a starving African tribe in which the elders who have outlived their usefulness are required to quietly go out into the desert and die.

That was what he felt like. He had delayed it as long as possible. Now it was his turn to meet his fate in the desert. The last scenes would be filmed in an area almost identical to the arid location where Shatner had nearly met his fate with a mysterious UFO a quarter century earlier.

Originally, it was planned to bring the entire classic *Trek* cast back for a fond farewell, but scripting such a complicated reunion proved an insurmountable task. No way could be found to bring back two different *Enterprises* that would make both crews look heroic.

Finally, a complicated, time-bridging plot evolved that allowed only cameo appearances by most of the original cast. For that reason, Leonard Nimoy and DeForest Kelley declined to be in the movie. Besides Shatner, only Walter Koenig and James Doohan would make it into *Star Trek: Generations*.

Being treated like an icon on the set did not give Shatner much to complain about. Director David Carson actually had to remind some of the newer actors to perform, so much in awe were they of Captain Kirk's presence on the bridge. Many of them had grown up wanting to be Captain Kirk, and now they shared the stage with him. But Shatner denied sensing any hero worship on the set.

"I was totally unconscious of it," he said. "I don't know what's the matter with them. How did they come to hire those simpleminded idiots?"

However, the regular cast members did not allow themselves to be caught up in hero worship. Michael Dorn (Lieutenant Worf) had worked with Shatner in *Star Trek VI* and was more concerned with what he believed was the poor production quality of *Star Trek VII*. Even Patrick Stewart complained that the season finale of the television series had a much better script than the movie. The other regulars were also upset with the script, which seemed to center around Kirk, Picard, and Data at the expense of other characters.

Marina Sirtis, who plays Counselor Deanna Troi in *The Next Generation*, admitted that there were "severe concerns behind the scenes" among some of the cast about Shatner being in the next film. They were all aware of his disdain for their characters and his reputation as a scene-stealer.

In fact, Sirtis blamed Shatner for having some of her own scenes cut in the movie. In the original script she had had only five small scenes and had gone to the producers to complain. Her character in the television series had grown very popular, and she felt she deserved a more important role in the movie. Reportedly, Shatner heard of her complaints and had her scenes cut to two.

She confronted Shatner at lunch one day and was told that she was lucky even to be in the movie. That was too much for Sirtis, who went straight to producer Rick Berman's office and quit. Luckily for her fans, she was talked out of resigning by the consolation that she would never have to work with Shatner again.

George Takei felt that since Leonard Nimoy and DeForest Kelley had passed on making the film, there was room to bring back his character (Sulu) and Nichelle Nichols's (Uhura). Although Sulu's daughter ends up at the helm of the *Enterprise D,* it was not enough to placate the man who "saved Kirk's ass" in *Star Trek VI.*

"One thing that is pretty obvious," fumed Takei, "is the line of demarcation that was drawn—the two minorities that represented significant demographics of the population of the future are missing from our generation in that time. I think producer Rick Berman made a serious mistake. Asians and African-Americans are missing, while there are a variety of aliens, including an Android."

Perhaps even more obvious was the fact that the only members of the original bridge crew not asked to be in the movie were the ones who had written books about their problems with William Shatner. But Shatner denied having any control over the selection of his cast mates and lamented the absence of Leonard Nimoy and DeForest Kelley.

"I missed them every day," he said. "Leonard, DeForest, and I were always buddies on the set and I didn't have my buddies around. It was nice working with Jimmy and Walter, but I worked with them for only a very short period of time. It was almost a nod and a kiss."

Would Shatner ever work with the "next generation" again? "The only way I could meet *The Next Generation* cast again," he told the *L.A. Times,* "would be to come back as

T. J. Hooker and bop a couple of them on the head—especially that Klingon guy [Michael Dorn]."

The film opens in the late twenty-third century with the three classic Trekkers, Kirk, Scotty, and Chekov, being welcomed onto the bridge of the sleek, new *Enterprise B*. But during the maiden voyage, the Federation vessel answers a distress call from two spaceships caught in an unusual space-time anomaly called the Nexus. During the ensuing struggle, Kirk saves the *Enterprise* but is sucked through a hole in the hull and is presumed dead.

The story then jumps eighty years into the future to the *Enterprise D*, under the command of Jean-Luc Picard. Picard slowly uncovers the plot of alien genius Dr. Soran to destroy an entire planetary system (and 200 million people), all to affect the path of the approaching Nexus (a rift in space outside time where our fondest dreams last forever) and allow Soran to return to the land of Never-Never.

Soran's evil plan is crushed with the help of psychic bartender Guinan (played by Whoopi Goldberg). She alerts Picard to Soran's intentions and suggests he get in touch with the great Captain Kirk, who was caught in the Nexus years earlier.

Picard finds Kirk cooking breakfast in a homey cottage deep in the woods. The former captain of the *Enterprise* is caught in a fantasy world but comes to his senses when he finally realizes that he is living in his own memories. The truth becomes clear after he jumps a dangerous gorge on horseback. He felt no excitement, no fear, as his horse glided over the chasm.

The horse in the film is one of Shatner's own, named Great Belles of Fire. The talented horse relays Kirk's emotions precisely as she circles Picard's horse and warily sidles up next to him. It is a marvelous display of Shatner's horsemanship.

Kirk agrees to accompany Picard and help him fight Soran. In what Shatner admitted was the hardest line he ever had to deliver, he says to his replacement: "Who am I, to argue with the captain of the *Enterprise?*"

It is hard to believe that at that dramatic moment, both men were wearing women's pantyhose. And it had been Shatner's idea. During a twenty-five-mile trip through the Santa Monica Mountains decades before, Shatner had found that wearing pantyhose helped reduce the chafing on the inside of one's thighs caused by horseback riding.

"I'd like you to hear about something very important," Shatner confided to Patrick Stewart. "I wear pantyhose a lot, and I was hoping you would."

What type did Shatner recommend? "Sheer, with the seam in the middle. It's a rather pleasant feeling, akin to scratching yourself all the time."

Malcolm McDowell, who played Soran in the film, did not care what Shatner was wearing, as long as he got to kill Kirk. The villainous actor, who starred in such films as *A Clockwork Orange* (1971), *Time after Time* (1979), and *Caligula* (1980), took glee in getting rid of Shatner's played-out character.

"I had the distinct honor of killing Captain Kirk after thirty years," McDowell beamed. "It felt lovely, I mean lovely. As I said to him: 'Half the country will hate me and half the country will love me.' And Shatner replied: 'Well, who's the half that's going to love you?' And, I said, raising a flattened hand up to my forehead: 'The people who are up to here with you—Captain Kirk!' "

The first scenes in the original version of the movie never made it into the theaters. After circling the earth three times in a high-altitude skydiving outfit, Captain Kirk parachutes to earth. He lands only 35 meters off target in a large field where he is met by Scotty and Chekov. His two officers plan to escort him to the christening ceremonies for the *Enterprise B*. But the futuristic space parachute designed for the scene nearly proved deadly. The device did not open until 2,000 feet from the ground and Shatner's stunt double hit with an ungracious thud. Fortunately, the man survived the fall, but it looked very haphazard on film and nobody wanted to try it again.

Another change was the way Kirk died. As first filmed, he was shot in the back by Soran's phaser. Trying desperately not to give in to the pain, Kirk staggers and falls. He dies in Picard's arms, saying only, "It was fun." However, test audiences were very dissatisfied with that ignoble ending, so the scene was changed and reshot in September.

In the new version, Kirk is more dramatically crushed by a catwalk and dies a lingering death in the arms of Picard. When Shatner heard they wanted to reshoot the death scene, he expressed the hope that the writers were changing the script to allow for the possible resurrection of Kirk in a sequel. Producer Rick Berman did not tell Shatner about the new scene, and he returned to the Valley of Fire location not knowing what to expect. Unfortunately, no such resurrection was planned and Shatner had to die all over again, this time with a little more gusto.

Although no one could take Shatner's emotional blows for him, stuntmen were taking most of his physical risks. Still, Shatner found his limited scenes in the movie a real chore. The scene in which Kirk climbs along a mountainside to reach Soran's remote-control device proved the most dangerous for Shatner.

"There was a lot of loose rock," he recalled, "and the safety man said it was unsafe. But we overruled him. It was very loose. Picking the right rock to grasp was pivotal—if it had given way, who knows what might have happened? It's not that important for me that I do my own stunts, but the audience is so wise to camera tricks and stuntmen that the director is forced to put the actor in some kind of position of jeopardy."

Once again, most of the filming took place in remote desert locations, not unlike the Mojave Desert terrain where Shatner's UFO encounter had taken place. He described location shooting as terrible, "a real nightmare," and complained that the desert sucked the energy right out of him. Part of the problem might have been that he was wearing what is known in the business as an "abdominal binder" or "waist cincher" (a girdle, to the rest of us). In any case, he was only too glad to be out of the area when his takes were finally completed.

Viacom, who had taken over Paramount from Gulf + Western, set the budget for *Generations* at $25 million and scheduled 50 days of shooting. It was not surprising that the film took 120 days to complete and went over budget by $10 million. Industrial Light and Magic wanted $8 million for the special effects, and Shatner's up-front fee was another $6 million, which was more than Stewart received. (Shatner's huge cut caused the supporting actors to end up with only half the salaries they were originally offered.) The final blow came when Kirk's death had to be redone. Reshooting the final scene cost $5 million more.

The film opened in November 1994 at 2,200 theaters. It had to buck the so-called *Star Trek* curse, in which odd-numbered films tend to do worse than the even-numbered ones. The curse was confirmed by our own survey, in which *Star Treks II, IV,* and *VI* were the best received, while *I, III,* and *V* were the "dogs." Yet despite the curse and lukewarm reviews, initial box-office receipts for the seventh *Trek* film were heartening enough to guarantee the continuing big-screen adventures of a whole new generation of *Star Trek* actors.

Chapter 10

Sex, Aliens, and Palimony

Anything done supremely well is an act of sex.
—William Shatner's personal motto

In "Amok Time," one of Shatner's favorite *Star Trek* episodes, Spock is seized by an uncontrollable urge to mate, and the *Enterprise* is forced to detour to his home planet so he can indulge himself. Although the Vulcan's sex drive peaks only once every seven years, Shatner never let Leonard Nimoy forget it. At parties and conventions, Shatner enjoys mimicking Nimoy's portrayal of the horny Vulcan. He believes there is a lesson for all of us in seeing the intellectual mind succumb to basic instincts.

Shatner himself is an example of breaking free of cerebral constraints and following one's passion, no matter where it leads. He has described his life as "a single-minded pursuit of the adrenaline rush," although other hormones are often involved, too.

He described the feeling as it applied to the sport of archery. "What could be more sexual than archery as a phallic symbol?" he told his two female biographers. "The arrow and the bow as you draw it taut, gathering the tension—your strength, your power pumped into it, behind the thrust, and then the release—like an ejaculation, thrusting the arrow forward to impale the target. The arrow arcs up and flies straight home and penetrates the center of the bull's-eye. I mean, it's like an act of sex."

He admits to experiencing dreams and visions of "making love to a whole audience—making them my lover, and I theirs." He believes there exists a special rhythm between stage and audience that can culminate in a sexual release shared by everyone present.

Fans sense Shatner's lust for life and powerful sexuality. Actress Mimi Rogers described the feeling on the *Tonight Show* when she told Jay Leno: "I've always loved James T. Kirk. He had unbridled passion. I liked it when he got laid."

Actually, Captain Kirk got laid more than any other science-fiction character on television. The captain's love interests ranged through a dozen alien species and several curvaceous Androids. Nearly every episode had scenes of Kirk flirting with or embracing some alien being. Many shows had Kirk beaming down to primitive planets and teaching some naive village girl what love is all about. Shatner often jokes about the challenge he had finding an alienette's erogenous zones.

"Kirk's success with women was uncanny," he told one reporter. "It was miraculous how well he did with women across the universe, especially alien women and the various techniques they require. It's not like he spent his off-hours reading how-to books on alien women."

Of course, it was Shatner's sensuality that made the scenes believable. His official biographers, Sondra Marshak and Myrna Culbreath, estimated from fan letters they accumulated that millions of people were fascinated with Shatner's butt, especially the way "he puts it up first when he gets up from a fight." Shatner responded that he always knew he played the part by the seat of his pants.

In many episodes, Shatner not only got to show off his butt, but also bare his chest and use his sexual charms to their fullest. Kirk falls deeply in love with an alien warrior bride pledged to a loveless marriage in "Elaan of Troyius," and he is proclaimed a god after marrying the high priestess in "The Paradise Syndrome."

In "Wink of an Eye," Kirk visits a planet inhabited by a race that has superaccelerated metabolism. The humanoid aliens are invisible to visitors until they drink the planet's water. One of the women sneaks into Kirk's room and plans to kill him, but the captain disarms her with a voluptuous kiss. Then there is a short fadeout, and when the camera returns, Kirk is sitting on the edge of the bed pulling up his boots, and the woman is combing her hair.

In a special *Star Trek* edition of *Entertainment Weekly,* writer Bob Cannon joked that Kirk's success with aliens was due to his insightful pickup lines, which included such gems as, "You have the most eyes I've ever seen!" and "What's a nice energy pattern like you doing in a quadrant like this?" And, "You really know how to activate my tractor beam."

When Kirk was given an illegitimate son in *Star Trek II,* Trekkers had no problem accepting it. "Everyone knew Kirk slept around," noted director Nicholas Meyer. "It shouldn't come as a surprise that he had an illegitimate child."

The *Enterprise* itself is strikingly female, nurturing 400 crewmen in an idealized womb suspended in space, complete with gigantic fallopian tubes connected to a mysterious antimatter energy source. She is Kirk's true love, his one mistress, and his commitment to her makes him sacrifice lasting and more satisfying relationships. His infidelity to his ship is what makes the captain's love affairs so scandalous—and so interesting.

The first interracial kiss on television (between Kirk and Uhura) occurred during the "Plato's Stepchildren" installment of *Star Trek.* Some critics have said that the sexual themes in that episode were almost overpowering. After receiving a distress call, the *Enterprise* landing party are enslaved and humiliated by the Platonians, a race with incredible psychokinetic powers.

The infamous kiss was originally between Spock and Uhura, but according to Nichelle Nichols, the scene was rewritten after Shatner got one look at the script and yelled at director David Alexander: "No, you will not! If anyone's going to be part of the first interracial kiss in television history, it's going to be me!"

In the scene, an alien force is coercing the two to embrace, and Shatner has said that the real controversy was not the kiss, but how far the aliens would force them to go. Both Uhura and Kirk were terrified because each was powerless to protect the other from his possessed body. For Shatner, the scene was not about interracial relations but instead depicted the terror of animal passion taking over our rational minds.

Actually, Kirk's relationship with Uhura did continue beyond just that one kiss. In a series of fan-written stories published in the long-running magazine *Delta Triad*, the captain's adventures with his communications officer went far beyond the call of duty. In fact, a flourishing underground network of Kirk pornography, available at *Star Trek* conventions, includes X-rated videos, audiotapes, and novels carrying the captain's adventures where no screenwriter has gone before. The romantic possibilities are endless. Shatner himself confessed that it would be a lot of fun to do an X-rated *Star Trek*.

So even off the air, Captain Kirk continues his liaisons with crew members and aliens. Over a hundred paperback novels, the last two dozen of which are bestsellers, continue the romantic adventures of Captain Kirk. Through the novels, Kirk's conquests have indeed become legend—firing the imaginations of a great many modern readers.

That Swinging California Dentist

Throughout his career, theater and film critics always seemed to have a hard time making up their minds about Shatner's acting abilities. Some were unhesitating in their praise for his unique stage presence and staccato oratory style, while others considered his acting to be nothing more than the boorish antics of a self-centered man showing off on stage.

One movie critic in particular was so convinced of Shatner's lack of talent that he refused even to call him an actor. But he did recognize Shatner's unbridled sexuality, seething just below the surface in many of his roles.

David Denby, film reviewer for *New York* magazine, started something of a craze when he began describing Shatner as "that swinging California dentist." Many confused fans began talking about Shatner's alleged background in dentistry, and several underground comic books and fanzines took up the theme. One of the more entertaining is Erin Lale's self-published series called *The Adventures of Dames T. Dork of the* USS *Dentifrice.*

Critic Denby had never appreciated Shatner's portrayal of Kirk in the television series and panned most of his other acting efforts. But when Captain Kirk hit the big screen, it was too much for the sophisticated New Yorker. Eventually, he expanded his exasperation to include the entire *Trek* cast.

"That scintillating group of players is back, every one of them," he wrote of *Star Trek II.* "William Shatner is Kirk—looking more than ever like a swinging California dentist in his tight-fitting space jacket. America's beloved players Nimoy and Kelley exchange huffy looks, like rival hatcheck girls vying to serve a big tipper, and Shatner is slightly less wooden than last time, but none of the others actually *does* anything. And why should they? They've become famous without acting."

Denby detected the same campy undertones in *Star Trek IV:* "Nimoy and Kelley are at their most amusingly snippy. They appear to be playing two aging gays dishing at each other at a party while vying for the attention of William Shatner. Maybe *Star Trek* isn't so square after all."

Denby's opinion of Shatner as a director in *Star Trek V* was not any better than his opinion of him as an actor. "William Shatner, the muscular dentist who unaccountably wandered into acting," he wrote, "has now wandered into directing, and despite recourse to divine sanction, he mismanages the climax of what is mostly an amiable movie."

A muscular California dentist who likes to swing? It is an image that will not go away. However, an even more startling image came into the minds of some fans.

Are the Rumors about the Captain True?

Kirk and Spock arrive for shore leave at a planet where the aliens have the ability to make any wish come true. It turns out the two Federation officers have the *same* fantasy, and for that reason, actually carry out their most secret desires with each other.

"Kirk smiled in assurance and reached out without words to draw Spock into a loving embrace. Spock stiffened automatically before realizing that it was, after all, his own fantasy that he was fulfilling. He let himself go in the warmth of the strong, somehow familiar arms."

When they realize their fantasies are real, Kirk and Spock return to the *Enterprise,* promising to talk about what happened only after they have cooled off and are "thinking more clearly."

The above scene is from a short story, "A Wish Come

True" by Caren Parnes, that appeared in a fanzine called *T'Hy'La* in 1985. It is only one of scores of self-published and mimeographed fan publications dealing with gay themes aboard Federation starships. Other popular fanzines that deal with the subject include *Nome, Blake's 7,* and *Warped Space.*

Most of the homoerotic fiction chronicles a love affair between the *Enterprise* captain and his science officer. *As I Do Thee,* a quarterly anthology published from 1986 to 1991, was devoted exclusively to short stories and poems about the gay relationship between Kirk and Spock, and another series of nineteen novels on the same subject are still sold at fan-sponsored *Trek* conventions. The underground code name for the material is "K/S" or simply "slash books."

Many of the stories begin with Spock trapped in the throes of "pon farr," the seven-year mating cycle in which Vulcans must find a sex partner or die. To save his dear friend, Kirk goes where few men have gone before and enters the realm of bisexuality. One twelve-hundred-page novel, *Courts of Honor,* is based on the relationship of the two men after pon farr is over. Spock is no longer interested in sex, but Kirk cannot control his yearnings. In the short story "Divorce, Vulcan Style," written by Mary Susskind Lansing, Kirk and Spock separate because their sexual relationship interferes with their duties. But Kirk always manages to return to Vulcan during the pon farr season.

In all the stories the basic premise is the same: there is no prejudice against sexual preferences in the twenty-third century.

That prejudice, however, is part of the twentieth century. Pocket Books had to pull Della Van Hise's commercial *Star Trek* novel, *Killing Time,* because word had gotten out that it contained allusions to Kirk/Spock sexuality. The revised edition omitted the offending passages.

But "Are Kirk and Spock Lovers?" is a regular topic on

America On Line and *Star Trek* computer bulletin boards across the country. "Your chance to voice your opinion on what has been whispered about for years" is the way one popular board describes the cyberspace rumor mill.

Gene Roddenberry admitted he designed Kirk and Spock as two halves which make one whole and understood the potential for physical love between the characters. He believed that some of the homoerotic poems and stories about Kirk and Spock were really quite well written. Once, he even joked that *Star Trek* could have had not just the first interracial kiss but the first unisex kiss as well.

Or perhaps it was Kirk's insatiable rompings with aliens or the *Enterprise*'s Horatio Hornblower seafaring atmosphere that first planted the seeds of the scandalous affair. Then again, maybe it was Shatner's own campy portrayal of his feminine side that provided such fertile ground for the stories.

"I am capable of an extremely wide range of sexual fantasizing," Shatner admitted in an early biography. "I have no particular list of things that are normal or abnormal, or anything like that. I have certain guidelines, but I don't have any forbidden ground in fantasy. No taboos."

There has been some speculation on just how far Shatner's "no taboos" philosophy goes. One persistent (and false) rumor about Shatner that he was working in a male burlesque show in San Francisco when Gene Roddenberry discovered him. On the other hand, Ron Asheton, guitarist for Iggy Pop's first band, is convinced Shatner made a pass at him one night in the summer of 1975.

"When I first moved out to L.A.," Asheton recalled, "I was living at the Hyatt House. I used to go in the bar every night to have a drink and listen to the weird jazz combo and stuff. One night William Shatner was there, and he was really drunk. I wanted to talk to him, but he kept looking at me like he wanted to pick me up or something. I was like, 'Whoa! I'm gettin' out of here, man!' It sort of freaked me out 'cause he was really fucked up. He wanted me to sit down, and then he got kind of grabby, and I thought, 'Nah, Captain Kirk can't be a fag.' I felt really awful. Probably if I'd been drinking I would have sat down just for the weirdness of seeing what would happen. But he never ended up chasing me around Hollywood, like some people said."

During an interview with *Playboy*, Shatner was reminded of his infamous portrayal of a woman trapped in Kirk's body in the "Turnabout Intruder" episode of *Star Trek*. His campy portrayal shocked many of his fans. He has admitted it was one of his favorite roles, but when asked which woman would he like most to exchange bodies with, Shatner declined to name anyone.

"I'm so content with being a man," said the star, "that I would miss the clanging of my balls."

So would most of his fans. However wide the range of Shatner's sexual fantasizing, he is very much a ladies' man.

Shatner met his first wife, Gloria Rosenberg, in January 1956, when he traveled to New York with the Broadway production of *Tamburlaine the Great*. The beautiful twenty-four-year-old had high cheekbones, large, wide eyes, and wheat-colored hair. For the twenty-five-year-old Shatner, it was love at first sight.

Though extremely talented, Gloria was having a hard time finding work acting, and Shatner arranged for her to be in a play he was directing for Canadian television. Later, he would help her get accepted at the Stratford Shakespearean Festival, where she had been trying to secure a part for the previous four years.

Then, in May 1956, he proposed marriage. They were wed on August 12 and went on a working honeymoon to Edinburgh, Scotland, where Shatner appeared in *Henry V*. Afterward, the two lovebirds took off on a whirlwind tour of London and Paris. As soon as they got back to Canada, Shatner moved his new wife to New York City, where his career blossomed on early live-television dramas.

Over the next eight years, the couple had three daughters. When *Star Trek* began, they moved to Los Angeles and eventually bought a home in Cheviot Hills, a posh section of Los Angeles.

Shatner tried to be a good father and provider, but the obligations and temptations of Hollywood were many. He usually left for the studio before the girls were awake and returned home after they were asleep.

"It bothers me," he confessed during his divorce proceedings, "that for years I haven't been able to give Leslie, Lisabeth, and Melanie the kind of time most fathers can give their children. I often think about it, and I often feel guilty. A large percentage of fathers of my age are at the peak of their vitality and earning power, and the demands on their time at this moment in their lives are the greatest. It's unfortunate that at this precise time, children need their father the most. And yet, that's the way it is."

Shatner made sure that the time he was able to spend with his girls was quality time. He was completely honest when he answered their questions about such things as God, good and evil, Vietnam, and nuclear war, and used trips to the zoo to teach them about sex. But more importantly, Shatner tried to imbue in them his own feelings about being open with one's emotions.

"I would prefer to see them express all the little hurts and joys openly," he told reporters. "I've been very aware of showing them as much love and affection *openly*—to show them emotion, whether it's sorrow or love or fear, whatever—to show it openly, so they can express themselves and not hide their emotions, as most of us do."

Of course, Shatner stayed true to his own emotions too. The good-looking leading man started spending more and more time away from home. After separating several times in 1967, the couple filed for a divorce June 1968.

David Ross, one of Shatner's closest friends, recalled what it was like for Shatner during his final months with Gloria.

"When Shatner was going through his first divorce," Ross told me, "he had this little rental house off Mulholland Drive, and we would sit over there and talk about what we were going to do with our lives. We were all going to sail around the world, live on the islands of Tahiti. Just get enough to live on comfortably. If you got a part, do it; if not, you're not worried. Depending on how long the show went, if it's a good run you could save enough or live off residuals. On weekends, a bunch of us guys used to go up there and hang around with him. He had a camper and sometimes we would go out and go someplace. But someone would eventually spot him, of course, and we'd have to take off.

"During those hard times, he was never a real depressed kind of guy, but sometimes you'd go to his house and, you know, things weren't absolutely great. But at least you knew it wouldn't be a downer when you went to visit him. He'd always joke around. We would get together and then, you know, eventually he found a steady girl."

Sex on the Set

There were always pretty girls on the set of *Star Trek*, and usually they were dressed in Bill Theiss's extremely revealing creations. So there was plenty of sexual tension, and sometimes a lovely young lady became the source of competition between Shatner and Leonard Nimoy.

"Leonard was more straitlaced," *Trek* actor David Ross told me. "He was more of an intellectual. You didn't see him smiling or trying to come on to a real good-looking girl who might have been an extra or something on the show. I mean, you didn't see that from him. If a girl came on to anyone, nine times out of ten it was to Shatner. It's the same today. You know, Bill has got a way about him. He knows how to be nice, all butter and honey. If there was any argument over women between Shatner and Nimoy, it was over a woman who was interested in Shatner over Nimoy. Shatner was the star, and he was the better looking. I'm just giving it to you straight. Leonard knew that."

Still, Shatner was very picky when it came to women. In fact, he had a definite wish-list. He admitted the first thing he looked for in a woman was how attractive she was. His usual preference was for long-haired gals with great figures, specifically 36-24-36. When asked what heavenly body he would most like to visit, Shatner replied, "How about Melanie Griffith!"

Next he looked for that "special something," a kind of animal magnetism that would add power to the encounter. He looked for women who were "real," who were not role playing or being coy. He believed that sex was a "celebration of our essential selves."

Last on Shatner's List was personality—he liked intelligent but unselfish women. If a woman met all three of his requirements, he found himself irresistibly attracted to her. Of course, he was not shy about making some of his requirements public.

"I am definitely in favor of the long hair trend for women," he told a reporter in 1968. "One of the glories of being a woman is long, luxuriant hair, whether it is used to run barefoot through or tie in pigtails. A girl who is particularly well built should wear miniskirts, *if* she has the right legs. If not, she should consider getting clothes to *overcome* these defects, not show them off for all to see."

Shatner's sexual appetite became increasingly predatory over the years. In the loose moral climate of Hollywood, when he saw something he liked, he went after it. His reputation as a ladies' man steadily grew. The phone in his office at the studio was always busy with calls from his female admirers.

"On location, when Shatner was single," Ross confessed, "everyone would hit his trailer. You could see that trailer at night bobbing all over the place."

After the cancellation of *Star Trek*, Shatner was on his own, both professionally and personally. He spent summers on the East Coast doing summer stock theater and the rest of the year working in any television show or movie that came his way.

Steamy scenes in Shatner films in the 1970s were obligatory. Critics agree his most degrading role was that of a child molester in *Want a Ride, Little Girl?* (1974), but his three nude love scenes with Angie Dickinson in *Big Bad Mama* (1974) were Shatner's favorite. He played a member of a gang of depression-era robbers led by an attractive widow and her dimwitted daughters.

"I got into my body makeup," Shatner told *Playboy*, "and wore my shorts under a kimono to the set. Angie was already there, in her dressing gown on the bed. I awkwardly took off my slippers and stepped out of my shorts and kept my robe clutched around me. That's when I noticed that her robe had spilled open a little, and she wasn't wearing any underwear. Then I heard the first assistant director say, 'All right, everybody, only the essential personnel will stay. Everyone else, please go.' A general movement began toward the door, when I heard Angie say to me: 'Oh, Bill, Bob's makeup; do you mind if he stays?' I said: 'Oh, no problem.' She said: 'Bob, you can stay, uh, George! Uh, Dick! Fred . . .' and gradually, one by one, she named them all, friends she had made during the first two weeks of filming."

To this day, Shatner talks fondly of his nude love scenes with Anne Francis during stage performances of *Remote Asylum* in 1971. The play was about a tormented Catholic homosexual who shared a villa in Acapulco with two other homosexuals. Shatner portrayed a tennis-playing gigolo who also lives at the villa. He is in the middle of a steamy affair with a film star, played by Anne Francis.

"I had to reach an orgasm," he reminisced, "at the

Ahmanson Theater, in Los Angeles, in front of 2,200 people, every night for six weeks. That was tough. Because how much do you reveal? Are you a screamer, or aren't you?"

In the summer of 1977, he co-starred with Yvette Mimieux in the Bergen Mall Playhouse in Paramus, New Jersey. There were all sorts of rumors about their relationship and reporters tried to find out the juicy details. All Shatner admitted was that they regularly sought to relieve their tensions together. He would give her deep back massages, after she "hypnotized" him.

Also in the late 1970s, Shatner went through a stage where he was enamored of rock artists such as David Bowie, the Rolling Stones, Elton John, and Neil Diamond. He even saw himself as something of a rock-and-roll performer himself with the debut of his *William Shatner Live!* album in 1977. The producer for his road show was Richard Canoff, formerly with the rock group Flock, and his guitarist was Mark Goldenberg, lead guitarist for the Al Stewart Group. The album was promoted by a top Hollywood rock publicist, although it never really caught on with the general public.

"A real sexual thrill takes place," Shatner confided, "hearing the hot beat of a rock number. The rock world today is where it's happening. Rock is expanding the horizons of our ability to entertain. Rock stars are dynamites of creativity and energy, and we have nothing but to learn from them."

Shatner's Second Marriage

"I knew Shatner when he was dating Marcy Lafferty," actor David Ross told me. "She was lots of fun. She lifted him up, and helped him, and wasn't competitive or jealous. She was not worried about Bill, because she knew exactly who he was."

Marcy was a dark-eyed, long-haired twenty-four-year-old brunette whom the thirty-nine-year-old actor worked with on the set of *The Andersonville Trial* in 1970. Her father was Perry Lafferty, a respected Hollywood producer. The two dated for nearly three years before getting married on October 20, 1973, in her father's Brentwood home.

The newlyweds bought a two-bedroom, one-bath ranch house at 2729 McConnell Drive in the Hillcrest section of Los Angeles. Their only real luxury was a swimming pool with a slide. In 1985, they moved to a beautifully landscaped home at 3674 Berry Drive in Studio City. The mountaintop house has a breathtaking view of Los Angeles. They also purchased an oceanfront cottage in Malibu.

"I can't think of many couples," said Marcy, "who are happily married and who have equally busy careers. I think one career has to take a backseat. We had children to raise from Bill's previous marriage, and he was already an established star. It was my decision that I'd see to our home. Considering Bill's schedule, it's inconceivable to me that someone not bred on this insanity would survive it. The only thing we argue about is not having enough time to ourselves. You are grateful for what you have, and you're ruthless about the four hours that you get on Sunday."

Shatner was able to find roles for Marcy in several of his projects. She had a minor role in *Kingdom of the Spiders* (1977) and played an assistant navigator in *Star Trek: The Motion Picture* (1979). She also appeared in two episodes of *T. J. Hooker*.

But as she said, her place was in the home. When they were first married, Shatner tried to keep his children separate from Marcy, but she persevered and became a wonderful stepmother. His three daughters eventually moved into their home, and she helped them grow into gracious young women.

The eldest daughter, Leslie, aged 37, pursued a career

in commercial art. On May 25, 1991, she married talent agent Adam Isaacs at ceremonies held in the Shatner home. Lisabeth, who is 33, attended college, then worked as a model in Los Angeles. In 1988, she wrote *Captain's Log*, the story of the making of *Star Trek V*.

Melanie, the youngest daughter at age 30, graduated from the University of Colorado with a degree in theater. She appeared with her father in a series of Oldsmobile commercials in 1988 and had a small part in *Star Trek V*. She played a shopgirl in Robert Resnikoff's *The First Power* (1990) and also appeared in episodes of *Knots Landing* and *General Hospital*. At one time, she owned a successful California jeans-decorating business called "Thou Art Jeans."

Both Marcy and Bill are passionate horse enthusiasts. They raised American Saddlebreds and quarter horses at their ranch in the Sierra Foothills and later at Belle Rêve, their ranch near Versailles, Kentucky.

Shatner's love of horses goes back to when he was fifteen years old and rode his bike to a stable near his Montreal home. Several times a week, he visited the stable to ride the horses or work in the stalls just to be near them. The teenager dreamed that someday he would own his own horse ranch.

Today, he spends as much time as he can at Belle Rêve, which is French for "Beautiful Dream," where he keeps more than a hundred horses. His favorites are world champion "Sultan's Great Day" and "Kentucky Dream," winner of the National Horse Show in 1986.

The Shatners also bred Doberman pinschers for many years, and even named one of their first dogs "Kirk." Three of his Dobermans had the run of their home. Stirling, the eldest male dog, once helped himself to a twenty-pound Thanksgiving turkey, and the Shatners had to serve cheese and crackers to a houseful of guests.

The couples' idyllic homelife has been featured on several television shows, including *This Is Your Life* (1989), *Lifestyles of the Rich and Famous* (1985 and 1986), and *Run-*

away with the Rich and Famous (1991). But there were signs of trouble. In 1985, when *Lifestyles of the Rich and Famous* visited the Shatners at their Los Angeles home, Robin Leach asked the star if he and his wife were any happier now than in the past. Shatner had a hard time finding the right words.

"We have been happy," he said, pausing for a few pregnant seconds, "—struggling together, bringing a family up, making a career, making a living. The things we built together have made us happy and in the building have made us happy, so it's hard to differentiate between whether we're happier now than before—but we're no less happy now."

"A husband and wife," Shatner told an audience at a British *Star Trek* convention, "live in a balance between humor and anger, ease and dis-ease. As with any relationship, there can be more positive or more negative elements. In my marriage there is tension, anger, and dissatisfaction. A director or actor can't have that balance, but a husband can allow himself to be angry."

In 1987, Marcy walked out on Bill in the middle of his 56th-birthday party, after she discovered he was having an affair and he refused to give up the other woman. Marcy moved in with her parents but returned two weeks later when he promised to try to be faithful. Shatner's daughter, Lisabeth, was less forgiving and continued to fight with him over the way he had two-timed her stepmother.

By the spring of 1989, Marcy realized her husband was up to his old tricks, and she moved out again. Communication between the two had broken down, and friends had convinced her she would never be able to curb her husband's adulterous tendencies. However, after staying away for several months, she returned to their home in Studio City to try one more time to make a go of their marriage.

The Perils of Palimony

Shatner is well known in Hollywood for his roving eye. In fact, he has displayed a sexual prowess unmatched by many of the most infamous of Hollywood's leading men. He has been linked romantically with a half-dozen different women, and some evidence suggests his thirteen-year marriage to Gloria Rosenberg ended because of his wandering ways.

Rumors of his affairs with such stars as Angie Dickinson, Joan Collins, Yvette Mimieux, Heather Locklear, and other female co-stars are common. Persis Khambatta, who played the bald-headed Deltan navigator in *Star Trek: The Motion Picture*, said her biggest problem in her love scene with Shatner was keeping him under control. "The man obviously loves women," Khambatta said with a grimace.

International model Iman, who played opposite Shatner in *Star Trek VI*, agreed. "It is very easy to have a man-woman relationship with William Shatner," she said. "He adores women."

Then, in December 1989, Shatner's former assistant, Eva-Marie Friedrick, filed a $2 million palimony suit against him. The thirty-something ex-model was hired by Shatner's wife in August 1986 to work as her personal assistant. After a few months, she also became Shatner's personal assistant.

Shatner promised Friedrick he would give her a chance to become a producer and gave her the title of associate producer with his production company. He even promised her a role in *Star Trek V* and told her they would travel, attend meetings, and work on other projects together. Three months later they were sleeping together.

After Friedrick was seriously injured in an automobile accident in October 1988, Shatner wanted nothing further to do with her. The following month he fired her. In one last act of cruelty, Friedrick said Shatner took all her belongings from his Paramount trailer and put them outside on the roof. The injured woman was forced to retrieve her belongings from the roof of the trailer by herself.

"I was fired when he got tired of me," she told a friend. "He thinks he's such a powerful celebrity that little me would simply let him get away with it. But I'm not!"

To make matters worse, Friedrick told reporters that Shatner was sleeping with her during the same period he was having an adulterous affair with Vera Montez. Marcy had walked out on Shatner in 1987, when she'd found out he was involved with Montez. She believed he had given her up and worked hard to patch up their marriage. Now, three years later, she discovered he had been seeing Montez all along. Shatner told a close friend that he loved Marcy but was wild about Vera and could not give her up.

The twenty-eight-year-old Mexican beauty said the fifty-seven-year-old actor had promised to divorce his wife and marry her. But Marcy's ultimatum to her husband was that either he break off entirely with Montez or she would sue him for divorce. Fearing a financial disaster like the one he'd experienced after his first divorce, Shatner quickly ended the affair and left Montez without any support. In January 1990, she filed a $6 million palimony suit against him, seeking $3 million in actual damages and $3 million in punitive damages.

Their relationship had begun in 1984, after Montez had landed a role on *T. J. Hooker*. Soon they were meeting in his Malibu beach home for romantic interludes. Then, he whisked her away to Vancouver, Canada, for several weeks, calling it an "unofficial honeymoon," and in December, took her to a celebrity ski tournament in Banff, Canada. His young companion had to pose as his niece when they were in public.

In 1986, Shatner bought her a home in the San Fernando Valley and started spending a lot of time there. Montez produced documents supporting her claim that Shatner spent more than half his time at the house. She said that despite his toupee and corset, Shatner was very romantic and a wonderful lover. For six years, Shatner had been "materializing in her bed and then beaming back up to his wife."

"But really," she said in a 1987 interview, "he would race around to see me. We would make mad love, then he would race back to his home in time for dinner. I heard he had lots of women, and the only thing I insisted was that I should be the only one apart from Marcy."

By this time, the tabloids had gotten hold of the story; Shatner lost control over the press. Hollywood was abuzz with tales of his problems, and everyone knew what was getting him in trouble.

In March 1993, in a hilarious skit on a Fox comedy show called *The Edge,* actors Tom Kenny and Wayne Knight played two tiny aliens who come to earth seeking Captain Kirk. From deep in space, they have intercepted the original *Star Trek* television transmissions and seek to bring back Kirk for an intergalactic peace conference. "Remember," one of them cautions, "even if he agrees to join us, *never* let him direct."

Unfortunately, the finger-sized aliens mistakenly beam down into Captain Kirk's shorts. In the ensuing panic to get out, one of them accidentally fires his ray-gun and dematerializes Kirk's penis. Kirk detects all the commotion in his underwear and takes a peek. "Oh, my God," he cries out. "Call 911!"

Both of the palimony suits were settled quietly out of court in 1992, and her wayward husband begged Marcy to forgive him. The two even renewed their marriage vows, and Marcy was just beginning to feel she could trust her husband again.

Then, in 1993, Shatner started seeing a thirty-four-

year-old model by the name of Nerine Kidd. He was
hopelessly in love. Reportedly, Shatner and the long-
haired beauty spent days at her house in Santa Monica
and eventually moved into his Malibu love nest.

Finally, in 1994, after agonizing over her decision for
five months, Marcy filed for a divorce to end her twenty-
year marriage. She called it quits after realizing that her
husband would never mend his wandering ways. Her
incredible loyalty had always amazed her friends, but now
she could no longer forgive the incurable philanderer.
Shatner flatly refused to leave their Studio City house, so
Marcy moved into an apartment.

Even Vera Montez, who filed a palimony suit against
Shatner, agreed that Marcy did the right thing. "Once a
womanizer, always a womanizer," she told reporters.
"He's a real tiger in bed."

A dignified Marcy told reporters: "Life took us apart,
and it was time to move on. We both share the highest
regard for one another and our loved ones." A prepared
statement released jointly to the press declared that "no
other parties are responsible" for the breakup.

Yet even before the split was made public, Shatner had
been seen taking Nerine Kidd to restaurants and charity
dinners. When Shatner was a guest on *Regis and Kathie Lee*,
Nerine waited for him in the show's green room. She also
accompanied him to Canada, where he was making the
film of his novel *TekWar*, and she showed up with him at
charity functions and horse championships. He even introduced his paramour to his three daughters.

Nonetheless, Shatner told some friends that he was
heartbroken over his wife's decision. He insisted he still
loved Marcy, but not in the same way he had when they'd
first met. Their love, as he described it, had developed
and matured over the years and had become something
entirely different. "Marcy's essence is good," Shatner admitted in a moment of unusual candor, "but I can be
evil."

When Marcy sued for half of Shatner's estimated $16 million to $20 million in assets, however, he was furious. To avoid the spectacle of a bitter divorce trial, Shatner agreed to an $8 million settlement.

Afterward, Shatner admitted to being emotionally excited about the prospect of a second divorce. He said he felt enthusiastic about the freedom, possibilities, and "chaos" that would inevitably follow the dissolution of his marriage. He was looking forward, like a renewed Captain Kirk, to a "whole new series of adventures."

Chapter 11

The Mystique of *Star Trek*

> I never really understood the mystique,
> the *thing*, of *Star Trek*.
> —William Shatner

There is no doubt that Shatner's portrayal of Captain Kirk has become part of the consciousness of generations of Americans. Today, there are more than two hundred *Star Trek* fan clubs, over five hundred fanzines, a half-dozen newsstand magazines, and hundreds of *Trek* conventions every year. Shatner's face is recognized throughout the world.

Nearly 70 million *Star Trek* books are currently in print in fifteen different languages (including Chinese and Hebrew). In America, thirteen *Trek* books are sold every minute, and two new *Trek* novels appear every month. No one knows the extent of fan-written materials, but *Trekindex*, a quarterly guide containing plot summaries of *Trek* stories published in fanzines, was created just to keep track of the latest 3,000 additions. That way, Trekkers can follow the most recent fictionalized exploits of their favorite characters.

Trekabilia includes the commonplace, such as plastic

models, dolls, mugs, T-shirts, backpacks, and trading cards, as well as specialized items like jewelry, video games, interactive board games, and screen savers. Original props, such as wooden phasers and communicators, go for thousands of dollars. In fact, original scripts can command as much as $10,000—more than the writers were paid to create them. Even copies of a fifteen-cent 1967 Gold Key *Star Trek* comic book now sell for $275.

Shatner's autographed picture (in his Starfleet uniform) goes for about $200, and photos of the classic bridge crew signed by all members of the cast sell for $5,000. The original *Star Trek* episodes are still broadcast more than two hundred times a day in the United States and have been translated into forty-eight foreign languages. There are scores of radio and television talk shows devoted exclusively to *Star Trek* topics. Even the 1974 animated series has been resurrected by the Sci-Fi Channel.

The billion-dollar *Star Trek* merchandising frenzy continues unabated, with thousands of new items created by new television shows and characters. *Star Trek: The Next Generation*, a syndicated series, premiered on October 5, 1987. The show was seen by more than 17 million people each week, making it the most popular hour-long syndicated drama on television. It won sixteen Emmys, the Peabody Award, and the Hugo Award for Science Fiction Achievement. The tradition continues with two more spinoffs: *Deep Space Nine* and *Star Trek: Voyager*, which are now seen in over a hundred countries.

Fans Are the Phenomenon

The first *Star Trek* convention was held at the Statler-Hilton Hotel in New York City on the weekend of January 21 to 23, 1972. Nearly 3,000 fans showed up—six times more than organizers had hoped for—and the convention has been repeated every year since. By the third year (1975), over 14,000 fans attended and conventions started springing up all over the country. In 1976, Trekkers had enough clout to get the name of the first space shuttle changed from *Constitution* to *Enterprise*. President Ford received over 400,000 letters asking for the change, and he instructed NASA to comply with the Trekkers' wishes.

Ten years after the cancellation of *Star Trek*, the captain of the original *Enterprise* was becoming a national icon. "Where's Captain Kirk?" asked the title of a hit rock single by the group Spizz Energi in 1979. Fans got their answer in seven *Star Trek* movies that have grossed over $600 million.

In 1984, fans in Bangor, Maine, built a complete mockup of the *Enterprise* bridge at a cost of over $4,000. That same year, the Movieland Wax Museum in Los Angeles built another full-sized model of the bridge that included wax figures of the entire crew. Wax figures of Kirk, Spock and other crew members are also on display at numerous other exhibits, including the Hollywood Wax Museum (since 1977).

In September 1990, the town of Vulcan, Canada, opened the first *Star Trek* theme park with the unveiling of a statue of the *Enterprise*. There are currently dozens of *Star Trek* rides in carnivals around the United States, as well as thousands of arcade games featuring Starfleet adventures. In 1993, a chain of "virtual reality" *Star Trek* entertainment centers opened across the country.

In July 1990, the New York City Opera announced the production of the first *Star Trek* opera. Perhaps fortunately, it never got off the ground. In 1991, Riverside, Iowa, was officially designated the birthplace of Captain James T. Kirk. He will be born March 26, 2228. (Oddly, that is Leonard Nimoy's birthday; Shatner was born on March 22.) A small container of dirt from his future birthplace costs four dollars—but it comes with an official certificate of authenticity.

As part of the twenty-fifth anniversary festivities, *Star Trek* was inducted into the Smithsonian Institution. The display, at the National Air and Space Museum in Washington, D.C., included the uniform Shatner wore in portraying Kirk, the captain's Naugahyde command chair, Spock's ears, the original six-foot model of the *Enterprise*, parts of the original bridge set, and an assortment of props, such as wooden phasers and fake scientific devices. There was even a special exhibit at the museum called simply "Sexuality" that chronicled Kirk's many interspecies liaisons.

"We're walking around not knowing we're icons," Shatner said at the opening ceremonies, "but coming here to this museum has actually opened my eyes."

"Star Trek was an important cultural artifact of the sixties," proclaimed curator Mary Henderson. "In the guise of science fiction, the series dealt with substantive concerns such as Vietnam, the Cold War, and civil rights. It explored many of the cultural conflicts of our society by projecting them onto an idealized future. Unquestionably, it influenced public attitudes about space flight, then and now."

That same year, the Oregon Museum of Science and Industry (Portland, Oregon) spent nearly a million dollars to assemble a six-thousand-square-foot *Star Trek* exhibit, featuring replicas of the *Enterprise* bridge, transporter bay, and engine room. The theme park at Universal Studios operates a *Star Trek* theater attraction, and every August, Paramount's Great America theme parks feature a *"Star Trek* Earth Tour," which traces the evolution of *Star Trek* from the original series.

Future Call Company, a Canadian firm that issues phone debit cards, was able to cash in on the *Star Trek* craze and enter the *Guinness Book of Records* at the same time, by setting up the largest telephone conference call ever attempted. Four thousand people paid $100 apiece just to eavesdrop on a live conversation between William

Shatner and Patrick Stewart. The massive party line was repeated three times on December 11, 1994. Stewart received $100,000 for participating, and Shatner, who is a part owner of Future Call, will end up with at least three times that.

In 1995, Paramount Parks and Hilton Hotels announced a joint venture to build a *Star Trek* entertainment complex in Las Vegas. The $50 million attraction will be housed in a fifty-thousand-square-foot addition to the Las Vegas Hilton and will feature virtual reality stations that allow visitors to participate as crew members in Starfleet missions.

The Success of *Star Trek*

Besides becoming an entertainment phenomenon, the original *Star Trek* series helped conceptualize space flight and spread an understanding of our place in the universe. Gene Roddenberry's concept of IDIC, "Infinite Diversity in Infinite Combinations," has become the guiding philosophy of generations. It is estimated that *Star Trek* has been seen by nearly half the world's population, and several doctoral theses and a dozen scholarly books have been written on the effects of *Star Trek* on our society.

"*Star Trek* is successful," explained Roddenberry, "because it's one of the few science-fiction stories done which has a happy ending. We also had real heroes, almost old-fashioned heroes, people who believed in their work, believed in honor, who believed that things must be done at the cost of great danger, and sometimes, your life.

"*Star Trek* not only says we're going to make it, but that we're going to make it in a very civilized way. Looking different and being different will be okay. We won't interfere with the evolvement of other peoples and civilizations. These are not warships going out, but spaceships exploring for new life, furthering the ideas of humanity.

Star Trek says, 'There is a future for us humans; the human adventure is only beginning.' "

But there must have been more than just good storytelling and optimistic philosophy to attract the average television viewer. What was it about the show that created such a vociferous block of dedicated fans?

A Sci-Fi Soap Opera

Star Trek was, in essence, a unique breed of television fare; it was the first sci-fi soap opera. The series combined the futuristic speculation and the imaginative glitter of science fiction with all the components of an old-fashioned television soap opera. There were strong sexual undercurrents and plenty of emotional scenes, and the characters and their relationships with one another evolved psychologically.

Almost every episode had some sort of sexual encounter, whether it was Kirk's bedding of an alien or just mild flirtation among crew members. With everyone on ship running around in very short miniskirts or skin-tight trousers, it was no wonder the level of sexual stimulation was high. Costume designer Bill Theiss revealed more flesh and physique than had ever been seen in a regular TV series. Network executives were gleeful, while censors were simply confounded. After all, who were they to dictate what trends future fashion would follow?

The uniforms were so close-fitting that many actors chose not to wear underwear. In fact, during Shatner's wrestling match with Gary Lockwood in the final scene of "Where No Man Has Gone Before," Lockwood's pants split wide open, exposing his unclothed manhood to the entire crew. To avoid similar embarrassments, everyone dieted or worked out so they could look good in the tight costumes. There was a set of barbells on the set, and Shatner was known to walk around wearing twenty-pound ankle weights. Most of the cast members also worked out in private gyms.

Of course, muscles were not all the stars were pumping up. Female bustlines throughout the ship were cleverly augmented, and several male cast members made use of rolled-up socks to increase their stage presence. The enhancements were common knowledge and became a running joke among the players. A favorite backstage putdown was: "Maybe you ought to try knee-high socks." But when asked what size sock Shatner wore, Bill Theiss replied: "Oh, you won't catch Bill doing that!"

Theiss regularly made adjustments to costumes to allow for a few extra pounds of weight gain, but Jimmy Doohan's ballooning figure almost cost him his job. Word was that the front office had politely informed him to shape up or ship out. After some effort, he got his weight under control. Shatner also had a weight problem and tried hard to keep it under control. He kept physically active, constantly dieting and working out whenever he had the opportunity. Nonetheless, the fluctuations in his weight became obvious on the television screen.

Another feature *Star Trek* had in common with soap operas was limited rehearsal time and frequent improvisation in front of the camera. Fortunately for *Star Trek*, that freedom gave Shatner a chance to take creative hold of his new character, as he had done in *Suzie Wong* and in other stageplays. Because *Star Trek* scripts were rarely completed on time, the show required a lot of fill-in by the actors.

"Doing a television show," Shatner revealed, "is walking a tightrope all the time. It's a madhouse. You are required to do twenty-two to twenty-six shows in a few months, the writers are never on time, and what happens frequently is you get pages handed to you as you're walking down to the set—and you've got to learn those lines. So the ability to make a choice as an actor is somewhat limited. You're just guessing and you're going by your instincts and imagination. So when I look at myself trying to perform as though a girl was in my body, and not having any time to even discuss it, let alone think about it or try it on somebody to avoid the obvious, I'd look at some of these shows and say, 'How could I have done that?' or 'What did I do?'"

It was exactly the kind of spontaneous acting environment in which Shatner did his best work. He fell back on the halting, searching style he had developed when playing in *Henry V* at the Stratford Festival. And even further, he reached back to that six-year-old boy bringing the audience to tears at summer camp.

"I was really being myself," he said, of the way he portrayed Captain Kirk. "I really do think that a man should have no problem in expressing an emotion to another man or a woman. Emotions are what we live by. There's nothing denigrating in feeling emotion. And yet at the same time, you can express an emotion and be in control of yourself."

True, the role of Kirk was a blend of responsible seriousness and swashbuckling cockiness. But what Shatner added to his character was a range of emotions not normally shown by the male leads of the day, let alone in what was considered the limited genre of science fiction.

In one survey of 40,000 television viewers, 90 percent said they believed that the way he portrayed Captain Kirk changed people's attitudes about sensitivity in men. In fact, Shatner was always very comfortable with his feminine side. His own life had always embodied both the tough and the tender, which was the central paradox of *Golden Boy*, his favorite play in high school. On the one hand, Shatner was a macho, sports-minded guy, and on the other, he was a tenderfoot actor whose success depended on how much emotion he could elicit from an audience.

Although the tension between opposing psychological forces was much more obvious in the character of Spock, there was a similar tugging of opposites taking place in the character of Kirk. While Spock's internal battle between Vulcan logic and human feelings became a prominent part of the plot, Kirk's balance of his masculine and feminine sides was a subtle addition that helped create the mystique of *Star Trek*. Beginning with the pilot episode, where Kirk is painfully hesitant to deal with a former friend who has become a deadly threat, then dispatches the man in violent hand-to-hand combat, it is the captain's curious combination of sensitivity and ruthlessness that fascinates us.

Shatner's intense performance in the fourth episode, "The Naked Time," reveals his character's almost spousal feelings for the *Enterprise*, which he admits has a mysterious hold on him. In the next episode, "The Enemy Within," a malfunctioning transporter splits Kirk into two people, one meek and passive, the other violent and aggressive.

In "What Are Little Girls Made Of?" Kirk is replaced with an android double by a crazed scientist, but the crafty captain has implanted false memories into the robot to alert Spock to the subterfuge. (Several stations on the East Coast thought that Sherry Jackson's android costume showed too much cleavage and censored scenes showing her.) The duality theme continues in "Mirror, Mirror," in which a sensitive Kirk meets his barbarian opposite in a parallel universe.

But nowhere are the paradoxical components of Kirk's personality more obvious than in the last episode, "Turnabout Intruder." He is taken over by a woman scientist who has learned to project her mind into other people's bodies. She wants to use the captain's body to hijack the *Enterprise*. The possessed Kirk's humorous efforts to hide his female body language is some of Shatner's best acting. The simpering, campy Kirk raises eyebrows all over the ship. Fortunately, an ever-observant Spock also detects the captain's feminized behavior and uses a Vulcan form of telepathy to probe his friend's mind. Together, they are able to restore Kirk to rightful control over his body.

Thus was *Star Trek* more than just an outer space adventure series. Like a continuing soap opera, it was really about the daily drama of emotions that played out between characters. The show was about people, and it never let the spectacle of advanced technology overpower that.

A Love-Hate Relationship

Although Shatner always appreciated the success he achieved in his role as the captain of the *Enterprise,* he also resented it. He always believed that he would one day be one of the world's most revered actors. Instead, the idealistic young actor from Canada sold out to Hollywood and became typecast in a role that determined the rest of his career. What is more, his fans were hardly the same kind he had encountered doing Shakespearean acting.

"These fans are like greyhounds racing to see who can get the rabbit," Shatner complained during the original series. "They only want to touch you or maybe get a souvenir, but if it gets out of control and reaches a flash point—well! They just start pushing and grabbing, and then it becomes hysteria."

Shatner's overzealous fans have tackled him in airports, chased him on freeways, and ripped the shirts and ties right off his back. He always travels disguised in dark glasses and a large hat, although sometimes even the best disguise does not work. Once, at the New Orleans Mardi Gras celebration, he donned a full-face leather mask, and several people still recognized him. But sometimes Shatner gets tired of acting like a scared rabbit.

"Once we were having lunch," Shatner's cast mate Dave Ross told me, "and a woman came up and asked Bill for an autograph. She didn't even have a pen. He looked right at her and said: 'I'm trying to eat, and you're shoving a paper in my face. I'm sorry. I think that's rude.' "

At a *Star Trek* convention held at New York's Statler-Hilton in 1976, Shatner made the mistake of stepping off the stage and walking up the center aisle of the ballroom. Security personnel panicked as hordes of fans immediately pushed toward the aisle to touch the star. Seeing himself inundated by fans, Shatner shouted at the top of his voice: "If you don't sit down right now, I'm leaving!" Fans sensed the captain's angry tone and everyone quickly returned to their seats.

Mob scenes like that are one reason Shatner rarely attends *Trek* conventions. Another is that he is genuinely amazed by people who pretend he is James T. Kirk. His unwillingness to give autographs infuriates fans, and his love-hate relationship with them ranges from telling them to "get a life" to begging them to write letters to Paramount Studios in support of his pet projects. In one effort, Trekkers tried collecting a million signatures on a petition to keep Captain Kirk in *Star Trek VII.*

"I look a little askance at them," Shatner admitted. "Obviously, they have a need of some sort and I understand that, and if we can fill it for them, fine. I try not to mock them."

But many fans have still not forgiven Shatner for his appearance on *Saturday Night Live* on December 18, 1986. In his opening monologue, he said "I hope *Star Trek* fans have a sense of humor tonight, or I'm in deep trouble." As it ended up, he was in deep trouble.

In a skit satirizing *Star Trek* conventions, Shatner fields a few stupid, trivia-filled questions from the audience, then loses his patience: "I'd just like to say, move out of your parents' basements and get a life! I mean, for crying out loud, it was just a TV show." Those words have been quoted time and again as proof of Shatner's disdain for

Trekkers. They may have represented his true feelings, but they were never his own words.

"We thought we were wasting our time with that skit, but Shatner did it," admitted writer Jon Vitti. "He was really a good sport about it. He didn't make us take anything out because it was too mean; he has always had a good sense of distance from the show. He wasn't difficult about it. He read it in character and we were waiting for word to come back that he would not do it, but we never heard a word of protest."

But when asked if he had heard any feedback after telling Trekkers to "get a life," Shatner replied: "They've threatened to take mine. I take karate lessons and walk around with Mace. They can be very violent people if you challenge their belief system."

After the poor reception of his *Saturday Night Live* skit, Shatner started trying harder to please his fans. Today, during his appearances at conventions and special events, he does his best to appear charming, even humble. As part of his contract with Paramount, Shatner is required to take part in certain publicity activities, including the annual *Star Trek* Earth Tour at Paramount's Great America theme parks.

Shatner's performance at the Santa Clara Great America on August 20, 1994, was one of the best received. He told behind-the-scenes stories about his experiences on *Star Trek* and accepted questions from the audience. (Fans were required to write their questions on cards and submit them before the show began.) Two couples asked Shatner whether he thought they should marry and promised to take his advice. He asked them a number of pertinent questions, but in the end, the twice-divorced movie star told them unequivocally to go ahead and get married.

The audience had a great time, but Captain Quirk was not so nice backstage. The auditorium production crew said he was very impolite and short with them. He refused to have anyone read questions to him on stage and insisted on prescreening the cards. Nor did he pay any attention to stage directions, designed for the benefit of a crew videotaping the event. Other personnel at Great America said it was common knowledge that Shatner was very bitter about going to Santa Clara in the first place. He said if he hadn't been contractually obligated, he'd have been at a Los Angeles dog show that day with his prize Dobermans.

Shatner has been quite successful at controlling bad publicity and is still considered one of the most difficult Hollywood stars to interview. Many personal interviews with the star have turned into outright farces, as he simply avoids questions by giggling or moaning to himself. Several television interviewers have shrugged at the audience in exasperation.

Typical is the reaction of one *Chicago Sun Times* columnist who tried to interview the star: "His initial air is one of annoying pomposity, and friendly conversation is nil. Answers to some questions are clipped and terse, while others elicit a bored condescension."

In televised interviews with Tom Snyder, Jay Leno, Larry King, and many other television talk-show hosts, Shatner has come off as arrogant, deceitful, and just plain bored. Sometimes he tries to be a smart aleck with lots of quick, thoughtless replies—which makes him seem a little weird. But for someone who has done as many as twenty-five interviews in a single day, the process can get a little tiresome.

"I knew the questions I was going to get," he explained, "I knew I would have the appropriate answers, and I would end up boring myself to death. So what I would invariably try to do was to bend the conversation around to the environment, horses, crippled children; *anything* so I wouldn't have to answer 'What's your favorite episode?' or 'How does it feel to be Captain Kirk?' one more time.

"Then, there are the times when the interviewer is

dumb or insulting or just hasn't done his homework. Those are the people I'll turn the tables on and go after just to make things interesting."

The Appeal of *Star Trek*

Shatner was always puzzled over the obsession some viewers had with *Star Trek*, and the continuing popularity of the series dumbfounded him. After the show started gaining popularity even after it was canceled, he admitted he had no idea what was going on with the fans.

"I really don't understand *Star Trek*," Shatner told audiences at his *An Evening with William Shatner* tour. "I understand the various levels of dramaturgy involved, the action and adventure, the science fiction, the family of players, the personal popularity of the individual actors, the underlying meanings of the stories, but I never understood the mystique that made it appeal so deeply to so many fans. Good drama plumbs certain universals and makes contact with the audience, but you only know that afterward. The fact is, nobody can know if a show is going to be a hit."

Nearly twenty years later, Shatner still is mystified by the *Star Trek* phenomenon. He keeps going back to the idea of something universal buried deep in the characters and concepts of the series.

"Nobody was sure, nor are they yet, what makes *Star Trek* tick," he reflected. "The appeal of *Star Trek*, it seems to me, is that it seems to tap a universal unconscious—the place where myths come from. There must be something about *Star Trek* that taps into that."

"Having done a quick course with Joseph Campbell," he said later, "I've realized that the magic of *Star Trek* is to provide a mythology that this culture doesn't have. As he pointed out, mythology relates man to his environment and tries to explain some of the inexplicable dilemmas and the dichotomies that face us. Because of the construction of our culture, we don't have time for that because all of us are busy solving these problems with science. I think mythology is best served by an individual, along with his hearty band of brothers, as was done so many times, so well, by the Greeks."

Of course, what the Greeks recognized were the classic archetypes of protagonist and antagonist, hero and antihero, and the importance of the elements of passion and dilemma in storytelling. Shatner believes those elements are absolutely necessary to any good story and is one reason he was against *Star Trek* becoming an "ensemble piece." He also faults *The Next Generation* for being a "story told by committee."

Beyond that, Shatner believes the success of the original series had a lot to do with an intangible quality that the actors brought to the screen. Over the years, he has attempted to isolate this elusive element in discussions with Leonard Nimoy and several of the producers of the show.

"Nobody has ever enunciated it," he said. "It's what everybody perceives instinctively. We talked about the themes and the people, but none of us ever said it was the *joie de vivre*, the 'tap dancing,' as Harve Bennett once put it." (Walter Koenig once characterized Bennett's idea as "putting on tap shoes, for the fancy dance.")

"Nobody talks about the 'tap dancing,'" Shatner continued. "When I was young many years ago, Tyrone Guthrie, who was a great English director, said to me I had 'happy feet.' I was wearing white shoes in a play, and I knew what he meant. The timing in comedy has to do with the whole rhythm, and the rhythm comes out vocally, with your head. In this case, the rhythm came out on these white shoes, and I was 'tap dancing.'"

Chapter 12

What Does God Need with a Spaceship?

To boldly go where no man has gone before.
—World's most famous split infinitive

The pivotal scene in William Shatner's own *Star Trek* movie, *Star Trek V: The Final Frontier*, occurs after the *Enterprise* passes beyond the Great Barrier at the center of the galaxy and finds a lone planet where God awaits them. Because of a transporter problem, Kirk, Spock, McCoy, and Sybok must pilot a shuttlecraft to the barren planet's surface.

There, they meet God, who is a bright shaft of pure energy which can take on a variety of godlike forms. God tells Sybok that he has been chosen to spread God's power throughout the galaxy using the starship *Enterprise*. It could become the *Enterprise*'s loftiest mission, but Kirk has reservations about giving up his ship, even to the Almighty. "Excuse me, what does *God* need with a spaceship?" he asks impudently.

Of course, the irreverent query exposes God as a powerful alien life form that wants to escape from its planetary prison, and Kirk must eventually battle it alone on the mountainous orb. But the question "What does God need with a spaceship?" is one that Shatner himself has been asking most of his life.

Hey! Mr. Tambourine Man!

While still a teenager, Shatner rejected the traditional Judeo-Christian concept of God and supplanted it with the belief that the supreme being was really a cosmic intelligence existing in the deep reaches of space. That belief inspired his participation in the filming of *Mysteries of the Gods* and was behind his interest in Roddenberry's communications with the Nine and his intense desire to meet people who thought they were in contact with alien intelligences. The central question of that film was whether mankind was being prepared for extraterrestrial contact. "Am *I* being prepared for this encounter?" Shatner asks at the end of the film. "Are *you?*"

After his close encounter with a UFO in the Mojave Desert during the *Star Trek* years, Shatner thought he *was* being prepared. It was easy for the egocentric actor to accept the idea that he was one of the chosen ones. His belief in UFOs and the shaping of human history by ancient astronauts became motivating forces in his life for many years.

But William Shatner got tired of waiting. For over a decade, he had searched for signs of the return of the alien God that had visited him in the desert. It never happened. Others were chosen—but not him. By the time Shatner returned to the *Enterprise* in *Star Trek: The Motion Picture,* his newfound cynicism had become obvious to all those around him.

Always an opponent of organized religion, Shatner now added UFOs and contactees to his list of targets. Just as in *The Final Frontier,* Shatner wanted to expose the alien God as a fraud. In October 1994, he was asked to comment about UFOs on a special presentation of *Larry King Live* called "UFO Cover-up."

"I think that people want to believe so much that it flies in the face of any logic," Shatner told the television audience. "People interpret what they are seeing as science-fiction because they want desperately to believe that *they* exist—that there is another intelligence out there that can, like Big Daddy, come and put his arms around us and gently say to the culture that has gone astray: 'Big Daddy is here. We'll set you on the path again and everything is going to be fine.'"

Shatner the Futurist

While Shatner does not believe in God, he has always believed in the future. He believes that only mankind has any control of our destiny, and because of that, we all need to be made aware of the effects of our actions and attitudes on future generations.

In the middle of filming *The Final Frontier,* Shatner took time off to fly to Nepal to film a ten-hour documentary for Turner Broadcasting about the environment. Called *Voice of the Planet,* the miniseries looked at everything from animal research and forced sterilization of people to pollution and the Gaia Principle, which postulates that the earth itself is a living organism.

In the fictionalized documentary, Shatner plays a writer contacted by Gaia, the spirit of the planet. (In past generations, she was known simply as Mother Earth.) Gaia communicates through a computer located in a Buddhist monastery high in the Himalayan Mountains. Shatner's character goes to the monastery and together, he and Gaia travel throughout the world. During their travels, Gaia speaks her mind about what mankind has done to the planet.

(Two years later, in a grim example of man's relationship with Gaia, the thousand-year-old monastery in which *Voice of the Planet* was filmed burnt to the ground.

The fire was caused by a short-circuit in an electrical generator brought to the site by an American film crew.)

As usual, Shatner performed his own stunts in the series, including hiking over glaciers and riding a killer whale, but he also got involved on a more spiritual level. In what he has described as an "epiphany," Shatner suddenly felt that the earth was truly calling out to him, and he became a passionate spokesperson for environmental groups and causes. When asked what video of any of his performances he would pass on to his grandchildren, he named *Voice of the Planet.*

"In defiling our planet," he warned, "we have given ourselves a life term, and the electric chair is slowly coming our way, and unfortunately, it would be an electric chair. It won't happen suddenly; we're all going to expire in a rather ugly way unless we do something about it."

Shatner hosted a syndicated television series called *The World of Tomorrow* in 1984. The show focused on futuristic gadgetry without considering the effect of technology on people's lives. But on June 1, 1993, he hosted the First Annual *TekWar* Symposium, in which prognosticators from around the world offered their views on what law enforcement, communications, entertainment, science, and sexual behavior would be like fifty years in the future. Most of the experts painted a rosy picture, but Michael Tobias, who wrote, directed, and produced *Voice of the Planet,* offered a darker portrait.

"In 2043," he told the Universal City meeting, "80 percent of the world's population will earn less than $350 per year, making the remaining 20 percent of the population an elite and vulnerable island of prosperity. Bombay, the second-largest city in India, has 14 million people, and 7 million of them live in tents on the streets or simply on the streets. This will be characteristic of 60 percent to 80 percent of the human population in 2043."

Author, Author

During lulls in the production of *The Final Frontier*, Shatner started outlining a science-fiction novel called *TekWar*.

"I always thought a police story was a wonderful venue for action," he told a fellow writer, "and I've always been intrigued by the pursuit of law and order and the way you can use the elements of crimesolving to tell a marvelous story. So when I was asked to write a science-fiction novel, I jumped at the chance to combine the genres. I would start writing very early in the morning. Then, I would work all day on the *Star Trek* movie and come back to the book at night."

He first named his hero "Jake Campus" and later changed his name to an equally improbable "Jake Cardigan." In any case, "J. C." is a futuristic policemen who, in many ways, seemed to be a combination of T. J. Hooker and J. T. Kirk. Like those characters, what distinguished Jake Cardigan was his vulnerability. Indeed, J. C. seemed to be crucified in every direction he turned. He has lost his family, his job, and his friends, and he ends up in prison under false pretenses. Like some futuristic Luddite, the moralistic hero fights impossible odds to thwart the spread of a computerized drug, a mind-altering computer chip with the street name "Tek."

Shatner's *TekWar* was released in October 1989 and within two weeks was on the top-fifteen list at both Waldenbooks and B. Dalton. Most reviewers found the book superficial though fast-moving and described his writing debut as credible. Sequels followed in quick succession: *TekLords* (1991), *TekLab* (1991), *Tek Vengeance* (1993), *Tek Secrets* (1993), and *Tek Power* (1994).

In 1992, Marvel Comics adapted his sci-fi novels for a comic book series called *TekWorld*. Ron Goulart, who wrote the novels with Shatner, took over the responsibility of coming up with original story ideas for the graphic novelizations, although Shatner maintains editorial control and writes a column in each issue.

"Shatner's a good storyteller," commented Goulart, "and he has a very good sense of how to reach a large audience. That's always helpful. All the suggestions he has made are toward making this thing work. They're not criticisms like, 'My way is better;' they're just suggestions on how to improve this product."

A syndicated television series based on *TekWar* began in January 1994 with four two-hour movies. That fall, the USA Network bought the movies and eighteen episodes of the series. Shatner intends to direct half the shows and has guest-starred in several of them.

After working together in *Voice of the Planet,* William Shatner and Michael Tobias also decided to collaborate on a novel. In *Believe,* master magician Harry Houdini teams up with novelist Sir Arthur Conan Doyle, the creator of Sherlock Holmes. The improbable team searches for proof of life after death in a worldwide contest sponsored by a respected science periodical. Houdini is a skilled debunker of physics and mediums, while Doyle is a firm believer in occult powers and communication with the dead.

The novel was published by Putnam in 1992. Shatner commissioned a script based on the book and hoped to present it at the Shubert Theater in New York, but his plans fell through for lack of financial backing. Shatner would have portrayed Houdini, and Leonard Nimoy agreed to play Doyle.

In 1993, HarperCollins Publishing paid Shatner $750,000 for the rights to his memoirs. He did over a hundred hours of interviews with people associated with the *Star Trek* television series for the first book, *Star Trek Memories.* His second book, *Star Trek Movie Memories,* was released the following year.

Just how much of Shatner's books the star actually

writes is a question of some debate in the publishing world. Ron Goulart, his acknowledged co-author on the *TekWar* series, is thought to work off outlines provided by Shatner. Shatner has admitted that Goulart did an enormous part of the work, but when asked about the extent of his contribution, Goulart will only say, "Whatever Bill told you, I'll go along with that."

The star's memoirs were co-authored with Chris Kreski, the editorial director of MTV and writer of episodes for the *Beavis and Butthead* animated series. The writer is used to working with Hollywood types and co-authored *Growing Up Brady* with Barry Williams. Kreski, who refers to the collaboration as "the Royal we," has also declined to comment on the extent of Shatner's contribution.

In September 1994, Shatner signed a contract with Pocket Books for two *Star Trek* novels dealing with the continuing adventures of Captain Kirk. He admitted to being "intrigued and enthralled" when the *Star Trek* books became a possibility, and he had always wanted to work in the wide-open environment of *Trek* fiction.

Shatner negotiated a six-figure advance, then went back and asked for a five-figure amount for Ron Goulart. Speculation on the plots centered around the rejected ideas Shatner had submitted for *Trek* films, such as the *Enterprise* finding the fountain of youth, and a falling-out between Kirk, Spock, and McCoy.

A Stellar Comedian

"I am essentially a clown," Shatner has admitted. "Anyone who has ever worked with me will tell you that. I love to make people laugh."

Some say that Shatner's comedy career took hold with some lighthearted humor on *Star Trek* episodes and evolved into full-fledged stand-up comedy routines like those he performed when he hosted *An Evening at the Improv*

on television in 1991. However, others maintain that
some of Shatner's serious performances were so bad that
people thought he must have been joking.

These include all his attempts at singing. Two songs
from his 1968 *Transformed Man* album were chosen for a
tongue-in-cheek collection of celebrity singers called
Golden Throats, released in 1990 by Rhino Records.

But Shatner could never really carry a tune and always
ended up embarrassing himself when he tried. The low
point came in 1977, during the Academy of Horror and
Science Fiction awards ceremony. He showed up on stage
with a sportcoat draped over his shoulder, looking like a
cross between Dean Martin and a traveling salesman.
Actress Susan Tyrell received an award at the ceremony,
but what she remembers most is Shatner's singing.

"I remember that hideous William Shatner singing
'Rocket Man,' " she said. "I was looking at his shoes; he
had these velvet shoes on with 'WS' on them. He couldn't
sing. He was smoking, so he would talk the lyrics between
puffs. It was horrible and hilarious at the same time."

At the MTV Music Awards in 1992, Shatner performed many of the nominated songs. His only background music came from a xylophone and a bongo drum.
He did an extremely unsexy "sexy" version of "Rescue
Me" and wore a lather-like white wig when he sang "I
Want to Sex You Up." People have been trying to figure
out what he was doing ever since.

Shatner honed his comedic talents with cameo appearances on *Mork and Mindy* and *Police Squad,* and as host of
Saturday Night Live. In 1982, he played Buck Murdock,
commander of Lunar Base Alpha Beta, in *Airplane II: The
Sequel.* The spoof of airport disaster movies takes place in
the future, when the lunar shuttle is threatened by a mad
bomber. Shatner's role is essentially a parody of Captain
Kirk.

Shatner has a cameo appearance as Captain Kirk in
Bill and Ted's Bogus Journey (1992), but his major comedic

role was in *National Lampoon's Loaded Weapon I* (1993). Shatner plays General Mortars, an evil South American military leader who tries to distribute cocaine in Girl Scout cookies. Emilio Estevez and Samuel Jackson team up to stop him. Although *Variety* accused Shatner of "hamming it up disturbingly," most reviewers found his antics genuinely funny.

"The most outrageously enjoyable turn is William Shatner's," wrote the *San Francisco Examiner*, "as the ludicrously toupeed, Banana-Republic–outfitted villain who gobbles piranhas with glee." *USA Today* agreed: "The closest thing to bedrock here is William Shatner, who, as mustached priss General Mortars, is the sinister mastermind."

Call 911!

Since 1990, Shatner has hosted a popular real-life drama series, *Rescue 911*, which won that year's People's Choice Award for favorite new dramatic TV series. The series was one of the first reality television shows, and it sometimes uses the actual persons involved in emergency calls to re-create the incidents reported. The show has been credited with saving over 300 lives because of the lifesaving techniques it portrays, and Shatner's face now graces the cover of the official *First Aid Handbook* issued by the National Safety Council.

Shatner was originally attracted to the show because of the excitement connected with it. He confessed to being fascinated by the intense drama generated by people who were totally oblivious to the camera because they were involved in life-or-death situations. But as the show progressed, Shatner felt his social conscience grow.

"*Rescue 911* is to me the best show on television. It makes me laugh and cry more than any other show on the air. It is a miracle show. It has saved a documented 300 lives, but on a radio show in New York, I heard a young boy tell the story of saving his grandmother's life with something he learned on the show. He didn't write a letter to say this happened, so there's some kind of multiple out there for letters written. I know there are thousands of people whose lives have been saved as the result of a television show being on the air. That's an extraordinary event. *Rescue 911* is something I'm extremely proud of."

Shatner has had to use 911 services on at least three occasions. In September 1983, he was walking on the beach in front of his home just north of Malibu when he saw a man and a boy struggling in the water. Shatner dived into the heavy surf and managed to keep the boy afloat while the man ran to call for additional help.

Another time, Shatner witnessed an automobile accident in which one of the occupants was injured. He called 911 on his car phone and called for an ambulance. When the operator asked for his name and he replied "William Shatner," he had a very difficult time trying to convince her it was not a joke.

But it was no joke when Shatner got to experience a 911 call meant for him. At a horse show in the spring of 1993, the mount Shatner was riding got spooked by a golf cart. The horse reared and fell on top of him. The muscles and ligaments in Shatner's left leg were badly torn and he had to undergo months of physical therapy. At first, he refused to admit he had been injured. He tried to walk and fell several times before he was forced to lie down. Then he refused to get into an ambulance and made one hell of a fuss on the way to the hospital.

"It was funny," he recalled. "The horse reared and rolled over on me, and when I tried to stand up, I couldn't. Then the ambulance arrived and they tried to give me oxygen, and I wouldn't take any oxygen, and they tried to put the intravenous stuff in me and the gurney slid from side to side. It wasn't like my television show *Rescue 911*. It was much messier. This guy, the EMT leaning over me, was sweating and perspiring and dripping on me!"

A Human Dynamo

Most of his friends agree that the idea of getting Shatner to lie down for anything is difficult to imagine. Relaxing is not his style, and he has always had a driving need to keep physically active.

"I like being physical," he told a reporter. "I believe that being one with yourself is the aim of everything we do. I admire people who go out and challenge nature; they have a willingness to experience. They participate; they don't merely observe life."

When Shatner took his first skydive, he jumped out of the plane in total hysteria. When he landed, his instructor, who had been falling alongside him, asked if the star was aware that he was screaming at the top of his lungs all the way down. Shatner replied that it was the only way he could get "this terrible feeling out."

An accomplished horseman, Shatner has twice won blue ribbons for the American Saddlebred Five-Gaited Class Competition at the National Horse Show, and in 1994, he won all four amateur class competitions for the breed. Not surprisingly, Shatner feels a sexual exhilaration in horseback riding.

"There's a real connection between love and riding a horse well," he admitted. "You've got to use your body, you've got to use your hands, you've got to make love to the horse, and she's a neat lady."

As was the case with a few of Shatner's female co-stars, his horses have not always responded kindly to his overtures, and he has taken a number of nasty falls. The real problem always is getting Shatner to accept the fact that he might be injured, like trying to get a sick horse to lie down. Many of his fellow actors have marveled at his physical stamina and ability to ignore pain.

The truth is, Shatner simply does not want to slow down. He feels that strenuous physical activity keeps him young, and he has spent much of his life searching for the fountain of youth. Always concerned about his appearance, he has undertaken a variety of cosmetic and health routines to ensure he looks his best.

At one point, he was spending over $2,000 a month to keep his hairweave looking fresh. In one Hollywood poll, Shatner tied with Sean Connery at the top of a list of actors who do the best job of hiding their "chrome domes." Shatner did such a good job that he started receiving requests for "hair grants." Dozens of financially strapped bald men have asked him for anywhere between $500 and $10,000 to buy wigs or start expensive hair treatments. Yet despite Shatner's active participation in a number of charities, the requests have all been denied.

Along with Sean Connery, Burt Reynolds, Tony Bennett, Rob Reiner, and Rip Taylor, Shatner shares one of Hollywood's best known "secrets." They are all bald. But Shatner would be the last to admit it.

In November 1994, while promoting *Star Trek: Generations,* Shatner agreed to a telephone interview on Florida's "Power Pig" radio station, WFLA in Tampa. Toward the middle of the interview, deejay M. J. Kelly brought up the forbidden subject: "I hope this is not a sensitive question—the hairpiece. It's the best I've ever seen." "I don't wear a hairpiece," said Shatner tersely. "That's the stupidest question I ever heard. 'M. J.' must stand for 'Most Jerk.' That's a stupid question by a stupid person." Thereupon, Shatner hung up the phone, abruptly terminating the interview.

He once said in an interview with *Playboy,* "There are a handful of people who, like me, have grown up in television. I've been on TV since the early fifties, and I've watched myself grow into the thing I am now. Seeing old photographs buried in the attic, that's one thing. But to see yourself walking around on a TV screen in one instant and then to compare that with your present-day form in the next is tough. However, I believe that if I can keep upping the limit of what I think I'm capable of doing, I can give myself the illusion that I'm not slowing down. That means I get up earlier; I attempt to do more things. I keep my mind open for new ideas. Perhaps this is an illusion, but I'm living on that illusion."

Shatner's Friends

One of Shatner's few friends from the *Star Trek* years is Leonard Nimoy. At one time, Leonard and Susan Nimoy were neighbors of the Shatners on a hilltop overlooking Los Angeles. The two men became very close friends after learning to complement each other's opposing personalities. There is great energy in such relationships, as was evident when Spock and Kirk worked on the bridge together, the perfect balance of reasoned logic and impulsive intuition.

"He's a very passionate guy," Nimoy says of Shatner. "He plunges into stuff. He's got his books and his horses. I like to tease him: Bill, why don't you do something with your life?"

"As we've become closer and closer friends," Shatner admitted, "the give-and-take between Spock and Kirk has increased, just out of the sheer fun of acting together. More and more, we've developed a shorthand, and when Leonard hears me fumbling around to try and explain why such and such bothers me or doesn't, again and again he will say, 'What Bill is trying to say is . . . ' I try to be diplomatic, but Leonard tends to be more forthright."

With friend Nimoy, Shatner hopes to produce and direct a limited television series for ABC called *Deadly Games*, revolving around the adventures of players of a virtual-reality videogame.

Nimoy and Shatner are also scheduled to work together in a television movie called *Underground.* Nimoy will star in the mystery whodunit and Shatner will direct. Atlantis Films has agreed to produce the movie.

Shatner is still friends with another of his male co-stars, Adrian Zmed, who played Officer Vince Romano on *T. J. Hooker.* Zmed quit the show rather than take a cut in salary when it switched networks in 1985, but the two have stayed in contact over the years.

Another close friend is David Carradine, who played Caine in the *Kung Fu* shows. The two men share an interest in Eastern philosophy and sometimes consult the same psychics. Shatner met Carradine when he guest-starred in an episode of *Kung Fu* in 1974. Nearly twenty years later, Carradine invited his friend to direct an episode of *Kung Fu: The Legend Continues.*

Who Is Bill Shatner?

"I am more than just an actor," Shatner confessed, in a moment of unusual candor. "I am William Shatner the human being. Who that is, I'm not quite sure. Possibly there are aspects to me which people see that I'm not aware of. I just try to be myself, with all the ineptitudes I have. I ask the fans to think of me as one of them. I happen to be an actor in the public eye, but I'm no less of a weak and hypocritical person, as are all human beings. I strive to be more, but I fall short of my expectations."

If we look to the stars for help in understanding this man's unique personality, we find that he was born in the sign of Aries. According to the position of the stars and planets at the time of his birth, he is "full of enthusiasm and creative energy, always ready to apply this energy to new enterprises, always ready to overcome obstacles and seek new challenges." On the other hand, he is very "self-willed and resents even constructive criticisms."

According to his natal horoscope, Shatner has a strong need to lead the way for others, to finish first and "prove himself through actions rather than words." But sometimes he can be overly competitive and starts things without giving the necessary attention to see them through.

Restless, full of energy, he is also emotionally volatile, tending to "react to events and people more through feelings than through rational thought." At the same time, he has difficulty expressing his own truest feelings. When speaking, he tends to use "energetic hand gestures and facial expressions."

His chart further states that his love of sports imbues him with great endurance, but he is impulsive in romantic relationships. He finds "standard moral strictures confining and seeks his own standard of conduct in personal relationships" and gives little consideration to the practical problems of maintaining long-term relationships.

Exhibiting common sense in all his worldly endeavors, he is quick-witted and gets things done with sheer willpower, though he also "has a vivid imagination and is sometimes melodramatic." Possessing a great talent in writing or art, this "creative, passionate" individual "may be inclined toward getting his way without considering others' opinions or feelings." People who have known, worked with, and had relationships with Shatner for decades could not have come up with a better description of his personality.

Shatner himself has always believed in the intuitive arts and confers with psychics regularly. One thing on which they all agree is that Shatner's aura is exceedingly strong. They say it swings from a metallic golden color when he is in a good mood to a black-spiked reddish hue when he is angry. But no matter what state he is in, his aura is always very powerful. Two psychics who have consulted with Shatner told me that his presence is so strong they can identify him over the telephone before he speaks or pick him out in a crowded room, even if he is disguised.

Of course, at one point in his life, Shatner believed he had experienced telepathic contact with an alien intelligence. It was one of the most amazing events in his life, and perhaps his legendary psychic presence had something to do with it. Though he was not chosen to be the emissary of extraterrestrials, Shatner's career has served to greatly increase our awareness and acceptance of space-age ideas.

In summing up his multifaceted career, he has said, "I suppose if I do nothing else in life, I've made a major contribution. Between *Star Trek* on TV and in films, if Captain Kirk has become part of the consciousness of a generation, that's not a bad thing to be remembered by."

The Death of Kirk

Despite his love-hate relationship with Kirk, it was very difficult for Shatner to give up the role. Filming Kirk's death at the end of *Star Trek: Generations* proved especially traumatic. Shatner had been fretting over the inevitable moment for many months, not sure if he was doing the right thing or would even be able to handle the death of a character he had brought to life for so many years.

In Shatner's mind, the death of Kirk would be the death of another part of him. He had just lost his mother, Anne, in 1993. The following year, he divorced his wife of twenty years, just as he was nearing retirement age. And it all started him thinking about his own demise.

Death and growing old were always touchy subjects for Shatner. Corsets, hairpieces, health fads, and working out were all part of his strategy to keep looking young. Amazingly, he never kept any personal photographs because he did not want to see "the harsh reality of the passage of time etched in the unforgiving stills."

"The prospect of my own death has always left me semihysterical," he confessed. "Of all the great fearful

issues in the world—abandonment, loneliness, helpless-
ness—death, to me, is the most terrifying. I can reason
with myself most of the time, but every so often, the fear
escapes my control, and I find myself breathless with
anxiety."

Kirk would face death in the 110-degree heat of an
ancient seabed desert, very similar to the spot where,
twenty-seven years earlier, Shatner had experienced a
close encounter with an unexplainable UFO.

What had Shatner seen? At this point in time, it is very
difficult to say for sure. Numerous sightings of strange
objects were reported in the same area in the months
before Shatner's experience, and his description was almost identical to that of a tambourine-shaped craft
sighted by Betty and Barney Hill, who claimed to have
been abducted by aliens near Niagara Falls five years
earlier. Though Shatner has never submitted himself to
hypnotic regression, he scores an impressive 85 percent
on an "Indicators of Alien Encounter Test" devised by
clinical psychologist and UFO researcher Dr. Richard
Boylan.

Interestingly, William Shatner was not the only member of the *Star Trek* cast to have a UFO encounter. DeForest Kelley, his wife Caroline, and a family friend came
across what looked like a flying spacecraft while they were
driving through Louisiana swampland toward Montgomery, Alabama. The event occurred in 1950 and was witnessed by dozens of other people in the Montgomery
area. Kelley was later contacted by a government UFO
investigator, who told him the UFO was never satisfac-
torily explained.

"It was the hackneyed story you've heard before," Kelley confessed at a recent *Star Trek* convention, "of a long,
cigar-shaped object with blue and green flames stretching
off the side of it. So I thought, nobody in the world will
ever believe this. We saw the UFO, measuring 500 or 600
feet across, pass in front of us, and I looked at it and it laid

down a jet stream. There were red identification lines flashing in the back. I know what I saw, but that's all I know."

"I am convinced that every one of the *Star Trek* regulars has had a similar experience," jokes Walter Koenig, who saw a spheroid UFO outside his bedroom window when he was ten years old. "We're not just eight or nine actors. We're special. We have been touched! It is our responsibility through *Star Trek* to bring our world into contact with other worlds. We are the chosen!"

But many people take Koenig seriously. After the cancellation of *Star Trek*, Gene Roddenberry was involved with a group who thought they were in psychic contact with extraterrestrials. For many years, Shatner pondered the question of whether he was one of the "chosen ones," and Leonard Nimoy has been approached on several occasions by people who thought he was sent here "as a vehicle for certain ideas that had to be transmitted to mankind."

Part of the mystique of *Star Trek* was the way it reached our deepest hopes and dreams as a species. If psychologist Carl Jung was right, that pool of psychic energy could even create sightings of flying saucers. UFOs very much like Klingon and Federation vessels have been reported from around the world. In September 1992, a UFO "strikingly similar to the Starship *Enterprise*" was sighted by dozens of witnesses at Cheesefoot Head, Hampshire, England. It was also seen and photographed hovering over mysterious crop circle sites, though the sites have since been proved to have been man-made.

It is impossible to say exactly what these strange objects represent, but in all likelihood, the human mind plays an integral part in the phenomenon. UFO experiences could be breakthroughs into other dimensions, some kind of superpoltergeist effect, or just our right brain trying to keep our left brain from giving us an overly rational picture of reality. The experience is surprisingly common, yet unpredictable, almost as if the phenomenon is in some way preparing human beings for something startling.

This preparation for the "right frame of mind" was exactly how Shatner interpreted his own close encounter. The experience changed his life in many subtle ways, but in none more far-reaching than the way in which he perceived his role in *Star Trek*. Shatner gained a new respect for the character he had poured his life into, for it was Captain Kirk who gave him the perspective to see the universe in a totally new way.

That connection to an exciting and optimistic part of his life was part of the reason Shatner had such a hard time letting Captain Kirk die. But late in the afternoon of his last day of shooting, Shatner was suddenly overcome with the feeling that he was ready to let go of Captain Kirk once and for all. He interrupted shooting on the set and asked director Dave Carson if they could film Kirk's death scene immediately. It would require turning the camera sequences upside down, but Carson agreed.

Shatner took his position lying face-up under the debris of a crashed catwalk at the bottom of a gorge near Soran's missile site. Picard rushes to Kirk's aid, but it is too late. With the camera over Patrick Stewart's shoulder, focusing down on Shatner's face, he mumbles: "It was fun," then gasps a feeble "Oh, my . . ." That final unscripted exclamation was inspired by something Shatner saw in the clouds high above him.

Just before he took his last breath as Kirk, Shatner gazed past the cameraman into the sky, like a dying man taking his last look at the world around him. There, high in the heavens, hovering without making a sound, was a silvery UFO. To Kirk, it might have been his last glimpse of the orbiting *Enterprise* or his first glimpse of the afterlife. To Shatner, as he described it later, the UFO might have been a distant jumbo jet cruising silently through the clouds. Or—it might have been that tambourine-shaped flying saucer finally come to take him to meet God.

Notes and Sources

Chapter 1

1. Personal conversations with William Shatner, September 1976; February 1977.

2. *William Shatner's Mysteries of the Gods.* 1977; Hemisphere Pictures, New York, NY.

3. *Official UFO,* July 1977. Countrywide Publications Inc., New York, NY.

4. *Ancient Astronauts,* July 1977. Countrywide Publications Inc., New York, NY.

5. "William Shatner's Amazing Cosmic Connection" in *UFOs Among the Stars,* by Timothy Green Beckley. 1992; Global Communications, New York, NY.

Chapter 2

1. "Still Many Unsolved Mysteries," by Ben Gross. *Sunday New York News,* January 6, 1968.

2. "William Shatner by Starlight," by Judy Michaelson. *New York Post,* May 4, 1968.

3. Personal conversations with Dr. Andrija Puharich, March 1977.

4. *The Making of the Trek Films,* by Edward Gross, Kay Anderson, et al., 1991; Image Publishing, East Meadow, New York, NY.

5. "Incident of the Nine," by Pat Jankiewicz. *Starlog,* July 1993, no. 192. Starlog Communications International, New York, NY.

6. *Gene Roddenberry: The Myth and the Man Behind Star Trek,* by Joel Engel. 1994; Hyperion, New York, NY.

5. *Gene Roddenberry: The Last Conversation,* by Yvonne Fern. 1994; University of California Press, Berkeley, CA.

Chapter 3

1. "No One Upsets the Star," by Michael Fessier, Jr. *TV Guide,* October 15, 1966.

2. "The Intergalactic Golden Boy," by Robert Higgins. *TV Guide,* June 22, 1968.

3. *The Making of Star Trek,* by Stephen Whitfield and Gene Roddenberry. 1968; Ballantine Books, New York, NY.

4. *Shatner: Where No Man . . . ,* by William Shatner, Sondra Marshak, and Myrna Culbreath. 1979; Grosset & Dunlap, New York, NY.

5. *Captain's Log: William Shatner's Personal Account of the Making of Star Trek V,* by Lisabeth Shatner. 1989; Pocket Books, New York, NY.

6. *The Trek Crew Book,* by James Van Hise. 1989; Pioneer Books, Las Vegas, NV.

7. "The Final Voyage of Captain Kirk." *Star Trek: The Official Fan Club,* May/June 1992, no. 85. The Official Fan Club, P. O. Box 111000, Aurora, CO 80011.

8. *William Shatner: A Bio-Bibliography,* by Dennis William Hauck. 1994; Greenwood Press, Westport, CT.

Chapter 4

1. "This Successful Actor Dreams of Becoming a Writer-Director," by Ben Kubasik. *Newsday,* February 1958.

2. "A Tale of Two Media: William Shatner Talks about TV and Stage," by Richard Shepard. *New York Times,* August 10, 1958.

3. "Backstage Differences Are a Family Affair: Actor William Shatner Sees Nothing Unusual in Differences of Opinion," by Anthony Shannon. *New York World Telegraph & The Sun,* April 18, 1959.

4. "When Does New York Actor Turn into a Hollywood Actor, and Why?" by Hal Humphrey. *Los Angeles Times,* August 22, 1961.

5. "High Purpose on a Low Budget," by Joseph Morganstern. *New York Times,* May 13, 1962.

6. "TV King of the Money Grabber? Don't Forget Movies, Theater," by Hal Humphrey. *Los Angeles Times,* February 9, 1964.

7. "Shatner Finds Dream Rules," by Henderson Cleaves. *New York World Telegraph & The Sun,* September 13, 1964.

8. "Shatner Bucks Movie Trend with Films of Social Criticism," by Kevin Thomas. *Los Angeles Times,* February 2, 1966.

9. "William Shatner: Mr. Versatility," by Steve Jacques. *Fighting Stars Magazine*, Summer 1974.

10. "Review of *The Celebrity Kosher Cookbook*," by James Bacon. *Los Angeles Times*, December 7, 1975.

Chapter 5

1. Television interview with William Shatner at Desilu Studios, Los Angeles, CA. August 1966.

2. "No One Upsets the Star," by Michael Fessier, Jr. *TV Guide*, October 15, 1966.

3. *The Making of Star Trek*, by Stephen Whitfield and Gene Roddenberry. 1968; Ballantine Books, New York, NY.

4. *Enterprise Incidents*, Collector's Edition no. 3, 1984. New Media Publishing Inc., Tampa, FL.

5. *Star Trek Interview Book*, by Allan Asherman. 1988; Pocket Books, New York, NY.

6. *Trek Classic*, by Edward Gross. 1991; Image Publishing, East Meadow, NY.

7. *Star Trek VI: The Official Movie Magazine*. 1991; Starlog Communications International, New York, NY.

8. *The History of Trek*, by James Van Hise. 1991; Pioneer Books, Las Vegas, NV.

9. *Great Birds of the Galaxy*, by Edward Gross and Mark Altman. 1992; Image Publishing, East Meadow, NY.

10. *Star Trek Memories*, by William Shatner and Chris Kreski. 1993; Harper, New York, NY.

11. *Star Trek: Where No One Has Gone Before*, by J. M. Dillard. 1994; Pocket Books, New York, NY.

12. *Beyond Uhura: Star Trek and Other Memories*, by Nichelle Nichols. 1994; G. P. Putnam, New York, NY.

13. *To the Stars: The Autobiography of George Takei*, by George Takei. 1994; Pocket Books, New York, NY.

14. *Gene Roddenberry: The Myth and the Man Behind Star Trek*, by Joel Engel. 1994; Hyperion, New York, NY.

Chapter 6

1. "William Shatner: Mister Versatility," by Steve Jacques. 1968; *Fighting Stars Magazine*, as reprinted in *Star Trek 74*, Galaxy News Service, New York, NY.

2. *Star Trek Interview Book*, by Allan Asherman. 1988; Pocket Books, New York, NY.

3. *Trek: The Lost Years*, by Edward Gross. 1989; Pioneer Books, Las Vegas, NV.

4. "The Cat with Nine Lives," by Kyle Counts. *Starlog*, April 1990, no. 153. Starlog Communications International, New York, NY.

5. "Star of Zetar," by Pat Jankiewicz. *Starlog*, February 1994, no. 199. Starlog Communications International, New York, NY.

6. *Star Trek: Where No One Has Gone Before*, by J. M. Dillard. 1994; Pocket Books, New York, NY.

7. Personal conversations with David L. Ross, August 1994.

Chapter 7

1. "The Intergalactic Golden Boy," by Robert Higgins. *TV Guide,* June 27, 1968.

2. "Bill Shatner's Trek with Heidi," by Connie Hunter. *Confidential,* May 1973.

3. "How a Star Treks to the Barbary Coast," by Shelley Andrews. *Movie Scene,* May 1975.

4. "William Shatner: Moving Right Along," by David Houston. *Starlog,* October 1977. Starlog Communications International, New York, NY.

5. "Shatner Treks on to Live Shows," by Mary Beth Crain. *Chicago Sun Times,* May 28, 1978.

6. *Shatner: Where No Man . . . ,* by William Shatner, Sondra Marshak, and Myrna Culbreath. 1979; Grosset & Dunlap, New York, NY.

7. *Star Trek 25th Anniversary Special.* Interviewer, Ed Naha. 1991; Starlog Communications International, New York, NY.

8. *Star Trek: Where No One Has Gone Before,* by J. M. Dillard. 1994; Pocket Books, New York, NY.

9. *William Shatner: A Bio-Bibliography,* by Dennis William Hauck. 1994; Greenwood Press, Westport, CT.

Chapter 8

1. "After Ten Years, Kirk's Back at the Helm," by Desmond Ryan. *Philadelphia Inquirer,* December 7, 1979.

2. "William Shatner Part II: I Am Kirk," by Steve Swires. *Starlog*, November 1981. Starlog Communications International, New York, NY.

3. "Star Trek's Straight Arrow Scores with a New Generation of Trekkies," by Gail Buchalter. *People*, July 5, 1982.

4. "Is He Admiral Kirk, T. J. Hooker, or William Shatner?" by Vernon Scott. *Evening Outlook*, April 27, 1984.

5. *Star Trek Memory Book*. Enterprise Spotlight Series, January 1985. New Media Publishing, Tampa, FL.

6. "Star Trek: The Motion Picture." *Starlog*, April 1978, no. 151. Starlog Communications International, New York, NY.

7. "A Space Age Captain Hornblower?" by Bob Sokolsky. *Philadelphia Bulletin*, December 9, 1979.

8. "William Shatner: I Am Kirk," by Steve Swires. *Starlog*, November 1981, no. 52. Starlog Communications International, New York, NY.

9. "Star Trek's Straight Arrow Scores with a New Generation of Trekkies," by Gail Buchalter. *People*, July 5, 1982.

10. "Walter Koenig on Star Trek II," by Steve Swires. *Starlog*, August 1982, no. 61. Starlog Communications International, New York, NY.

11. "Film Stars Linked to Laos Raid," by Marc Kalech. *New York Post*, January 31, 1983.

12. "Enterprising Leonard Nimoy Directs the Search for End-Ear-ing Spock," by John Stark. *People*, April 1984.

13. "Star Trek's Nine Lives," by Charles Leershen, Peter McAlevey, and Janet Huck. *Newsweek,* December 22, 1986.

14. *Trek: The Lost Years,* by Edward Gross. 1989; Pioneer Books, Las Vegas, NV.

15. "Insider Grapevine," by Lawrence Eisenberg. *TV Guide,* June 10, 1989.

16. *The Making of the Trek Films,* by Edward Gross and Kay Anderson, et al., 1991; Image Publishing, East Meadow, NY.

17. "Hollywood Report: Trek Talk," by Martin A. Grove. *The Hollywood Reporter,* September 25, 1991.

18. "The Undiscovered Kirk," by Dan Yakir. *Starlog,* February 1992, no. 175. Starlog Communications International, New York, NY.

19. *Trek: The Making of the Movies,* by James Van Hise. 1992; Pioneer Books, Las Vegas, NV.

20. *Star Trek Movie Memories,* by William Shatner. 1994; HarperCollins, New York, NY.

21. *Star Trek: Where No One Has Gone Before,* by J. M. Dillard. 1994; Pocket Books, New York, NY.

Chapter 9

1. "After Ten Years, Kirk's Back at the Helm," by Desmond Ryan. *Philadelphia Inquirer,* December 7, 1979.

2. "William Shatner: Directing Star Trek V," by Dan Madsen. *Star Trek: The Official Fan Club,* October/November 1987, no. 58. The Official Fan Club Inc., P. O. Box 111000, Aurora, CO 80011.

3. "The Ultimate Trek: Search for God," by John Stanley. *Datebook*, June 4, 1989.

4. "Star Trek V Turns Metaphysical in Outing to the Final Frontier," by Harry Haun. *New York Daily News*, June 7, 1989.

5. "Another Day, Another Voyage," by Caryn James. *New York Times*, June 9, 1989.

6. "William Shatner: Shakedown Cruise," by Marc Shapiro. *Starlog*, July 1989, no. 144. Starlog Communications International, New York, NY.

7. "James Doohan: Daredevil of the Skies," by Kathryn Drennan. *Starlog*, September 1989, no. 146. Starlog Communications International, New York, NY.

8. *Star Trek V: The Official Movie Magazine.* 1989; Starlog Communications International, New York, NY.

9. *The History of Trek*, by James Van Hise. 1991; Pioneer Books, Las Vegas, NV.

10. *The Making of the Trek Films*, by Edward Gross, Kay Anderson, et al. 1991; Image Publishing, East Meadow, NY.

11. *Great Birds of the Galaxy*, by Edward Gross and Mark Altman. 1992; Image Publishing, East Meadow, NY.

12. *Trek: The Making of the Movies*, by James Van Hise. 1992; Pioneer Books, Las Vegas, NV.

13. "The Undiscovered Kirk," by Dan Yakir. *Starlog*, February 1992, no. 175. Starlog Communications International, New York, NY.

14. "In Producer Country," by Marc Shapiro. *Starlog*, April 1992, no. 177. Starlog Communications International, New York, NY.

15. "The Making of Star Trek VI," by Mark Altman. *Cinefantastique,* April 1992.

16. "Warp Speed Ahead," by Rick Marin. *TV Guide,* July 24, 1993.

17. "Trekking Onward," by Richard Zoglin. *Time,* November 28, 1994.

18. "A Farewell to Kirk," by David Resner. *TV Guide,* October 8, 1994.

19. *Star Trek Movie Memories,* by William Shatner. 1994; HarperCollins, New York, NY.

20. *Beyond Uhura: Star Trek and Other Memories,* by Nichelle Nichols. 1994; G. P. Putnam, New York, NY.

21. *To The Stars: The Autobiography of George Takei,* by George Takei. 1994; Pocket Books, New York, NY.

22. "Taking the Fall," by David Kronke. *Spirit,* December 1994.

23. "Generations," by Michael Beeler and Sue Uram. *Cinefantastique,* December 1994.

24. *Star Trek: Where No One Has Gone Before,* by J. M. Dillard. 1994; Pocket Books, New York, NY.

25. Personal interviews with Nichelle Nichols, George Takei, and Walter Koenig, August and September 1994.

26. "Star Trek: The Ultimate Trip Through the Galaxies." *Entertainment Weekly Special Edition,* January 18, 1995. Time Inc., New York, NY.

27. "Captain's Finale," by Ian Spelling. *Starlog Platinum Edition,* vol. 5, January 1995. Starlog Entertainment Inc., New York, NY.

28. Interview with Patrick Stewart on KCRA-TV, November 19, 1994.

Chapter 10

1. "William Shatner's Personal Tragedy," by Roger Elwood. *TV Star Parade,* April 1968.

2. "Was This Divorce Necessary?" by Milburn Smith. *Photoplay,* July 1968.

3. "Star Trek's Shatner: His Many Enterprises Leave Him Facing a Void," by Jan Hodenfield. *New York Post,* September 3, 1977.

4. *Shatner: Where No Man . . . ,* by William Shatner, Sondra Marshak, and Myrna Culbreath. 1979; Grosset & Dunlap, New York, NY.

5. "Shatners Live Life in the Fast Lane, But One's in the Back Seat," by Isobel Silden. *Los Angeles Times,* February 24, 1985.

6. "My Superlover Shatner—By His Mistress," by Carl Pinter. *Star,* May 5, 1987. World News Corporation, New York, NY.

7. "Twenty Questions: William Shatner," by David Rensin. *Playboy,* July 1989.

8. *Enterprising Women: Television Fandom and the Creation of Popular Myth,* by Camille Bacon-Smith. 1992; University of Pennsylvania Press, Philadelphia, PA.

9. "Interview with Ron Asheton," *Motorbooty,* no. 5, Spring 1994. Motorbooty Worldwide Communications, P. O. Box 02007, Detroit, MI 48202.

10. "Secret Heartache Behind Bust-Up of Shatner's Marriage," by Peter Kent and Alex Burton. *Star,* February 22, 1994.

11. Personal interviews with David L. Ross, August 1994.

12. "Star Trek: The Ultimate Trip Through the Galaxies." *Entertainment Weekly Special Edition,* January 18, 1995. Time Inc., New York, NY.

Chapter 11

1. "Shatner Treks on to Live Shows," by Mary Beth Crain. *Chicago Sun Times,* May 28, 1978.

2. "Shatner Interview," *Enterprise Incidents,* Fall 1986. Pop Cult Inc., Granada Hills, CA.

3. *Star Trek Interview Book,* by Allan Asherman. 1988; Pocket Books, New York, NY.

4. "William Shatner: Captain's Discretion," by Marc Shapiro. *Starlog,* August 1989, no. 145. Starlog Communications International, New York, NY.

5. *Star Trek 25th Anniversary Special.* 1991; Starlog Communications International, New York, NY.

6. "Shatner Night Live," by Pat Jankiewicz. *Starlog,* February 1992, no. 175. Starlog Communications International, New York, NY.

7. "Smithsonian Premieres Star Trek Exhibit," by Virginia Lister. *Starland,* Spring 1992.

8. "Star Trek Stars Trek," *People,* July 20, 1992.

9. "Star Trek Convention," by Joseph Barclay Ross. *Fate,* August 1993. Llewelyn Publications, St. Paul, MN.

10. *William Shatner: A Bio-Bibliography,* by Dennis William Hauck. 1994; Greenwood Press, Westport, CT.

Chapter 12

1. "Shatner Has Fan Troubles," by Earl Wilson. *Los Angeles Herald Examiner,* September 23, 1967.

2. *Chekov's Enterprise,* by Walter Koenig. 1980; Intergalactic Press, Longwood, FL.

3. "William Shatner: I Am Kirk," by Steve Swires. *Starlog,* November 1981, no. 52. Starlog Communications International, New York, NY.

4. "William Shatner, Schizoid Superstar," by Ed Naha. *Starlog,* July 1983. Starlog Communications International, New York, NY.

5. AstroQuest Desktop Astrologer. 1988; One Step Software, Charlotte, NC.

6. "Twenty Questions: William Shatner," by David Rensin. *Playboy,* July 1989.

7. "William Shatner: Captain's Discretion," by Marc Shapiro. *Starlog,* August 1989, no. 145. Starlog Communications International, New York, NY.

8. "The Undiscovered Kirk," by Dan Yakir. *Starlog,* February 1992, no. 175. Starlog Communications International, New York, NY.

9. "Warp Speed Ahead," by Rick Marin. *TV Guide,* July 24, 1993.

10. "Looking Ahead: Shatner Leads TekWar Symposium," by Veronique de Turenne. *Los Angeles Daily News,* June 2, 1993.

11. "Tek World," by Bill Florence. *Starlog,* September 1992, no. 182. Starlog Communications International, New York, NY.

12. *Star Trek Movie Memories,* by William Shatner. 1994; HarperCollins, New York, NY.

13. *The William Shatner Connection,* Winter 1994, vol. II, no. 4. WSC, 7059 Atoll Avenue, North Hollywood, CA 91605.

Acknowledgments

A work of this nature is not possible without the input of many different individuals who are willing to share their personal experiences and private collections. I am especially grateful to the former cast members of *Star Trek*, who took time out from their busy schedules to allow me to interview them: Nichelle Nichols, George Takei, David Ross, and Walter Koenig.

I am also grateful to Jim Ivers for sharing his extensive collection of Shatner video clips and movies with me. I am indebted to Will Valentino, for sharing his wide-ranging collection of celebrity videos and newsclippings, and to Jeff Nelson, who provided me with material from his amazingly complete *Star Trek* scrapbooks. Greg Allen, editor of a Shatner newsletter in Anchorage, Alaska, also provided many original articles.

My special thanks goes to Bruce Schaffenberger, for his assistance in researching the mounds of material I accumulated. Likewise, I am indebted to Christian Merciari of Montreal, for his thorough research into Shatner's childhood there.

Finally, I would like to personally thank all the hundreds of *Star Trek* fans who shared their opinions about William Shatner and participated in the surveys whose results are reported in this volume.

WARBOTS by G. Harry Stine

#5 OPERATION HIGH DRAGON   (17-159, $3.95)
Civilization is under attack! A "virus program" has been injected
into America's polar-orbit military satellites by an unknown enemy. The only motive can be the preparation for attack against
the free world. The source of "infection" is traced to a barren,
storm-swept rock-pile in the southern Indian Ocean. Now, it is up
to the forces of freedom to search out and destroy the enemy.
With the aid of their robot infantry—the Warbots—the Washington Greys mount Operation High Dragon in a climactic battle for
the future of the free world.

#6 THE LOST BATTALION   (17-205, $3.95)
Major Curt Carson has his orders to lead his Warbot-equipped
Washington Greys in a search-and-destroy mission in the mountain jungles of Borneo. The enemy: a strongly entrenched army
of Shiite Muslim guerrillas who have captured the Second Tacti-
cal Battalion, threatening them with slaughter. As allies, the
Washington Greys have enlisted the Grey Lotus Battalion, a
mixed-breed horde of Japanese jungle fighters. Together with
their newfound allies, the small band must face swarming hordes
of fanatical Shiite guerrillas in a battle that will decide the fate of
Southeast Asia and the security of the free world.

#7 OPERATION IRON FIST   (17-253, $3.95)
Russia's centuries-old ambition to conquer lands along its southern border erupts in a savage show of force that pits a horde of
Soviet-backed Turkish guerrillas against the freedom-loving
Kurds in their homeland high in the Caucasus Mountains. At
stake: the rich oil fields of the Middle East. Facing certain annihi-
lation, the valiant Kurds turn to the robot infantry of Major Curt
Carson's "Ghost Forces" for help. But the brutal Turks far out-
number Carson's desperately embattled Washington Greys, and
on the blood-stained slopes of historic Mount Ararat, the high-
tech warriors of tomorrow must face their most awesome challenge yet!